MISTS OF IGA

D1607668

Mists of Iga

Book One Of
Sons Of Yōkai
By
Kyle Mortensen

Mists of Iga Copyright © 2020 by Kyle Mortensen
Book Cover Copyright © 2020 by Kyle Mortensen
Maps Copyright © 2020 by Kyle Mortensen

This book is based on actual events and persons. However, this is a work of fiction. Names, characters, places, and incidents either are the product of the author's imagination or are used fictitiously.

All rights reserved. No part of this book may be reproduced or used in any manner whatsoever without written permission of the copyright owner except in the case of brief quotations embodied in critical articles and reviews. For inquires or permission to use content contact Info@Kyle-Mortensen.com

Printed and bound in the United States of America
First paperback edition published 2020

The Library of Congress has catalogued this edition as follows:
Mortensen, Kyle.
    Mists of Iga: a novel / Kyle Mortensen. 1st ed.
        Sons of Yokai: series
    LCCN 2020917717
    ISBN (9798654917843) (paperback)
    First Edition 2020

www.Kyle-Mortensen.com

"Without destruction there is no creation, there is no change."

-Nobunaga Oda

Contents

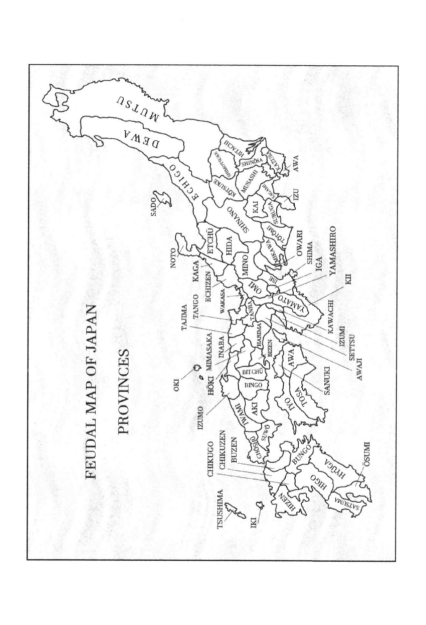

FEUDAL MAP OF JAPAN

PROVINCES

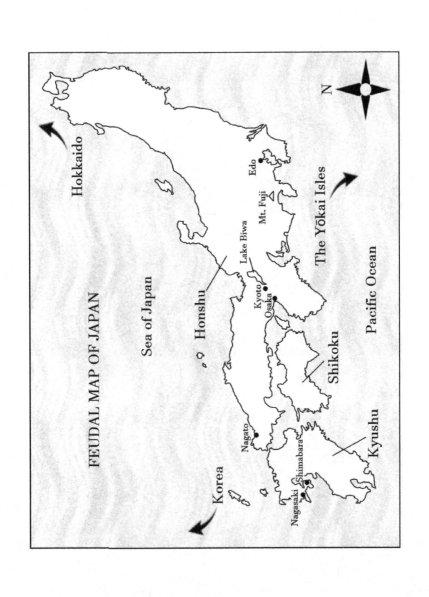

FEUDAL MAP OF JAPAN

Hokkaido

Sea of Japan

Honshu

Korea

Nagato

Shimabara

Nagasaki

Kyushu

Shikoku

Osaka

Kyoto

Lake Biwa

Mt. Fuji

Edo

The Yōkai Isles

Pacific Ocean

N

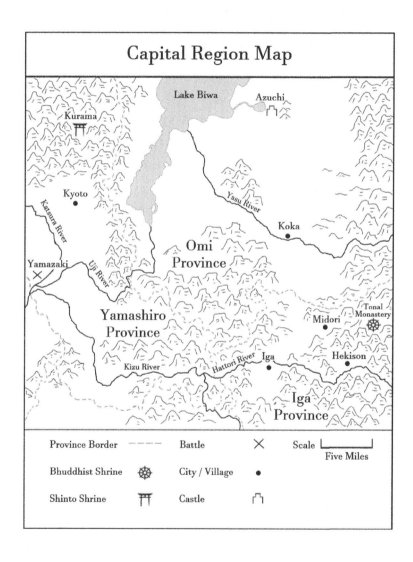

Capital Region Map

Lake Biwa

Azuchi

Kurama

Kyoto

Yasu River

Koka

Omi
Province

Tonal
Monastery

Yamazaki

Uji River

Yamashiro
Province

Midori

Hekison

Kizu River

Hattori River

Iga

Iga
Province

Province Border	- - -	Battle	✕	Scale
Bhuddhist Shrine	☸	City / Village	●	Five Miles
Shinto Shrine	⛩	Castle	⌐	

List of Definitions

In Japanese to English translation there are words that do not have an equivalent interpretation. For this reason, some words were kept in the Romaji Japanese form for integrity of meaning. The below list is to help the reader understand the titles and terms that are frequently used. Names and places are not in the below list as they are not needed for story comprehension.

Bushidō	Code of honor and ideals used by samurai
Chūnin	Middle rank position of a shinobi
Daimyō	Feudal lord and governing land ruler
Genin	Lowest rank position of a shinobi
Jōnin	Leader rank, highest position of a shinobi
Kami	God or deity of Shinto
Kanpai	Toasting of drinks, "Cheers"
Katana	Japanese curved long sword
Kitsune	Fox
Kunai	Diamond shaped dagger with ringed pommel

Kunoichi	Female practitioner of ninjutsu
Kusarigama	Sickle and weighted chain weapon
Oni	Yōkai in the form of an ogre
Tantō	Japanese dagger
Tengu	Yōkai in the form of a human and bird
Samurai	Japanese warrior class
Seppuku	Ritual suicide of samurai class
Shamisen	Three-stringed instrument with neck and body
Shinobi	Practitioner of ninjutsu, ninja by modern naming
Shinto	Native religion to Japan
Shōgun	Military dictator and de facto ruler of country
Wakizashi	Japanese curved short sword
Yōkai	Creatures of Japanese folklore taking the forms of sprits, animals, monsters, & demons

1

Mist on the Mountain
-Iga Province, Iga Mountains-

Itsuki and Noboru ran from the chaos that would consume their commander and brother in arms, Kazuki Yukimura. They had grudgingly withdrawn, knowing full well that they were leaving him to die. Nobunaga's heavily armored forces were slowly gaining ground toward the central stronghold of the Iga Province. Itsuki paused briefly to rub the sweat off his bald head and gaze down the wooded slope to their rear. "Noboru, how many kunai bombs did you give him?"

"Three kunai bombs, and one black powder dragon. It's all I had left," Noboru called back.

That should buy us enough time, Itsuki thought. Nobunaga's invasion had kept them occupied on the front lines for months, but now a matter of minutes could mean survival for what remained of the Iga shinobi clan.

It had been almost two years since Nobunaga's troops had made the initial attack under the leadership of his son, Nobukatsu. At first, forces had been repelled easily, but now with 40,000 soldiers on their doorstep, the shinobi were struggling

1

desperately for their lives. Deceptive guerrilla tactics and difficult mountain terrain had enabled the 4,000 Iga warriors to inflict massive casualties upon the advancing samurai. Battles were hard fought as Nobunaga's forces met shinobi traps and ambushes with brute force. At times men were sacrificed by the hundreds in the advance. Cursed as cowards by their enemies, the shinobi would scoff at the foolish soldiers who put their honorable fighting above the mission; after all, Noboru and Itsuki were alive while the mountainside was littered with bodies of dead samurai.

Noboru sucked in air, his long-bounded hair flowed behind him, his lungs burning as the pair climbed. "I guess four hours, maybe less if we hurry, but Nobunaga's men won't be far behind."

Boom! The two spun toward the echoing rumbles far below where they had left their commanding chūnin officer. Kazuki had used the first kunai bomb to distract the samurai. "You think the old man will make it to the rock pass?" Noboru asked.

Itsuki closed his eyes, sorrow tensing the muscles of his scarred face. "If anyone can, it will be Kazuki." When he opened them again, his eyes were clear and vibrant. "Let us not linger. He gave us a mission to complete, we will honor his sacrifice with swiftness."

The shinobi had been steadily losing ground for days, laying traps, killing a squad or two at a time, then falling back to regroup. Kazuki had been an astute chūnin, expertly commanding Noboru and Itsuki in battle. One man would make a distraction to draw troops in pursuit, while the other two would circle in attacking fiercely from behind. The unconventional and highly inventive tactics were effective, both in overpowering larger forces and in filling the enemy with dread. Yet the samurai kept coming like unending waves upon a rocky shore.

2

Kyle Mortensen

Dozens of other shinobi squads had been scattered throughout the hills to engage and confuse Nobunaga's forces as they made attempts to advance. One by one, the squads had fallen to the samurai hordes, beheaded when possible as a show of power and pride. When it became clear to Kazuki that the battle was lost, he had dispatched his two younger genin subordinates to the stronghold of Hekison, a final desperate effort to urge a total evacuation into the high forest. Kazuki would stay behind to lead the invading soldiers off their trail, buying some much-needed time for those fleeing the village. Kazuki had asked only one other task of the two shinobi as they parted ways, the secondary request being more precious than the first.

Boom! Another kunai bomb echoed in the distance. Noboru gave a broad smile, knowing that the old man was making good use of the dangerous gifts he had so lovingly constructed. Noboru had been well trained in all the shinobi arts but held a special place in his heart for kayakujutsu, the study of fire and explosives. A standard kunai, a slender diamond shaped dagger with a ring at the end of the handle for tying cordage was altered by Noboru for his invention. The handle was fitted with a cylindrical wrapping of black powder and metal shards, the wrapping was then sealed with resin and fitted with a fuse. The result was a deadly throwing bomb that detonated shortly after making contact with its target. Continuing through the dense undergrowth that blanketed the mountain foothills of Iga, Noboru wondered at the quick successive explosions. *How many could the old man take down with him?*

It would be a steep climb of just over an hour before the slope softened, followed by a three-hour trek over riverbanks to the fortress of Hekison. The journey would take a fully outfitted soldier in top condition nearly twice that long. However, men of Iga traveled light and routinely ran great distances. They would make short work of such a daunting journey. Speed, among other things, made them an elusive foe, and while neither Itsuki nor Noboru were considered fleet-footed by shinobi standards, they nevertheless could push themselves with incredible stamina when needed.

"Pick up your feet, my friend," Itsuki encouraged, "Make like the wind!" Such expressions were commonplace in Iga, helping to keep spirits high even in the most desperate hour. They were a people raised on warfare and hardship, weaned from childhood on the virtue of endurance in every aspect of life. Even the name shinobi, by which they called themselves, short for shinobi-no-mono, meant "one who endures."

"You be the wind Itsuki, I'll be the fire lapping at its heels," Noboru growled.

Itsuki permitted himself a grin. He was glad to be in the company of such a man. At age twenty-four, Noboru had a gruff humor that filled the heart and strengthened the resolve. Itsuki was one year older than Noboru, but they had been friends ever since they became subordinates to Kazuki. The grin faded as Itsuki's thoughts turned to the task ahead. It had been a sorrowful decision for Kazuki to issue the order, and a sorrowful act to leave him, but they had been charged with a task of utmost importance. Those in command at Hekison did not share the beliefs of Kazuki Yukimura and could hardly be expected to throw their support behind his plan.

"Will the Jōnin agree to evacuate the village?" Itsuki mused to himself as much as to Noboru.

"That man is stubborn as an ox, pride alone may stop him,

Yamato may deny the plan purely because it is Kazuki who has advised it. Yamato has never respected Kazuki's views, and he damn sure won't start—"

Boom! The third kunai bomb had gone off, this time much farther south. The samurai had taken the bait, and Kazuki would be nearly to his goal. Itsuki climbed with renewed vigor. "Kazuki is almost to the pass. We had better pick up the pace if we are going to make his sacrifice worth it."

The sun was beginning to drop, and temperatures with it. The shinobi's breath billowed like smoke from their lungs as they reached the summit. Autumn had lingered late that year, and the promise of a bitter cold winter was on the wind. When the snows did come, they would hit hard and fast. In the past, harsh winter weather had turned back many invading armies, but Nobunaga had gambled well and there would be no blizzards barring his way tonight.

Itsuki was thankful to have the difficult climb behind them, and the promise of fresh water ahead. Sniffing the cold air, he looked out across the valley below. Proud stands of pine, spruce, and cedar crowded the slopes, concealing all evidence of battle in a great canopy. Scattered among the alpine forest, painted ribbons of colorful maple shined like flickering gold stars in the evening light and ominous cold mists rose from the abundant streams, flowing through the trees like ghostly rivers.

Kaboom! The sound of a huge black powder bomb erupted across the mountain face, followed by what sounded like a rockslide. Wide-eyed, Itsuki shot a look at Noboru. "How big did you make the last one?"

Noboru smirked with pleasure. "I wasn't about to let the old man die without making an impression."

Dazed and with ears ringing painfully from the blast, Kazuki Yukimura watched in awe as a cascade of rock poured from the mountainside, crushing the soldiers below. A dense cloud of earth rose from the landslide obscuring the carnage. A long silenced followed, the dust enveloped Kazuki's position as if shrouding him by the power of the old gods. An old friend had come to strengthen his resolve, a familiar tremble of fear that Kazuki had not felt in years crept through his arms. Kazuki knelt with intense concentration, interlocked his fingers making three distinct hand formations, and prepared to make his final stand.

2

Enter Nobunaga Oda
-Iga Province, Iga Mountains-

"So shall fall all men of Iga." Blood dripped from the glimmering blade held by the Daimyō Nobunaga Oda as he stood over the lifeless form of a battered shinobi. At age forty-seven, Kazuki's body gave testament to years of applied ninjutsu, muscles lean and sinewy beneath his skin. A warrior's grimace was plastered on Kazuki's lifeless face, his hard jaw peppered with white and black stubble.

With a snap of his arm, Nobunaga flung the shinobi's blood from his katana, then produced a square strip of cloth and thoroughly wiped the blade clean before returning it to its scabbard. A samurai warrior who had been tested many times over, Nobunaga led his men by example, fiercely engaging enemies on the battlefield as well as in the halls of the imperial court. He threw his helmet to the ground in fuming disbelief, only then did he notice that a few droplets of blood fell from his face. In wonder of how close he came to death; Nobunaga thumbed a small cut on his jawline where Kazuki had nearly made a deathblow.

Nobunaga spat. "One Man? How could one man have defeated so many?"

Lieutenant Ito bowed. "Lord, the peasant scum was equipped with powerful explosives; he used one to set off the rockslide... such dishonorable cowardice."

Nobunaga wheeled around in anger to meet the lieutenant. "Cowardice? Can you explain to me how such a coward managed to take down nine more men after the rockfall?"

Lieutenant Ito stammered, "I... there's no excuse, sir."

Nobunaga eyed the lieutenant aggressively, moving in close. The daimyō was an intimidating man, made ever more so by full battle garb: elaborate leather plating, dyed a deep black with a slight sheen of crimson, and fastened together with woven bands of black silk layered over a heavily embroidered kimono. The Oda crest, a flowering Japanese quince, was painted on the chest piece in exquisite black and gold. Below the waist, the flexible armor fanned out as overlapping panels, offering protection to the level of the knees. The helmet laying in the dust next to Kazuki was masterfully crafted of iron and leather with a flared skirt that protected the neck. A bronze family crest adorned the brow, and two long water buffalo horns rose ominously at its sides. A pair of gently curved swords was tied at the man's waist with a length of gold silk. The longer of the two was a katana of immeasurable value, forged by the legendary Goro Masamune. The three-foot long katana was coveted by all samurai for its masterful craftsmanship and near mythical origin of its maker. At nearly 300 years old, the katana had known many owners, yet still it shined with terrible fury when unsheathed in battle. Nobunaga kept the relic sharp as the day it was made, and had it fitted with a new scabbard and a hilt lacquered black with crimson details to complement his armor. Nobunaga's sword set was completed by a shorter wakizashi blade sheathed in matching colors yet lacking the impressive pedigree of its partner.

The strength of my enemy is multiplied by incompetence in my ranks, Nobunaga thought. "Lieutenant!"

Ito shifted nervously under the daimyō's scrutiny. "Sir!"

With lightning speed, Nobunaga assumed a warrior's stance. He firmly planted his feet shoulder width apart, pulling the katana from its sheath he drove the handle forcefully into the lieutenant's stomach. The samurai folded in half from the painful blow.

Nobunaga slowly sheathed his sword. "Next time I will use the sharp end, and you will join the men that you so carelessly let die."

Lieutenant Ito grasped the hilt of his sword, wheezing in pain. "As you say, sir, but should I fail you again, I will save you the trouble."

Nobunaga gave a curt nod. "Attend the men. I want the troops organized for the final assault."

Despite Ito's admission of guilt, he could hardly shoulder the blame for the lost men. In the dust and confusion that followed the rockslide, Kazuki had taken up his bow and rained arrows down on the charging soldiers with deadly precision. He felled six before the samurai were able to close the distance. The first man to reach the shinobi caught a jabbing kick to the side of his knee, buckling his leg. A swift blow to the temple sent him tumbling headlong down the slope, breaking his neck in the fall. Drawing forth the wakizashi lashed across his back, Kazuki slayed another two soldiers before facing Lord Nobunaga. All paused and none dared to disturb the clash of blades between the two masters. Time slowed and the only sound was steel against steel paired with the yells of fury. For a slim moment Nobunaga had felt a jolt of fear run down his spine, a phenomenon as rare as the skill of the shinobi that he battled. The two masters paused, their eyes met, and for a moment they were more familiar than any kin. A small breeze danced through the leaves of the forest and in one final move the shinobi fell by the masterful skill of Nobunaga Oda. In a gush of blood, the flashing tip of the Masamune blade had pierced the shinobi's chest.

Nobunaga's son, Nobukatsu, stepped forward and broke the deep pondering of his father. Nobukatsu wore a deep red armor with a gold painted familial crest on the breastplate that showed his status. Like all samurai two blades hung at his waist.

"Father, if it is disappointment you see in your commanders, let me lead the front lines for you. I would paint the hills red with the blood of these farmers."

Nobunaga was known as a man of explosive temper, a mar on the otherwise pristine slate of the illustrious daimyō. Yet many believed that great daimyōs possessed an equally great character flaw, a touch of evil to temper their more noble qualities. Nobunaga tightly shut his eyes, drawing a slow breath he let the anger within him return to a simmer.

"That won't be necessary; they are already defeated. I have dispatched a lightly armored auxiliary group ahead of our main force, a ghost squad. They have followed game trails up the mountain and will be far ahead of us by now. We have taken the foothills and broken their primary defense. The remaining shinobi will now retreat to the fortress village of Hekison to make their final stand. Our path will be clear on the march tonight." Nobunaga opened his eyes turning to face his son. "I now understand why you failed in your past attempts to flush out those men of Iga; they play cowardice against honor, vanishing into the mist at the first sign of danger. Once you draw them out into the open, they fight like men possessed until they drop in utter exhaustion."

"Father... no one respects your stratagems more than I, but why do you burn so to uproot Iga? They are no more than simple farmers defending their homes with scythes and bows. They play the part of would-be assassins with secluded lives in these high mountains. The only time they come down is to do mercenary work that a daimyō may offer. Has the price in blood been worth this conquest?"

Nobunaga's fist tightened. "You are very young. Many years ago, there was a similar dilemma near Osaka. A group of militant Buddhist monks began to gain prominence, hidden from the consciousness of the nobility in their monasteries. The local daimyō thought little of the threat they posed, convinced that conquest of these monks was not worth the trouble. Eventually that foolish man lost his head when the monks rose against him, plunging the province into chaos. A bamboo forest starts with a single stalk. Do you understand?"

Nobukatsu hesitated only but a moment. "The seeds of rebellion must not be allowed to grow."

Nobunaga nodded. "Exactly. It is because of their independence that they must be uprooted. The history of Iga has been a secluded one and the people believe themselves above the laws of this country. They believe that they can rule themselves in their mountain villages with no regard for the codes by which peace for many can be maintained. If I hope to bring the whole of this island under one banner, I cannot abide an independent

11

people whose loyalty can be bought and sold. They must be governed, they must be broken, and they must come to fear the word as much as the sword."

Nobunaga's gaze turned toward the mountain. "And then there is the matter of a debt unpaid. I suppose blood will have to suffice." Gesturing his son forward, Nobunaga spoke quietly, "When Hekison falls, I want you to personally secure both the village armory and personal quarters of Yamato Akiyama. No one is to remove a single item from any structure without my leave. Take the head of any man who attempts to do so."

"I shall see it done, father. What is it that you seek from these farmers?"

Nobunaga gritted his teeth. "Only what is owed… vengeance and steel."

3

Hekison
-Iga Province, Hekison Village-

Nestled among the rocky folds of a small canyon east of the city of Iga, the village of Hekison had been home and haven to the Iga shinobi for centuries. Built into a triangular notch of gray rock that cut deeply into the craggy mountaintop, Hekison was a natural fortress with but a single accessible side open to the gently sloping hill below. During times of war, barricades could easily transform the town into a citadel capable of repelling massive armies. A row of heavily reinforced structures typically used for storehouses formed the basic framework of this barricade. Stout stone walls, chest high as thick as two men, standing shoulder to shoulder spanned the gaps between these buildings. These walls formed an unbroken border, save for three unhindered corridors that provided access to the village. Bamboo fencing, manicured vegetation, and a dozen cleverly placed sheds served to conceal the stonework and break up the uniformity of the blockade. In times of peace, the town would appear as placid and vulnerable to attack as any other farming community, easily deceiving unfamiliar eyes.

When the threat of invasion loomed, the disguise could be quickly thrown off, revealing Hekison as a military stronghold. The heavy timbers out of which the decoy buildings were constructed could be disassembled by a handful of men and fitted atop the stone walls to complete the barrier to twice the height of a man. Similarly, thick wooden frameworks were posted into sturdy footings and buried deeply into the roadway to seal off the open passages. This clever design allowed the convertible fortifications to be stored and hidden in plain sight.

Outside the barricade other preparations would greatly amplify the effect of a defending force. A slow winding river made for a bottle neck shape for those wandering up the canyon. The natural slope of the dell in which the village was perched provided a high ground advantage, while a dozen paces out the ground dropped sharply into terraced rice patties that radiated down from the village to the tree line in the distance. The terracing not only gave Hekison greater dominance on the hillside but added challenging obstacles for soldiers advancing from below. The layout of Hekison was a masterpiece of shinobi methodology; every aspect was so intentional, every defense subtlety integrated, that it was at once unassuming and effortlessly beautiful.

The name Hekison simply meant "the remote village," and was fittingly understated. The place was nearly impossible to find for those who did not already know the way, and for this reason had become the nerve center from which all directives to shinobi were dispatched. In the two-year siege of the Iga Province, the face and spirit of Hekison had changed greatly. Oda's forces had subjugated all the outlying villages of the Iga Province, killing whom they could and leaving the rest to take flight deeper into the hills. As the samurai led forces from one town to another, leaving them in waste, Hekison had become as much a refugee camp as it was a command post. Homes were converted into medical stations, workshops into barracks, and the heavy barricade that enclosed the town became a permanent fixture on the landscape. All residents were pressed into the war effort, sharpening weapons, packing explosives, working tirelessly to keep everyone fed and healthy.

Over the past two months it had become increasingly evident that despite the great perseverance of the shinobi, they were being overcome, and soon would be flushed completely from their mountain home. Little by little, the women had begun to flee the village accompanied by their young children, with vague ideas of finding asylum in neighboring provinces where they could leave the name of shinobi behind.

Night had fallen when Noboru and Itsuki emerged from the forest's edge. The mist had enveloped the forest and the sentry lanterns along the wall of Hekison had come into view in the form of ghostly spirits dancing to the night. They had already met several shinobi scouts as they made their way through the woods, warning them of the coming forces. The scouts were under strict orders to hold their ground, well camouflaged and lying-in wait. As they drew near the village perimeter Itsuki issued forth a whistling birdcall, expertly imitating the rapid high-pitched squeaks of a robin as a signal to those on watch. A mimicking answer came back, confirming the received call. Itsuki scowled in the darkness; the call was effective, but far from convincing. He turned quietly to his partner. "What are they teaching these kids?"

They were tired and dirty from battle, and the hard trek of the last several hours had done little to improve their mood. "How to get caught apparently," Noboru quipped back. Noboru's hands shook wearily as he loosened a small hook at his waist attached to a long cord. Exhaustion had set in, but adrenaline had kept them going. Coiling the line methodically in his left hand, he held the pronged metal hook it was tied to in the other hand, preparing for a throw. They could hear sounds of bowstrings creaking under tension.

Itsuki peered to the tops of the walls. "The night watch is definitely on edge."

Noboru lobbed the hook just over the wall, catching its sharp points into a thick timber with a tug. After dark, the gates along the barricade were not opened for any reason, not that it did much to slow the shinobi. Within moments, both men were up the line, over the battlements, and on the ramparts between two young guards, bows still drawn and aimed for a killing strike.

"Oi, do we look like samurai to you, boy? Best check those eyes of yours," Noboru barked as he rewound the climbing line around his mid-section.

The ill-tempered warriors were garbed in the worn outfits of guerrilla mercenaries, shinobifukus, that each had mended innumerable times. A dark ragged coat with rolled sleeves was layered over a brown shirt that tied just below the elbows and a dark pair of roomy trousers that tied below the knees. Gauntlets reinforced with leather paneling protected the forearms and the backs of the hands. On their feet they wore straw sandals with a notch between the first and second toe for climbing. Around the neck, each had wrapped an earth toned three-foot square cloth, a versatile scarf that could be utilized for several functions. The outfit was completed by a kind of harness constructed of thin leather bands that strapped about the waist and shoulders. To this harness was secured a wakizashi, a curved short sword that hung diagonally across the back, as well as several pouches slung at the hips. The contents of the pouches varied from one shinobi to another, but typically consisted of food rations, medical supplies, camping gear, and tools for entrapping an enemy.

The sentry was startled as light from the lantern revealed Noboru's face. "My apologies, sir. We... did not expect you. One cannot be too careful."

Itsuki was out of breath. "It's fine, you are right to be wary, and you shall certainly need those arrows soon enough. Where is the Jōnin? We must speak with him immediately."

"In his quarters I believe, taking council with the elders."

"You mean the Hall of Four Rings," Noboru corrected with obvious disdain.

The young man scanned the surrounding area, nervously scratching his eyebrow. "Eh... yes, yes you are right sir, the Hall of Four Rings."

"An honor we gave to our head Jōnin. Something you would know nothing of, Noboru Tsukino," a man barked at Noboru in defiance.

At the mention of Noboru's name there was a murmur of the guards, men gave whispers of both disdain and praise. One guard that had been previously smiling to see comrades from the front lines spat on the wall in disgust.

The man who had spoken was Masanari Hattori, master of arms, charged by the village elders with the direct defense of Hekison. Masanari was a raspy voiced man, with a broad chest, suntanned skin, and a black as coal beard. The man was six feet tall, considered a tower by Iga standards; his mere appearance invoked respect amongst the troops.

Masanari looked like royalty as he barked at the war-torn Noboru. Noboru's shinobifuku had rips, dirt, and mixed stains of his own blood from several enemies. Despite Noboru's appearance, he met Masanari's gaze with defiance and hate.

"Masanari Hattori..." Noboru growled.

"Careful of that insolence, or I'll put you on the outside of the wall to fight. Probably be safer for my men if you weren't on this side."

"We have news for Yamato Akiyama," Itsuki butted in, trying to ease the tension.

Masanari wheeled around to face Itsuki, redirecting his wrath from Noboru. "Itsuki Hayashi, why you stand with Noboru is beyond me. I would have thought you a shrewd man. Give me the message. The head Jōnin should not have to deal with the likes of you two."

"Our orders," Itsuki stated calmly, "come directly from Kazuki Yukimura, and we are to give the news to Yamato directly, no one else."

Only respect for Kazuki was the reason that Masanari let Noboru and Itsuki pass, but not without great grudge. Noboru and Itsuki intentionally did not mention Kazuki's death, for the news of the final stand of the Hundred Shadow Man would be an ill omen for the morale of the troops.

Noboru and Itsuki arrived at the entrance to the Hall of Four Rings, pausing a moment in reverence for their fallen leader. Time and mystery hung thick about the place with the presence of sprits past. For the two shinobi, the hall was a sacred place, a shamanic temple that whispered secrets to those who would listen. Kazuki had instilled in them profound respect for such places. Ancient, and much larger than any other structure in Hekison, the building predated the town itself by hundreds of years. Stories passed down from generation to generation told of the mountain spirit who had helped the first Iga settlers build the hall with great tree trunks gifted by the Iga forest. Four solid wooden pillars and immense lateral beams supported a broad tiled roof that swept to a curve on all four ends. Beneath the extended roof, steps rose to an elevated veranda that wrapped the building's perimeter. Flanking the steps were two guardian spirits, matching stone carvings of seated wolves with tall trees sprouting from their upturned tails.

Noboru looked at the two wolf statues and gently placed a hand on one. "He'll hate this news, Itsuki, especially coming from us." Itsuki didn't respond. He was quietly gazing into the night, lost in some distant memory. "But to be fair, this is a very nice house," Noboru jested patting the closest statue. "I wouldn't want to leave it behind either."

"Who does Yamato think he is?" Itsuki forced the words through clenched teeth. "Using this hall as his personal quarters. He insults the very ground we stand on!"

Noboru's eyes glowed with intensity; it wasn't often that his companion let emotions get the better of him. Noboru felt the blood rise in his veins. He loved nothing more than being a witness to the rare occasions when Itsuki really let loose; unfortunately for him this was neither the time nor place for an outburst, they had a mission to complete.

Reaching up, he placed a calming hand on the tall shinobi's shoulder. "Easy. Lower your voice." Noboru hated the words he was saying. "There will be plenty of time for rage later. Right now, we have orders to carry out, and I need you to be the cool one. The gods know I can't play that role."

Itsuki's muscles relaxed with an effort. "You are right... thank you my friend. Let us be done with this." Snapping back to his usual self, he turned, and bounded lightly up the steps toward the hall's entrance. In a brief second Noboru followed, treading heavily, feeling the stiffness from the long trek.

The entryway contained no real door; only a heavy curtain that could be pulled across. It was presently barred by two armored soldiers bearing spears. The guards quickly recognized the faces of the approaching shinobi, and bowing with respect, let them enter unchallenged. Itsuki returned their kindness with a gracious nod.

Inside, a few elders who had refused to leave the village shuffled about lighting incense and relighting the hanging lanterns. Focused intently on their work, the old men took no notice of the shinobi. In front of a large deposit of scrolls, the Jōnin was sitting cross-legged at a low table, studying a pile of maps and dispatches. He looked up with eyes but did not raise his head, eyeing the pair with disapproval as they entered. "What brings you here genin? It is your chūnin officer that should be reporting to me," his voice echoed powerfully in the large room. "From the looks of you two, I should say that we have already been beaten."

Noboru and Itsuki crossed between the pillars that served as the main supports for the curved ceiling and rafters visibly far above. The interior of the hall was a single open room with wooden floorboards that had been polished to a high gloss shine by ages of care. Despite the incense that was burned daily, the hall always smelled of the forest, the musky aroma of crushed pine needles and damp earth. Dozens of soft glowing lamps dangled happily from long ropes secured to beams overhead. The lights gave the hall a certain intimacy despite its grand scale. The warriors knelt before the table at which the Jōnin was still seated.

"Kazuki Yukimura is dead, we bring his final message," Itsuki stated plainly.

The Jōnin signaled the elders to leave, which they did after a feeble protest and some grumbling about the youth these days. Yamato Akiyama, or the Jōnin as he was more commonly referred to, was in his mid-fifties, and far from a young man. His hair was heavily grayed along the temples of his head, and his face had been deeply creased by age and duty. A strong thick nose and a small scar that ran at an angle from his lower lip across his square chin gave him the look of a fighting general, though in reality he was long retired from such work. His hands showed the evidence that he was more at home wielding a writing tool than a sword, yet he possessed a certain dignity that enticed the respect of men and gave one the sense that he was quite wise.

Yamato scowled, drawing a hand across his shaven face. "So... the Hundred Shadow Man has fallen, and yet the two of you made it out relatively unscathed." He studied their filthy blood-stained garments for any evidence of wounds. "Certainly says something for your spirit."

Itsuki kneeled in respect. "All squads along the front line are scattered or dead. For all we know we were the only ones left. Kazuki sacrificed himself to give us all a chance to escape. We believe that he was able to delay Nobunaga's main forces at the rock pass. Hopefully, he brought down enough of the hillside to bar their passage. If so, it would take them several more hours to move troops up an alternate route."

Yamato's face remained calm. He retrieved a small white stone from a pocket in his kimono, rolling it between his thumb and index finger; a nervous habit the shinobi had seen many times before.

Noboru was growing impatient. "Oda's numbers are beyond count; his men cover the foothills like an ocean, and that ocean is rising. Our last orders were to report this news in the hope that we may still have enough time to evacuate Hekison... sir."

The Jōnin rolled the stone in his fingers with consideration. "How long till the first wave arrives?"

"Three, maybe four hours at the most... if the soldiers we saw were the tip of the spear."

Yamato took a deep breath, holding it as he studied the two men. "If you and your unfortunate chūnin had not botched the mission that Nobunaga had hired us for, perhaps we would have avoided this horror. Entire villages have been burned; our people routed from their homes." Yamato eyes locked squarely on Itsuki's gaze. "And many dear to us have been lost."

A twinge of pain showed on Itsuki's face. Yamato replaced the stone in his pocket, his voice became a tired whisper. "Our defenses are strong. We are well provisioned and have many strong men to hold the town. For a thousand years, men of Iga have held ground against every enemy who dared to claim these mountains as their own."

Noboru clenched his jaw, preparing for a fight.

"Forgive me," the Jōnin sighed. "We must begin evacuations immediately. With any luck Nobunaga will find nothing but a deserted village when he arrives." Yamato shook his head. "This goes against my better judgment, but there are too few shinobi with experience to lead, and even less time. Noboru Tsukino, Itsuki Hayashi, as Jōnin of Hekison, and keeper of the Hall of Four Rings, I promote you two to the rank of chūnin, placing upon you the honor and responsibilities that come with this title. Now rise and be recognized, there's no time to waste."

Speechless, the newly dubbed chūnin rose to their feet, following Yamato as he hurried from the hall. The last thing they expected today was to receive a promotion from Yamato Akiyama. In front of the hall was a courtyard, featuring a large rectangular gravel pit neatly framed at its center. Tradition dictated that the pit was not tread upon with the exception of specific ceremonies for which it was created: public hearings, trials, promotions, and tests. The residents of Hekison strictly avoided the patch of ground as if an invisible force bound it, making the long trip around when traversing the courtyard. The trio moved quickly down the steps of the hall and into the lantern lit yard, skirting around the pit with familiar routine.

Yamato spoke over his shoulder as he walked. "We must see Masanari Hattori. As master of arms, he has been charged with overseeing the defensive forces. Itsuki, you—"

"Incoming!" a soldier's cry interrupted Yamato mid-sentence.

The faint whir of arrows in flight was instantly recognized by the two shinobi who dropped into crouched positions, making themselves small targets in the unprotected courtyard. The Jōnin, who had not seen real combat in years, was slower to react. A cloud of projectiles peppered the courtyard, several hitting the roof of the hall with a distinct thwack! Two arrows plunged into the chest of Yamato, driving him forcefully backwards, causing him to fall into the gravel pit. Noboru growled in pain as an arrow struck him in the meat just above his left collarbone. With a grimace, he grabbed for the shaft, and pulled the arrow free with surprising ease.

As soon as the volley ended, the crouched men sprang into action, lifting the injured Yamato by the legs and under the arms. Noboru winced under the weight of the man as they rushed him to cover. The Jōnin coughed up blood as they set him down. Itsuki tended the Jōnin as Noboru began to inspect the severity of his injury. Sliding his leather utility harness off his shoulder, he noticed the strap had been sliced nearly in half; the arrow had cut through when it made contact. The leather strap had given Noboru just enough armor. No wonder it had been so easy to pull out. Blood poured down his chest as he pulled open his shinobifuku, using the long cloth around his neck Noboru tied off the wound. Noboru gave a violent yell as he finished the dressing, pulling the bandage tight.

"Noboru," Itsuki blurted out at seeing his friend bleeding from the shoulder.

"Don't worry, I'll live," Noboru stated almost unconcerned. "How could they already be here?"

As Yamato lay on the ground, he clutched Itsuki's arm with a trembling hand. "The book..." he wheezed, "Kazuki's book... you must destroy it." His breathing was shallow, a steady trickle of blood running from his mouth. "Wrapped in cloth, under the b-b-bed... Nobunaga must not..." Yamato's voice sputtered to a stop as he began to choke on his own blood.

"The book," Noboru whispered. Then in realization, he grabbed at Itsuki's collar with wild excitement. "The book! He... I thought the old goat had burned it years ago."

Itsuki reluctantly let go of the Jōnin, knowing the book was of a higher importance than the dying Jōnin. Noboru had a wild look of excitement and an obvious lack of care for the dying elder.

"Noboru, this changes everything."

The warriors exchanged glances. With a slight nod, the two sealed an unspoken agreement between them. The roar of fighting rose from the edge of the village, the beating of war drums layered upon command shouts and cries from the injured. The shinobi sped into the darkness toward the Hall of Four Rings, leaving Yamato Akiyama to die alone.

4

The Yukimura Brothers
-Iga Province, Hekison Village-

Silhouetted against the moonlit sky, two sentries along the far western stretch of the Hekison wall shivered with nervous anticipation. They were wrapped in heavy woolen cloaks and huddled tightly against the cold. The taller of the two leaned in speaking, "Fine, tell it to me again." His smooth face contorted in concentration as he sucked his cheeks. The boy next to him grinned with delight.

"Alright Tsubasa, pay attention this time." The boy paused for dramatic effect, resting his bow across his shoulder. "Bound I walk, and loosed I stop. What am I?" The grin quickly returned to the boy, exaggerating his youthfulness. "Come on, it's an easy one. Hell, I bet even that beast Masanari could figure it out."

Tsubasa glared at the young guard. "Watch your tongue, little brother. If the commander heard you mocking him, he would beat your teeth out." A roll of Kaito's eyes pushed Tsubasa to anger. "I'm not joking, Kaito! He's a brutal man. I've seen him lash a man's back raw for less. Do not cross him." The young guard turned away in frustration. Quiet hung between them for a long

26

time as he stared out across the darkening sky that loomed over the terraced rice paddies.

The paddies were a sight to be seen at night in the moonlight. In spring each paddy was a one-foot-deep flooded pool with tiny sprouts protruding through the surface. When the water was still, it could reflect a perfect image of the night sky above. The hundreds of paddies were like large mirrors made by the footsteps of giants as they made their way to the base of the hill. With the autumn season being upon Hekison, some grass grew tall and wild due to neglect of harvest, a biproduct of the long siege.

"When do you think we will see father again?" Kaito spoke, breaking the silence.

"I don't know."

"It's been two months already; he should have been back weeks ago. Do you think he's all right?"

"I don't know! Keep your mind on your post."

Kaito wiped at his nose with the edge of his cloak. "I think he's fine."

Nudging the boy with his bow, Tsubasa gave a half smile. "I'm sure of it." At age seventeen, Tsubasa was only two years older than his brother, but at times the age difference seemed much greater. As one of the prominent shinobi of Iga, their father had been absent for much of their young lives, and Tsubasa had stepped into his role from an early age. For this reason, he had developed quickly, and now at seventeen he shouldered more responsibility than men many years his senior. He had participated in low-level field operations for nearly five years now, having been inducted as a full shinobi much earlier than his peers. Tsubasa had soon earned a reputation for being one of the deadliest and swiftest fighters with a sword for his age. The young man was no stranger to battle, keeping notches on his scabbard for every man he had killed. After two years of invasions by the Oda clan, the scabbard was beginning to run out of space. Apart from his skill, Tsubasa took after his father physically; his face and body were long, angular, and well proportioned. His coal black hair was perfectly straight, and just long enough to tie back in a short ponytail.

Despite being on the verge of shinobi initiation, fifteen-year-old Kaito made no attempt to hide his boyish character. Sheltered to a considerable extent by his brother, he had retained a child-like spirit that endeared him to all but the most hardened of soldiers. He had made friends easily both in and out of training and would frequently approach strangers without hesitation. Tsubasa often remarked that he possessed more qualities of a priest than a warrior. Kaito shared his brother's physique, though shorter, and his round face had the soft gentleness of his mother. Like Tsubasa, his hair was straight and dark; he wore it short but unkempt.

For brothers, the pair could not have been more opposite. Aside from their voices, which were nearly indistinguishable, they had little in common. In training, Kaito excelled in disguises and espionage, while Tsubasa's talents excelled in stealth and assassination. Kaito had mastered the bow at a young age while Tsubasa preferred the sword and close quarters combat. The two were opposite sides of the same shinobi coin.

"I give up. Kaito, what's the answer?"

"It's a riddle, giving the answer ruins the game."

"Come on, it's driving me crazy. I can't concentrate in this cold."

Kaito yawned, stretching his arms back. "Maybe you should

spend less time sharpening your sword and more time sharpening your mind."

A moment later a rush of wind flew by, and Kaito was on his back looking up at his brother standing high above him on the rampart. He gasped for breath and his temple burned. Reaching up Kaito felt his head, warm and wet blood stuck to his palm. The fall from the rampart had knocked the wind out of him, it was nearly ten feet high, and he found his head bleeding. He looked up at his brother with accusation, until he realized that Tsubasa was ducking behind the battlements with his mouth wide, yelling something that Kaito couldn't make out. Rolling slowly to his feet, the dazed sentry climbed to the platform where he had stood moments before. When he reached the top, his brother pulled him down violently.

"Keep your head down!" The words seemed muffled and far away even though Tsubasa was shouting them close to his face. Kaito wiped at the blood that was dripping down his brow.

"What happened?"

"Happening! What's happening," Tsubasa yelled back.

"Huh?"

"Arrows! We're being attacked." Tsubasa grabbed Kaito's head, turning it to see the wound. "Damn, you're lucky. Just a graze." Tsubasa quickly grabbed a strip of cloth from his shinobifuku and wrapped his brother's head, creating a bandana to stop the bleeding.

Kaito blinked in confusion. "Graze? Who?"

"Get it together. You're lucky to be alive; that'll have to do," Tsubasa stated as he cinched his brother's bandana tight.

The older brother threw off his cloak, notching an arrow into his bow. Shouts and commotion had broken out all along the

Hekison wall. The attack had come without warning, a barrage of arrows riddled the barricade and the village behind it. As soon as the alarm had been sounded, all sentry lanterns had been covered. The shinobi knew better than to provide the enemy with easy targets. War drums came to life from the direction of the armory, issuing forth auditory commands with coded beats and patterns. The drums were calling men to bolster the wall's guard. After the first massive volley was a short pause, then came a second volley like hail. Another pause and the arrows began to rain with a light but steady flow.

Tsubasa shifted behind the battlements several paces to his right, and then rising up in the darkness he peered out toward the tree line of the woods. Straining his eyes, he could just make out the forms of troops moving along the trees' edge. He also noticed movement along the ridges that divided the terraced paddies. Taking aim, he let fly an arrow at the nearest ridge, receiving a grunt of pain in response. He ducked back down, shifting farther to the right, and then beckoned Kaito toward him with a hand while loading another arrow. "Alright, little brother, time to put all that target practice to good use." He raised his voice over the clatter of battle. "There are men along the tree line that are advancing along the terraced berms."

Kaito smiled. His head was beginning to clear, and the excitement of battle flooded over him in waves. "I got hit." His smile widened. "Now let's hit them." He removed his cloak and drew his bow. He stole a quick glance over the wall, then he rapidly loosed three arrows. Three cries rose above the din of the war drums. Kaito shot a grin at his brother. "Sandals. That's the answer to my riddle." He loaded another arrow. "Sandals." Tsubasa clapped him on the arm. The Yukimura brothers were fighting side by side for the first time. Several arrows struck the battlements in front of them, and several more flew over the top, sailing into the night.

"Kaito, take up position to the left of where you were hit. I will hold down this end. Fire, move, then fire again. Keep quiet as possible. We don't want to give them anything to shoot at."

Tsubasa moved down the rampart while his brother fired another shot, this time at a group of troops that were creeping forward along the bottom edge of the rock face that comprised Hekison's western border. The leading soldier fell wounded and several of his comrades picked him up, rushing back toward the woods. Kaito hit one of the rescuers in the back of the leg as they fled. The remaining troops returned arrows in kind, forcing the boy to take cover. Tsubasa dropped another man, drawing their attention. Kaito felled another two before the soldiers withdrew their advance. Reinforcements were beginning to arrive with full quivers of arrows.

Tsubasa frowned; something was wrong. He hurried down the platform to his brother. "This isn't the main force. There are no more than a few hundred men from the looks of it. And these soldiers are not that aggressive... they seem to be merely probing our defenses."

Kaito nodded. "A scout force to wear on our nerves with a long night of harassment, paving the way for Nobunaga's army. Or maybe..." His voice trailed off as he looked to the edge of the forest. "I'll be right back," Kaito stated, and then fluidly leaped down from the rampart, rolling to soften his landing, and sprinted off toward the village center.

Tsubasa gaped as his brother sped off. "Where are you going?" he asked the wind, knowing his words were landing on deaf ears. The older brother shook his head, reprimanding himself for letting his brother out of his sight.

Dodging through buildings and tight passageways that crowded the backside of the Hekison wall, Kaito passed dozens upon dozens of men and boys rushing to strengthen the defenses. He scanned the faces as he ran, noting how many shinobi were missing from their numbers. Most of these soldiers were young boys and old men. All the shinobi with experience had been positioned out beyond the barricade, and now it could be assumed that they had fallen under the swords of Nobunaga's samurai. Kaito was glad that his brother had been stationed on the wall during the last several months, and not out with the scout forces. Even so, he was worried about the prospect of a siege by the samurai. The shinobi were strong in their guerilla tactics, not for open field battle, and had little experience in massing large forces. Nobunaga's troops, on the other hand, had seized castles a hundred times over.

When he reached the armory, he could hear the gruff voice of Masanari Hattori barking orders at a group of men carrying spears. The men jumped at his every word. At age thirty-nine he was respected by most, feared by all, and had been a natural choice to take lead under conditions of a siege. A black-bearded man with thick shoulders and callused hands who had seen more action than most. While he was neither the subtlest nor cunning of warriors, he was hard as steel and possessed the relentless determination of a starving wolf. He wore an aged shinobifuku like the others, and had an excited look on his face, his eyes shining as though welcoming death.

"Yu-ki-mur-aaa!" Masanari's voice roared with fury. "You better have a damn good reason for leaving your post!" The commander's stare froze the boy dead in his tracks. His large fists clenched powerfully at his sides. "If not, I will gladly end you myself."

Kaito dropped to a knee. "Forgive me, sir. I have urgent news. In the woods off the western wall, the enemy is forming up for an attack. I saw men with tall shields, and I saw the soldiers loading spheres into clay casks." The boy went silent, cleverly allowing the commanding shinobi to put the pieces together.

Masanari stroked his beard in thought. "Incendiaries... they mean to bring down our wall by making the casks into a bomb. That's why they've been hitting so hard along the eastern wall, it's a diversion. They want to draw away our forces for the assault."

Kaito stood. "We could bring them down with a dozen good archers."

"A dozen good archers..." Masanari snorted. "We don't have five decent archers left in Hekison. Run back to your post where you're needed." He turned his back, beckoning over a nearby shinobi with a wave of his arm. "Yukimura, you will regret it if I have to repeat those orders." The boy could not help but feel a jolt of fear; one did not willingly draw the commander's wrath. When Kaito arrived at his post, he was welcomed by a smack to the head from his brother.

"Fine time to leave! If you wanted to send a message, that's what the children are for," Tsubasa scolded.

Kaito pushed back. "Leave me alone. Give me my bow." He snatched up the bow, hastily loading it. Peeking out, he saw the formations of men; three holding large shields in front, followed by two carrying clay cask containers that were beginning to make their way from the wood's edge. He could make out five such squads spread across the western flank. "The fool," he mumbled under his breath as he loosed an arrow at the nearest formation of advancing shields. His shot was high and flew harmlessly into the trees. In frustration he took aim at a closer target, fired quickly, and missed again.

Tsubasa caught him by the elbow. "Calm down, you're going to waste all your arrows in anger and have nothing to show for it. Where did you go? What happened?"

Kaito pulled his arm away. "Nothing, it doesn't matter anyway." He reached down for another arrow.

His brother blocked his hand. "No, you always miss when you get mad. I need you on point. I need you to calm down." Suddenly his attention was drawn by a large procession of soldiers moving toward them from the direction of the armory. "What have you done?" he asked. Forty archers were flooding their position. They all carried arrows readied with points wrapped in oilcloth.

Kaito's obnoxious smile returned. "How's that for on point?" The soldiers climbed up to the platforms along the western stretch, hauling lit torches.

A voice called up to them. "Kaito Yukimura? What is our target?" Tsubasa stared in disbelief. His little brother nudged him playfully with his elbow.

Kaito looked down noticing that the voice belonged to the same shinobi that Masanari Hattori had waved down. "There are formations of men moving across the field under cover of large shields," Kaito stated, gesturing to the targets. "The soldiers behind them are carrying clay casks... explosives."

The head archer nodded and started pacing down the line, shouting orders to the archers to light their arrows. With the commanding archer's hand wave and accompanying battle cry, the night sky was streaked with flaming arrows. The large, overlapping rectangular shields of the advancing troops were barraged with missiles. Light provided by the burning arrows showed that the shields were large screens made of tightly bundled reeds secured to a bamboo frame. The benefit was that they provided a large amount of cover and could easily be carried by a single man. The drawback was that the screens were extremely flammable. Soon the screens were crowded with arrows and blazing brightly. Several formations fell apart. The soldiers abandoned the burning shields, while several more continued to advance, flames and all. Kaito drew his bow with a flaming arrow, aiming carefully at a formation that was nearing the wall. He exhaled slowly, loosed his arrow that landed with a thud in the neck of a soldier bearing a cask. The man tumbled to his left, knocking down the soldier running next to him who had been carrying a banger. The pair crashed to the ground, a burst of red embers leaping from the arrow as they fell. For a moment, the uninjured soldier fumbled for something on the ground, but only for a moment.

Boom! An explosion of fire and earth erupted where the soldiers had been. The blast shook the battlements, rattling the timbers. Debris erupted into the air and rained down on the archers in great chunks. They looked in wonder at the crater that had been cut into the field, not fifteen paces from the barricade.

A mighty cheer erupted among the guards of Hekison who felt they had stopped the enemy's plan. Tsubasa and Kaito grinned as they silently congratulated one another for performing their duties well. A moment of elation washed over the fighters before a second explosion interrupted them.

Boom! Five hundred paces east of the Yukimuras' position; the wall was suddenly ripped apart. Men were thrown from the rampart as the battlements in front of them splintered, opening a small rift in the barrier. Arrows rained in, forcing the archers to take cover. Several were hit and fell to the ground. The flaming arrows served as unmistakable targets for the enemy. Men scrambled to help the wounded and form ranks in the damaged barrier. *Boom!* Another roar of a well-placed banger echoed from the eastern wall. Men and fragments of timber soared into the night air, creating a visibly large breach in the barricade. Smoke began to billow from the far side of the village.

The Yukimura brothers watched the enemy soldiers abandon their siege on the west wall and sprint toward the direction of the blasts. Many men on the defending side of the wall began running east as well, leaving only a handful of archers, aside from the Yukimura brothers. Tsubasa and Kaito continued to fire, picking off nearly a dozen in the chaotic scene.

Tsubasa turned. "We should fall back to the armory… join up with the main force. If the eastern wall is broken, we'll be easy prey. We won't stand a chance."

"If we leave, there will soon be a hole in this part of the blockade as well," Kaito protested.

"It will happen anyway; the only difference is if there will be two more corpses if we stay."

The brothers loosed a few feeble arrows hoping to thin out the samurai before dropping from the platform to make a run for the armory. It was madness on the ground. Children cried, women wailed, and men screamed in death. Tsubasa saw one woman defend herself with savagery, but all that did was attract the attention of more samurai and her sword arm was quickly lopped off, leaving her to bleed and shriek. The samurai were making examples of anyone resisting. The slaughter had begun and smoke from some unseen fires was starting to fill the narrow village streets. Many young soldiers were rushing in all directions. Tsubasa led the way, urgently weaving through buildings, hoping to bypass the commotion that had broken out along the barricade.

As they turned a corner to cut deeper into the heart of the village, they nearly collided with a group of enemy foot soldiers, armored in green with swords drawn. The eight men were led by a ninth, a samurai commander painted with the golden Oda crest. The closest soldier excitedly charged at Tsubasa with the point of his blade aimed at Tsubasa's breast.

With lightning speed Tsubasa unsheathed his wakizashi and deflected the attack, simultaneously grabbing the wrist of the enemy's right hand. Twisting the arm, the agile shinobi spun his body, dropping his weight to break the forearm as he threw the soldier to the ground. The freshly sharpened wakizashi pierced the man's neck, fulfilling its deadly purpose. Kaito wasted no time, unleashing an arrow into the chest of the next adjacent soldier. The remaining troops, slightly startled by the violent skill of the young men, fanned out to encircle them. The head samurai lifted his katana in command, and the circle began to close in on the brothers.

Just as the enemy soldiers moved to strike, the shining point of a steel sickle plunged deeply into the shoulder of the man flanking Kaito. The chain attached to a sickle's handle was pulled taut, and the soldier was yanked off his feet in a spray of blood followed by a belligerent war cry from the mysterious attacker. At the chain's other end was a well-built shinobi with long wild hair that hung in thick tangles concealing his face. The attention of all was drawn to this dark figure, head slightly forward, feet firmly planted in a wide stance in the shadows of smoke and fire.

At that moment, a second shinobi dropped from the roof of an adjacent hut, pounding his feet into the back of one soldier and cleaving the neck of another with the edge of his sword, his bald head shining in the moonlight. A swift downward thrust silenced the grunts from the man underneath him. Pulling his wakizashi free, he quickly rolled to the outside of the encircled men, dividing the focus of their attack. A heavily clad soldier calmly turned to face him.

The longhaired warrior threw his kusarigama again, a ten-foot-long chain with a deadly forearmed-sized sickle at the end, this time encircling the chain around the waist of a soldier. Kaito jumped into action, sending an arrow into the ribs of the entrapped enemy, just below the armpit. He screamed as the sickle tore free from his lightly armored abdomen. Tsubasa spun gracefully to evade an enemy swing. With an overhead chop, he drew the man's defense up. Then with a flash, he retracted and sprung forward, forcing the sword into the enemy's chest. The soldier fell with a look of surprise on his face.

Kaito's quiver was spent, and he dove away from the last remaining foot soldier, narrowly escaping his thrust. The chain end of the kusarigama looped around the charging soldier's neck, stopping his forward motion. The wild hair of the shinobi flailed as he cinched the chain tight, crushing the victim's windpipe, dropping him to the ground in a heap.

The head samurai and the bald shinobi were focused intently on one another. Tsubasa wiped the blood from his blade while he watched the duel unfold. The samurai moved with the strong confidence of an expert swordsman, wielding his katana as an extension of his body. His strikes were quick and precise, and he was clearly determining the pace of the swordplay with aggressive action. Yet, despite the samurai's skill, the bald shinobi seemed to anticipate his every move, evading his swings with confounding subtlety. The samurai's frustration was evident, but although he could not land a blow, neither could his opponent. Tsubasa made a movement to join the fight, but the mysterious longhaired shinobi grasped his shoulder.

"Watch and learn something."

Tsubasa turned his attention back just in time to see the shinobi throw a concealed hand of dust into the samurai's eyes. The samurai cursed the dirty trick, but it was too late; the shinobi's blade had pulled cleanly across his throat. The shinobi at Tsubasa's side nodded his head in approval, clearing the hair from his face. "So, you must be the Yukimura brothers."

Tsubasa stared intently. "Yes... How?"

"Well for starters, you have the face of your father, and we were told that you would be posted on the west wall." He pulled back his long hair, tying it into a knot. "Anyhow, let's get out of here before we have to kill another dozen." He flashed a friendly grin.

Kaito grinned back nervously. "Sounds good to me. We were just on our way to the armory ourselves. I feel much better with you two here."

The bald shinobi shot a look to his partner, shaking his head. "I'm afraid not. We have other orders that must be carried out... your father's orders."

Tsubasa frowned with disapproval, but Kaito's face brightened with the mention of their father. "Father's orders?" he asked excitedly. "What orders?"

The bald man spoke up. "To get you safely out of Hekison." He finished cleaning his blade and skillfully sheathed it. "And we will complete our orders." The noise of fighting rose in the distance, several more explosions sounding off.

"What of the village?" Tsubasa stated, his pride and anger rising. "Are we just going to abandon our comrades and our home like cowards?" Grabbing Kaito by the sleeve, he moved the boy behind him, firmly gripping the handle of his own sword. Nervous sweat began to bead at his brow. It was hard for Tsubasa to think clearly with adrenaline from the fight still pumping through his blood. "And where is our father if these are his orders?"

"He's dead," the bald man stated bluntly. "Sacrificed himself in order to buy some time for the village. You can trust us, Tsubasa, this is not the first time we have met."

The longhaired shinobi interjected. "We don't have time to argue. The village is lost. If you want to honor Kazuki, then you must live. We can explain everything later, but now we must go." Tsubasa and Kaito looked at each other and grudgingly nodded.

The two mysterious shinobi led the Yukimura brothers deeper into the village, stopping at a small grain storage shed. Prying a board from its side, the bald headed one pulled out four fully stocked packs, the kind shinobi took when they were headed to the front lines or on a mission that required significant travel. He handed a pack to each of them. Then reaching inside the hollow where the packs had been, he retrieved another object. It was rectangular and wrapped in white cloth. This he placed carefully in his own bag, removing several packets of rations to make room for it.

"Let's get this over with before more enemies come, and my shoulder stiffens up," the longhaired shinobi groaned.

"You used the hand seal again," the bald one said. "You know the consequences."

The Yukimura brothers had no time to ask questions. They did as they were told and tried to keep up as the shinobi ran ahead. Pandemonium raged in Hekison as enemy troops flooded through the decimated eastern wall. Fighting spilled into the village streets, and fires were set to the roofs of homes. The village battle was converting more into a slaughter while the enemy pillaged, burned, and killed. The group moved swiftly, and soon the sounds of war became muffled as they circled around the western edge, sneaking back toward the wall where the Yukimuras had been stationed. The group boosted themselves up the wall to make their escape.

Tsubasa helped lower the bald shinobi down. "You said we've met before, but I don't remember."

The bald shinobi looked up; his face covered in sweat. "You were young, still in training. We came by to speak with your father, my name's Itsuki Hayashi, my friend is named Noboru Tsukino."

Just before the Yukimura brothers lowered themselves down the wall they saw in the distance what seemed to be master of arms, Masanari Hattori, killing an enemy soldier and to the brothers' shock, pointing while cursing in their direction. Lowering down the wall, the four were quickly over the battlements, dropping silently into the shadows of the forest beyond. Kaito stared at the bodies of dead enemy soldiers as they passed, many of which still bore his arrows. A soldier moaned in pain as they stepped over him; without hesitation, the longhaired man stepped on his throat, producing a kunai dagger from his belt that he slid soundlessly into the man's neck. No movement could be detected along the western tree line, but the four were taking no chances.

Escaping into the night, the shinobi cut a path along the mountain rock face to the safety of the thick woods. The spreading flames from the village cast narrow sheets of light through the trees, and the Yukimura brothers turned to look for a final time on the place they had called home. Hekison had fallen.

5

Gray Dawn
-Iga Province, Iga Mountains-

Gray ash fell like snowflakes and cold light crept over the mountaintop as morning came to Hekison. The stale smell of smoke lingered in the air. Timbers smoldered, and the bodies of the dead littered the streets, leaving blood-stained trails of their final acts. Once a haven for free people, the crushed village only contained sorrow and ghosts. A perimeter had been established around the Hall of Four Rings, which only a select few were permitted to cross. Dozens of soldiers, handpicked and under the direction of the young Nobukatsu, had emptied the armory and were now scouring the village building by building for every weapon they could find, both large and small. Floorboards were ripped up, tiles torn from the roofs, and every conceivable hiding place overturned. By command, all items discovered and taken from the dead were transported immediately to the hall for inspection by Lord Nobunaga Oda. The men conducting the search had been stripped down to just their sandals and undergarments. Nobukatsu was not about to let any prize walk off hidden amongst the layered battle dress of his troops. Soon enough, they would be rewarded for their loyalty, but not before the daimyō had his turn.

Nobunaga calmly sat cross-legged at the same table Yamato Akiyama had occupied the previous night. The candle lanterns that had been diligently lit by the elders of the village still hung from the ceiling but had almost burned out. Aside from the exterior that resembled a pincushion filled with arrows, the Hall of Four Rings had remained untouched throughout the siege. The daimyō sat quietly in the large room as if he were a guest waiting to be served tea. Beside him sat his helmet, like the severed head of some terrible demon, horns curling up from the floor. He was studying a katana, holding the blade close to his eye, inspecting its graceful curve from guard to tip. Running his fingertips over the metal, he became enchanted at the delicate swirling patterns where the swordsmith had laboriously folded steel over steel.

Nobukatsu entered to find his father gently cradling the sword, eyes wrapped in emotion. "It's quite beautiful."

"Yes… yes it is," Nobunaga replied, clearing his throat.

Nobukatsu removed his helmet. "Where do you think these farmers acquired such a blade?"

Flipping the weapon to study the other side, Nobunaga pointed it toward his son. Then meeting Nobukatsu's eyes he replied, "Stolen, most likely. From a dead samurai, one of the many shinobi contracts… maybe from one of the many men under my command. Regardless, it is just like all the rest." He sheathed the blade and threw it across the room in frustration where it crashed into a growing pile of discarded swords. Arranged next to Nobunaga's helmet were two blades that had been previously examined along with various books, scrolls, and letters that had belonged to the Jōnin of Hekison. Lifting his helmet, the daimyō rose to his feet. "We cannot afford to dawdle here any longer than need be. You must press your men in their search. While we toil in these cursed mountains, my enemies conspire against me."

Nobukatsu stepped forward. "You are the most powerful warlord in Japan. You command the loyalty of many daimyōs, and you wield one of the greatest swords ever made. No one will forget the strength of your will, or the reach of your katana. Hashiba, Tokugawa, Mitsuhide, and all the great houses believe that you can bring Japan under a single banner. Why do you worry so? The success of these men depends on your success in this campaign. Surely they will keep your enemies in check during our absence."

Nobunaga approached his son, smoothing his mustache. "Ah, but would you trust a man that always keeps one hand behind his back? Sure, he may bow and give praise... he may call you the savior of an empire, but what of his hand? You must always trust that in it he holds a dagger. Yes, use him! Give him land, title, and the command of troops, but never turn your back to him, for he will plunge with the dagger at first chance. Face him and let him see that you always keep one hand on the hilt of your sword. Only by fear of being struck down will he choose his actions carefully."

Admiration shone in Nobukatsu's eyes as he bowed. "Someday, I hope to be half as wise. Your counsel, I always take it to heart."

Nobunaga smiled graciously, placing an arm around his son. "You will be twice as wise! But only half as handsome." He broke into loud laughter, leading Nobukatsu to the door. "Now, have envoys sent ahead to each of the daimyōs in my service. Have them deliver letters reporting our victory over the Iga shinobi. Furthermore, issue a command that all available generals are to take part in a war council to discuss the campaign to unify Japan. Reports to be given by every general and preparations to be made during the winter months while my enemies sleep behind the snow."

The son and father emerged from the hall into the chill of the early morning. "What of the prisoners, have any of them proven useful?"

Nobukatsu walked with his father down the steps to the center of the gravel pit beyond. "This one might, though he's been nothing but trouble so far."

In the middle of the ceremonial pit, Lieutenant Ito was interrogating a broad-shouldered shinobi bound at the wrists and ankles. A short way off, a few battered men, women, and young children were tied up, waiting to be questioned.

Lieutenant Ito gave the back of his hand to the bound shinobi. "You will tell me what I want to know or drench the pit you kneel on with blood."

The man looked up at Lieutenant Ito with wild bloodshot eyes and spat. His shinobifuku had been pulled down around his waist, and a rivulet of blood leaked from a wound in his chest. Injuries on his arms and across his back were swollen and crusted over. Ash caked and cracked about his eyes, and his beard was matted with blood. "That's a piss poor slap. When I hit a man, I make a fist." Lieutenant Ito was winding up for another swing when he saw Nobunaga striding forward.

Nobunaga looked down at the shinobi. "And whom do we have here?"

Grabbing the shinobi by the hair, Lieutenant Ito yanked the kneeling man's head back to show his face. "This man put up quite the fight during our siege; I am told that he took out four of our best samurai before we could subdue him. Though he would deny it, another prisoner confirmed his identity; his name is Masanari Hattori, master of arms of Hekison."

The daimyō stepped closer with interest. "Is he now... Well then, perhaps we can help each other." He leaned his face in toward Masanari. "If you help me find what I'm looking for, I will oblige you to a quick death, maybe a chance for life if your information is valuable. If not, well, things will get considerably more painful." He let his words sink in for a moment. "Where are Jōnin Akiyama's personal belongings? I would like to collect them now."

Masanari shook his head. "Yamato was a man of many secrets. If you think a few trinkets will help unlock them, you must be dumber than you look."

Dropping to a crouch, Nobunaga placed his palms together. "I know how fond you shinobi are of your deceptions. Shadows, mist, some say magic. But I know it's just tricks, and I can't help but think that even now I am being played for a fool."

Masanari snorted in laughter, spraying blood from his nose. "The Fool of Owari Province, the great Nobunaga. Yeah, maybe, maybe you are being played. Maybe we all are. You want a dead man's toys? Go take them." Masanari nodded his head toward a slumped body with a pair of arrows protruding from its chest. "He's waiting for you."

Nobunaga studied Masanari Hattori for a long moment, ash lazily danced toward the earth in the silence of the courtyard. Masanari could not help but admit, Nobunaga in his full battle garb looked like the underworld itself had come to Hekison.

"Kill me and be done with it, but if I'm going to be slapped by a girl at least give me a better looking one than your concubine over there."

Lieutenant Ito clenched his fists while his face turned red with rage.

Underneath his mustache Nobunaga permitted a smile, curious to see if Masanari's resistance was true courage or a defense mechanism to hide his fear. *If anyone knows it's him,* Nobunaga thought. "Defiant to the end. You would have us beat you to death rather than give up the information I seek. Very honorable... but misguided." He pressed his thumb against the shinobi's chest, pushing his wound open.

In pain Masanari struggled to pull away. "There is nothing I can help you with, samurai, and if I could... I would take pleasure in denying you."

Nobunaga chuckled to himself. "Well, Masanari Hattori, I have no reason to trust you." He nodded to lieutenant Ito, who kicked Masanari to the ground. "But in a few moments, I will trust anything that you say."

Nobunaga gestured toward two soldiers with lit torches and the once proud Hall of Four Rings started to take flame. Soon the heat could be felt by all present, the few villagers left alive gasped at the scene and a child began to cry. The two soldiers who had set flame to the Hall of Four Rings dragged Masanari to a wooden bench at the border of the gravel pit, forcing his head onto the smooth wood. Masanari struggled the whole way and cursed the men for not fighting him properly. Nobunaga went to a nearby smoldering fire and took out a discarded red-hot dagger. Masanari spat at Nobunaga's feet as the bright orange steel made its way to his face.

Masanari Hattori screamed in pain, and the corpses of Hekison watched.

6

The Forest Trail
-Iga Province, Iga Mountains-

A long night of running gave way to a swift sunrise, and as the sky gradually brightened, the four shinobi were glad for the headway they had made during the dark hours. Pale light mixed with morning mist filtered through the trees, giving off a low visibility to the group. Such weather was considered by shinobi to be brought by the spirits of the forest. The men's legs were weak and quivering with fatigue. Anticipating a rest, Itsuki signaled with his hand for the group to slow their pace. In several minutes, they neared a clear running stream, and came to a full stop. The group dropped their packs to the ground, panting. The noise of running water was barely audible over the pounding of blood in their ears, but just the sight was enough to refresh each shinobi.

The Yukimura brothers laid out flat, taking deep even breaths. Noboru crouched to the water and splashed his face and neck while Itsuki remained standing for a few minutes stretching his legs. "You should all stretch as well… keep your muscles warm. We will stay here for an hour."

Noboru began undressing his wound, grimacing every time he moved his shoulder too much. The cloth he had used to wrap it was soaked through with blood. He dunked the cloth into the stream, scrubbing it against the smooth stones and wringing it repeatedly until the water ran clear. Draping it from a branch to dry, he riffled through his pack for his medical pouch and began to thoroughly wash the wound with handfuls of clean water. With the coat and shirt of Noboru's uniform pulled back, Kaito noticed the mess of scars that decorated the man's chest and shoulders. In particular, Kaito noted one scar on Noboru's back, a brand in barely legible kanji script between the shoulder blades. Kaito tried to distinguish the mangled brand but quickly diverted his eyes, seeing that Noboru took notice of his gaze.

Noboru grumbled to himself as he cleansed the opening. "Eh, I'll make those samurai pay for this."

Itsuki walked over, inspecting the shoulder and sniffing the wound to check for a stink. "You did make them pay, several times if you remember. You're luckier than Yamato at least. The wound is clean and shallow, it'll just be a tale to match the rest of your scars."

In a small bowl, Noboru began to combine some ingredients from his medical kit, mixing them clumsily into a chunky paste. Kaito watched the process with concern. "It's too dry; you're doing it wrong."

Noboru gave a dismissive grunt. "Am I? What would you know about medicine, boy? Probably never had a real wound yourself."

"He knows what he's talking about. He may not share your experience, but he is careful and observant, and he's got a real knack for mixing herbs," Tsubasa said.

Noboru stopped mixing the medicine, annoyed by the teenager's attitude. "I have treated more wounds than most men would see in three lifetimes. I don't need some fresh-faced tadpole giving me advice on how to make an ointment!"

"Yes, clearly," Kaito said sarcastically. "Judging by all those scars, which look like they were dressed by a blind man with feet for hands."

Noboru tossed the bowl down. "I'll show you feet for hands."

"Enough," Itsuki said lazily. "Kaito, you may be good with herbs, but mind your tone." He turned to Noboru. "And we both know you're better at blowing things up than treating wounds. Even I can see you're making a mess of your shoulder. Let the kid try."

Noboru shot a death stare at Itsuki, who in response put his hands in the air to indicate that he would push the subject no further. Folding his arms with silent defiance, Noboru sat cross-legged with a scowl for several moments, then picked up the bowl and shoved it toward Kaito.

Kaito eagerly seized the concoction and knelt by the stream. He skillfully dipped his hand into the running water, lifted it, and guided several drops as they rolled down his fingers into the bowl. He methodically mixed the paste until it was smooth. The boy produced some delicate green leaves from a neatly folded pouch in his pocket, rolling them in his fingers until he was able to squeeze a few drops of white liquid into the mixture. Itsuki watched every movement closely as Kaito finished mixing the ointment and moved toward the scowling shinobi to apply it to his wound. Noboru grunted once before allowing Kaito to delicately apply the dressing. Afterwards, he securely wrapped and tied the shoulder off with a fresh cloth and a perfectly made knot that would lay flat, preventing irritation from rubbing. Noboru eyeballed him suspiciously as he worked.

Kaito placed a warm hand on Noboru's arm. "Try not to move it for a few days or the wound will reopen." Noboru nodded in gruff acceptance and pulled a sake gourd out of his pack. He took out the wood stopper and dipped his head back for a long swig of the liquor.

Itsuki's eyes smiled at the interaction of the odd pair and began to fill a gourd with water from the cold spring. "There is a small pool a short way up the stream if you would like to make a try at catching fish."

Kaito's face lit up, and he scrambled for his pack. He may have been exhausted, but the prospect of fresh fish gave him new energy. With the invasion, it had been months since anyone stationed at Hekison had been rationed fresh fish, all meat being cured for the shinobi on the front lines. In a flash, Kaito was hiking upstream, bow in hand, a kunai tucked in his waistband.

Tsubasa remained seated while staring into the rippling water until Kaito was out of earshot. "How did my father die?"

Noboru studied the teenager. "He died, giving us time to help you and Kaito escape. He died as he lived... a true shinobi."

Tsubasa skipped a rock across the stream. "Save your vague and honorable stories for my little brother; he will appreciate them. I want to know how."

"He stayed behind to block the rock pass with a landslide. He knew that it would cut off his escape. He probably died surrounded, alone, and against odds," Noboru stated solemnly. "Before we parted, I gave your father a bag of explosives; we heard every one of them go off. Your father wasn't called the Hundred Shadow Man for nothing."

Tsubasa stared at the older shinobi pondering the truth of their words. "Yet you weren't there to watch him fall."

Itsuki met Tsubasa's gaze. "Noboru and I were under your father's command for years before the invasions of Nobunaga. We shared many missions." He paused in reflection. "Kazuki Yukimura was the finest shinobi I have ever known. By the name of my family, I promise you he died well."

Tsubasa gave a solemn pause. In many ways these two men knew his father better than he did. Kazuki had been a good father to the boys but his duties as a shinobi often led him far abroad, and having lost their mother to childbirth of a stillborn, the brothers were raised by the village to a considerable extent. "So... that's where he was," Tsubasa stated with no emotion, lying down to rest, letting exhaustion get the better of him.

Noboru glanced toward Itsuki from the corner of his eyes, his dark brow slightly arched. The bald shinobi reached for his pack, placing the faded gray bag between his knees. It was a simple leather bag of sturdy construction, waterproofed with beeswax, and just large enough for the essentials of the traveler. Untying the top of the bag, he reached in and removed the cloth bound parcel from Hekison. Itsuki handed a leather book with strange markings on its cover to Noboru. Tsubasa could hear the men mumbling, mingled with the flipping of pages as sleep overtook him.

The sun was starting to scare off the morning mist as Noboru thumbed through pages of the book. "Kazuki would never make anything easy. Half the book is encrypted. This best not be an elaborate trick to confuse Yamato. I don't think I could handle him fooling us even after death. I thought Yamato would have destroyed it himself long ago, but instead he asks us to burn it with his dying breath... Why? Why wait?"

Itsuki thought for a moment. "Leverage over Kazuki and the influence he held among the villages I suppose. If the book stayed intact, Yamato could keep Kazuki under heel. He was probably trying to decipher it himself... learn the secrets Kazuki withheld, learn the truth of the years he went missing."

"What is that book?" Tsubasa's tired voice interrupted.

Noboru did not look up. "None of your business. Go back to sleep. This book isn't for all eyes," he said, flipping a page.

Tsubasa was sitting up now. "You have done what my father asked; my brother and I escaped the village and are safe. We have friends and relatives that have fled to Osaka before the fall of Iga. Kaito and I could easily make our way there, start new lives. I need some answers if we are to stay and follow you."

Itsuki sighed and closed the book, replacing it in his pack. "You're right. You two are free to do as you please. You are free men, and you must choose your own fate." Absentmindedly he reached up, touching his face where two parallel scars crossed his left eye. "We trusted your father as our chūnin commander for years. We bled, we sweat, and we killed with him. What we didn't do was question his motives... doubt his wisdom. If you choose to follow us, we will expect the same."

Tsubasa considered the offer. "And if we were to follow you... to what end would you lead us?"

Itsuki stood up, stretching his long legs, "We are shinobi; we endure no matter what happens, but we will not endure long under the hammer of Nobunaga. We will eliminate him, and we will rebuild."

Tsubasa shook his head. "Two men, rogue without support. An army surrounds Nobunaga, and his castle at Azuchi is an impenetrable maze of traps designed to foil assassinations.

Besides, they say that no man has ever defeated his Masamune blade. They say that it is sanctified."

"Sanctified blade," Noboru stated sarcastically, followed by the mimic of a large fart. Noboru unwrapped a small rice cake of compressed rice, grains, and honey from his supply pack and hungrily began eating. With his mouth still full he said, "They also say that we shinobi are yōkai given power by dark magic. People will always fear what they don't understand."

"Yōkai, huh? Demons, monsters, and spirits from folklore. Is that what the common folk think of us shinobi? I suppose our methods of stealth will create that effect," Tsubasa stated slightly amused.

"I'm not complaining. Fear like that will work in our advantage when the four of us go after Nobunaga." Noboru gave Tsubasa a wink and took another bite of his meal.

Reluctantly, Tsubasa smiled, weighing his options. The sight of food made his mouth water, and he began rummaging in his own pack for a rice cake. Finding one, he broke off a small piece, savoring the sweet nourishment, and then he looked expectantly upstream. With a high whistle that dropped a vibrating note at the end, Tsubasa called for his brother. The older shinobi snapped to attention.

Itsuki blinked. "That is your father's call."

"Of course. He taught it to me when I was very young to keep track of Kaito. It has come in handy more than once." The younger Yukimura could be seen making his way back along the stream.

Itsuki nodded with approval. "I have never heard anyone mimic it so closely."

Tsubasa straightened up with pride, wiping his hands on his

pants as he finished his rice cake. He cinched his pack shut. "So, how about that book?"

"Trust first. Knowledge will follow." Itsuki was growing impatient with the young shinobi's impudence. "You are now part of a select few that know of this book's existence. Consider yourself privileged." He put his hands on Tsubasa's shoulders. "I promise you; the journey will be worth it."

Kaito bounded down the stream bank, a line of fish dangling from his hand. "This place is known as Last Haven, is it not?"

Noboru admired the boy's catch. "Yes, a name given by the shinobi of Hekison. This is a common stopping point before embarking on a mission, long treasured for its rejuvenating water and abundance of iwana, the type of trout you have there. Well done."

Kaito beamed at the praise, holding up the line to show off the haul: two large fish, nearly the length of his forearm, and three smaller specimens that would still make good eating. The boy grinned as he handed the line to Noboru. "We will eat well tonight!"

"That's up to you." Noboru felt the weight of the line, handing it back with a nod. "Your brother thinks that maybe the two of you would be better off on your own. Make your way to Osaka alone... of course, we wouldn't mind the company if you chose to stay."

Kaito turned to Tsubasa in protest. "Leave? They saved our lives! We owe them our loyalty." He searched his brother's hard face with worry in his eyes. "Please, brother, don't make us go. Besides, I remember our cousins who left for Osaka. They're mean... and the big one smells."

Clearing his throat, Itsuki spoke up. "Noboru and I cannot complete the task ahead of us without the both of you. If you truly be the sons of Kazuki Yukimura, we would be honored to have you by our sides."

All eyes were fixed on Tsubasa, waiting for a response. After a moment of resistance, he cracked under the pressure and grudgingly nodded his surrender. Kaito gave a yell of youthful delight.

Laughing heartily, Noboru slapped Tsubasa on the back. "Kanpai! Let's seal it with a drink and be on our way." Toasting with the gourd slung from his shoulder, he passed it around making sure everyone took a good long drink.

As the day wore on, the four held a steady course to the north, following a worn game trail that wound along the mountain ridge. After the break at Last Haven, they did not stop again, except to occasionally catch their breath and readjust their packs. They had far to go before the cover of night, and the older shinobi were wary that scout teams sent by Nobunaga could well be in the area, hunting down survivors. Kaito and Itsuki led the way briskly, the young boy eagerly chatting to Itsuki with an unending flow of questions and curiosities. Itsuki did his best to humor him, stressing repeatedly that breath would be better served powering their legs; there would be plenty of time for questions once the day's journey was complete. Noboru and Tsubasa followed behind, mostly in silence, aside from a few crass jokes that Noboru was fond of telling. The jokes always featured either a deviant, women, or both, and Tsubasa couldn't help but laugh as the gruff man delivered his well-practiced punch lines in the absurd falsetto imitation of a lady's voice. Along the way, Tsubasa noted that the longhaired shinobi repeatedly paused, stuffing handfuls of herbs, and leaves into a pocket sewn into his pants above the knee.

When the sun was nearing the western horizon, the four

stopped to make camp, picking a spot well off the trail and relatively flat that overlooked the valley floor miles below. While the Yukimuras were unloading their packs, Itsuki began building a little pile of twigs and chips of dry wood. From the satchel at his hip, Noboru removed a small box made of iron; inside were left over embers from some previous fire. Pulling the dried kindling he had collected from his pocket; he shook the cold embers from the box into their center and began to softly blow. He held the whole bundle in his hands, continuing to blow till little puffs of smoke appeared, followed by a glowing flame. Quickly he introduced the flaming handful to Itsuki's pile, and skillfully nurtured the whole into a conservative cooking fire, taking care not to allow too much light to escape. Without proper precautions the fire would easily reveal their location to anyone nearby, but considering the dropping temperatures, Noboru judged it worth the risk.

Kaito unwrapped the previously gutted fish from Last Haven. Luckily, the trout had stayed fresh with the cool air, he began to cook them over the fire. Kaito planned to cook half his catch and smoke the rest. Meanwhile Tsubasa helped Itsuki clear spots to sleep and construct a simple tent by lashing together the large beeswax coated capes that were rolled up and tied to the outside of each man's pack. The tent would sit very low to the ground, supported by bent green boughs and lengths of strong chord anchored to the ground by wooden spikes. The men would sleep close together, side by side to conserve body heat; in this way they would last the frosty night.

Soon the smell of cooked fish filled the air, and the group was happily eating hot food for the first time in days. Their brief joy was soon replaced with a solemn silence as they ate. Each one stared into the fire with a deep sense of loss and sorrow, remembering the path that lay behind them. For two years Nobunaga's invasions had hung over them like a foreboding shadow, and now the finality of defeat had started to set in. From this point on, there would be no support or guidance except for that which they drew from one another. Kaito stared into the darkness to the south where a single flickering light could just be made out along the same trail they were on. "Look, a fire! You think it could it be survivors like us?"

Itsuki spoke without looking. "Not like us, shinobi would not make themselves so visible. Most likely it is a team of Nobunaga's men, sent after us. We will have to take extra care in hiding our trail."

Noboru chewed a bit of trout. "They are at least a day behind. We will be far ahead of them by tomorrow night."

Itsuki grunted his agreement with less conviction.

Tsubasa saw the unease on his brother's face and changed the subject. "Itsuki, no disrespect, but back in the village, how were you able to fight the samurai while moving so slowly?"

Noboru nudged the young shinobi, making a gesture with his hands at the sides of his head. "He read his mind."

Tsubasa smirked. "Or the samurai was much slower than he seemed."

Itsuki sat very still. "Speed is not everything. Your quickness may be enough to confuse a clumsy foot soldier like the one you killed in Hekison, but a true samurai would not have fallen for your simple trick so easily."

"Speed is not a trick! It is a skill, prized by all shinobi."

Itsuki nodded in agreement. "Don't take offense, and don't think of tricks in a negative light. You are correct, speed is one of our greatest tools, but it is only a means to an end, and that end is deception. Deception is that which we most highly prize. A good deception can overcome the fastest sword, the strongest army, or the most desperate odds."

"Even so, a samurai is just like any other man; when his blade is too slow, he falls," Tsubasa retorted.

"From the way you talk, I know that you have never crossed blades with a master. Many of our comrades have been bested by samurai." Itsuki prodded the fire. "You see, the title samurai is used much too regularly, the average foot soldier is either a slave, or a man for hire that grabbed a sword and decided to play war. Fighting a man with little or no true understanding of combat is not the same thing. Do not underestimate a true blood samurai."

"And what makes these men so different?" Kaito questioned.

"Simply put, true samurai are specialized in open combat. From the age they can hold a sword, they are given two of them. They know these swords as an extension of their very spirit, and do not part with them till death." Itsuki rubbed his hands together before the flames. "They are well educated in culture and trained in all aspects of war. Of course, you know that we shinobi are trained to kill in other ways, but there are precious few of us who can confront our enemies head on."

"That's interesting, but you have carefully evaded my question of how you defeated the samurai in Hekison," Tsubasa pressed.

Itsuki grinned. "You catch me in my deception. Experience and training are how I evaded the samurai's strokes."

Tsubasa stood up. "Show me."

Noboru let out a low-bellied laugh. "This kid's brave, I think he's starting to grow on me."

Itsuki poked Noboru's hurt shoulder. "Don't encourage him. All right, Tsubasa. You are a shinobi... I will show you as your father showed me."

Itsuki closed his eyes for a moment, concentrating. Then making a symbol with his fingers intertwined, he stood, drawing his sword. "Strike me if you can. Hold nothing back." Tsubasa unsheathed his wakizashi in the firelight and came at Itsuki with blinding speed. With a series of short jabs, he attacked while the bald shinobi lazily deflected the blade's trajectory. Every time Tsubasa took a swing, Itsuki seemed to be one step ahead, as if it was a game and he was cheating. Tsubasa charged fiercely in the dark, but soon he had been thrown to the ground with the tip of Itsuki's blade at his throat.

Tsubasa was breathing hard. "How?"

Itsuki put out a hand to help the young man up. "Like I said, training and experience. Two things you lack much of."

Kaito watched the older shinobi as he returned to the fire. "The sign you made before you sparred, our father spoke of the nine Kuji-in hand seals, was that one of them?"

Itsuki nodded. "Few practice the Kuji-in anymore, but your father insisted that we learn; he believed the seals to be essential to the development of every shinobi."

"Which seal did you use?" Kaito was excited to hear about his father's teachings.

"I have trained in the seal of Jin, the awareness of the thoughts of others. With years of training, I have learned to read the subtle movements of my enemies; eye movements, feet positioning, the way they grip their handle, all clues to a man's intentions."

"How about Noboru?" Kaito spoke eagerly.

Itsuki sheathed his sword. "Sha, for healing."

"How does one learn all these hand seals?" Tsubasa asked.

"No shinobi has ever mastered all nine hand seals," Noboru stated. "But we can help you both choose a seal that will compliment your strengths. First comes an understanding of the entire Kuji-in, then training."

Itsuki began making his bed. "Alright, that's enough on the subject for tonight. We have a three-day journey to our destination, lots of time for questions."

"I have noticed that we have started to take a long route backtracking eastward higher into the mountains. What's our destination?" Kaito asked.

"Yes, an unfortunate precaution, as our escape from Hekison forced us away from our destination. But if you must know, it is a monastery to which we are headed." Itsuki took an exhausted yawn and closed his eyes. "Known for its chants."

7

Kitsune
-Omi Province, Azuchi Castle-

In the Omi Province of Japan on top of a large hill that bordered the shores of Lake Biwa stood Azuchi Castle. The night fog was blanketing the lake but did not reach the peak of the inlet where the castle stood. Broad stone steps curved upwards from clusters of homes at the bottom of the large hill that trailed from the lakeshore up to the elaborate castle grounds. The foundation was of mortar and large stones, the building itself was several stories of masterfully assembled wood. The center of the structure rose without a ceiling up to the fifth floor, which highlighted a stage used for theater and councils. The top roof was a large curved gabled structure containing red clay tiles. At the end of each center roof beam was an elaborately crafted emblem containing the Oda family crest.

Azuchi Castle was made to be a military command center but held the form of a luxury palace. The seven-story castle was strategically near Kyoto and in the center of Nobunaga's rule. Nobunaga Oda had the ability to effectively manage the communications and transportations of the rival warlords of

Japan; naturally, this became the meeting place of many of his generals. Nobunaga had recently returned to Azuchi from his conquest of the Iga Province and was currently holding a meeting with his eldest son Nobutada. The luxury and security of their surroundings put them at ease, and they did not notice that they were being spied upon.

A soft yellow lamplight glimmered across a slick lacquered tabletop littered with empty sake bottles. The table had been made into a map; the outlines of the Japanese islands were inlayed with gold against a shining sea of ebony. The stern countenance of Nobunaga Oda reflected in the table as he hunched over tracing the outline of the main island of Honshu. With a thick callused hand, he covered the region of Iga, little zigzag lines peaking from the edges of his palm in depiction of mountainous terrain. Slowly, the fingers drew in, curling underneath to form a fist.

From the opposite side of the large dimly lit table, a voice probed. "Father?"

With terrible power Nobunaga drove his fist into the table, violently rattling the sake bottles and cracking the lacquered finish in a spider web that radiated from Iga.

"Their laughter echoes even from the grave." He cracked a wry smile, hunching forward onto his elbows. "And I am the joke." Clumsily reaching for the nearest upright sake bottle, Lord Nobunaga took a long drink and wiped the excess from his lips with the sleeve of his fine silk kimono. "What'd you say? Come boy, speak up! And empty your cup while you're at it." He slid the bottle down the table toward his eldest son. Nobutada, by request was the only person attending the great daimyō this evening aside from the ever-present servants that waited like statues just outside the elaborately carved doors.

"We celebrate yet another victory for the Oda family!" He boomed, hiccuping between words. "Drink with me."

With only a moment's reluctance, Nobutada raised his cup toasting his father's success, and then drained it in a single swig. "Kanpai. May our house last a thousand years."

At twenty-four, Nobunaga's eldest son and heir had learned when to give in to the daimyō's wishes. Some battles were better left not fought. "I take it that Iga proved an elusive conquest."

His father grunted. "A strong enemy. Surprisingly so."

The young man poured himself another glass. "Perhaps Nobukatsu was not so incompetent in his previous attempts after all... simply outmatched."

"Your brother is a good man. He loves the soldiers as he loves himself. He will make a fine general one day if only he learns to trust his intuition, as I should more often trust mine." Nobunaga was now gently swaying back and forth, his elbows teetering on the table's edge, his head cradled between his rough hands.

"And you didn't trust your intuition with the men of Iga?"

"Trust has no home in Iga. Honor is a stranger in that land." Nobunaga's voice dropped with disgust. "Such a fool am I to think that those hill rats would provide me with the key to an empire. They would just as soon run a blade through my back as place it in my hands. I should just kill the prisoners we brought back. Not even worth the scraps." He slipped into a whisper and lazily began singing an obscure song from his childhood, an odd tune about yōkai, heroes, and times long past.

The tune drifted like a feather on a night breeze, sneaked through the sliding doors, danced across the gilded balcony, and landed upon the sloped tile roof of Azuchi Castle where a pair of small, perked ears patiently waited. Tucked tightly into shadows beneath the balcony of the uppermost level of the seven-story keep, the ears had been silently waiting for the better part of two hours, as still as one of the many sculpted dragons that decorated the fortress. In the scant moonlight, a pearly smile emerged between the ears. The long wait had paid off. The talk of a mysterious prize and new prisoners in the castle meant new information to be learned. Faint singing lingered for quite a while until the clear young voice of Nobutada Oda spoke up, suggesting it was time for a proper dinner. Light thumping footsteps and the creaking of steep staircases could be heard as servants hurried to the lower levels, presumably the kitchen. Now that food was on the mind, there would be no more talk of campaigns.

A dark form nimbly uncoiled itself from under the balcony and glided like a wraith, dropping from one roof to the next, and vanishing into a window port where one of the bars had been pried loose. A bony child would have struggled to make the squeeze, yet the agile figure slid through effortlessly. The graceful figure belonged to a young woman named Rin Kurosawa.

Steam billowed from the kitchen doors in great hot clouds as a dozen bustling men hauled heaping baskets of vegetables, wielded cleavers, and sweated over massive clay ovens that glowed with red flame. The din of cooking and the shouted orders of the head chef echoed in the tight quarters. The walls seemed to drip with perspiration. With the sleeve of his soiled shirt, a gangly chef's apprentice wiped the sweat from his brow as he tirelessly stirred the contents of a large wooden bowl. There was no forgiveness for burned rice in this kitchen. His mouth gaped, and his wooden spatula stopped mid-stir as the slender form of a young woman emerged from the shadows of the main doorway.

Even through the thick layers of dull colored fabric, her youthful shapeliness could not be hidden. The apprentice caught her eye as she anxiously scanned the kitchen's frantic activity, and he quickly looked away in embarrassment. He resumed his stirring, then slowly and involuntarily, his eyes drifted back to her fidgeting near the threshold. She looked to be in her late teens, petite and very fair, with keen eyes the shade of sandalwood. Her shining hair was carefully wrapped and held up with a simple black comb set with a single white stone. He caught her glance again, and this time held it, beckoning with a wave for her to enter. With a timid bow, Rin drew near, moving gracefully with small footsteps.

Forgetting his stirring, the apprentice turned to face the young woman. "How may I help you?" he asked with a smile.

No sooner was his greeting finished did a dirty wet rag hit his face with a loud thwap! Pulling away the limp rag, the apprentice tensed to see the old grumpy head chef scowling with great bulging eyes that burned like hot pokers. Going pale, the apprentice snapped back to his task, stirring with renewed vigor and focus.

The old chef crept over, eyeing his underling. "Next time you leave your work to flirt with a girl I'll have your finger!" he snarled, mumbling something about the proper way to season a finger. The chef muttered a string of obscenities as the apprentice returned to his work. Turning to Rin, he cracked a sneering smile and looked her up and down. "Well, my lovely, what brings you to my kitchen at this hour?" The head chef placed a hand around her shoulder and quickly lead her away from the chastised apprentice.

"I apologize for entering without your leave, chef," Rin stated.

"I can see that you are quite busy, I truly do not wish to trouble you, but some of the lords are growing restless and I fear that if their growling stomachs are not appeased, they might become quite unsavory."

"I see," said the old chef, stroking his chin with his free hand. "I can understand your concern, but as you can see, we are already in the midst of preparing a very fine meal for all the lords and ladies of the house! All will be dining well in less than an hour." He walked her through the bustling kitchen toward the far end where heavy sacks of rice were piled amongst barrels filled with rice wines and crates of rough-skinned root vegetables that had been carried up from the cellars below.

Looking about in wonder, the young woman praised the chef facilitating her plan of seduction. "What wonderful smells your kitchen contains. Chef, you are surely an artist in your craft! I am quite certain that the entire household will relish your meal. I would ask only that you might spare some small morsel to whet the appetite so my lord may appreciate your talent the better."

Flattery was not wasted on the old chef, and with satisfaction he began to nod, musing to himself. "Yes, yes indeed. Just a taste to make them salivate." His hand drifted slightly to the woman's back, just between the shoulder blades. "I suppose I could snatch a few dumplings from the oven."

"Oh!" she exclaimed with joy. "You are so gracious, master chef." She turned with a light dancing in her eyes, and gently placed her hand on his arm. "How wonderful you are. And if they could enjoy a sip of your rich and fragrant sake as well, their hunger would be quite piqued by the time the meal was ready!"

The old chef's eyes bulged, and a grumble began to rise in his throat, but the young woman squeezed his arm playfully and giggled with delight. Her strawberry lips parted and pulled back to reveal a wide dazzling smile marred only by a front tooth with a tiny chip in the corner. The chef could not help but give into her request.

Unfortunately for the head chef, Rin had never planned to use the food given to her on the lords of the castle. Padding quietly down a dark corridor that led deep into the stone foundations of Azuchi Castle, Rin pulled a comb from her hair, letting it fall thickly about her shoulders. Pausing briefly, she set down the food basket to untie her plain kimono; she flipped it inside out, revealing a flowered pattern in luminous shades of pink and blushing orange. From a concealed pocket she produced a small brown vial and a delicate pouch tied at the top with string. Undoing the pouch she dipped in her little finger, then carefully rubbed it across her pursed lips, giving her smile a fresh beam of color. She carefully poured the contents of a separate vial into one of the sake bottles. Her eyes closed, and with deep even breaths she inhaled the damp stale air. Reaching out with her consciousness she envisioned the path before her: the heavy stone walls, the thick hewn timbers of the prison cells, the rancid stench of the imprisoned, and the leering eyes of the dungeon gate keeper. When her eyes opened again, they flickered in the gloom with a seductive cunning. Then lifting the food basket to her side, she strode into the darkness like a cat prowling in the shadows of the night.

The prison guard stiffened his stance at the presence of someone coming by and then looked surprised when Rin came around the corner. The guard eyed the beautiful girl with suspicion. "And what is a serving maid doing in this part of the castle?"

Rin put on the mask of the maiden and glowed as she smiled. "Nobunaga is in good spirits. He has commanded that all his forces be rewarded," she said in a flirtatious tone.

She pulled out a white clay sake bottle, displaying it toward the guard and unstopping the top for him. The guard leaned his spear against the wall and grabbed the bottle but paused in thought. "Nobunaga in good spirits? That's hard to believe."

Rin stepped closer to the guard putting a hand on his chest and smiled. "I know it's hard to believe, yet here I am with sake. Take a drink. If you're willing to share maybe I'll keep you company for a while," she baited.

"Oh?" The guard seemed amused. "I am on duty."

"Doesn't mean we can't have some fun," Rin jested seductively.

At that, the guard smiled and took a long drink, never taking his eyes off Rin. Shortly after, a glazed look came over the man's face and his eyes fluttered. Rin pushed the man's head away from her as he passed out on the floor. When the guard would wake, his head would pound like a battle drum, and he would be dazed with a blurred memory. He would recover, if his commanding officer didn't discover him napping on the job; a severe headache would become the least of his problems.

Rin sprawled the guard's body upon the dungeon's admitting chamber, a narrow room between the hefty main doors and the barred gates that lead to a long row of holding cells. His water skin, which had been emptied and then partially refilled with fresh sake, laid in his clutched hand.

Before entering through the prison doors, Rin took a piece of cloth from the basket and wrapped it around her face so that only her eyes showed. The figure of the young woman could faintly be made out in the pale light of a single lantern.

The dirt floors and damp stone walls were reminiscent of a cave, the thick crisscrossed wooden barred cells showed the only signs that it was a prison. Rin walked down the row of cells, seeing various men garbed in tattered shinobifukus, fatigued and ill fed. Rin studied each cell as she walked by, making note of the men inside. Most men seemed starved, dirty, or sick. The final cell contained only one man sitting alone, unique, as all the other cells were crammed with three or four men.

This is the one, Rin thought.

Sitting against the far wall with his knees pulled up to his broad chest, the prisoner did not raise his head, nor make any indication that he took notice of the visitor, yet the woman could tell that he sensed her presence. A long silence stood between them. Rolling back his shoulders, the man raised his head and the lamplight gleamed on a single shining eye.

"Are you here to poison me like you did the guard? Or have you come for my other eye?" the prisoner spoke hoarsely. The prisoner turned his head to the right, so that the light fell on a gaping charred socket that had been robbed of its precious orb.

Rin smiled under her face covering. "If I truly wanted to harm you, I would simply let you rot here in the dungeons. Cold and dark would do more to you than make you blind, shinobi. And do not worry yourself for the welfare of the guard; he is merely catching some needed rest. However, I do wish to offer you hot food and drink if you would perhaps share your tale. It is direct from Nobunaga's own kitchen, and I promise to be as attentive an audience as you could desire." She sat down cross-legged at a safe distance from the bars.

The one-eyed man scoffed. "Words can be very costly, and I

am a dead man regardless. Why should I spend my breath on you, woman? Or better yet, kitsune."

She tensed at that word: kitsune, or fox. Kitsune were considered by all to be shapeshifting tricksters, able to assume human form at will. The word was meant to be an insult as the prisoner had no belief that the woman was a spirit. Rin had not been called that for years beyond memory and it stung like an old wound.

"Yes, I may collect information for my patron, and I use every tool at my disposal to do so, but I am no blundering maid servant with big ears and open legs. And I never betray my lord," she stated with finality.

The prisoner studied her eyes. "Like I said, words can be expensive... and they can also give you away. I can see your mind, little kitsune. What is your name?"

Rin was unphased by the prisoner's banter. "As you say, Kitsune. But if you like, you can call me Kit for short." Unwrapping the bundle that sat next to her, she produced a small clay bottle of sake, and by now a few not quite hot dumplings, and held them under the lamp.

"Now, if we are done with the teasing, would you like to eat something?" she asked. The starved shinobi wetted his lips despite himself as the young woman placed the small meal through the bars. A small wood saucer lay near the bars, and this she filled to the brim with sake, then drained the remainder of the bottle herself. "Come," she said, "food and drink for your story and your name."

"What does it matter," the shinobi sighed. "My tale is a long one, longer I suppose than you wish to stay here waiting for that guard to wake up from his nap." The shinobi smiled for the first time.

Rin shifted to get comfortable. "All the same, I would hear you speak your own name, and as for the tale, I care only to know of your dealings with Nobunaga. If I work for him then I already know everything you would tell. So, what's to lose?"

Grumbles of discontent came from the shinobi as he crept forward and suspiciously picked up a dumpling. "Most likely this is some complex game of Nobunaga, to squeeze every drop of information." He took a reluctant bite, chewing thoroughly, but not swallowing. Once he was satisfied that it was not poisoned, he began to nibble none too quickly, but with great delight. "Nonetheless, one cannot tell what one does not know to begin with. I don't know what Nobunaga seeks, and if by any chance my information can work to the detriment of that murderous torturous dog, I suppose the trade would be in my favor. I cannot betray a village that no longer exists." He held the dumpling before him and nodded his thanks. "My name is Masanari Hattori, but of course Nobunaga already knew that when he gave me this little love-tap." The shinobi pointed to the black crater where his left eye had been stolen. He lifted the saucer of sake to his dry lips, taking a long draft.

"Why were you singled out for questioning?"

"I was the master of arms of Hekison, the last stronghold of the Iga shinobi. Nobunaga naturally believed that I would have knowledge of all weapons of war kept by the shinobi of my order. He seemed dissatisfied with the stock and quality of the arms he had collected from our armory and pilfered from the bodies of our dead. Perhaps he was baffled that men with such meager weapons had proved such a strong resistance to his mighty samurai."

"And he desired great spoils of war," Rin suggested.

"Yes. His men scrutinized every inch of my ruined village and brought the daimyō every weapon of superior craftsmanship they could find; mostly swords stolen from rich households or defeated samurai foes over the years. Nobunaga seemed convinced that our leader had kept a hidden stash somewhere. They tore Yamato's house to the ground and dug up the earth all about its foundation in their search. Apparently, Nobunaga is obsessed with whatever he's looking for."

"Why was Nobunaga so convinced the shinobi had what he sought?" Rin probed.

"Only Jōnin Akiyama would have known." Masanari peered at Rin, weighing the consequences of his words. "There was a rumor years ago, that a shinobi squad was charged to find a certain sword, some say a demon sword for none other than Nobunaga. But there are always rumors, and we do not discuss active missions with each other. One cannot divulge information one does not know if ever caught by an enemy. In any case, as you can tell from my face, I was resistant to Nobunaga's hunt," Masanari stated, sounding out every syllable of the word resistant. "Probably the only reason that I am still alive."

"This leader of yours, this Yamato, was he not questioned?"

Masanari frowned. "Alas, he was slain in the assault from arrow fire. Rumor has it two shinobi left him to die… I'll kill the cowards if I discover their identity. Nobunaga would never have permitted Yamato's immediate death. Any secrets the old man held died with him."

In the dark, Rin thought in silence for a long moment, then gathering her composure she feigned interest. "I would kill such cowards in the same situation. Leaving one's leader to die is a disgrace worthy of a fate worse than death. Yet… your tale has a flaw. Nobunaga has no need of swords; he wields the sword of Masamune!"

Masanari scratched at his shaggy beard. "Be that as it may, he wants more. There has been more than one swordsmith in the long ages, and relics from forgotten times may still linger in dusty hollows. Masamune was a swordsmith of order; Nobunaga wants an equally valuable blade of chaos."

She waited expectantly, but the shinobi grew silent and would say no more on the subject. *Nobukatsu will know*, she thought. "What of the survivors of Hekison?" Rin questioned, looking at the other cells.

"My people have been annihilated. Nobunaga ordered all men, women, and children killed. The only reason the few of us were kept alive was for his search for a sword, and soon we will be dead as well. I'm sure there are a few remnants out there from previous evacuations, mostly women, children, and... deserters," Masanari spoke the last word with disgust.

"Deserters?"

"Yes, deserters!" Masanari's anger flared suddenly. "I saw men fleeing the village even as it burned. Cowards, filthy rats jumping from a sinking ship that they had sworn to protect. Two-faced sneaks that ran away into the night like those damned Yukimura brothers and two others."

Rin did her part to appear sympathetic. "It... it is unfortunate to see comrades from your village betray you, but you should never use names."

Masanari finished the last dumpling and wiped his hands on the legs of his tattered shinobifuku. He peered into the darkness beyond the lantern, straining to see the woman's face more clearly, only to see a sandalwood gaze. "How do you... Who are you Kitsune?"

"As you say, just a shape shifting fox here to play tricks." Snuffing the lantern light, Rin became a shadow. "Thank you for your time, Masanari, but I'm afraid I must now make my exit." Then turning to leave, she paused for a moment and softly spoke over her shoulder, "Do not give up hope, Masanari Hattori, you may endure this yet."

Dinner in Azuchi Castle had come and gone, and now dressed once again in the demure attire of a serving maiden, Rin passed quickly through the lower gardens toward the viewing terraces that ran along the western edge of the fortress. Like a stone carving, there stood Nobukatsu Oda, second son of Nobunaga, overlooking the moonlit waters of Lake Biwa. Feeling the presence of another person, he turned around to meet the sandalwood gaze of a young woman. Nobukatsu stared as one in a trance. "Rin... you always have a light step. What brings you here? You should not be shirking your responsibilities of attending Lady Hashiba."

"She is in Kyoto; I was left in Azuchi to take care of her affairs here in preparation for her return. She watched for her subtle words to take effect. "I have come to see if there is anything that you need." Rin stepped closer. "You do not seem tired, so perhaps I could offer some company." She put a hand on Nobukatsu's arm. "Especially after all the hard work in the Iga Province."

Nobukatsu retracted his arm from her grasp. "Glory and councils among the wise are not to be my fate. My brother is the eldest, and it is right that he should enjoy the company of my father. I had plenty of time to claim it for myself, but that I have squandered. It shall be long years, if ever, before I am given another chance like that." He turned sadly back to the dark waters of Lake Biwa.

"All these plans and conquests are far beyond the understanding of a handmaiden," Rin admitted. "I can only perceive what is plainly set before me, what I can see and touch." She pressed close to Nobukatsu's side and leaned against the railing to share the view of Lake Biwa. "I often wonder what great treasures have been brought back from the field of victory."

"Hmph."

"Rich kimonos, silks, and jewels that glitter like stars in the heavens," Rin dreamed aloud. "All things that sparkle and dance in the light!" She giggled modestly and fluttered her fingers as if tracing the lines of rippling waters in the distance. "Even the elegant swords that you samurai wear, as sleek as a calligraphy brush, more beautiful than gold!" Her eyes drifted to the handsomely adorned swords tied at the lord's side. The lacquered finish of the scabbards shone like a black pearl.

Nobukatsu's eyes lit up at the mention of swords and his hand drifted down to finger his katana. With his thumb he could feel the Oda crest emblazoned upon the tip of its hilt, an adornment as familiar as his own face. "I must admit that I too am drawn to adore great swords captured in battle. They are the immortal embodiment of great warriors and artists. There is no finer treasure than the instrument of a worthy foe."

"Were there any worthy men defeated in Iga?"

Nobukatsu nodded. "Indeed, many. Though my pride and the pride of all samurai would say otherwise, there were many warriors slain on the mountainsides worth honoring in memory."

"Yet, no worthy swords?" pressed Rin.

Considering the question for a moment, Nobukatsu replied, "Their weapons were simple for the most part, yet cunningly wielded. But these people were little more than farmers and had no easy means to possess fine works of artistry. Very few would have been worthy of anything other than stockpiling."

Rin's eyes brightened hopefully. "But some were worthy of a daimyō's interest?"

Nobukatsu eyed her sharply. "What are you getting at?"

"Oh, nothing really, I just heard that some beautiful swords might have been found after the final siege." Rin tried to sound casual. "Perhaps even the work of a master…" Her conversation with the shinobi prisoner echoed in her mind; his words of a demon's sword had somehow triggered long forgotten memories, and now a name floated to the top of her consciousness. "Even swords made by the demon-smith Muramasa."

Gripping her shoulder Nobukatsu cautioned. "Careful with your words, Miss Kurosawa. It is dangerous for a handmaiden to take interest in such things. Where did you hear this?"

Rin laughed playfully as if amused at such an outrageous reaction. "Forgive me, my lord, I would not presume to step above my station. It is just that I get so intrigued by stories of war that I hear from you samurai."

Nobukatsu's suspicions faded at the display of feminine deference. "Many soldiers talk of what they do not know… they start rumors. I am sorry Rin, but you are misinformed."

Rin bowed respectfully. "That is why I came to you lord. A son of the Oda clan can always separate truth from fiction. I have always trusted in your judgment."

Nobukatsu returned to his view of the lake. "You may be the only one in this castle that can say that. If only my own family were so confident."

"Are you sure there is nothing I cannot do for you? Would you like some sake perhaps?" Rin proposed.

"No, Miss Kurosawa, the quiet night holds the solace I seek."

"As you wish," she conceded, bowing low. She turned and made her way into the moonlight, leaving Nobukatsu to his thoughts. Only when her back was turned did her deadly smile with the tiny, chipped tooth appear. Rin had a skill for reading the truth behind the words. *Misinformed indeed,* she thought.

8

The Monastery
-Iga Province, Iga Mountains-

Shadows grew long on the streets of Midori, Itsuki's former village. Itsuki stood alone in the rice fields that spread from the edge of the village like waves from a shore. He was dressed in his familiar shinobifuku, but it was clean and freshly mended. The Iga mountains rose in the distance, purple in the evening light, and the air held a sharp frost with a vague sense of foreboding.

Ground passed beneath his feet and the familiar streets of Midori blurred by in a monotone haze as he moved forward. Forms of people passed by as they went about their daily business, ignorant of Itsuki's presence. Whispers on the wind whirled around Itsuki, but no matter where he turned the owners of such words were unseen, fear beckoned him forward. The shuffle of elderly feet could be heard, an old man hunched under a bundle of wood strapped to his back slowly stepped by and then whipped his head up in a surprising unhuman movement. The villager had no face, but only a mask of skin covering the openings where eyes, mouth, and nose should be. Terror struck Itsuki as he could see that underneath the skin of the villager were the indents of a face as if trying to protrude itself through the barrier of tightly wrapped skin. The old man did not speak, for he lacked the mouth to do so, but pointed with a long thin finger to a house ahead. Itsuki became aware that the street was now filled with faceless villagers all pointing in the same direction.

The shinobi walked toward the house slowly and carefully gazed at the faceless villagers. Several glossy black feathers lay upon the entryway of the home, which he cautiously avoided. In a flutter of wings, a crow gave a great caw and flew from the roof of the home. Entering, Itsuki found the interior charred black and caked with ash. In the main room he found the huddled corpses of an adult and child. Their flesh was burned and cracked, as brittle as the creaking house in which they lay. He reached out with a trembling hand to caress the child's cheek, but at his touch the brittle skin gave way, collapsing in on itself. A gust of wind came, and the tiny home began to rattle furiously, the wood structure started to groan in strain. At the moment when Itsuki thought that his home would be torn apart, the corpse belonging to the burned child sat up staring with black holes and gave a shrill shriek no human could make, deafening Itsuki's ears with pain.

Itsuki woke up gasping for air as if reemerging from water. His heart pounded in his chest and sweat beaded on his brow.

Noboru was sitting cross-legged next to Itsuki as he honed the edge of a kunai dagger. "The dead still speak to you," he stated unsurprised.

Itsuki wiped the cold sweat with his sleeve. "No, there was no speaking this time."

Dawn had arrived, and a pale pink light illuminated the mountain landscape. The air was crisp and tasted of pine, and the cold dew of morning clung to the turf about them. Kaito and

Tsubasa were beginning to stir in their blankets as the sky brightened.

Noboru stood up stretching, then gave the brothers both a nudge with his foot. "C'mon you two, I'm sick of sleeping in the woods and I'd like to feel clean linens against my skin. We are less than a day's journey from the monastery."

The four shinobi packed quickly and erased all signs of their stay. After three days of unbroken travel, they had become highly efficient at setting up and breaking down camp, the actions becoming instinctual. They took off down the trail at a brisk pace, resolute to reach the monks' haven by day's end.

The day passed quickly with little talk and much forward progress. Noboru had to stop once to cinch his sling tighter to keep his wounded shoulder from jostling, and Itsuki once needed to gather the group's bearings at a split in the trail. As the sun began to fall in the sky, the shinobi arrived at a heavily wooded dell that opened to the west. The trees here had long skinny trunks bearing branches only at the top that spread up more vertically than horizontally, and although they were packed more tightly together than the conifers that covered the surrounding slopes, rays of light streamed down against the tree shadowed floor. A stone statue covered in moss stood at the wood's edge, a seated depiction of a round cheeked man with a single forward-facing open palm in meditation.

"The Buddha," Noboru stated, "the enlightened one, so they say." He turned to face the other shinobi. "Your guard must be up around these monks. Though they are no enemy to Hekison, their beliefs differ from our own and they will seek to cause doubt in our hearts. I have never fully trusted these Chinese immigrants anyhow."

"You forget that our own people were once new to this land, and in very similar circumstance," Itsuki stated.

Noboru eyed him with skepticism. "I admit that the teachings of Buddha have merit, but these monks leave the old gods behind. They forget the creators Izanagi and Izanami, the wild and secret. A heresy I'm unwilling to forget." He then looked to the Yukimura brothers. "They are peaceful if not provoked, but they will not be mocked either. Do not expect them to understand our gods and customs."

Itsuki nodded with approval at the words. "Furthermore, we have dealt with these monks before, but they have never known our names. They knew your father quite well, and his face shines well through your own; we cannot hide that, but we will be mindful of what else we choose to reveal." He looked for understanding in the eyes of the brothers.

"We never use names," Kaito responded.

"Well taught."

Tsubasa gave a laugh. "You made it sound like we were making for refuge, now it sounds like walking into a trap."

Noboru grunted. "Just as a shinobi should always think. In our line of work, we are often invited inside as friend and soon realize that we are under the roof of an enemy. The monks may view us as an unwelcome sight; they too understand the long reach of Nobunaga's arm. No more words now. We will enter this realm with caution."

From the statue it was only a short winding path to a narrow stone stairway that led up to the shrine's gate. A bundle of rope, woven as thick as a man's thigh hung above the door. They climbed the steps, and at the landing above, found a singular monk dressed in simple orange robes, sweeping the entryway.

The monk squinted his eyes. "Shinobi-no-mono… we saw the smoke rising in the distance. We did not expect to see any of you again. Even in this remote place, we know of Nobunaga's wrath, but this is still a haven of peace." He paused considering his words and returned to his sweeping. "You haven't brought war here, have you?"

Itsuki stepped forward, placing a hand on his chest. "No friend, we honor this sacred land, and would not dare bring war upon it. However, war may yet come of its own accord. I ask you, tell Daisuke Miayamoto that the scarred shinobi has come for his help."

The monk gripped his broom with worry, then nodded warily and gestured the shinobi to wait. After what seemed a very long time, a heavyset monk with a shaven head and orange robes drifted from the gate, staring intently at the weather worn shinobi. His voice was like a low echo accented by ages of Chinese ancestry. "You? Ha! I'm surprised to see you here, for it is not safe to be a shinobi in these times." His face was stern, but behind the wrinkles and folds of dark skin, a faint humor lingered.

Itsuki bowed. "So we have found. Greetings! Daisuke, I have no desire to bring trouble to your temple, but we seek shelter and council. I ask you to remember our old oaths of friendship and permit us to rest here for a short while."

Daisuke gave thought. "I will let you enter the shrine for the help that Hekison gave in winters past when our food stores had gone rotten, but only for two nights. It can be assumed that Nobunaga's men are roaming the mountains looking for refugees like yourselves. It would not be wise for you to linger here long, or for us to harbor you. Come inside quickly now, for we must get you out of those clothes. You might as well paint a target on your back and put Nobunaga's sword to my neck."

As they entered the monastery, many monks stopped their various tasks and gaped at the strange procession. Since before Nobunaga's siege there had been no interaction with the men of Hekison, and few could remember a time when any shinobi had stepped foot within the confines of the temple. Some were surprised by the warriors' appearance, and others grumbled with discontentment, shaking their heads at the intrusion.

Daisuke led them directly to the bathhouse, swaying lightly as he walked. "You should bathe first. You stink of death. The brothers here at the temple will look kindlier upon you when you are clean. We will set fresh clothes outside for you." The monk gestured to Noboru's bandaged shoulder. "We can redress that wound of yours, although you don't seem the worse for wear."

Promptly, the large man swept round and left the shinobi to disrobe, his robes following like wisps of smoke in his wake. They were glad for a bath. The water was clean but cold, and with the application of a little soap, effectively washed away both dirt and fatigue, leaving them refreshed. The sweet piney scent of the soap lingered on their skin and calmed their minds. Outside the bathhouse the simple garb for four religious pilgrims was folded and waiting. Fresh clothes were a welcome change from the soiled shinobifukus that had been like a second skin for weeks. The only items not discarded for cleaning were the swords that each shinobi never let out of arm's reach.

Outside the bathhouse, Daisuke was waiting patiently, humming to himself with deep melodic tones. He bowed as the newly washed men emerged, now hardly recognizable as warriors, aside from their weapons.

Daisuke smiled. "I assume the clothing is adequate. If you would like to leave your battle clothes behind when you depart, we will be obliged to burn them. I hope you understand that we cannot permit any evidence of your stay."

Itsuki moved his hand over his bald head. "Yes, I understand... we thank you for the hospitality. These garments are a most helpful disguise. But none the less, we will take our clothes when we leave. But a chance to clean them would be appreciated."

Daisuke smiled graciously. "Now it is time for some tea. I would be honored if you would all join me, and perhaps tell me why you have come. No doubt you know better places for refuge than our humble monastery."

Itsuki bowed. "You shall learn all you wish, and more."

The monks took their tea quietly in the sparse dining room where they took all their meals. To offer some privacy and avoid spectacle, Daisuke suggested the shinobi be served in the small courtyard behind the kitchen. They were more accustomed to the outdoors than strange interiors of Buddhist monasteries and took no offense at the consideration. They sat themselves around a low crude table and the fat monk filled their cups with a steaming fragrant tea that swirled about in golden eddies. He hummed to himself as he poured, bobbing his head lightly as if to a song that the tea played only for him.

Daisuke cleared his throat. "So, what brings you to this place? Apart from your obvious need to avoid Nobunaga's wrath."

Itsuki felt the warmth of his cup. "We seek items which are precious to the shinobi. The ones that knew their location perished in the defense of Hekison." Itsuki took a small piece of parchment out of his pack and looked at Noboru as if weighing a decision. The parchment was a copy made during their trek from a page of the mysterious book. The Yukimura brothers watching, did not say a word but listened attentively, hoping for answers to questions that had begun to fill their minds.

Noboru scratched his sideburn with the back of his hand. "We need him, let him see the page."

In agreement, Itsuki handed the parchment to Daisuke. "This is sacred to us we... trust you with what you will see."

Daisuke took the parchment with a puzzled look on his face and began to study it. Written in a fine script was an elaborate sequence of musical notes belonging to an instrument unknown to the men of Hekison.

Daisuke furrowed his brow. "This is a musical notation for overtone chants."

"What are overtone chants?" Kaito questioned eagerly.

"A sort of music you could say, and a talent that few know," Daisuke explained. "Evidently it brought you to us, this monastery studies it, yet few still have mastered it. An overtone you see, requires producing two distinct tones from one's vocal cords simultaneously."

Kaito cocked his head in confusion, but the monk just looked back to the parchment. "Maybe you will have a chance to hear some chants for yourself before you leave." He looked ever closer at the page. "These are very complex... yes... how you came about such chants is a mystery in itself. It seems this particular tune is to feature four monks with their chants overlapping. Hmm, quite curious indeed."

"Four chants at once?" probed Kaito.

Daisuke lifted his head. "Why yes, and it gets more curious still. I can't be sure, but I believe the overlay is intended to sound as spoken words. Most unusual."

The two older shinobi exchanged knowing looks.

87

"Well," said the monk decidedly, "you have caught my interest. I assume you would desire for me to translate these chants. A true challenge, but one that I shall savor all the more. I will need to study the parchment more closely and share its contents with a few of the brothers here… with your permission of course."

Itsuki nodded. "Your wisdom rivals your kindness. Permission gladly granted."

"It will take some time to decipher. I have three brothers of the monastery who are adept at overtone chanting. We shall gather tomorrow in effort to unlock your riddle. In the meantime, you must be weary from travel; many days lie between here and Hekison, though I suspect that men such as you have made short work of the journey. You may stay the night and share our hospitality."

All four shinobi bowed their heads in thanks.

Daisuke shifted his bulk, letting out a melodic sigh. "But now I would like to hear of what happened at Hekison, if the telling is not too painful."

Noboru had a knack for weaving tales, and he told of the fall of Hekison, carefully omitting that which he did not trust to Daisuke. Occasionally Kaito or Tsubasa chimed in with minute details of their own. Itsuki listened in deep silence and thought. The large monk provided a captive audience, asking questions and giving looks of shock and horror at the more gruesome parts.

At the story's conclusion, Daisuke shook his head gravely and quietly spoke words long forgotten. "The fall of Hekison, the death of free men, from the mists of Iga yōkai rise to roam these lands again."

"What is that from?" Itsuki questioned, surprised at the verse.

"A shinobi," Daisuke answered, ignoring Itsuki's gaze and looking at Tsubasa. "It has been many years. I remember him wise and gracious, but he could not hide the solemn burden he carried about him. But as you shinobi always say. We never use names."

9

Training
-Iga Province, Buddhist Monastery-

Noises of preparation drifted like visions in the minds of the Yukimura brothers as they began to stir in the cold of the early morning. The hard stone-floor, made more hospitable by cloaks and spare blankets, prodded at the sore bone and sinew of the young travelers. Better rest than the forest undergrowth, soft in the hazy memories of the boys, though undoubtedly chillier.

Breakfast in the monastery was sure to be a bland and simple affair despite the great clatter of dishes, slopping of rags, and stoking of fires, the heat of which soon compensated for the predawn disturbance. The shinobi had bedded down in a corner of the dining hall near the hearth. As darkness had drawn in the previous evening, the air was crisp with the promise of snow. Daisuke had generously offered the shelter of the hall; the large hearth was a long-forgotten blessing of warmth to the shinobi. But now, as morning light began to break, the monks had seen fit to turn the dwindling embers to a roaring blaze to rouse their sleeping guests. Noboru and Itsuki were long awake, their bedrolls neatly folded and presence missing from the hall.

Kaito gave a long yawn, stretching his arms high overhead. "Do you think it snowed during the night?" he asked.

Tsubasa rolled nearer to the small fire, pulling a blanket around him. "I don't know. If it hasn't, our trail will be easier to follow. If it has, we may be stuck here."

"You are always the optimist," Kaito mocked. "I was thinking that if it hadn't, we might get to explore the grounds, and if it had, well... we might get to explore the grounds in the snow."

"And you are always so damned negative." Tsubasa grinned reluctantly. "I doubt that there will be much time for hide and seek. Those two friends of our father have something in store for us today; of that, I am sure."

"I hope so. Perhaps they will teach us what father taught them."

"Do not be so quick to trust these men. Skilled shinobi such as they deal heavily in deceit and misdirection. They will use our emotional attachment to father to play us as pawns in the game of their choosing."

"They were students of our father, if they followed him, should we not follow them?"

"We may have known our father well, but I don't think we ever knew the Hundred Shadow Man. There may be things that were kept from our knowledge intentionally, to protect us. We have no way of knowing where this errand of theirs might lead."

"I trust them," Kaito said. "There is truth in them."

"It's not that I mistrust their intentions, just their wisdom. One grunts like a bear, the other thinks himself a guru," retorted Tsubasa.

A beastly grunt drew the boys' attention to the kitchen door where Noboru had appeared holding two steaming bowls. "Rouse yourselves," he said, nodding to the bowls, "breakfast."

The four shinobi ate in silence along with the monks. The meal given was a simple vegetable broth with some unknown root, though adequately warm and filling. The simplicity somehow fit nicely into the setting created by the Buddhists. The monks ate slowly, chewing with purposed focus. Yet, the famished shinobi lingered long after the others had finished, tucking away second and third helpings. The nourishment was badly needed and eagerly welcomed. They knew not when they would eat this well again. A particularly thin and fragile looking monk began clearing away the last of the dishes, and Kaito lost no time in bombarding the monk with many questions pertaining to their daily activities. He asked about their cooking and cleaning, about rest and exercise, and particularly about their meditation periods and the purpose it served. The monk smiled kindly at the boy's inquisitiveness, glad to answer and to teach.

"There are many questions and many answers," the skinny monk spoke with a voice like a scratched whisper. "And every answer is a doorway to more questions. When we quiet the mind, we see through all doorways, lined up and overlapped as one. We see only one question and one answer."

Kaito wrinkled his brow searchingly. "What is the question?"

The monk smiled with his old eyes. "I understand you will be here for a short while, perhaps you would like to spend the day asking yourself that. Our beautiful monastery is an ideal location to practice if you would like."

The boy opened his mouth to respond but before he could, Noboru interjected. "We appreciate the offer monk, but he will be very busy today."

Kaito looked to Noboru curiously. "Doing what?"

Noboru produced a tiny blade from his mass of bundled hair

and began picking his teeth. "If you are looking for something to train in, we will train you in shinobi arts, not some idle Buddhist meditation."

Returning to his cleaning, the thin monk scuttled away with hands full of dishes and his face cast with irritation.

Tsubasa chimed in with skepticism in his voice. "What kind of training do you propose?"

Noboru gave a wink. "Training in the arts that Itsuki used to put you on your back at the campfire."

Hand seals! Thought Tsubasa. Before he could push the subject, the fat monk Daisuke entered the room with a flourish and a chiming resonance seemed to ripple from the flow of his robes. He approached the table, and clasping his hands behind his back, began to rock gently back and forth.

"Scarred One, Long Hair," Daisuke addressed the elder shinobi in his peculiar manner. "I hope that our humble lodgings have been adequate for you."

Itsuki nodded in approval. "Many thanks."

Daisuke smiled. "I am most interested to begin deciphering these chants with the other monks. To be honest, many seasons have passed since I have felt such an excitement. Something of this riddle speaks to me in ancient tongues; it should take many hours to unravel. You are all free to meditate and use our monastery while we work."

"May we train?" Kaito blurted out.

Daisuke pursed his plump lips in consideration. "No weapons please. I assume you shinobi train in other things besides slitting throats." Swaying gently, he bowed a little toward Itsuki. "I'll leave it to you to make sure the boys don't get overzealous." He shot a wary look at Noboru who was still picking his teeth. Promptly, Daisuke turned gracefully on his heel and drifted from the dining hall.

Itsuki took Noboru off to the side to privately consider the matter away from the two boys. "You know they aren't ready for such training," Itsuki said in disapproval.

"Ahh," Noboru gave a sly smile and playfully hit Itsuki's chest with a backhand. "Call it a test of their potentials and strengths. They need something to do while we're here and we need to see if they carry the seeds of their father; you know the challenges we may face."

"Clever," Itsuki agreed. "Tsubasa would never submit to a test willingly, but under the guise of battle training, he may trade his arrogance for instruction."

"A good chance to bring him down a notch or two," Noboru winked. "You can have Kaito."

Kaito bounded forward as if called. "So, we will train?" he asked eagerly.

Itsuki ran a hand over his bald head and resigned himself to the boy's youthful impatience. "Very well. We will teach you in your father's ways."

The four shinobi crossed a small bridge over a running stream and came to a clearing that seemed to be a place of meditation that the monks kept very pristine. The elder shinobi sat down cross-legged, gesturing the other two to follow. Tsubasa stood defiantly.

Noboru looked up at Tsubasa. "Sit."

Tsubasa rolled his head exhaustedly to one side. "I've sat enough for one day, I thought we were going to learn fighting techniques."

"Sit!" Noboru barked. "Shut up and listen. You just might learn something of value."

Tsubasa resigned his fight and stubbornly sat.

Itsuki took a deep breath and thought a moment. "First off, do you know the core concept of the Kuji-in hand seals?"

Kaito scratched his head. "I've heard from the old men that the seals can pull magic from nature to intensify one's natural abilities. When you used the seal at the campfire you seemed to be able to read Tsubasa's mind."

"Half-truths I suppose. There are nine hand seals in total, corresponding to the nine essential virtues of the shinobi. Every one of us possesses a share of each virtue, and usually a larger share of at least one of the nine. For generations, our ancestors honed their gifted virtue by using the hand seal meditations. It can take years to master even one, but when you do, your natural gifts will be augmented into powerful tools and weapons."

"So, we spend years mastering a single hand seal, and then we can do magic?" Tsubasa snorted.

"No," Noboru stated bluntly. "There is no guarantee that you will ever master a seal, and many shinobi long die before they can wield real power. Most never make the attempt."

"Why not?" Kaito stated confused.

"It is a tradition of the old ways, ways that have been forgotten and hidden from all but a few. Your father was perhaps the last great master before his passing. He perfected more seals than any shinobi in living memory."

"How many?" probed Tsubasa with a creeping interest.

"Three," answered Itsuki.

Tsubasa scoffed slightly.

"It may not seem like many to you but considering the years of dedication it takes simply to understand one seal, and that your father did it all without a teacher... astonishing. Each seal can only be completely unlocked from within a state of extreme mortal danger and emotional transcendence. His accomplishment was truly extraordinary." Itsuki forgot himself and smiled warmly at the memory of his master.

"What do you mean by completely unlocked?" Kaito asked.

"What I mean is that training can only take you so far. For the seal to fully unlock your dormant potential you must experience a moment of total mastery, a phenomenon that cannot be brought out in training alone, and more often than not that will only occur when your life is dangling from the thinnest of lines."

Kaito squirmed. "Hmm, I'm not sure that I understand."

"That is not terribly important for now. First comes practice of the seals."

"And how do we do that?" asked Tsubasa.

"It is done by recalling specific emotional or bodily states at will, states you've experienced in your life that will aid you in battle. You will learn to link each seal with your own firsthand experiences." Itsuki gathered his thoughts. "Have you ever lain in wait to ambush an enemy? Do you remember the feelings you had at the time?"

Kaito eagerly nodded. "Many times, in training and once in combat. We were told to be totally aware of our surroundings, to listen for any sounds, to watch for any movement so that we would know the enemy's intent."

"Your muscles tense with anxious excitement and blood beats loudly in your ears. Silence requires total focus," Tsubasa stated.

"Exactly." Itsuki looked deeply into the boys' eyes. "Now in that state your mind was completely concentrated on intuition and premonition of danger. This feeling is linked with the hand seal Kai."

Noboru chimed in. "You must learn to associate your heightened senses with the hand formations. In your everyday state of consciousness, you are unable to draw out these senses at will, but with repetition and training you can condition your mind and body to trigger these senses when you perform a seal."

Tsubasa's eyes grew bright. "So what people interpret as magic is really the conjuring of extreme senses and emotions at will."

Itsuki nodded, slightly impressed at Tsubasa's perceptive comment. "Yes, most of these emotional states are only felt in moments of intense harmony or stress. A shinobi's life can cultivate such moments. Your father, Kazuki, was a master of extremes."

"You have just been handed a large piece of the secret of The Hundred Shadow Man. He left a path for Itsuki and me to follow, had he still been alive he would have taught you two the old ways as well, it is fitting that we now instruct you," Noboru stated.

Kaito sprang to his feet. "Ha! I want to learn one of the hand seals you two know."

Itsuki held up a calming hand. "Slow down. We have been observing you and your brother since we first met. The first hand seal learned should reflect your own natural talents."

Tsubasa frowned. "Why did our father not attempt to teach us such secrets?"

"Too young of course, this is not training for children," Noboru half lied. *There is a cost to learning such things, things a father would try to spare from his sons,* Noboru thought.

Tsubasa fell silent, somewhat satisfied with the answer. For an hour, the discussion of hands seals continued, elder shinobi instructing the younger with interlacing finger combinations of each assigned hand seal. When satisfied that they could perform the contortions correctly, each teacher took a pupil, splitting the group for personalized instruction.

Near the monastery the sound of overtone chanting could be heard drifting on the wind like bellows of some great and mysterious forge. The shinobi paused for a moment to listen to the musical monks at work. Noboru came back to reality from the hypnotic effect of the chants, his hair fluttered in a small breeze as he turned. He smiled carelessly as he gently prodded and massaged his bandaged shoulder. Something in the music put him at ease, with a healing to the mind and body alike.

"You are amazingly fast, Tsubasa, like a blustering wind through tall grass. Wind is perhaps the most powerful and elusive of all elements. Wind cannot be seen, but only felt, its effects in the ripples on a pond, or the devastation after a great storm. No other element can boast such mastery over the others, feeding or starving fire, capable of freezing water, able to tear mighty trees from the very earth. Few shinobi possess such a large share of wind as I see in you. Therefore, you will be trained in the hand seal of Retsu, the mastery of time and space. It is the second hand seal that I have begun to master, and it will help you to control your speed."

Tsubasa grinned back. "You find my speed too dangerous?"

Noboru laughed. "I thought you might like that. Personally, I like danger. Don't tell Itsuki I said that, but you will be vastly more dangerous when you can learn to use your speed with exacting precision. Essentially, the aim of Retsu is to enhance your reaction time and in turn your movements by exercising precision."

The fingers on Noboru's hands twisted expertly into place forming the hand seal Sha.

Tsubasa tilted his head in consideration. "What are you doing?"

Noboru suddenly shot his free fist blindingly forward, stopping a hair's width from the tip of Tsubasa's nose. In a panic Tsubasa tripped, landing with embarrassment on his rear.

"Your shoulder?" Tsubasa looked at Noboru in surprise. "Did it magically heal?"

"Ha, I wish," Noboru laughed. "The hand seal Sha represents healing, or more accurately, the ability to ignore pain. The riskiest of all the hand seals, but the one I have mastered. Now come. Show me what you got."

Tsubasa quickly rolled to the left, regained footing, and sprang recklessly toward Noboru with his right fist clenched for a crippling blow. With surprising grace, the longhaired shinobi glided backward and turned his body, catching the youth's punch mid-strike, and pulling him off balance as he spun. Once again, the young man found himself on the ground. Noboru rotated his injured shoulder as if testing its power. "You must place new limits upon your perception of time and space. You must see the space between spaces."

Tsubasa spat and rose slowly to his feet, warily eyeing his opponent's shoulder. *No restraint at all,* he thought.

"The feeling that you must draw upon to perform Retsu is of when time seems to slow down during battle, the expansion of normal temporal perception experienced when one is afraid." Noboru stretched his arm with fluid control. "This phenomenon can be conjured at will once you learn to recognize it."

Tsubasa swept sweat from his face. "Right… sounds simple."

Noboru held forth his fist, slowly uncurling an upturned hand, "I will instill fear in you that you may understand." He signaled the boy forward with a wave. "And you shall turn fear into a weapon."

Not far away, on a stout bridge spanning a shallow rocky stream, Kaito and Itsuki were in the midst of a similar conversation on the Kuji-in seals. Itsuki leaned far over the railing, scanning the streambed.

"Tsubasa has told me about how the two of you defended the wall of Hekison during the final siege, how you were aware of many things on the battlefield before anyone else." Itsuki turned to look at the boy. "You are more observant than most, and possessing a certain grace, which is why you will be trained in the seal of Kai. It is the discipline of intuition, or the premonition of danger." He gestured Kaito to take a seated position near the bridge. "Mastery of Kai will allow you to sense danger before it comes to you, just as you did in Hekison. For now, you will sit here in meditation, and I will try to approach without your knowledge. You will be blindfolded."

"What? Why?" Kaito stated as Itsuki produced a cloth over the boy's head.

Itsuki fastened the knot, a faint smile emerging. "Because you must learn to rely on your other senses. Each training period a physical sense will be taken away to force your mind to rely on the others. Since it's such a sunny day we shall start with sight. Each time we start you must make the hand seal first, then try to predict my location before I get to you. You will attempt to call out my position if you believe I have revealed myself."

"Attempt?" Kaito scoffed. "You act as if I'll never know."

"Let's get started shall we," Itsuki stated, rolling his eyes at the boy's comment. Itsuki walked to the far end of the clearing, some thirty paces away. "Make the seal, we start now."

Kaito made the hand seal of Kai then waited patiently, trying to ignore the commotion of his brother and Noboru. He concentrated on every noise, every flutter of wind. Only a minute had passed when Kaito smiled at the faint sound of the creaking of wood.

"You're on the bridge," Kaito stated triumphantly, only to be interrupted by a hit on his head from a small stick.

"I'm not on the bridge," Itsuki stated not a foot from Kaito.

Kaito tore off the blindfold in disbelief. "How did you do that?"

"That is another lesson, concentrate on the task at hand. Let's start again, shall we."

As the lesson went on, Kaito failed miserably in sensing Itsuki's position. Kaito became paranoid and would call out locations from the slightest of sounds, steadily becoming more nervous of a coming hit on the head from Itsuki's stick or a tossed rock.

"Why do I have to get hit every time?" Kaito stated in frustration, tearing the blindfold off.

"If you want it to be more realistic, I can use a dagger or arrowhead like the enemy," Itsuki stated without care. "Your mind will not learn if there are no consequences to your failure."

"The stick is fine," Kaito submitted, putting the blindfold back on and making the hand seal of Kai once again.

In these ways, the shinobi trained till midafternoon. Tsubasa was battered and bruised but had made progress in his training. Kaito similarly had impressed Itsuki, and while the Yukimura brothers were nowhere near mastering their hand seals, they had both started following in the footsteps of their father. As the sun grew low in the sky, the shinobi were called back to the monastery by the chiming of a gong.

Daisuke shook his head disapprovingly at the ragged state of the young warriors. "Playing rough today? I hope you have not worn yourselves out." The monk wrung his hands nervously. "I must tell you, Scarred One, Long Hair, as we made the chants and translated the notes... we all agreed that the meaning was foreboding a great evil. A dark omen lies upon that which you seek. I fear the merits of Buddha do not—"

Noboru began to grow impatient. "We do not fear the evil monk. Tell us what you found."

Daisuke frowned and then grudgingly handed the shinobi a slip of parchment. Noboru opened the paper, the other shinobi crowded around to see.

Itsuki looked up at Daisuke. "We will be leaving at dawn."

10

Winter's Snow
-Iga Province, Iga Mountains-

The translated chants that the shinobi received were only five simple words, "The Shrine of Mount Kurama," a holy place real enough on a map, yet known to the warriors only through the whispers of legend.

They spent a second somber night at the monastery and woke before the sun had crested over the eastern peaks. Daisuke saw to it that the four travelers were well provisioned and appropriately dressed. Their packs were filled to the brim with honey rice cakes, fish cured in salt, dried fruits, and nuts; he even sneaked a small gourd of sake into the bottom of Noboru's pack. The shinobi saved their newly washed shinobifukus, but gladly took the garb of pilgrims that would provide a disguise as well as added warmth. Robes of simple blue and beige were well made from linen woven fibers, layered over soft warm wrappings for the arms and legs, and round straw woven hats. From their battle outfits, only the robust well fitted shoes and the large multi-use scarves were worn openly. In addition, each shinobi was gifted a long wooden staff to help him on his journey, a tradition of monks of the high mountains. When fully outfitted, the shinobi perfectly portrayed the appearance of four traveling monks dressed against the oncoming winter cold. Daisuke gave them a gracious farewell, but under his smile a glimpse of relief could be seen to be rid of the shinobi.

Winding westward from the mountain home of the monks, the path of the shinobi stretched ahead of them following a small river through the Iga mountains, many days of trekking in fair weather, slowed doubly by the growing cold. The early hours passed in silence on the trail. A light wind began to blow, and the shinobi were glad that it blew at their backs, a blessing on their journey. In the shady places of the trail the earth was frozen solid beneath their feet. Not until the morning sun was well placed in the sky did any venture to speak.

Young Kaito was the first to break the silence and when he did his words predictably pertained to Kurama. "It's real?" he exclaimed in wonder.

The older shinobi exchanged a knowing glance. "In a sense," Itsuki said, "but Kurama is probably not the place we may expect."

"Enough," Tsubasa sighed, "just tell us what is going on. What is Kurama really, and why are we going there?"

Noboru raised his thick eyebrows. "I think it is time we tell them Itsuki. We can't expect them to follow us to the ends of the earth without a good reason, can we?"

Itsuki did not break stride but looked up at the mountains and drew a long-measured breath. "Kurama is a holy mountain off the western shores of Lake Biwa, and while the stories of our ancestors say a great many things, the only certainty is that it is home to some very ancient shrines." He cleared his throat with a sound that betrayed his reluctance on the topic. "And we are going… to retrieve weapons."

"Swords," Noboru stated with a wink. "If we have interpreted the book correctly."

Itsuki shot an irritated glance toward Noboru.

"I already have a sword!" Tsubasa exclaimed. "I can't believe this. We're on a fool's errand when we should be planning an attack on Nobunaga. Now is the time to strike, while his judgments are thrown off balance by the thrill of victory."

"Nobunaga has fought and won greater battles many times. I can promise you that any attack now would be soundly defeated." Itsuki ran his fingertips over the thin parallel scars that crossed his left eye from temple to cheek. "And the fool of whom you speak is your own father."

"What?" Tsubasa stated.

"Your father," Noboru said, "wrote many pages of the book we have carried from Hekison. It was he that led us to the monks, and now he directs us toward Kurama."

"The book!" Kaito's eyes bulged out of his face. "My father wrote the book?"

Noboru shook his head. "Yes, well, he wrote some of it. Most of the pages were written long before your father ever received the book by a man named Sengo Muramasa."

"Oi! Noboru, discretion, please!" Itsuki had planted his feet and was firmly grasping the top of his pilgrim's staff.

"Oh, come on, Tsubasa is right." Noboru waved a dismissive hand and kept walking with the boys. "They need to know. Anyway, I'm tired of all the secrets." Noboru pushed the straw hat back from his head and lightly nodded side to side in thought. "Yes, they will know, and we will be rid of questions. Where was I?"

Tsubasa was now trailing closely at the heels of the longhaired shinobi. "You were speaking of Muramasa."

"Right, well the volume was originally the diary of Sengo Muramasa and while much of the writing is confusing, he recorded many secrets of his smithing that no other living person has ever seen. Your father studied the diary like a holy script and added his own contributions, in time it became much more than a journal. Now…"

"Wait, hold on," Tsubasa said. "Do you mean the Muramasa… the demon swordsmith?"

"One and the same," Noboru stated with a sly grin. "Although much like Kurama, the story and the real thing are not equal. I don't mean that the legend outshines the man, much the opposite, but a story does not contain all that is within a man."

"You have met him?" Tsubasa laughed. "Impossible. He is known to have died long ago."

"Oh, and who told you that?" the voice of Itsuki crept up like a cat. "The same legends that describe his evil black eyes and the way he entrapped the souls of men within the blades he forged."

The boys were spooked by the words, for although they knew the stories well, something in the tone of Itsuki's voice told of horrors beyond mention. For all knew that the only blades to rival that of the legendary Goro Masamune were the swords forged by Sengo Muramasa.

"He was ancient," added Noboru. "Well preserved, though his mind was troubled."

Kaito thought hard as he walked. "All right, so what do father's entries say?"

"Something of great value," resumed Noboru. "And that is just the thing. You see, the vast majority of his writing seems to be coded beyond our skill to read. The small legible bits are mostly side notes, one of which led us to the monastery."

"Which in turn is leading us to Kurama!" Kaito said excitedly.

Noboru nodded. "Precisely."

"So, tell us about the swords you expect to find when we get there," Tsubasa stated, trying to sound casual.

"I thought you already had a sword," chided Noboru sarcastically.

Tsubasa fingered the hilt of his wakizashi which protruded from his pack, carefully wrapped in linen. "Yes, well," he stated nervously. "I do, it's just that, um well if what you say is true then the blades at Kurama might be actual Mur—" He was cut short by a strong hand clasped solidly over his mouth.

"Silence!" whispered Itsuki in his ear. "Keep walking, but speak no more, someone approaches." The faintest sound of footsteps could be heard ascending the path ahead. Without an additional word, the four shinobi slowed their pace to one that seemed more natural for a band of pilgrims and relaxed their posture, allowing their shoulders to hunch forward and feet to drop more heavily with every step. Even the muscles of the face eased from their normal intensity to present a more docile disposition. Within moments the warriors had utterly transformed, with the exception of their lean muscular fingers that protruded from the cloth wrappings that protected the backs of the hands. Each one adapted his attention to the oncoming footsteps, equally ready to attack or to talk.

Soon they spotted a solitary figure trudging steadily up the trail. It was a small man carrying a very large bamboo framed pack that was laden down with a great many parcels wrapped and tied down with twine. He was bundled tightly in furs, and his unkempt beard blended perfectly into his garment. Keeping his eyes to the ground, the man seemed to take no notice of the shinobi until he had walked within two paces. He hailed them with a hand containing only three fingers: a thumb, forefinger, and a middle finger.

"Good brothers," he croaked in a hoarse voice that reminded one of a toad from a swamp. "Winter is near at hand. I see from your staffs that you have come from yonder monastery; it would be wise of you to either return there or make great haste on your way." He shifted the weight of the pack, breathing heavily from the effort of speech. "The snows will come quickly and there are more treacherous things in these mountains than storms. Not a place to be caught without shelter I assure you."

Itsuki bowed low. "It is for this very reason we hasten our stride to get over the mountain pass. The monastery is less than a day's trek from here. We would stay and chat, but for the fear of snow we must keep moving."

"I do not mean to keep you." The pilgrim shifted as if weighing his words. "But have you seen a man traveling these mountains? A man of my height, short, peppered hair, wears clothes of black and gray, with a string of bones about his neck."

The shinobi looked at each other quizzically.

"We have not good traveler," Itsuki stated. "What business do you seek with a man who wears bones?"

"I have been tracking him for years, but I will keep my reasons to myself. I mean no offense, but there is danger in sharing one's mission," the traveler stated.

"A belief we share in common," Noboru replied.

Scanning the distance with his narrow dark eyes the pilgrim

made a slight bow and added, "I will say this, if you should come across such a man, do not keep his company and do not let him linger. Peace be with you... and the spirits as well."

"Peace be with you," Itsuki spoke.

Then with a turn, he was on his way as simply as he had come. The shinobi exchanged curious looks, eyebrows were raised, and shoulders were shrugged, and they resumed their course with no words spoken.

When they had put some distance between themselves and the traveler, Itsuki hissed with deadly seriousness. "That is why we walk in silence."

The group traveled with redoubled speed after the ominous warnings, Itsuki leading on at a merciless pace. None had extra breath for words even if they had dared to speak. They kept the pace steady until twilight, and they found a protected spot amongst some large boulders to camp for the night. All were glad for the rest.

Dinner was made and as they ate, stories were told of the past and better times. Noboru took a comb from his pack and began brushing the knots out of his long hair that had accumulated during the travels. Itsuki watched him from the other side of the fire.

"You brush your hair more than a geisha," Itsuki taunted.

Noboru continued to brush, tossing his hair with a flourish. "You're just jealous that you have none, your head looks like a dumpling."

Itsuki rubbed his head and grinned. "Maybe it does, but you know your hair gets you into trouble. Remember Osaka?"

Noboru gave a frown. "That wasn't my fault."

At this point the boys, who were drifting off to sleep, began to pay attention.

"What wasn't your fault?" Tsubasa asked, drawing his knees into his chest.

Noboru stopped brushing his hair and looked directly at the brothers. "Nothing," he grumbled. The Yukimura brothers grinned expectantly at Noboru and then at Itsuki.

Itsuki gave a chuckle. "Almost blew our cover. We were tailing a target through the market when an old merchant woman yanked Noboru's hair from behind and accused him of stealing an item from her cart. She threatened to cut off his hair and sell it for a wig. When she pulled a knife to cut it, Noboru punched her square in the jaw." The Yukimura brothers snickered and Itsuki joined in.

"I'll have you know that I stole from another cart, not hers. Besides, the crone had a mustache. I thought she was a man."

Noboru's defense only caused an uproar of laughter, sleep was the only thing that eventually put an end to the taunts and teasing. In the morning, the shinobi rose early and once again were on their way before the sun had risen. In hopes of beating the winter snows their pace had increased, and the frigid air burned their faces as they bounded down the rocky path one after the other. In the early light they saw darkening clouds had indeed started to surround the mountains and while it was not yet cold enough for snow, all feared that it soon would be. In an effort to defend from the windburn, the shinobi had drawn their large neck scarfs about their heads and mouths while tightly cinching down their straw hats. In this fashion they stayed warm and comfortable as they raced against the day, yet every hour that passed brought dropping temperatures.

We must stop," Kaito called to the others.

"What? Why?" Tsubasa said, peering over Kaito's shoulder.

"Shh!" Kaito held a finger to his lips. All took note of Kaito's tone and dropped to a silent crouch, eyes wide and attentive. "What is it that you see?" Itsuki stated while peering down the path. "Nothing," Kaito stated as he removed his pack and pulled forth his small bow, setting an arrow to the string. "It's what I hear. We are not alone."

Closing his eyes, the youth waited and listened patiently, then aimed at a tuft of brush fifty feet ahead and just off the trail. He released his arrow and the missile cut the air with a shallow arch and plunged cleanly into the shrub, disappearing with an audible hit. With a gurgling yelp, a massive dusty brown wolf stumbled from the brush, took a few drunken steps, and fell heavily to the ground with a bloody shaft lodged in its neck.

Tsubasa patted his brother's shoulder. "Good shot, that wolf could have—"

Five massive wolves crept from the brush, bristling and snarling as they sniffed their fallen comrade and eyed the shinobi with bared fangs. Kaito fumbled to reload his bow with the last arrow of his quiver. He loosed it, hitting a second wolf in the breast, knocking it to the ground. Snapping their jaws, the four able beasts sped forward quickly encircling the shinobi while growling and drooling through teeth. Snow flurries started to twirl and dance around the shinobi as if the wolf pack had summoned some vile magic. Throwing their packs to the ground, the shinobi formed a circle with backs together and unsheathed their swords. Only the shinobi's eyes could be seen through their covered faces, deep breaths billowed out like clouds rising above their conical hats. Snow whipped about the huddled shinobi, enveloping them in a white cloud. The wolves circled round as if carried by the wind, fading from view, darting just within reach, taunting an attack.

"Steady!" yelled Itsuki through clenched teeth. "Wait for them!"

Noboru gave a wry laugh. "Oh come on, I'm hungry!" The wind stung and tore at their clothing and the shinobi braced themselves against the torrent with wide stances. With a splintering crack, an overhanging branch from a nearby tree crashed to the ground and in that same instant the wolf pack closed in as if controlled by a single mind. With an explosive swing, Noboru thrust his hefty kunai dagger into the neck of the nearest wolf, killing it in a spray of blood.

With a flash, one wolf leapt toward Itsuki's crouching form, striking at his neck. With a sickening thud the wolf's head impacted the rocky ground, pinned by a thunderous blow from the blunt tip of Itsuki's staff. A thick red liquid oozed from the downed wolf's clenched jaws, sending the remaining pack into a yammering frenzy.

With both hands, Kaito gripped the handle of his sword as a sinewy brown wolf glided forward with an air of predatory confidence. A low growl resonated from the animal's throat, and he weaved casually around Kaito's swings as if playing a game. Then with a dodge and a bounding leap, the wolf was upon the boy, snapping at his face and knocking him backwards. Kaito sacrificed his forearm to the wolf's jaws and with an effort plunged the wakizashi into the animal's chest pushing savagely. The wolf squirmed until the sword tip emerged from the other side of the ribcage and the body went limp.

Meanwhile Tsubasa was engaged in a brutal fight with the largest and foulest beast of the pack, an old, grizzled alpha with a thick brown coat and a snout hatched with scars. Both the boy's sword and the wolf were dripping with blood, but no fatal wounds seemed to be apparent, the wolf moved with a slight limp. Unblinkingly, Tsubasa stared into the eyes of the beast, taking a deep breath to master his fear. His posture began to relax, and his sword hand slowly dropped to his side as he observed the wolf's muscles contracting. Then with blinding speed, the wolf leapt, and Tsubasa leapt right, sweeping his blade along the suspended animal's abdomen, spilling its entrails. The wolf crashed headlong into the earth and the boy rolled to his feet in the place where his opponent had crouched a moment before. He breathed hard, his lungs expelling massive clouds about him as he sat in silent reflection. The snow flurries had ended with the conclusion of the fight.

Wiping his blade clean, Tsubasa turned to the others. "I've never killed a wolf before. Do they always fight like this, to the last?

Itsuki pulled his blood-stained staff free from his enemy's carcass. "I have never witnessed this, nor have I ever heard stories of wolves doing as such." He prodded the lifeless form. "This is a bad omen, a very dark day. The wolf spirit is a guardian of our people... or at least, it was. It seems that even the kami have turned against us."

"Not all of them." Kaito pointed. "Look."

A lone black crow had landed on the head of the wolf that Kaito had first struck with his arrow; it had pecked out the eyes and was happily preening itself. Itsuki shook his head with a look of disbelief. "Could it be?" he mumbled to himself.

Noboru tucked away his freshly cleaned dagger. "In any case, we are still alive. That was good work." He tussled Kaito's hair.

113

"If not for you the wolves may have had us for dinner. How did you know they were waiting for us?"

Kaito managed a smile. "The Kuji-in hand seal training I started at the monastery with Itsuki. I have been trying to read all the signs of nature, all subtle movements and sounds. I thought I had heard something following us for a while, then suddenly I heard nothing."

Noboru gave a gruff laugh of approval. "A well-played hunch! It seems Itsuki whacking you on the head with that stick improved your senses. Now come here. How is that arm?"

"Nothing more than scratches," Kaito stated proudly.

Inspecting the arm, Noboru smiled, for he found only a single puncture wound with a small stream of blood. "Scratches indeed, you may be stars with a bow, but your swordplay needs work. Clean the wound quickly, animals breed sickness for man. But at least we will be eating well tonight."

"We should be going," Itsuki said while hunching over to retrieve his pack. "There is no time to spare if we are to beat this weather." Even as he spoke, the icy wind rose carrying the snow in great waves through the air. He adjusted the scarf about his mouth and nose to keep out the cold. "Let's get to it!" he commanded, but the others made no move to follow his lead.

"We should make an advantage from the merits of our kills," Noboru argued. "And who knows what else might hunt us on this cursed trail. Next time... we may not be so fortunate."

"The meat will help us in the long run," Tsubasa suggested.

"And a wolf skin cloak would certainly keep us warm," added Kaito hopefully.

Itsuki leaned on his staff in visible frustration. "Tanning hides takes days. The pass will get snowed in and we will be trapped up here in the mountains. If we quicken our pace, we may yet make the foothills before it's too late."

Noboru scratched at his sideburn. "Camping here for the night will not make a difference, and as for the hides, you know we can at least start the process. We are already moving as fast as we can and Kaito needs to properly dress his wound. Suppose we go without taking advantage of these welcome provisions and then we are snowed in regardless. We would be in serious trouble then."

"Waste of time," snapped Itsuki.

"We will put it to a vote," Noboru said. "All those in favor of eating some wolf, raise your hand." All except Itsuki eagerly shot a hand up. "Well there you go," Noboru stated while pulling out a knife. "Let's get to it."

Luck seemed to be on the shinobi's side as the storm clouds fled and the wind died down. With a bit of protesting from Itsuki, they made short work of the four healthiest looking wolves. Each shinobi carefully skinned the hide of a wolf. Small drying racks were made from nearby wood; the wolf furs were attached and stretched appropriately to dry. They then cracked open the skulls to access the brain oils, a precious commodity to help the future curing process. The brain oils were poured into a small cooking container and put over a fire. Soon after, wolf meat was crackling for dinner, and the extra was put on for smoking for the future journey.

"It doesn't taste half bad." Noboru mumbled with a mouthful of wolf meat.

"If only all food was so easy to catch," Tsubasa stated sarcastically.

Kaito's wound was properly wrapped with some of the medical herbs from Hekison. The spirits of all were raised by the hot food and the comfort of the small glowing flames. Noboru told a story based on the stars in the sky and the boys listened intently, enjoying his rich and animated voice. Itsuki sat in a gloom of his own brooding, barely touching his food and staring deeply into the fire. Noboru finished his story and turned to Itsuki.

"What's wrong? We are alive with our goal in sight, and you sit sulking like a starving peasant."

Twirling his meat on a shaved spindled of wood, Itsuki's voice came as if from far away. "I do not believe those wolves came by chance. I feel... I feel they were sent."

"Sent? How do you mean? They seemed nothing more than wild beasts."

Itsuki looked up from the flames. "Even you have never seen wolves fight like that, to the last? And the way they moved with the wind, with the snows..." Itsuki stopped in silent thought.

Noboru gave a grunt of consideration, but no more was said on the topic. The words had brought a somber silence to the night, making real the fears that none had wished to acknowledge. One by one sleep took them, though it was a cold and troubled sleep.

The shinobi were awoken hours before dawn to the falling of a heavy snow. They quickly packed up camp and resumed the trek. They attached the drying racks of wolf furs to their packs; the furs could prove more precious than ever now. It was a slow and difficult journey as the terrain had become quite steep, and in places the trail was hidden by fresh, ankle-deep snow. The shinobi were forced to stop and make camp under trees, having made little progress. During the night, the snow had stopped and gave the shinobi a false hope of reaching the mountain pass.

On the morning of the second day a great storm struck, and the boys feared that they would be drowned and buried in snow. Yet the older shinobi led on more determined than ever and growing ever more serious. By noon they came upon the charred remains of a tiny village, nestled into a cleft of the mountainside. A few shacks still held their structure, but the place seemed more like a graveyard than a settlement. The black of the timbers stood out starkly against the newly blanketed snow, giving the village a look both beautiful and ancient. The shinobi's pace slowed to a crawl as they kept their limbs tucked into the interiors of their body to conserve heat. Noboru and the brothers stopped to investigate the shelter, but Itsuki marched on paying them no heed.

"Oi!" Noboru called out, but Itsuki ignored the call. "Itsuki, stop!" he called out again. Finally, Noboru was forced to run after Itsuki, catching him by the shoulder. Itsuki's face was hard as stone and his eyes red with tears.

From a distance, the Yukimura brothers shivered and watched a conversation that they could not make out. The older shinobi exchanged heated words; their voices barely heard over the howling wind.

"L-l-look." Tsubasa's teeth chattered as he pointed at Noboru.

It was hard to see, but through the falling snow Kaito could make out Noboru slowly shifting his hand to his kunai at his side. For what seemed an eternity, Noboru held his stance to Itsuki, preparing for a fight, the howl of the wind was the only entity that spoke. Itsuki spat at Noboru's feet, and finally marched toward the welcome shelter, eyes fixed on the ground.

Noboru returned to the brothers giving a large sigh. The boys dared not ask what had been discussed, but Kaito could not help a twinge of curiosity.

"So, where do you suppose we are?" He tried to ask through chattering teeth. "What is this place?"

Noboru drew a long breath. "It was called Midori," he stated with reverence. "And it was Itsuki's home. Come, it seems it will be his home again till winter passes."

11

The Game of Go

-Omi Province, Azuchi Castle-

Winter had come to Japan, and a soft snow covered the high rooftops of Azuchi Castle. Smoke billowed from the structure, showing evidence of the lit hearths from within. The previous night had left a new snowfall on the surrounding terrain, leaving the world in a silent white blanket. A few puffy clouds blotted the otherwise flawless blue sky, and small ice crystals glistened in the sun as they fell to the earth. The surface of Lake Biwa reflected a pristine image of the surrounding terrain, wispy clouds flowed through the ridges of the snow-capped mountains in the distance. A serene landscape for a somber day to take place. After Nobunaga's conquest of Iga, he had summoned a war council of all available generals. The winter and adverse weather conditions had brought a stalemate in his conquest of Japan, a time for planning and punishing.

In one of the upper levels of the castle in an octagonal room sat two daimyōs named Hideyoshi Hashiba and Ieyasu Tokugawa. They were sworn allies, but fierce rivals regardless. Between them was a woodblock board game called go. On top of the block was a grid containing nineteen by nineteen squares. White and black stones spread across the board in strategically linked chains. The object of the game was to carefully place your stones turn by turn to encompass your enemy's pieces while avoiding being ensnared yourself. The game required an acute mind and a cunning for entrapping one's opponent, much like war.

Both men sat playing, wearing casual clothing opposed to their usual military garb. Ieyasu wore a solid blue kimono, where Hideyoshi wore a similar black kimono. But despite the simplicity and comfort of the garments, both were of superb quality that befitted the status of the wearer.

Both men were contemporaries of their liege lord, Nobunaga Oda, Ieyasu being just shy of forty years old and Hideyoshi being just past forty. Ieyasu was thicker of bones with a clean-shaven face and a long head of hair tied in a knot at the crown of his head. His eyes were dark, complimented by a hard-narrow jawline.

One would not say Hideyoshi was a handsome man, with average looks and loss of hair. Furthermore, Nobunaga on more than one occasion referred to Hideyoshi as monkey faced, a title given when he was a mere foot soldier, but occasionally was brought up regardless of his status of a general. Nevertheless, he carried himself with a sense of wisdom and dignity. Hideyoshi stroked his goatee looking at the game and scratched his head where it was balding, a trait that had started at a young age. His long forearms showed sinewy muscles underneath, revealing his pedigree of a warrior.

Ieyasu placed a white stone game piece. "You always challenge me, Hideyoshi. It is good to have you around to keep me on my toes."

Hideyoshi gave a sly smile and placed a black stone. "One

must keep your wits sharp in these times of war. A mind is more dangerous than a sword."

Ieyasu chuckled. "Don't let Nobunaga hear you say such words. His obsession with swords and the power they bring is well known; some say it has made him reckless. Some say the campaign he led against the Iga shinobi was about a sword."

"And some say you shouldn't talk about the lord you serve so recklessly. The walls have ears in Azuchi Castle."

Ieyasu grinned. "Most likely all the ears belong to you."

No sooner had Ieyasu finished his sentence did the door slide open with a woman kneeling. It was the very same Rin Kurosawa who had spied on Nobunaga Oda for an unknown master in Azuchi Castle.

"My lords, sorry to disturb you, but there is an urgent message from Lady Nene."

Hideyoshi leaned to the left to see past Ieyasu and waved a hand. "Ahh, Rin. Come. What tidings do you bring?"

Rin Kurosawa was a fair woman, with an enchanting smile, and a flirtatious aura to match. The one difference that set her apart from most women was that her body was a bit leaner and more gamey, unusual for a handmaiden. She strode across the room as gracefully as a geisha but hidden underneath her façade was the subtle movements of a tiger waiting to pounce. She wore a simple flowered kimono with her hair held up by a small black comb with a polished white stone.

Rin had been employed as a serving maid in Azuchi Castle in her early teens. The general, Hideyoshi, had seen the potential in the young girl; he originally paid her for the secrets she obtained amongst the castle traffic. Eventually he had found further use of her skills for espionage and thievery. Officially,

Rin was a handmaiden to Nene Hashiba, Hideyoshi's wife, but that was the façade used by them to give her royal access to gather secrets.

Rin stepped toward the two men; Ieyasu gave a look to Hideyoshi and raised his eyebrows twice.

"Well?" Hideyoshi questioned impatiently. "Do not hesitate woman, out with it."

"It is not publicly known, your wife heard of it and instructed me to tell you immediately," Rin stated. "It seems that the war council will be preceded by a seppuku."

"Seppuku, of who?" Ieyasu interjected, shocked by the news.

"My lords, of Haruto Watanabe, the first captain of Mitsuhide Akechi. I am sorry, my lords, but that was all the information given to me."

Ieyasu gave a long look of disbelief at Rin and then at Hideyoshi.

"I know that Mitsuhide Akechi failed numerous times while he battled with you against the Mōri Clan, but for Nobunaga to put the blame on his first captain is harsh, an outright insult," Ieyasu contested.

Rin bowed. "I should let you discuss such matters in private."

"Tell my wife that she is as shrewd as she is beautiful for giving me this information ahead of the official announcement," Hideyoshi stated.

Rin smiled and bowed. After Rin had slid the door shut, Ieyasu looked at the go board in thought. "I stick by my words; our Lord Nobunaga is getting a tad reckless with his discipline."

"Nobunaga wishes to show that failure is not an option, and that loyalty is to be first priority. You don't want to end up like the Iga shinobi or like poor captain Haruto, do you?"

Ieyasu shook his head. "Not even a true rebellion if you ask me, the Iga shinobi never swore fealty to Nobunaga or even to the Shogunate when it still existed. They came in beneficial use from time to time, and all they wanted was their precious mountain tops. Shame to have such assassins go to waste."

Hideyoshi placed a black stone on the go board. "Yes, but Nobunaga's ruthlessness sends a message. The more victories he wins, the more fear is driven into his enemies, and the more likely they are to submit without resistance."

Ieyasu placed another stone piece on the go board. "You were once his sandal-bearer. You probably know the man better than most. In any case, Mitsuhide will be furious over losing his captain simply because Nobunaga will not tolerate failure."

Hideyoshi looked at the go board in thought. He was a man of great cunning; many rival generals detested him for being a man of lowly birth. Hideyoshi had been born a peasant and had started out as a mere foot soldier of Nobunaga Oda. Through victory, cunning, charm, and marriage he had worked his way through the ranks to become an advisory general to Nobunaga Oda. One of the few men to rival him was his current opponent across the go board, Ieyasu Tokugawa.

Ieyasu was not as ruthless as Hideyoshi but was famous for his victories through patience. He had received traditional samurai training from a young age, and despite his noble bloodline, he had experienced his fair share of hardship to earn his position of daimyō and general to Nobunaga. Most recently he had become victor over the southern provinces of the powerful Takeda clan, earning him respect among all.

Hideyoshi placed a black piece on the board, winning the match against Ieyasu. "Game," he declared.

Ieyasu swatted the game board in frustration. "You are a cunning man, Hideyoshi. I ought to watch my back around you."

Hideyoshi stroked the goatee hanging from his chin. "That's the smartest thing I've heard you say yet."

Ieyasu stood up composing himself and smiled. "I always enjoy our games together. Next time my patience may overcome your aggressiveness."

"Next time," Hideyoshi mused.

"Well till our next game, news of the seppuku of Haruto changes things. I must prepare for the war council that is to come. No doubt, Nobunaga will want thorough reports."

Ieyasu abruptly left the room and slid the doors behind him. No sooner that he closed the door did Rin enter through the door rolling her eyes. "I wasn't gawking, merely looking for a signal if you wanted Ieyasu to know the news of the seppuku. Information is my business in case you forgot."

Hideyoshi sternly stood up. "Watch it now, I'm still your lord. Besides, the reason you're so useful is because we keep up the charade that you're just a simple handmaiden. If the other daimyōs new of your other unique skills, there would be questions asked and unnecessary deaths would occur."

Rin gave a flirtatious look while acting like a naive young girl. "You want someone killed?"

Hideyoshi stepped closer. "When the time comes, but right now I need you to keep an eye on Ieyasu, and an even closer eye on any oddities that Nobunaga may have brought back from his siege. Prisoners, spoils of war, anything out of the abnormal, understood?"

"Like usual I am one step ahead of you, I have already probed into the prisoners of Iga and Nobunaga's trinkets."

"Good," Hideyoshi stated impressed. "Just don't get into too much mischief while spying on Ieyasu."

Rin pulled the black comb out of her hair, revealing it to be a small dagger and began adjusting her hair to better conceal the disguised weapon. "Understood."

Seppuku was a form of ritual suicide adopted by the samurai in alignment with their code of honor, Bushidō. To an outsider seppuku would seem like a cruel demeaning death, but to the samurai it was a way of keeping their honor in death when they had failed in life, redemption through bravery of taking one's own life. Instead of being publicly killed by crucifixion like some common criminal, a samurai could keep his title and his family would keep all status through seppuku.

The ritual was to take place in the center stage of Azuchi Castle. Nobunaga Oda himself had sentenced the samurai to seppuku. The samurai was a vassal of a general, Mitsuhide Akechi, who had been paired with Hideyoshi Hashiba on the siege of the Mōri clan in Bitchū Province. Unlike Hideyoshi, who had made grand headway with his battles in the north of Bitchū Province, Mitsuhide had met fierce resistance in the south and was battered with defeat after defeat. Mitsuhide had delivered a formal report to Nobunaga Oda on the efforts. Enraged of the setbacks, Nobunaga Oda looked for someone to blame for the cause of the unsuccessful battles. Nobunaga would have commanded Mitsuhide himself to commit seppuku but would not dare place the blame on a daimyō for fear of rebellion. Therefore, Nobunaga put the blame on Mitsuhide's right hand man, Haruto Watanabe, a skilled samurai and battle tested.

In all, the situation was of ill taste, Nobunaga Oda had to keep the respect of his generals by proving that failure could not be tolerated, a sign of weakness would give his fellow generals cause to question Nobunaga's authority in the great civil war of Japan. Reluctantly, Nobunaga sentenced Haruto to seppuku with full titles, the ceremony taking place in Azuchi Castle, a rare honor to be given. Nobunaga had hopes that the gesture would appease Mitsuhide Akechi, but the daimyō had at best an ill tolerated look on his face as he entered the room.

In attendance were all the head generals that could be spared from their military duties of battle for a brief period. The occasion was solemn and silent; nobody dared to speak as if it were to give dishonor to Haruto's death. When all were in attendance, Nobunaga gave a curt nod to the administrator. The administrator was in ceremonial garb, a clean kimono in all white from head to toe.

The administrator bowed toward Haruto. "For your failures in the Bitchū Province you have brought disgrace to yourself and your family. Lord Nobunaga has given you the right of seppuku that you may regain your honor with a true death of a samurai in front of your lords."

In the center of the room was a large thirty by thirty-foot mat covered by a white cloth backed by a white curtain against the wall. Haruto was also in a complete white kimono, as was his number two. The man holding the title of second, or number two, was the younger brother and fellow samurai of Haruto, a look of solemnity was upon the young man's face. To fail at the duties of second would give great disdain upon one's household. A second's duty was to assist the first in completing his death.

Haruto unraveled a small scroll, revealing his prewritten death poem, a sort of parting last words, and began to read.

Like the waters of autumn
My life flows to winter
I do not fear for my soul
But I fear for those who are left behind
May the gods bless these islands
That they may be guided out of the chaos of war

Haruto gave a solemn nod and handed the death poem to one of his ceremonial assistants. He then knelt and unraveled his kimono, bearing his chest and abdomen. Haruto's brother unsheathed his katana in one swift elegant motion. The sound sliced through the silence of the room, bringing a startling reality of death to the moment. Haruto's brother held the sword upward with a two-handed grip, positioning for a masterful stroke. Haruto grabbed the ceremonial dagger, his hand started to tremble in anticipation. Even though Haruto had faced death dozens of times in battle, ending himself with his own blade was a feat in which he was not prepared. Plunging a blade into one's abdomen went against every instinct of Haruto's being.

Haruto took two large breaths to calm his soul and shaking hand. Haruto opened his eyes and plunged the tantō deep into his abdomen, with what little strength he had left he began disemboweling himself. Haruto tried to stifle his scream, but the pain instinctively made him yelp. The second, Haruto's brother, gave a large war cry and without hesitation decapitated Haruto's head in one fell swoop. Haruto's lifeless body slumped over while the head landed on the floor to look up at his brother. The white mat quickly became stained with a stark, deep-red pool of blood that was slowly growing larger. An assistant picked up the head and wrapped it carefully in white silk and began to clean up the corpse. The ceremony had been completed and a long pause of silence amongst the audience was held in reverence. A single tear betrayed Haruto's brother, the man quickly composed himself as he watched Haruto's corpse cleaned and carried off.

Mitsuhide Akechi stormed out of the room, an obvious social slight to Nobunaga. Mitsuhide left mumbling in anger and when he exited the room, yelling could be heard in the corridors. As the crowd left the chambers, Mitsuhide's outburst went unnoticed, except from a few.

"He should have more prudence not to make offense," Ieyasu whispered to Hideyoshi.

"The man is rash… but has a right to be angered. A discussion to be had away from so many ears. Come, we must not be late for the war council," Hideyoshi whispered while making his exit.

The ceremony of seppuku cast an ominous sense of foreboding over the members of Nobunaga's war council. The generals did not know what to make of the mixed message, and no longer knew what was expected of them when they went to war. Only one clue could be deciphered from the events of the day, the general Mitsuhide Akechi was furious.

12

The Crossing
-Iga Province, Midori Village-

The former village of Itsuki Hayashi had been a haven to the shinobi for winter. The weather had been harsh, and snow had barred the mountain pass. Midori was the name the villagers had called it, and it simply meant green, referring to the lush greenery it had in the spring months. The village had once been a peaceful place, a home where Itsuki had planned to grow old with his wife, Yuna, and raise his young daughter, Natsumi. The fires that Nobunaga had brought put an end to the village and Itsuki's hopeful future.

There was one home in particular that escaped the fires of Nobunaga; the group had taken residence in it to survive the ominous winter that had come. They had immediately taken account of any usable supplies. The shinobi at first survived on the monastery rations and cured wolf meat. As time went on, they were forced to be more creative. They found some volunteer plants of mainly roots and leafy greens from a past garden long run with weeds. They were even more fortunate to find an unspoiled storage of rice grain, necessary sustenance for survival. Although the shinobi were lucky with the found food, they had all dropped in weight due to the necessary rationing of provisions. Furthermore, in the first two weeks Tsubasa and Kaito had run a high fever that kept them close to a fire and not far from a bed.

The winter was mainly devoted to survival. The wolf furs were cured and made into cloaks, a welcome commodity for any outside work. The home they lived in was repaired with the remaining parts of other homes. Hunting and foraging were an almost daily practice. When essential tasks were completed, time was spent on training the Yukimura brothers. Their isolation gave them much to reflect on and much to prepare.

Throughout their stay in the dead village, Itsuki had avoided the burned-out husk of his former home with the upmost diligence. Noboru had given the Yukimura brothers the bare minimum details of what had happened in the raid, emphasizing not to question Itsuki about the matter. Itsuki's countenance had darkened almost every day that they had stayed in the village. The only distraction was to help the Yukimura brothers in training.

The sound of wooden practice swords could be heard echoing in the dead village, the snow had melted and next would be the pass, a welcome sight to the coming spring.

"You've gotten better," Noboru stated, "but you still lack patience."

"Just like you," Tsubasa quipped back.

Noboru could not help but laugh. Tsubasa's style was somewhat similar to his own; he had a natural tendency to take the first strike in battle, always staying on the offensive. They only differed in that Tsubasa excelled in a barrage of quick small blows whereas Noboru would go for the long lightning-fast swings backed by large brunt force. The two shinobi continued to clack their wooden practice swords, at one-point Tsubasa even made Noboru stagger, but Tsubasa was soon tripped, followed by a wooden point at his throat.

"Almost," Noboru smiled.

Tsubasa shook his head. "Just when I have the upper hand you pull out another one of your tricks."

Noboru gave out his hand to help the young man up. "My tricks have kept me alive." Noboru smiled through a large and unkempt beard that had grown through the winter. "Come let us check the pass."

They both grabbed their wolf furs and put them over their shoulders. Noboru and Tsubasa checked a small vantage point to see the mountain pass, as suspected, today would be the day that they would leave. They quickly returned to the small house where Itsuki and Kaito were studying a map near a small hearth. This is how most of the days had been spent in winter. The older shinobi honing the skills of their younger comrades: climbing, combat, stealth, and the Kuji-in hand seals. Often the physical lessons came at a price; Kaito and Tsubasa had fresh bruises and calluses as proof of their work. The training was good for preparation and to fight off idleness in the winter months.

"The pass is clear, at least clear enough, there will be snow," Noboru stated bluntly, closing the door behind him.

"Excellent," Itsuki stated. "Are you two ready to leave."

"We're leaving?" Kaito spoke excitedly. "Finally?"

"Yes, Mount Kurama," Itsuki stated, pulling out a map.

"Kurama? Is it on the way to Azuchi Castle?" Tsubasa sat looking at the map.

"No, it is beyond Azuchi, north of Kyoto. First, we must make our way north to the Yasu River, we can resupply with rations at a river village. Then we follow the river up to Lake Biwa and cross the neck of the lake. Here," Itsuki stated, pointing to a spot on the map. "Then travel west to Mount Kurama."

Tsubasa shook his head in frustration. "Why not get the swords after, why pass Azuchi and Nobunaga?"

"And what if it's full. Do you plan to kill all 1,000 garrisoned in that castle?" Noboru mocked.

"If I have to." Tsubasa knew he sounded foolish as the words came from his mouth.

Noboru sighed. "We have no idea when and where Nobunaga will be. We must find an ample opportunity to strike. Kyoto is the Capital, hub of information and best place to start."

"I have finished mapping out our trail, I am leaving this graveyard, with or without you," Itsuki stated with a tone of finality in his voice.

As the shinobi left the village only Itsuki betrayed one reluctant glance at the charred husk of his former house. The group traveled for two days, making their way through the last of the Iga mountains and finding lush green lands with tall grass on the other side. The travel was slow, the shinobi avoided main roads where they could and always took the guise of unarmed travelers. The warring provinces of Japan had made travel a risky ordeal and authorities could question anyone on the roads. As planned, they resupplied with any necessities through trade and what money they had near the river village of Koka. Their stay was brief, taking extra precaution to get in and out without staying the night in the village. When the shinobi had made it to the shores of Lake Biwa, they made camp in front of the setting sun. Only a few miles separated the shinobi from the ever-watchful Azuchi Castle upon its high hill overlooking Lake Biwa. The shinobi made usual accommodations to their camp and started a small fire by the lakeside reeds.

"We should be heading toward Azuchi, not crossing this lake," Tsubasa complained.

"We don't even know if Nobunaga is there," Kaito stated.

"It would not matter. To penetrate Azuchi Castle, we would need a year's planning, funds, reconnaissance, and luck; even then I wouldn't bet on us," Itsuki sighed, sounding somewhat defeated. "We are only four of a scattered tribe."

Tsubasa decided not to push the argument and leave the matter be, he did not doubt Itsuki's motives on Nobunaga's life.

The four sat around the fire and discussed their next day's travel of how they would cross the waters. Lake Biwa was the largest lake in Japan, a length of fourteen miles at some points, for this the shinobi chose the lower half of the lake at a narrow neck crossing. They had argued which would be riskier, to pay a ferry and be questioned, or steal a small boat and risk pursuit. They all agreed that it would be better to decide come morning when they could survey the nearby ferry crossing.

In a moment of silence Itsuki seemed lost in thought and then pulled the mysterious leather-bound book of Muramasa from his pack, a sight the Yukimura brothers had seen many times. This time to Tsubasa's surprise, Itsuki walked over and handed it to the young shinobi.

"Read it," Itsuki said plainly. "I know you have been frustrated through this trek; it will give you insight into what we seek."

"Why haven't you told us the tale yourselves?" Tsubasa asked.

"We told you what we could already, without revealing..." Noboru thought for a moment. "Kazuki made us swear by the gods to never speak of the things we saw outside the three of us, we would not condemn our souls. We swore by our names."

"This is the only way you may learn while we do not have to break our vow; it is only part of the story. I believe your father made us promise to ensure the secrecy of such issues," Itsuki stated in agreement.

Tsubasa looked at the book for the first time in detail, inspecting the craftsmanship. It was a handmade simple leather-bound book with twined pages. A single kanji like calligraphy symbol was stamped on the front of the book, similar to the native language of Japan, but the text eluded his understanding. Tsubasa thumbed through the book finding the beginning journal entries legible in his native tongue, but the latter portion of the book was written in a jumble of words speaking nonsense, an encoded message.

"Start from the beginning," Itsuki said while sitting down. "And before you ask, no we don't know what's in the latter portion, but we know it was your father who wrote it, the encoded message."

Tsubasa looked at the book quizzically and thumbed to the beginning. Kaito was staring at the book as if it were some form of a portal to the future. Tsubasa read aloud so his brother could hear.

The stars shine brightly tonight, and I feel as if I'm pulled by some unknown force to the sea. I write these words to make sense of my life's pursuits, and for what I fear is a blind hope that these words will reach those who may understand. With haste I recall my journey, for I fear my sanity has started to fade.

Kyle Mortensen

My name is Sengo Muramasa,

I was born long ago on the island of Honshu, In the Ise Province, in a small village of extraordinary craftsmen. I was brought up in the tradition of sword craft under the expert tutelage of Master Heianjō Nagayoshi, and guided in the ancient secrets for producing blades sharp enough to cut through man or demon, but beautiful enough to display as art. From a young age I had a disciplined hand, a keen eye, and a seeking heart, all of which I poured forth into my apprenticeship with Master Nagayoshi. For five years I worked and learned every aspect of the craft, until at long last I was ready to forge my own blade with the blessing of my master.

For two months I sweated, folding steel over steel, working its grain into long graceful lines, and hammering its surface by the light of my volcanic furnace. As my hammer pounded the metal, I felt my very being and the blade tune together in harmony until it reflected my soul. And for another month I polished and sharpened my blade until its side shone like clear water under silver starlight. The blade's edge was tapered to a sharpness that would make a razor scream with envy.

At the end of the third month, Master Nagayoshi, having not yet seen nor asked of the sword's progress, held a ceremony to personally inspect the finished work, and to induct me as the newest swordsmith of the school. The ceremony, a most solemn of occasions, fell on an auspicious full moon evening in the cold dead of winter, and was strictly between master and student. Both of us dressed in the richest of white, reflecting the purity of our craft which fit perfectly with the light snow fall around the school. When I presented my blade, Nagayoshi eagerly received it wrapped in a bundle of fine white silk; but as the bundle passed hands, darkness came over the master's countenance. Nagayoshi hung his head and was silent.

After an age, he raised his eyes and cast a sympathetic gaze upon me

135

while I showed an earnest expression that betrayed no misgivings. With reluctance, Master Nagayoshi unwrapped the silk and inspected my blade. In a forced smile my teacher handed it back and told me that it was a work of transcendent beauty and that another should never be made. My confusion of my master's statement was only surmounted by my disappointment.

Second entry,

Disregarding my master's advice, I began crafting under my own name. By the time the cherry blossoms had begun to bloom that spring, the reputation of my sword craft was known throughout the central provinces, and I had begun work on my first commissioned sword for a powerful daimyō. Additionally, I had accumulated a list of orders that would take three years to fill. With the extraordinary prices I charged for my blades, I quickly established my own forge and hired on apprentices of my own to help with the abundance of work.

While the quality of my swords as well as the satisfaction of my patrons was supreme; I felt nothing but discontent as the warning of Nagayoshi festered and grew. The master's warning struck a deep chord that would resonate deep within my soul, as if the single thought was a note that once played would inextricably drive me to a lifetime of proving my master wrong.

Later I had confronted my former teacher to the meaning of his warning. Nagayoshi had said that when he held my first blade, swaddled in its robe of virgin silk, he felt the chill of 10,000 cold nights pierce his bones, and that the cold had hardened his heart. While the blade was physically flawless, its spirit was dark and clouded with the envious desire of one that cannot know peace. The master explained that many years earlier he had beheld a perfect weapon much like mine, but that when it had been handed to him, Nagayoshi had been overcome with such tenderness that he was compelled to hold the weapon as he would a baby bird. He held the sword, and it held him in the void. The sword was one of the lesser-known masterpieces forged be the late Goro Nyudo Masamune, undisputedly the greatest swordsmith in all the ages of the land of the rising sun. His blades were famous not only for their superior craftsmanship, but also for their purported capacity to still the wielder, and in moments of battle bring them as one with the void.

I was in fact not merely familiar with the artistry of Masamune, but fanatically obsessed. I had been chasing the elusive legend of Masamune my entire life. Having my blade now compared to the specter and found it equal in quality, but wicked in contrast, opened a wound in my soul that would never heal.

For years I worked tirelessly, turning out dozens upon dozens of swords, filling the orders of daimyōs and samurai whose requests fell upon the forge like a monsoon rain that would never end. Despite ever-growing demand and unceasing urgings from my clients for speed of production, I stuck resolutely to my craft with each new forged blade surpassing the last. Yet never once did a patron upon receiving their long-awaited sword remark on the serenity or benevolence that had been imparted therein. Rather, the warriors and chieftains who hungrily took possession of their new blades would praise the craftsman for the grace with which each masterpiece would elicit but a single thought of victory. The vitality of this fact was undeniable, as the very air would tingle with anticipation as a Muramasa blade was unsheathed for battle. These were blades of action to be wielded with ferocity. As naturally as the fish takes to the waters of Lake Biwa, so too do the blades of Muramasa take to human blood.

Third entry,
As the years passed, and the reputation of my school grew, so did my

reclusiveness. My work became my obsession and because of it I lost my family and my love, but that is another story. I became ever more withdrawn and secretive with my work, insisting that none but my closest aides be allowed near the forge, particularly during the earliest stages of the forging. I immersed myself obsessively, not just in the physical processes, but also into study of ancient writings on my most beloved craft. I would stay up long hours into the night, pouring over scrolls and texts of any kind that might reveal to me secrets of long departed smiths. On many occasions, I would completely halt work in order to take lengthy trips to remote and distant provinces merely to view a document or speak to a particularly distinguished sword maker. So frequent and disruptive became the expeditions that in time my blades became as well known for their scarcity as for their lethality. My actions did not go unnoticed by the public and the rumors started that I used dark magic, human bones, and other nonsense to forge my blades. The time of civil war in my country brought many a person to be acquainted with the effectiveness of a Muramasa blade. To the common folk, how else could I have created such lethal blades, and so my title of demon-smith started to spread across the land like wildfire. However, this served only to build upon a mystique that already hung thick like a bank of fog around the fires of the Muramasa forge.

One day in autumn, just as the leaves of the maple trees had begun to drop, I announced to all in my employ that I would make only twelve more blades, completing one each month for the next year. Once all twelve blades had been forged, I would close the doors of the school, pay each pupil an extra month's wage, and lay down my hammer. I instructed that any back orders, beyond the twelve to be forged, were to have their deposits refunded in double as an apology for the inconvenience.

Fourth entry,

In the summer months, I commenced work on the first of the twelve blades. With a greater fervor and passion that would have rivaled any youth on the beginning of their apprenticeship, I set to making what was to be the pinnacle of my career. I completed the forging in exactly one month, and by the time the blade had been polished, it was generally agreed upon within the school that its equal had never been seen. That is until my second month's toil was completed. The second month's blade was every bit the twin of its predecessor, except that it somehow seemed to shine more brightly and deeply in comparison. And all within the school marveled at its beauty and agreed that it would never be surpassed.

And so, it went for a year. At the end of each month, all were convinced that my opus had peaked, and at the end of the next all chided themselves for their lack of faith.

At the end of a year all twelve blades had been forged, one per month as promised. They were all of surpassing allure. They were my masterpiece and I fancied myself every bit the equal of the legendary swordsmith Masamune.

The recipients of the swords coveted the blades lustfully, for they knew that they possessed not only the finest blades forged in two centuries, but an added allure of being the final works of the Master Muramasa. My final works tainted only by my solidified title of demon-smith by the public, for at this time my true name was hardly used outside of the people I knew. Alas, my furnace had gone cold, and the news of my retirement carried by the coming winter winds spread across the lands.

Fifth entry,

The furious year of production had taken its toll, and as I went about setting my affairs in order for the closing of the school. It was murmured that the light had gone from my eyes, and that I appeared diminished in both stature and virility. I had blossomed in an explosion of brilliance and was now fading into the twilight. I loaded up a small cart with clothes, personal effects, and a bundle of my most treasured scrolls on which was recorded all the findings of long years traveling the provinces. Lastly, I packed in a set of my favorite hammers, tongs, and smith tools. While they would be little more than keepsakes in retirement, they were an extension of myself, and I could no sooner leave my tool set as I could my left hand. When all had been arranged, and I felt confident that my school would be well kept and continued by my apprentices, I took to the road. I made my way southeast to the sea, and I traveled alone.

As my ox lazily pulled my possessions, I found myself settled in a village on the coast of the Sagami Province, south of Edo. It was no accident that I chose this particular town to take up residence in my old age. This was in fact the very same village in which the legendary Goro Masamune had worked more than 200 years earlier in the time of the great swords. It was here that the man became a legend, here that man became immortal by the work of his hands and the sweat of his brow.

I hoped that it would be in this coastal village that I would find peace, but peace was not to be my fate. I had secured an unassuming residence nestled on a rocky outcropping, which overlooked the great waters of the Sagami Bay. Neighboring houses were speckled down the coastline, but the cliffs were all mine, keeping me for better or worse isolated from the surrounding villagers. From the garden I could watch dawn creep slowly over the horizon, far beyond the gilded outline of islands silhouetted against the rising sun. I took to settling in, and as soon as my last stitch of luggage had been unpacked, the fatigue of my age had caught up with me.

For the first time in half a century, I had no work to fill my hands.

Now, with nothing but unburdened time before me, I found myself terrified at the prospect of living in memory and introspection. I knew what awaited me and had no desire to confront it, a long retirement of introspection. My work which had produced a new generation of blades that cut down a generation of young warriors, death was my legacy.

Sixth entry,

Fears of regret haunted me, but I did my best to stay occupied. Every morning while the sea fog was still fresh in the dawn air, I would hike down to the beach, and walk the shores to still my mind. On my walks I would often meet fishermen setting out to troll the deep waters of the bay and others just returning with some early morning catch. So consistent were my strolls, that within a month I knew most every boat, captain, and crewman by name for miles in either direction. Most days I purchased fish for meals, but on occasion I returned home empty handed except for perhaps an odd or particularly inviting stone picked up along the way. I missed the feel of heavy steel, and the raw heft of firing coal. So, I took to hunting and collecting stones, which occupied my nervous hands, and fostered communion with the earth.

As the months passed, I began to accumulate a large number of stones, so many so that they mounded in the garden as if it were a quarry. There were stones of all sizes, though most were larger than a man's head, as they were sufficiently heavy to afford some amount of physical exercise in their carrying and a sense of accomplishment. Deciding something must be done with all the clutter, I commenced to building at the far end of the garden. I began without intention, simply mortaring into place one stone at a time as they happened to fit together. Every day I worked, binding the stones together, and every day the structure grew. At first the stones fit clumsily, with excess mortar spilling out of the joints like rice pudding. But soon enough I gained an understanding of

141

this raw material, and little by little, the stones joined more naturally. I followed no plan, yet each stone seemed to know its place, to know where it was needed.

Days turned to weeks, and the seasons passed, and still I worked. The structure, which I dubbed The Shrine had grown from a small pile into a small shack entirely of stone, with flowing walls that seamlessly arched overhead to form a ceiling. Besides the doorway that allowed entrance to the shrine, there was a small opening in the ceiling near the back that acted as a skylight. There were shelves and a small bench built into the walls, and below the skylight, what looked like the makings of a hearth. Whether guided by subconscious desire, or by the will of unseen forces, I had indeed built myself a forge, as unconventional as it may have been.

As fate would have it, I completed this shrine on the fourteenth day of the seventh month, laying the final stone just in time for the celebration of Obon, which would begin on the following day. For most, Obon was a joyous three days, honoring the beloved departed ancestors, but for me it had always been a dark reminder that I would not be honored once gone.

Just as Tsubasa finished the sentence Itsuki snatched the book from his hands and snapped it shut.

"Hey!" Tsubasa exclaimed.

Itsuki paid no heed to the young shinobi's clamor and had soon packed the book away in his pack. Noboru was up and about quenching the fire by urinating on the embers, the loud sound of steam erupted from the fire and then all was dark. The two older shinobi had obviously seen something that the Yukimura brothers had not.

Noboru retightened his robe and crouched next to the lakeside reeds, looking toward the water.

"Look over there, do you see?" Noboru pointed.

In the faint darkness a small incoming rowboat was floating between the patchy lake fog.

"I thought we were far enough from the main road that we would go unnoticed. Quickly, grab your things," Itsuki whispered.

Instead of running the opposite direction, Itsuki gestured the group to follow slightly south and into the lake. The frigid water crawled up their legs as they went in thigh deep. The group crouched in the water with their heads below the lake reeds, their packs carefully on their backs to keep dry.

"What are we doing?" Kaito whispered, but the older shinobi only gave him gestures to hold his tongue.

When the small boat landed, four shadowed figures came out, soldiers from their manner of speech. "Split up, two by two, signal if you find them," the leader of the pack barked. "Traverse through the grass to see if they're hiding."

The intruders lit torches and started searching near the shinobi's campfire. Itsuki put a finger over his mouth and winked at Noboru. Noboru only smiled and nodded while the Yukimura brothers waited quietly in the water. As the four soldiers' search stretched from the coastline, the shinobi quietly walked with hunched backs toward the boat. The vessel was a simple wooden pontoon with four oars. In a fluid motion Itsuki and Noboru threw their packs in the boat and hoisted themselves inside. The Yukimura brothers swiftly followed in fear of being left behind.

The shinobi silently started to row, creating distance from the coast, the slightest wind made their drenched clothes cold to the skin. The lake was a pristine reflection of the night sky with only the ripples of the boat slightly distorting the reflection of the moon and stars upon Lake Biwa. The silent night was broken by a loud cry near the coastline, the sounds of a man cursing something or other about a boat.

A slight smile cracked upon Itsuki's lips followed by a growing laughter from Noboru, eventually all four shinobi were bellowing thunderous laughter as they rowed into the darkness of Lake Biwa.

13

Hideyoshi Hashiba
-Omi Province, Road to Kyoto-

In the distance behind Hideyoshi Hashiba's caravan the sun was setting behind Azuchi Castle, creating a black silhouette in the skyline. The military council of Nobunaga Oda had ended and after a month, Hideyoshi Hashiba had received his orders to return to the war in Bitchū Province. Spring had arrived in full bloom for the lower valleys, but the mountain peaks showed streaks of snow. The caravan followed a road that split the waist-high grass field, a brown scar in an ocean of green, leading to the Capital city, Kyoto.

Hideyoshi was riding on a white horse groomed to perfection with a gray mane and matching tail. He rode with his head high in his military garb; the caravan held a group of 500-armed men befitting Hideyoshi's status as a general of Nobunaga Oda. At the front and back of the lines the men were holding banners containing the family crest of Hashiba. Hideyoshi came from a lowly birth, so the crest and surname had been given to him in later years as an honor; Hideyoshi wore the banners with pride.

Hideyoshi's wife, Nene, rode beside him on a full white horse that shimmered in the sunlight. It was custom for her to ride in a palanquin befitting her status, but she enjoyed riding a horse on occasion. Since their marriage, Nene had been Hideyoshi's closest confidant. Daughter of a high-level samurai, she was well connected and well versed in politics. Her knowledge was crucial to the rise of power of her husband. Nene made up for her husband's lowly beginnings and legitimized his family for the noble courts. Nene was thin and slender with prominent cheekbones and high arched brows. Her hair was black as night, but it shimmered in the sunlight, topped by a silver jeweled brush. Her silk white kimono matched her horse and was as pale as her skin. She held an umbrella to protect her complexion and did so with the utmost diligence. She held a presence that demanded respect but always conducted herself with a kindness that even made Nobunaga Oda himself give every courtesy.

Behind the Hashibas rode Rin Kurosawa upon a black horse from head to toe. She had changed into a kimono for traveling but rode with her head high, befitting the status as one in Lady Nene's confidence. Foot soldiers gave scowls, for they all suspected Rin a spy, but would never question openly that she was a handmaiden to Nene. Nene gestured Rin to ride close and the three of them put distance between them and listening ears.

"So, I take it your time in the castle was not wasted?" Nene stated with a casual look on her face as if talking about the weather.

"More fruitful than I had hoped, my lady," Rin smiled.

"Well do not keep me waiting, what did you find," Hideyoshi said. "Spare me the usual gossip I'm well aware of war matters."

Rin looked over her shoulder. "He's after a blade, a blade made by Sengo Muramasa."

Hideyoshi and Nene could not help but chuckle as if on some inside joke.

"Ha, I would expect no less from Nobunaga," Nene stated. "He wishes to mirror the blade of Masamune already in his possession."

Rin furrowed her brow in confusion. "But why the obsession? Nobunaga has more important matters, it's not like a sword will give him armies or win wars for him."

"It may," Hideyoshi said thoughtfully. "For the same reason he built that monstrosity, Azuchi Castle, he wants those two swords. The castle is a military outpost, yet Nobunaga insisted on having it be made to look like a palace. You saw the daimyōs, how they praised Nobunaga for his palace. How could one doubt a leader with such visible success?"

"But the swords?"

"Symbols to the masses," Nene assured. "Nobunaga knows how to play the game."

Hideyoshi nodded in agreement. "He contains a sword of Masamune; the people say that the sword can bestow wisdom to the wielder as well as still the soul of the warrior. In contrast, the blades of Muramasa are said to bring death and destruction. Two blades in the hand of one man to unify Japan, two blades for a mighty shōgun. It has been over seventy years since civil war erupted and the last shōgun actually held any power. Nobunaga dissolved the last Shogunate himself, he is biding his time to create a new one and unify the daimyōs under one rule. Superstitions such as mythical blades can cause men to rally to such a leader. You have to hand it to my liege lord for his cunning, wars can be fought in other places than the battlefield, my dear."

"Well, in any case, he did not want anyone knowing about it,"

Rin stated. "I had to go to quite a bit of trouble to find out. I don't know why the man is so secretive over such trinkets."

"Why does Nobunaga do anything that he does," Hideyoshi scoffed. "The man does not trust anyone but himself. People called him the Fool of Owari Province in his youth, but the man is no fool. Japan is in a state of chaos and war; a daimyō that got hold of the last sword forged by Muramasa could leverage the weapon against Nobunaga to trade for land and titles, no matter I suppose. This information is of little consequence to my plans, although I am curious to how you came about it."

Rin batted her eyes and gave a cunning smile, showing her devious smirk with the small chip in her front tooth. "You keep your plans secret, my lord, but I keep my methods secret as well, curious you shall stay."

Hideyoshi gave a smile as he watched the young woman ride off to put distance between them. "Always the attitude, if she wasn't so useful…"

"But she is useful," Nene stated. "Do not fret my husband, I will make sure she keeps proving herself to our benefit, and to our plans. Speaking of plans, how are things going?"

Hideyoshi gave a long sigh. "Progress, progress, the unexpected seppuku of Mitsuhide's subordinate can be used to our benefit. I am most grateful, my dear for sending me that information ahead of time."

Nene smiled, pleased with herself. "Of course, my husband. You keep winning battles, and I will keep the noble courts filled with allies."

The caravan traveled until they reached a small town to lodge for the night. The town had an inn large enough to house Hideyoshi and his confidants, but the rest of his garrison camped on the outskirts of the village. The innkeeper had a humble abode but was using every resource he had to appease Hideyoshi Hashiba. During the warring years of Japan, the common folk were the ones who suffered the most. Yesterday's friend could be tomorrow's foe depending on which daimyō was ruling what province. Many of the common folk had to adjust by showing their allegiance to whoever happened to stroll through town at the time; this innkeeper was no exception.

In a small private dining room sat Hideyoshi and Nene with a number of their servants. Rin was sitting, eagerly awaiting her food while speaking with Hideyoshi's number one captain, Kenji, about the battles in which he had participated. Rin was playing her usual part of the maiden and acting very interested as the captain spoke proudly of his bravado.

Kenji was a warrior to the bone, in and out. Rin found him one of the easiest men to toy with. *A man who only thinks of fighting, glory, and then bedding a girl,* Rin thought.

Kyou, the man in charge of Hideyoshi's effects was eating the humble appetizers that the innkeeper had laid out.

The innkeeper slid open the door looking at his guests with a smile. "I trust the appetizers are to your liking. Is there anything more I can get for you?"

Hideyoshi looked up. "More sake, and I expect the main course is coming soon."

The innkeeper bowed. "Grilled vegetables, rice, bass, dumplings, and sake on its way."

The innkeeper clapped and two young girls entered. They appeared to be his daughters, sharing his arching eyebrows and wide mouth. They served bottles of sake and a basket of dumplings, which were remarkably good for a provincial kitchen.

149

The girls were wearing kimonos beyond the wealth of a common peasant, they were creased with fold lines, indicating that these were rarely worn garments that had been hastily pulled from a trunk and donned to impress their guests.

The servants laid out the appetizers and the innkeeper bowed. "My inn is here to serve the house of Hashiba." Shortly after, he slid the door shut.

Kenji took a shot of sake. "The man certainly knows how to flatter."

Hideyoshi ate a dumpling. "Out of fear, not respect. No matter, fear is sometimes just as good."

"Respect is better," Nene chided. "We should pay him amply, loyalty grows into a tree that bears fruit, and fear grows into a weed that becomes a thistle in your side."

"Right as always, my dear. He is showing manners regardless, so I won't have to kill him for this bland food," Hideyoshi jested sarcastically.

Although Hideyoshi came from a lowly birth, he played the part as a man that was born to be emperor. Through his own cunning he had risen through the ranks of Nobunaga's forces. Once Hideyoshi got a taste of respect he lusted after it, always striving for more. *Keep acting like a noble and eventually they'll treat you as one*, Hideyoshi often thought.

Hideyoshi rolled one of the dumplings between his chopsticks in thought. "Kenji, as you know, Nobunaga has ordered that I will be the one to finish off what I started with the Mōri clan. Nobunaga has disgraced Mitsuhide Akechi with the seppuku of his captain and has reserved him from Bitchū Province like a leashed dog. I will be facing the Mōri clan alone and I will need more troops to do so. I will be having business with Chuugo when we reach Kyoto. If all goes well, we will be receiving a number of arms and mercenaries to add to our forces. I will need you to keep the mercenaries in line and keep them well informed of what is expected of them in battle."

"Cutthroats and thieves with no discipline." Kenji replaced his furrow with a smile. "But perfect for the front lines, they have their uses."

Hideyoshi raised a cup. "I'd expect no less, and if they die in battle there will be less to provide for after."

"But what is to stop other generals from using Chuugo's mercenaries?" Kenji added.

"Leave that to me," Nene stated. "I will be in the noble courts of Kyoto making sure we have full support and making sure no other entities take from what we need."

"No offense, Lord Hideyoshi, but your wife seems to be the true power behind your victories," Kenji stated.

"I wouldn't disagree," Hideyoshi raised a cup of sake in agreement.

Rin shuddered. "Chuugo disgusts me, I have had the displeasure of meeting him once. He would not stop ogling at me, and his weird humming? It disgusts me."

Kenji could not help but laugh. "Agreed, the man is repulsive if you ask me. I mean no disrespect, Lord Hashiba, but aren't their other routes we may go to get weapons and men."

Hideyoshi gave a half smile. "I do not deny Chuugo's strange behavior, but he is good at what he does. Although I wouldn't be surprised if he already has dealings with the Mōri clan."

Kenji drank another shot of sake as his cheeks reddened. "Chuugo will do what's best for Chuugo, the man knows the Mōri clan's days are numbered."

"I'm counting on that fact," Hideyoshi agreed. "Chuugo will back the man with the most swords, and I will be buying a lot of men."

Kenji thought a moment. "A pity to not use the Iga prisoners, free bodies to put on the battlefield."

Hideyoshi had an angry look about his face. "The Iga shinobi would have escaped at first chance if let out of Azuchi Castle. My rival, Ieyasu Tokugawa, suggested the very same notion to Nobunaga, our lord would not hear of it. From what I have heard the prisoners will be sentenced to death soon, they have outlived their usefulness."

"Such characters cannot be trusted anyway," Nene chimed in. "You cannot trust a people that put their loyalty to the highest bidder. A pity none the less."

"A pity," Rin mouthed without creating a noise, her thoughts taking her to the prisons of Azuchi Castle.

The sound of sliding doors interrupted the conversation. The daughters of the innkeeper came in with serving plates in both hands carrying the fish, vegetables, and rice as promised. The travelers began to eat their meal.

14

Mount Kurama
-Yamashiro Province, Mount Kurama-

Dawn came as the shinobi made their way to a crude stone walkway. The gray morning began to take light and the shinobi could hear the rippling of running water through small stones. Although the four comrades had been traveling for days, the welcome sight of the shrine gave them a burst of energy as if coming home from a long journey. The four shinobi stopped in front of a massive torii, two-pillars connected by two offset horizontal beams. The lower beam sat plane and extended through the pillars, while the uppermost sat on top of the pillars and arched upward at each end. A torii was a monument to Shinto, the way of the gods, a gate that stood twenty-five feet high. Faint evidence of red paint had been applied to the ancient gate, the color had faded, and chipping was evident. Shinto belief stated the gate separated the terrain between the natural earth and sacred ground.

Noboru put a hand on the massive pillar and smiled. "We are here."

Itsuki smiled back. "We are indeed." Itsuki then pulled a large,

153

braided cord hanging in front of the torii that rang a bell, a ritual to tell the kami of a mortal's presence.

The four shinobi walked through the torii, following the crude stone path upward into the shrine. The Yukimura brothers looked up at the massive horizontal pillars and saw glimmers of sunlight poke through the tall trees overhead. The shinobi walked with caution as they made their way deeper into the sanctuary. Parallel to the path appeared a running brook that spread into a web of miniature waterfalls and ponds. The dark gray rocks were blanketed in thick green moss and the sounds of aqueous creatures could be heard among the ponds. The earth was dark from decomposition, made darker by the shade of the trees. The trees varied in size, but the large ones had massive roots coming out of the ground that twisted through the earth as if the tree spirits were sprouting legs to walk. The overhead branches of the trees acted as a natural ceiling, creating a dome with their massive greenery filtering the overhead sunlight. Occasionally a piece of floating leaf or insect would beam out in the air as it danced through the sunlight. The smell of fresh water, earth, and foliage rejuvenated the air, giving a fresh feeling of spring.

Itsuki paused to take in the land. "This shrine is not what I expected," Itsuki whispered. "This place seems…"

"Old… untouched," Noboru stated in almost a whisper, looking around with disbelief.

"Yes, older than man," Itsuki responded. "It's as if this place was a shrine built by the kami."

The shinobi continued their walk up the beaten path that looked to be created more by nature than man. The only way the shinobi knew they were on sacred grounds was because of the torii at the entrance. Unbridled nature was the master of this shrine.

The Yukimura brothers followed their older comrades, wide-eyed and curious they walked. The brothers could feel the presence of the shrine, as if a physical weight was on their shoulders. Each did not speak but only gestured, believing that the use of speech would blow away the infant flame of magic within the shrine. As the shinobi made their way up the path the sound of running water became ever more encompassing.

"If this is a shrine, where are its keepers?" Tsubasa spoke nervously.

"Good question," Itsuki responded.

Noboru rubbed his chin in thought and looked around. "This must be where Kazuki hid the blades."

"A fitting place as ever," Itsuki spoke. "Kaito, Tsubasa, I don't suppose your father ever mentioned a place such as this to you?"

Kaito shrugged looking at his brother. Tsubasa thought a moment and then spoke, "Years ago my father spoke once of a shrine he had traveled to, he never mentioned the name. But when he spoke of it, he would talk of it as if it were a place of dreams that one would be blessed to find. The description fits our surroundings."

The four shinobi sat by a pond, trying to be contemplative but each struggling against confusion and fear as they wondered if their quest had reached a dead end. They decided to search the area, pairing off, for over an hour they looked for any signs of the keepers. The brothers came back only with news of finding a large waterfall. The two older shinobi only found old stone faces covered in moss and some unmarked graves. The search was fruitless, man or spirit was not found in this place, so the shinobi sat confused as ever on what to do next.

Noboru scratched his head. "The blades were meant to be

found. We shouldn't have to solve endless riddles to find what's ours."

Kaito started to become frustrated. "If they were meant to be found by you, why did my father hide them without consulting you?"

Noboru's eyes flared at the young shinobi's impertinence. "You weren't there, if you were, you'd understand." Noboru threw a rock in frustration. "Unmarked graves, a shrine with no priests, and Kazuki's lost trail. There's nothing."

Noboru's angry tirade was interrupted by echoing laughter that encircled the group from all directions.

"Where is that coming from?" Kaito stated, twirling around. The four shinobi instinctively drew weapons with tensed muscles preparing for a fight.

The laugh echoed once more, mocking them. "Right in front of you, shinobi," a voice beamed from every tree.

"What is this trickery," Noboru said as he grabbed a kunai dagger from his side.

"How do you know we are shinobi," Itsuki spoke calmly.

"Ding-dong, I have been watching you since you rang the bell at the torii," the voice said bluntly.

"Show yourself," Noboru spoke with authority.

A man suddenly appeared in the middle of the path the shinobi had just followed. He was dressed as a Shinto priest, wearing robes of a dark mossy green that blended with the greenery around them. The shinobi turned around in disbelief, surprised that a priest could get the best of four men trained in stealth.

The priest carried a wood staff of a man's height, at the top of the staff was a large brass ring ornament. Interlaced in this ring were four more brass rings that jingled in the air as the priest walked. The priest also wore a large conical hat almost too large for practicality and it covered the man's shaved head but for a thick braid of hair that swung at waist height behind the priest. The man's face was weatherworn, tan, and contained smile-line wrinkles. The priest seemed to be young and old at the same time, his age was indistinguishable.

"If one has eyes, he only needs open them to see me," the priest spoke as if it were a riddle.

"Good to see a priest still guards this shrine," Itsuki spoke. "We were starting to think that the place was deserted. Where are your brothers?"

"Brothers?" The priest spoke as if trying to recall a lost memory. "Brothers, others? Brothers... oh yes, I am the last, the last to keep this shrine, the rest have all gone."

"Gone?" Kaito said unbelievingly. "Where?"

"To the other side of course," the priest frowned in sadness, recalling a frightful memory. "But that is a long story yes, a story I must complete."

The priest walked up closer and studied the Yukimura brothers' faces, he stopped at Tsubasa and peered into the young man's eyes. "I have been alone, alone to think, alone to bode. Since the last shinobi came. Your father by the looks of these two, you have his face," the priest said, pointing at Tsubasa.

"Our father, Kazuki?" Tsubasa stated impatiently.

"Kazuki, Kazuki, yes man of wind and ice, man of many shadows... that was his name," the priest riddled. "It has been a long time, alone, alone, alone."

"It seems you have plenty of voices in your head to keep you company," Noboru taunted.

The priest only blurted into laughter. "Yes, yes, more friends than you, I speak with the kami that I do."

Itsuki tried to probe the priest's broken mind. "Why do you stay at this shrine alone? What dealings did you have with Kazuki?"

"Stay? I stay because I am the keeper, it is my purpose, it is my charge. I serve the Gods, Izanami and Izanagi I do, creators of all," the priest spoke while jingling his staff. "I counseled with Kazuki on many a thing, we shared much with each other."

"And how do we know that this is true?" Noboru questioned skeptically.

The priest joking smile turned to a menacing grin and his tone became serious. "I know that you ate from the hearth of Yomi-No-Kuni, Noboru Tsukino, and I know that Itsuki Hayashi stood for you." The priest cackled menacingly.

In a flash of rage Noboru pulled his kunai dagger to the throat of the priest while grabbing the priest's robe with the other hand. "Why would you speak of this?"

"Proof you wanted, proof I gave. Secrets to tell, secrets to keep, I told you that Kazuki and I shared much with each other," the priest riddled. "Why do you cower at your shame, it made you strong, it gave you fame. The hand seal Sha the hearth gave."

Noboru's grip loosened and his eyes widened in surprise at the knowledge of the priest.

"He's right, only a handful know of that tale," Itsuki admitted grudgingly. "That is proof enough for me. It doesn't matter; it is in the past, Noboru."

"Hmph." Noboru released the priest's collar knowing that he had met Kazuki in person.

"It matters to me. What's he talking about?" Tsubasa butted in. "The hearth of Yomi-No-Kuni?'"

"Nothing. None of your business," Noboru and Itsuki responded simultaneously with authority.

"Are there any shrines here priest, one's that the last shinobi visited?" Itsuki stated, changing the subject.

"Yes, many shrines for those who have eyes, but how many have come? Is this all of you?" the priest questioned.

"Just the four of us, priest," Noboru stated still distrustful.

"Four, four..." the priest mumbled to himself. "Come shinobi I have time for four, but no more, no less."

The priest started walking up the main path, his staff and rings making a metallic jingling sound as he walked. The four shinobi looked at each other, not knowing what to think of the odd priest, the man seemed highly knowledgeable but insane at the same time. The priest would mumble to himself as if having a conversation with someone not there. With no other choice the four shinobi followed the priest as bided, hoping for answers. The priest led the shinobi farther up the path toward the sound of running water. They came upon the large waterfall, the very same one the Yukimura brothers had previously seen in their search of the area.

"Up, up, up we go, to the cave of Sōjōbō," the priest would rhyme in a growl.

The waterfall was just over twenty-five feet high and fed into a large pond. The water was crystal clear, calming more in motion farther away from the falls. The priest led them up above the falls on a hidden path of wet stones and slippery earth. The five men climbed until they came to a small stony hillside covered in grass and moss. In the clearing the treetops ended, letting the sky open

159

to all, revealing a small cave entrance that was camouflaged into the hillside by hanging moss.

Serious for the first time, the priest's expression became grim and seemed to age as he pointed his staff toward the cave. "Lord of the Tengus, Sōjōbō is who you seek."

15

Hanzō

-Omi Province, Azuchi Castle-

Underneath Azuchi Castle, Masanari Hattori sat in his dank cell with the smell of vomit, blood, and feces assaulting his nostrils. The muscles in his body had started to atrophy from disuse and his wits had begun to fail him. *A pitiful state for a man, why don't they just kill me,* Masanari thought. The eye that Nobunaga had burned away had luckily scarred well, for what good it did him. The flesh had been cauterized upon impact, destroying the eye, but at the same time sealing off infection. The burn scars crawled out of his eye socket like a blight attempting to escape from his soul. His beard had become long and unkempt; he had not seen daylight for what seemed forever. A feeble tortured soul remained of the great arms keeper of Hekison. *A shinobi is one who endures. If they expect me to take my life, I will not give them the pleasure.*

The outline of the cell door was the only light Masanari had received; the walls were made of solid stone and the wood bars of thick unbreakable oak. The last shinobi that was caught scratching at the wood had his hands chopped off; only after the poor soul had

161

begged for death was the request given. That was when Masanari had still shared a cell chamber with his comrades. A week ago, a month, he could not say, but the guards had taken him to a solitary cell with a new set of shackles for his wrists and ankles; the chain length was cruelly designed to be just short enough to impede the prisoner from standing up straight. Masanari was left only with thoughts; for what purpose he did not know.

Prison is the poison of courage where strong wills become weak. I am here because I defended the village to the last. I am here because I am a true shinobi. I endured to the end. I am here because of the deserters. My back aches. Damn these chains. The deserters should be sharing this cell. The Yukimura brothers should be in this cell with me. How long has it been since I've seen light, a day, a month... more... less?

The faint sound of footsteps down a stairway could be heard.

The woman came, the woman came, an eternity ago asking about Nobunaga. Asking about a sword...no, the village. Why would a woman ask about Hekison? Who was that woman!

Two men could be heard outside the cell door. Masanari came out of the conversation he was having with himself. *Only one person delivers my food, maybe they have come to kill me, I still have strength to kill one of them, when they try, they will not find me easy prey.*

The door, which was no more than a secured hatch, was pried open and a flood of light shined upon Masanari's face. When his eye adjusted, he could see that it was just torchlight from the adjacent room.

A man in a formal kimono came through the door, of high birth from the looks of it. He had dark eyes, a strong jaw line, and a deep voice. He carried a single basket with him and had two swords at his waist. *A man of soft hands, a man that sends others to die for him.*

"Leave us," the visitor said to the guard with authority.

162

The guard hesitated only for a moment, and then bowed. The guard glared at Masanari in disgust before heading up the stairway, only when the sound of footsteps disappeared did the visitor come forward.

"Have you come to kill me, fancy man? You're as well-groomed as the last—" Masanari began a coughing fit, his voice muffled and croaked from disuse.

The failed insult did not affect the visitor. "Your missing eye gives you the appearance of an oni the underworld spat out."

"Thanks to your Lord Nobunaga Oda. I will take both his eyes and tongue for what he did."

"What is your name?" the visitor asked as if pondering about the weather.

"We never use names... I am a prisoner. My name is Prisoner," Masanari grumbled.

The visitor frowned. "The men in the other room say otherwise. The men... the shinobi say you are Masanari Hattori and that you are their leader."

Masanari blurted a laugh. "Me? Ha, Yamato Akiyama was the last jōnin, and was the last leader of the Iga shinobi."

The visitor slid the basket of a water gourd and a single rice cake toward Masanari. "They say that when the village fell that you were the one that held everyone together. That you fought to the last. That you would have died fighting had you not been knocked out by one of Nobunaga's men."

Masanari looked at the rice cake in skepticism. "What do you want, fancy man?"

"What do you want?" the visitor calmly replied.

Masanari made his weak hand into a fist. "I want out of this cell. I want food. I want a woman in my bed again. I want a sword in hand. I want revenge on Nobunaga Oda, and I want to kill the deserters of Hekison."

The visitor could not help but smile. "Prison has made you honest, I'll give you that. And what if I could give you those things?"

Masanari started eating the rice cake and almost retched it up, it had been so long since he had eaten proper food. Masanari slowed his eating to keep the food down. "I would say you are a fool. Nobunaga put me here, I don't think he's likely to release me."

"Correct," the visitor spoke. "He told me that there is no more use for the Iga shinobi in his cells and ordered that all be killed by week's end."

Masanari spat at the ground. "So get on with it then, you don't want to disappoint your lord, do you?"

The mysterious visitor looked around and lowered his voice. "Maybe, maybe not. I opposed him when he started his campaign on the Iga Province. I said that the Iga shinobi could be our allies, but Nobunaga would not hear of it. I would still believe that a mutually beneficial pact is possible."

"You say you are no friend of the Fool of Owari Province," Masanari scoffed.

The visitor furrowed his brow. "I believe in Nobunaga's dream of a unified Japan, but I do not believe he is the man to be shōgun. He makes enemies by killing anyone who does not share his exact views. The man insults his friends, multiplying enemies while his allies dwindle. Nobunaga is good at war, but not at peace, and a shōgun must know how to keep the peace."

Masanari gulped down water. "So release me then, and I will slit his throat for you."

The visitor shook his head. "You misunderstand, I do not wish his death, I merely know it is eminent. Rumors... insults... there are people sharpening daggers for him, that much is true. Besides, things are not that simple. Do you wish to throw your life away so quickly? You could not hurt a child in your weakened state. Furthermore, he is gone, and I do not know his whereabouts, the man has been secretive in his plans. I will not promise that I can deliver all that you desire, but I can give you freedom. In exchange, I only ask you consider being my ally."

"Surely you jest. You want me to change these iron shackles for a life of servitude."

The visitor shook his head. "A partnership, I would not see good men go to waste. Restore your shinobi, lead them, in return I would have you help me unify Japan."

Masanari looked at the visitor suspiciously. "The Oda clan was once a friend to Hekison. How do I know you will not betray us like them?"

The visitor gave a stern look and pulled a dagger from his kimono. Masanari recoiled ready for an attack, but the visitor slowly handed the blade to Masanari. Masanari gripped the blade with a familiar deadliness.

The visitor knelt. "I swear by the gods that I will not betray the Iga shinobi should they come into this pact with me." The visitor grabbed his kimono and loosened it, baring his chest. The shackles around Masanari's arms clinked as he moved the blade toward the visitor's heart.

Masanari looked at the blade and then the visitor's eyes. *This man is not the pampered noble I thought him to be. He does his own dirty work.*

After what seemed like an eternity, Masanari Hattori spoke, "Who are you?"

"Does it matter?" the visitor replied. "In this moment you are a prisoner, and I am a visitor with a dagger to my heart."

"I should kill you." Masanari stared at the tip of the blade. "But I will trust you... for now."

Masanari handed the blade, hilt first, back to the visitor and leaned back against the wall in his shackles. The visitor's muscles loosened, and a single drop of sweat rolled down his neck; he readjusted his kimono and stood up.

"That is good," the visitor smiled. "Your execution has been scheduled for week's end. So, we must perform an elaborate ruse so that I may have my reputation intact. I have an idea—"

"That won't be necessary, how many of my men still live in the cells of Azuchi Castle?" Masanari grunted in his raspy voice.

"I believe there are eleven."

"So few of us. If I am to trust you, we must save all of them."

The visitor furrowed his brow at the prospect. "What do you suggest?"

Masanari smiled from the thought of actually being free again. "First, we will need a man that you can trust not only with your life, but with your wife as well; a man of honor that would not betray you for money, gain, or status. Do you have such a man?"

The visitor nodded.

"Good." Masanari continued looking at the visitor with his one eye. "If you are to stay clean of this situation you must use him to carry out your part of the plan. I will need a small bowl, a pestle, parchment, a sack of green tea leaves, a small bottle of bufo toad ointment, a bundle of oni root, and a large bundle of the valerian herb."

"Bufo toad ointment can be toxic... and cause visions. What for?" the visitor questioned.

"A paste," Masanari spoke with reservation, "that dissolves into water. It was invented by my people, brings a person to a deep sleep, to an inch of death. If the ingredients are not mixed correctly, it can be fatal. We call it the Cup of the Reborn. When you take our bodies from the prison no one should be the wiser in thinking that we are dead. You can slaughter beasts and wipe blood on our throats to give no cause for suspicion... and feces."

"Feces?" the visitor sneered.

"Keeps anyone suspicious from coming close. Everyone knows the bowels can loosen at death. Best done at night," Masanari stated, accepting his fate.

"I'm impressed, shinobi. I knew there was potential in your people," the visitor nodded in approval. "I will need a few days to change the guards to men I can trust and get you your materials. You will have to play the part of a prisoner again. The bodies are typically disposed of in a swamp outside Lake Biwa, that is where you will wake up."

"Yes... hopefully." *Many men are not reborn, but simply die.*

The visitor started to make his leave and paused. "Till your rebirth... Masanari Hattori."

The cell door was secured back into place with the guard returning to his post. Masanari closed his one eye and slouched uncomfortably on the cell wall, the shackles chaffed his hands and ankles. He fell into a restless sleep of pain, dreaming of a blazing demon burning his eye out repeatedly with a hot iron, laughing with pleasure.

A day passed, and Masanari woke to the cold stone of his cell. Rice and water were all he saw slide through the cracked cell door. He passed the time pondering of his escape.

Another day passed, rice and water had been delivered at his door again. This night Masanari had the same dream of the demon burning out his eye again and again. The pain was like poison through his veins. Every time he would attempt to see the demon's face but was always blinded before he could see his torturer. When he woke, he would touch where his eye used to be but would only find a scarred mess of flesh and skin. The wound had healed but the ghost pain still existed, festering, and cultivating thoughts of hate.

On the third day rice and water was delivered again. *Am I really going to escape, or did I dream of a man coming with an offer? Is it like the woman that came with the shadows, talk of Hekison and the outside world?*

The cell door opened again but this time a large sack appeared with a wooden bowl and pestle. Masanari crawled to the sack and pulled out a piece of small parchment.

"Make it fast," the note read.

I make it too fast, and I'll never wake up.

Masanari began separating the materials, counting roots and leaves by the tiny light that beamed in through the cell door. Judging the ratio needed between ingredients, Masanari mashed the materials together. When he finished one dosage, he would put the paste inside a small piece of parchment and twist the ends. Repeatedly, Masanari made the paste until he had finished them all for his fellow shinobi. He put all the pieces but one back into the sack and made a light knock on the door. A hand from the cell door promptly took all evidence of Masanari's work.

Masanari closed his one eye and pondered on his ambitions. When he woke, there was rice and water at the cell door. Masanari took the piece of parchment containing the paste and took a long look at it with his eye. He unraveled the paste and put it into his water bowl. Slowly the paste dissolved into the water to become an ominous dark liquid.

Masanari did not wait for his nerves to unsettle, he held the cup up to his lips resolved, and then fear struck his heart. In the corner of his eye, a figure could be made in front of the cell door, crouched in the shadows watching. Masanari slowly raised his eye to the figure, knowing full well it was the demon from his dreams. The demon's features were concealed by the dark shadows, but Masanari made out a small saucer of liquid the creature held. The demon held the saucer to its lips, light reflected on it, revealing it to be a bone saucer filled with blood.

"Kanpai." The demon toasted the bone saucer in a low growling baritone voice, then with great pleasure slurped down the blood.

Masanari rubbed his eye in disbelief. When he looked again, the demon was gone.

"Kanpai," Masanari whispered in fear, and then drank the liquid as fast as he could.

Darkness.

Masanari was surrounded by darkness. No wilderness, no room, only black oblivion, and emptiness. At first, he thought the elixir had failed, that he had met the gates of the afterlife, but as Masanari turned around, he could see a dim flickering light. He made his way to what seemed to be a campfire in the distance. When Masanari arrived at the fire, he saw the same demon that had been in his previous dreams that had regularly burned out his eye. Unlike previous dreams, Masanari could make out the demon's image. The demon had the body of a man, but his shirtless red tinted skin showed the menacing heritage of a yōkai. The demon was crouched with his back to Masanari, poking the fire with a broken femur bone. Two small black horns could be seen protruding above the crest of his forehead; long tangled black hair blanketed the demon's red tinted back. The demon wore baggy brown pants, with a large black belt, and his shoeless feet showed small black claws in place of toenails.

"I'm glad you shared a toast with me," the demon spoke while poking the embers of the fire. "Shall I burn your eye out again?"

This time Masanari was not afraid as he had been in his previous dreams, only anger filled his soul. He ran at the demon with the intent to kill. When he came in contact, he gripped his hands around the demon's throat. Flames burst from the demon and crawled toward Masanari, turning darkness into inferno.

The demon's face contained black eyes without irises. A long two-inch nose pointed like a dagger and a mouth with teeth as sharp as blades clawed their way toward Masanari. The mouth contained an underbite with two particularly large protruding canine teeth decorating the demon's dark smile.

"What are you?" Masanari screamed.

The demon laughed in a low cackle that shook the ground, a voice that made Masanari's ribcage shake in fear. "I am that which has freed your eye so you may see. I am Hanzō!"

Fear had replaced anger upon hearing the demonic voice. Masanari saw that the flames of the demon began to spread over his body. The flames crawled their way up to Masanari's eyeless socket and poured down into his soul.

Masanari screamed in pain as he was grappled awake. When he opened his eye, he found that his hands were wrapped around a man's throat with a death grip. Two men ripped Masanari's grasp free, wrestling him back to reality.

"Sir, sir!" One of the shinobi said as they saw Masanari regain sanity.

Masanari looked around to see that it was night. The stars were out, and he could see Lake Biwa in the distance. *The heavens my roof once again,* Masanari thought and gave a nod to the shinobi that was standing next to him.

"We thought you dead," the shinobi spoke.

"Yes…" Masanari responded. "I was lucky."

"Not all of us made it." The shinobi pointed to a few bodies that were now corpses. Some of the shinobi had not been reborn, but simply died from the drink.

"But you are free," a voice called out.

Masanari looked out to see a figure on a horse in the dead of night.

The visitor was clothed in common garb to hide his status of a noble. Another horse was riding next to his.

"Here, a gift," the visitor stated, holding out the reins of the horse.

Masanari was hoisted up onto the horse by the hand of the visitor and found that it was callused and strong from sword use. Masanari could not help but feel grateful and bowed in respect.

"You and your men will need new clothes and time to recover from the cells," the visitor spoke. "We will need to travel swiftly to go unnoticed."

Masanari looked at the heavens as if looking at them for the first time. "We are shinobi, we endure."

The visitor nodded. "Good. We will be touring the southeastern provinces in the areas of my victory and establish a new rule."

Masanari eyed the visitor, guessing his identity for a second time. "Victory... who are you?"

"I am no shinobi, so I have no problem giving my name now that we are beyond the eyes of Nobunaga," the visitor smirked. "I am Daimyō Ieyasu Tokugawa, general of Nobunaga Oda and victor over the great Takeda clan."

Masanari knew the daimyō by reputation, but at this point did not care. "To the south we go then."

"You will need a new name," Ieyasu stated. "Nobunaga mentioned you more than once to his generals, and that eye of yours will get you noticed as well."

"My eye... what did you say in the cells about it?"

Ieyasu hesitated a moment. "I said it made you look like an oni, a demon."

"Well then, you may call me Hanzō Hattori if you like." The newly dubbed Hanzō spurred his horse to a fast trot, and felt the cool night wind, and savored every drop of the feeling of freedom.

16

Lord of the Tengus
⁻Yamashiro Province, Mount Kurama⁻

The cave of Sōjōbō blended into the landscape and the entrance was a large chiseled rectangular doorway. Outside the opening at each top corner were two sculptured crows; each head was pointed as if watching any person who entered the cave. On the rock face to the side of the entrance hung a single oil wrapped torch ready to be lit.

Itsuki grabbed the torch. "Noboru, if you will."

Noboru pulled out a small stone container of flint; with his usual skill he wielded his fire tools like magic and the torch came alive.

"Stay close, who knows what's in here. I trust the priest, but he's... odd," Itsuki stated, thinking of no better word.

"That's an understatement," Tsubasa stated sarcastically. "The man has been secluded too long."

"But he has more friends in his head than Noboru does," Kaito snickered, recounting the priest's joke.

Noboru waved a hand. "There will be time for jokes later. We must be vigilant; we don't know what's inside."

173

The four shinobi entered the cave one by one, the hallway narrowed quickly. Itsuki lead the way, side stepping through the narrow cave. A man of girth would have had trouble passing through. The cave had naturally formed due to running water, the walls of the cave felt cold with moisture and the ground was slick. The yellow torchlight flickered off the wet walls, giving the stone a glassy look. If a person had claustrophobia the cave would have been a nightmare. The only sounds that could be heard was the flicker of the torch, the stepping of the shinobi, and the occasional droplets of water into a puddle. The pathway widened as the group descended into the cold darkness for what seemed to be forever, until they came to what could only be an opening in the cave.

Noboru paused for a moment and inspected an uncommon dry spot on the walls by touching and licking the contents.

"What is it?" Itsuki asked concerned.

"Blood," Noboru stated. "But old, a duel from long ago. It leads to the opening."

The four shinobi stood in front of what seemed to be oblivion; the torch gave little light, sufficient only to reveal a five-foot radius.

Noboru slid his hand along the wall and found a standing stone lantern. "Here, Itsuki. Light it."

Itsuki lit the new lantern increasing their illumination. The shinobi found another lantern not ten paces from where the previous one hung.

"They seem to be lining the walls. Let's spread the light, shall we," Itsuki suggested.

The four shinobi worked the stone lanterns and started lighting the cave until a rough circular-shaped room started to appear by firelight. The domed ceiling was at least three stories high, and the room could have housed at least one hundred men. On the wall opposite of the entrance of the dome was an ornate carving of various Shinto gods, starting with Izanagi and Izanami and the creation of the islands of Japan. Moreover, were their children: Susanoo god of storms, Amaterasu goddess of the sun, and Tsukuyomi god of the moon. Various depictions of demigods interacting with mortals in famous legends furthered the carving. The tale would be a treasure to read if the centerpiece of the cave had not dwarfed it. Kaito gasped in fear when he abruptly walked into a scowling face. The light revealed a dark and ominous wood statue standing one story high in the center of the cave.

"W-w-what is it?" Kaito stammered.

The other shinobi turned to see the statue, and all were shocked with fear as if the legends of old had formed life.

"Sōjōbō, Lord of the Tengus and Mount Kurama," Noboru solemnly observed.

A tengu was a creature considered a demon by some, a demigod by others, but all agreed them to be harbingers of war. The statue depicted a hybrid bird and man like creature holding a staff with four intersecting rings, similar to the mountain priest that led them to the cave. The tengu held the staff with two bird-like talons resting its weight on the rod with a slightly hunched back. The face was more bird than man with a long beak and dark holes for eyes. The wings came out of the back, mimicking an aggressive bird, and each wooden feather protruding out became an individual spike. The tengu's feet were bird talons sitting on a large platform, below the platform sat a sword hanger holding four sheathed swords.

"They're here," Kaito spoke as he pointed at the swords.

Noboru hurriedly came over to the statue to inspect the findings and unsheathed the top sword. As soon as he saw the shimmer of steel, he sheathed the sword. Noboru hurriedly repeated the inspection on the remaining three swords, unsheathing and cursing at the shimmering steel each time, throwing the last sword on the ground.

"What are you doing?" Tsubasa stated confused. "No man can know a sword by a mere glance. How do you know they are not the ones you seek?"

Noboru spat. "The color is wrong, they're decoys."

Tsubasa looked at Noboru in confusion. "The color is wrong?"

Itsuki broke in. "The swords are decoys, and your father would have never made it this easy. Come let us look for clues."

The four shinobi looked around the cavernous room for clues or secret compartments, but none were to be found. Noboru was getting frustrated while the Yukimura brothers succumbed to boredom; Itsuki simply sat in front of the tengu statue and stared eye to eye with the harbinger of war. Itsuki glanced down at the floor, finding more evidence of old blood from a past duel. He rubbed his chin in thought.

An hour went by as the four discussed the motives of Kazuki and where he could have hidden the blades. The older shinobi probed the Yukimura brothers regarding their father's past, but nothing seemed relevant. In silence, the four shinobi sat as the faint sound of water droplets fell into nearby puddles.

Noboru began to eat a rice cake from his pack while Itsuki brought out the book of Muramasa.

"You have read the story several times, what makes you think it will give you the answer?" Noboru stated with a mouth full of rice.

Itsuki turned to the page where the Yukimura brothers had left off. "Do you not notice?"

"What?" Noboru said with a mouth full of food.

"The statue, it fits the description that Muramasa gave," Itsuki stated, looking at the words of the book. "I believe Kazuki made, or at least had an influence in this statue."

"That would explain the rough craftsmanship," Noboru joked. "I am sick of these riddles. Read it, perhaps it will shed some light."

The Yukimura brothers stopped their conversation to listen and Itsuki began to read aloud the words of Muramasa by the dim firelight of the nearby lanterns.

Seventh Entry,

In the past months, my time on the seaside town gave me nothing but days of depression and reflection on my past life as a swordsmith. Being in the midst of the holiday of Obon, this fact only fueled my feelings of darkness instead of commemorating my ancestors like all others had.

When the sun rose the next day, I remember sitting on the cold little bench in the smith shrine I had made, as still as the rocks all about me. In one hand was a massive earthen jug of sake, in the other was a shining ten-inch tantō, unsheathed and held with the tip pointing inward toward my abdomen. I gazed out beyond the stonewall, beyond this world entirely, into dark recesses.

For the three days of Obon, there I sat with little food and less sleep, contemplating to end my life through seppuku. My depression fueled by my legacy of going down as a demon swordsmith. Each day I only removed to relieve myself and to fetch more sake from my stores. When night fell, I lit an oil lamp and wrapped myself tightly in a light linen kimono, for even in the dead of summer the wind off the ocean brought a chill in the black of night.

On the third night of the shrine vigil, surrounded by empty broken jugs, I began to weep. I wept for the ancestors I did not know, for those killed by the swords I had made, those who wielded them, and for myself.

Reaching out through my tears I grasped the burning oil lamp, hurling it violently onto the hearth, where it burst into a great fireball that lapped the stones and singed my sleeve. Staring into the flames as they leapt and danced on the rock and shattered porcelain, I was suddenly comforted. My face which previously had been contorted in agony, relaxed into tranquility.

Rising from the bench, I staggered out into the garden, quickly collected what kindling I could find by the light of the summer moon and returned to the shrine. I then carefully introduced tinder to a tiny flaming puddle of oil that had not yet burned out. Once the kindling was ablaze, I made another wobbling trip to the garden, and returned with a load of proper tinder from the wood stack. Building a large fire on the hearth, I curled up next to it on the ground and began to feel at home.

As flames burned low, and the embers glowed a brilliant red, I was enveloped by sleep like the heavy fog that was climbing from the bay to my stone forge.

Darkness overcame me.

When I opened my eyes, I found myself lying before a pile of smoldering ashes whose flames had long burned out. All about me was the sort of impenetrable darkness that one only finds in a deep cavern or a dense forest on a moonless night. I was still wrapped in my kimono, the cuff of its sleeve was still yellowed and crisped by the previous fire. There was a scent on the wind that vaguely reminded me of childhood, but I could not place it.

Rising to my knees, I felt about for something with which to coax the flames back to life. I felt a strange sense of urgency, as if there were an imminent danger very near and the fire being my only protection against it. I moved my hands desperately across the ground, hoping against hope to feel some twigs or maybe some dry grass to pull up, but my heart sank as all my fingers felt was dry earth.

A slow tapping in the distance caused my head to jerk up instinctively. I strained my eyes to pierce the darkness, but it was no use. I could hardly make out my hand in front of my face as I probed into the black. Again tapping, this time much closer, my head pulled sharply to the left. Now on the verge of panic, I groped aimlessly while flailing my arms about. A sudden rustling of what sounded like feathers just a few paces behind caused my body to jump, but the terrified yell that I strove to summon seemed trapped in my throat. Swinging my right hand wildly across the earth I felt a sting as my right palm tore against a small, jagged object. Ignoring the searing pain, I snatched up the object and threw it recklessly into the ash and ember.

In a spectacular explosion of blue, the fire burst into a seething tangle of flames that writhed like the tentacles of a blazing squid. I was bathed in azure, and light spilled out all around me, revealing a circle of carefully spaced trees with massive trunks that disappeared into the heavy dark canopy overhead. The blue magic settled and returned to the center, leaving a well-built campfire with felled logs for sitting. But to my horror I heard a creature that was walking to the clearing from the forest just outside of the firelight, as if drawn by my disturbance. I will never forget the voice, the voice of a being not of this world, mimicking the language of man.

"That's the way," I heard it growl in a low baritone voice.

As the beast came into the light my eyes grew wide, and with quivering lips I uttered the single word. "Monster."

Standing only a few paces away a large feathery creature watched with black caverns for eyes and a beaked snout that gleamed in the firelight. Tumbling backwards in fear, I lay trembling in the dirt before a terrible beast. It was the size of a large man, made larger by the wings that loomed behind its shoulders. Its head, which bobbed slowly side to side in a lizard like twitch, was that of both bird and man, a menacing beak protruding forward framed by torn ragged ears. Its posture was vaguely human, and in its clawed hand was a twisted wooden staff with four intersecting gnarled brass rings extending from a center top ring. A faded gray kimono hung loosely around its body and its boney limbs were wrapped in worn strips of cloth. I was paralyzed, gaping in awe and disbelief. I gazed with large, fixed eyes but made not the slightest noise or movement.

The creature straightened, planting its staff firmly into the earth. "Are all man creatures this rude? It is very disrespectful to stare."

The creature sounded like an old, grizzled warrior with a gravelly voice of rocks rolling across its words, making it difficult to understand.

"Who... who... who are you?" I remember stammering. "What are you?"

"Dumb questions get dumb answers." The creature stepped carefully past me, taking a seat near the fire. I nervously took the other felled log for my seat at the opposite ends of the fire from my host.

I now realized that the tapping I had heard earlier was the result of the tall geta, stilt-like wooden sandals that the creature wore on its scaly feet. Clattering geta filled the memory of my younger years, and always reminded me of the monks who inhabited the high mountains. The footwear was also known as tengu-geta and was a trademark of the most infamous of all yōkai creatures. A yōkai whose stories frightened toddlers and grown men alike.

"You're a tengu." I could hardly believe my own words.

"Names. Just names by the tongues of men. I have been given many. Men give names as the winds blow. What will men name you, Muramasa? What will they call you when you have gone?"

I found it hard to look directly at the creature, averting my eyes to the ground and glancing up every few moments to confirm it was still there.

"I... I don't know. They will say I made swords." I could not help but lie.

The creature stood up as if it could read my thoughts, anger filled its eyes while the creature ruffled its feathers. When the foul beast spread its wings, showing the full span of its demonic stance, I felt as if the creature permanently scarred the memory into my mind with dark magic. It then bellowed a hellish gargling squawk a crow often gives, but the sound was a much lower tone and made my chest shake in agony.

"They will say you brought death. They will call you the demon-smith! And they will be right. For all your sweat, they will only remember your blood. That is the blood your swords have spilled. The hatred of men is like the falling rains."

My brow furrowed deeply, I glared resolutely into the fire. "I have never shed any blood but my own." My words sounded small and did little to convince me or the creature.

Anticipating my answer, the tengu thrust the base of his staff into the earth, the rings jingled into the forest with a dozen echoes. In response to the tengu's call, ghostly balls of light started to dance in the dark forest beyond the clearing of which I stood. The lights did not illuminate much, but as they danced in the forest, they swirled around thousands of objects which I soon made out to be people, dead people to be precise. All without life, but all standing next to the thousands of trees with the help of some yōkai magic. Fresh wounds were upon the bodies, some without heads, some without limbs, some missing a torso entirely, but all similarly cut by an instrument of absolute efficiency.

"Behold your work, Muramasa. It is most impressive," the tengu spoke with pure admiration.

I swirled in every direction, seeing the same multitude of horror in the dark forest. "Enough," I quietly spoke, resigning myself to the tengu's presentation.

The tengu stamped his staff again and the corpses vanished as the ghostly lights disappeared, leaving only the campfire between the creature and myself.

"Do not deceive yourself, blade master, that is the greatest of all follies. Be as you are, be complete. Better to be all of a snake than half of a pheasant. These are the old ways. This is the way of the mountain and the forest, before the man creature walked on soil."

I stared into the yōkai's sunken eyes, gathering my courage for the first time. "Resign to being demonized? Bask in the tears and curses of generations? I have given up my work. I will not add corpses to your forest."

The monster gave whatever twisted version of a smile it had as if amused by my answer. The tengu then stoked the embers with its staff and growled. "You will never know peace without the hot flames of a forge and the ringing of steel at your side. The potential of man is like this fire, capable of such wonders and terrors, in need of stirring from time to time."

To my horror and surprise the tengu thrusted his arm into the fire, elbow deep, as if reaching underneath the dirt. Then with great effort, the tengu slowly pulled a bright yellow object out of the coals, the flames roared as the object was reluctantly let go from the fire. It was a hammer, but I recognized it as my forging hammer, knowing its shape better than my face. Despite the immense heat, the handle of the hammer did not burn, and the creature held it with ease. The tengu threw the hammer at my feet, the steel burning the forest undergrowth beneath. The tengu *gave no word, only a nod and a grunt as it slowly rose to its feet.*

After ruffling its feathers, the yōkai whispered into the end of its staff in its low demonic coughing language for the first time. "Brrrocach stasss rrropag." As the tengu spoke the incantation, blue flames leapt excitedly from the rings of his staff.

"I, Sōjōbō, will help you, Muramasa, I will impart four of my feathers to you," the tengu cackled. "Four rings for four seasons. Four seasons for four swords. Four swords for my sons. Soon they will come."

I saw that a shard of the rock, which had ignited the embers earlier, was now lodged in between the metal rings, glowing brightly amongst the blue flames of the staff. The tengu walked to the edge of the clearing, touching its flaming staff to a giant tree trunk. A burst of heat hit my face as the bark was engulfed in fire. The tengu then walked to the next tree, touching the staff to it as well. Within moments the forest all about us was ablaze. A terrible heat like the hottest embers at the heart of a smelter's furnace radiated over my body.

"What are you doing?" I yelled over the din of the roaring flames.

Calmly the tengu replied, "Stoking the fire, the creature called man must be moved from time to time. Remember this, Muramasa!"

Brothers bound in blood
Others bound in shame
Each protected by their yōkai name
Sharp claws made of tengu feathers
To restore the old ways and break this nation's fetters
Beware the demon revived by flame and fire
He will see the future and join the oni's ire
The first brings war, the second hates
Only when my sons unite will the third create

In a panic that I would be consumed by the blaze, I instinctively grabbed my forging hammer as if it would provide me with some sort of protection. As I gripped the handle, my fear was washed away, and I remember stepping with unknown purpose into the raging inferno.

I awoke from my drunken nightmare with a burning sensation in my hand and the creature's warning still in my mind. Indeed, the tengu was a harbinger of war. A faint gray light leaked in, and the smell of old stale smoke filled my senses. I instinctively pulled my hand toward my chest, finding that the burning sensation was from my hand touching a still hot coal. Through a pounding headache I forced myself to my feet. At least I was alive, surely no one could hurt this much in death. Shuffling forward slowly, I was surprised to find my path blocked by a solid rock wall. What yōkai magic was this? Had the creature somehow saved me from a fiery death only to imprison me in a stone tomb?

The abrupt cry of a bird brought me to my senses. As my eyes cleared, I recognized the prison, my own forge. Standing amidst the shards of a dozen broken sake jugs and a shattered oil lamp, I was alone, swaying in the wake of my drunken stupor. A wall of cold morning fog met me as I shuffled from the shrine; like white smoke, it hid the landscape from view, and I meandered cautiously forward in the direction of the breaking waters against the shore.

I saw a wailing bird perched on my garden fence nearest the cliffs. In its beak was what looked like a short twig, no bigger than my smallest finger. As I walked toward the bird, I was overcome with the sense that this winged creature knew me and that it was here for a visit. Approaching the fence, I slowly held out my hand, palm facing up to indicate my good will. Twisting its head severely to the right, it fixed me in the gaze of a shiny black eye. My hand trembled. Then with a great fluttering, it leapt into the air, drawing skyward. "Caw!" it screamed powerfully, letting the small piece of wood slip from its mouth. The scrap landed square in my shaking hand. The bird quickly vanished from view into the dense fog, though the continuing cries and the clear beating of its wings told me that it was headed out to sea, into the wide Sagami Bay. I listened intently until the squawking had faded into the distance, and only then did I turn my attention to the gift in my now tightly clenched fist.

I relaxed my fingers which revealed the wooden fragment, now stained in blood. A sharp end had apparently punctured my palms when I squeezed it so tightly in awe and wonder. Wiping the blood carelessly onto my kimono, I inspected the stick more closely. It was not merely a stick, but a root ball from a very young sapling. A single small trunk emerged from a ragged tangle of miniature roots. It was bone dry and nearly petrified, the reason it had cut me so easily. The little roots wound twisting in graceful loops, and there snagged in its delicate tendrils was a single jagged stone, a remnant of the soil in which it grew.

My mind flashed to an image that I half remembered, like a shadow of a dream. Then examining it closely, the simple grain of rock revealed itself to be of a dark blue hue, nearly black. The stick had a much too eerily resemblance of the tengu's staff. Fear had struck my heart as I had made the connection and I instinctively turned around as if the yōkai was standing behind me, watching. Did the tengu follow me into the world of men or did I merely concoct a nightmare made from my everyday surroundings and drunken stupor? The tengu's staff indeed had resembled the twig I now held cautiously to my eye. The rings on the staff, and the stone, and the blue flame! This was far beyond coincidence.

To this day I am still unsure.

I pressed my thumb deep into the puncture of my wounded palm. Pain shot through my hand and up nearly to the elbow. No, this was no dream. Closing my fingers protectively around the twig, I walked back to the house to contemplate what I had seen and heard.

Upon this moment is when I had begun to write in this very book to try and make sense of my life's connection with the warning I had received.

Itsuki stopped reading and closed the book; his mind was blank with only more questions.

"A terrifying tale, do you really think he met a tengu?" Kaito stated as he shivered as if a ghost spoke to him.

"Only Muramasa knows," Noboru spoke. "When we met him, his mind was at a loss, perhaps a tengu did appear to him to commission these blades, perhaps not. Maybe the yōkai is what drove him mad. The entries of the book soon after show the deterioration of Muramasa's mind."

"What does it mean, the tengu's warning?" Tsubasa asked.

"Warning?" Itsuki pondered. "It could be a tale made up by Muramasa's troubled mind for all we know."

"Four swords for four sons," Kaito whispered in deep thought.

"Your father contemplated the meaning, that much I know," Itsuki stated as he weighed the book in his hands. "But you two are the only ones that are brothers between the four of us. Whatever the meaning I will have those blades."

Kaito began to mumble, "Four swords for four sons. I will impart you my…" Kaito looked up excited. "The feathers!"

Noboru and Itsuki both looked at Kaito, understanding what the young man meant. The two men seemed to read each other's mind as they stood and walked over to the statue. Itsuki and Noboru started probing the wings of the tengu statue.

One wooden feather moved.

"Loose?" Itsuki said as he wiggled the feather more.

With a large grin Noboru took out a kunai from his side and gestured Itsuki to stand clear. Noboru carefully put the tip of the dagger at the base of the wooden feather and began chipping around the wood. Eventually the feather became loose from the wing to reveal that it was no wood feather at all, but a sword sheath. The sword handle had been hidden in the statue itself wrapped in fine silk. Noboru pulled the sword with a large grin and held it two-handed from tip to handle.

"This one is yours Itsuki," Noboru said, handing it over. "I will know mine when I find it."

Itsuki normally could keep his calm but the excited emotions he felt could be plainly read on his face. "I'll wait, but not for long."

Noboru hastily inspected the feathers, guiding his hands until he found another loose feather. Noboru repeated the steps to pry open another sword. Noboru held the sheath and dropped his kunai to the floor. He slowly moved his palm to the handle; finger-by-finger he tightened his grip. Together the two shinobi unsheathed the swords in unison, showing the Yukimura brothers the prize they had sought.

Tsubasa and Kaito soon realized why Noboru had previously said that the decoy swords were the wrong color.

"Black?" Tsubasa whispered.

The blade of the sword was the color of a pure black that contained no shine against the firelight, opaque like steel but black as obsidian. To stare into the blades was to stare into oblivion; the blades contained no reflection or sheen and seemed to suck in whatever light touched the dark metal. Only a thin, dark-gray line at the very edge of the blade showed the elements of a traditional steel.

Noboru gave out a large laugh as he wielded his new weapon and Itsuki could not help but smile as he inspected the blade.

The sheath was a plain, dark brown wood, a stark contrast to the masterpiece inside. The sword itself had been forged in the form of a long wakizashi, a two-foot curved blade made even longer by the handle, any longer and it would have been considered a full-fledged katana. The sword guard was a simple dark black oval, with a matching black sword collar. The handle was wrapped in a black cloth that mirrored the rest of the black blade.

The Yukimura brothers looked at the blades in astonished envy.

Noboru finally looked up to see the young shinobi's faces and laughed. "You don't think we dragged you all the way here to gloat, do you?"

Itsuki gestured the Yukimura brothers to the back of the tengu statue. Two more loose feathers were found and soon the young brothers had pried out two more swords.

Itsuki gestured he be given both blades in each hand and looked at the Yukimura brothers. "Kneel."

The Yukimura brothers knelt. Itsuki closed his eyes for a moment, contemplated, and then switched the swords to opposite hands.

"Sons of Kazuki Yukimura. I will give these swords to you because I trusted your father. I owe him my life and much more. If you accept these swords, you will accept the role that your father would have chosen for you, to follow in his footsteps, to follow the ways of old; to commit to the ways of a true shinobi leaving the ways of your youth behind and stepping into the responsibilities of men. Do you accept?"

The Yukimura brothers spoke in unison, "We accept."

Itsuki hesitated. "And will you use these blades to avenge Hekison with us, following Noboru and I in this task?"

Tsubasa grinned happily at the thoughts of avenging his father. Kaito mimicked his older brother. "We accept," they said in unison again.

Itsuki smiled. "Stand and be recognized."

Itsuki handed both swords to the brothers while they excitedly looked at each other. Together they had unsheathed their new wakizashis to reveal the new black blades.

"I'll prefer this over a bow any day," Kaito spoke.

Tsubasa laughed. "It only took you a blade forged by Muramasa to convert you, brother."

"Not just any blade Muramasa forged," Noboru said, sheathing his new sword. "His final creations, the pinnacle of his life's work."

Tsubasa gripped his sword tighter. "Yes, there is much to know about this mysterious blade. Why the metal is black and why it is so light."

"True, I have never held a sword so light." Kaito said as he looked over the blade. "Nor masterfully crafted and well balanced."

"Shhh," Itsuki whispered.

From the entrance of the cave the sounds of men speaking could be heard.

17

Yōkai

-Yamashiro Province, Mount Kurama-

"We hear you in there," a voice called out.

"We're waiting," another voice mocked, followed by a group of laughter.

Itsuki cursed under his breath.

"Who is it?" Tsubasa questioned.

"Were we followed?" Kaito said nervously. "What do we do?"

"Oi, come out or we'll bury you in there." The joking had ended.

Noboru looked at Itsuki. "That is no bluff, it could easily be done. It seems we have no choice."

Itsuki nodded grudgingly. The cave was indeed a tomb, the entrance was narrow, and the earth on the hill could easily be moved. There was no point in waiting out the unexpected guests or goading them into the cave. Against the tenets of a shinobi the group exited the cave to confront their visitors.

The shinobi were somewhat blinded by the sun that hung low in the sky. The greenery of the landscape had received a blanketed golden sheen with extending shadows from the trees. Near the cave they found four soldiers sitting nonchalantly and talking outside the cave entrance. They were samurai from the looks of it, but they were lightly outfitted for travel, a handpicked specialized unit loyal to Nobunaga. The four shinobi were somewhat taken off guard by the leisure composure of the samurai.

One samurai was writing a letter paying no mind. A large nosed samurai smiled and pointed at the shinobi. He mumbled something to his comrades, followed by a low laughter as if they were in on a joke the shinobi did not know. In any case, the samurai did not see the shinobi as a threat.

A broad-shouldered samurai started clapping his hands. "Good to see you. I almost thought we lost you."

The shinobi looked at each other somewhat confused.

"And why would you be following us? We are but simple priests of this shrine." Itsuki knew the ruse was a long shot, but he gambled regardless.

The samurai only laughed. "Simple priests that traveled from the south of Iga, simple priests that make campfires near Azuchi Castle, and simple priests that steal boats to cross Lake Biwa." The samurai's tone became stern as he finished his speech. "Your trail was easy to follow."

This group of men had been the very samurai that had almost come upon them when they had camped at Lake Biwa; they had obviously held a grudge for the loss of their boat.

"So..." the samurai smugly spoke as if catching a child red handed. "As you can imagine, Lord Nobunaga can't have renegade shinobi wandering the mountains near Kyoto. What are we to do with—"

Noboru cut the samurai off mid-sentence, fed up with the game he was playing. "You will die first."

The four samurai stood up, unsheathing their swords for battle.

The leader spoke again, this time his voice was grim and embittered. "The only reason you four are alive is because you fled Hekison when we sacked it."

Itsuki glared at the four enemies. "You will soon learn the reason we are alive. You will do well to remember this, samurai."

The four shinobi unsheathed their new black wakizashis. Each shinobi had a wild look in their eyes as if hungry for blood. The four samurai looked upon the blades in disgust, noting the color of the blades that seemed to suck the light from the very air.

"Tainted swords." The long-nosed samurai spat at the ground.

"Black? Looks like you shinobi burnt your swords in a fire. I will show you how a—"

Before the samurai could finish his sentence, Noboru lead the attack with a scream, his hair flowed behind him like a cloak. The three other shinobi followed, each approaching their targeted foe.

Noboru came at the samurai leader with a powerful two-handed upward strike, aiming for the samurai's chest. The samurai instinctively parried with a perfectly timed downward blow, but his masterful skills did not have an effect. Noboru's strength combined with the speed of his new black blade caused the samurai's sword to fly wildly from his hand. The samurai's only defense was his hands in the air and a wild look of surprise upon his face. Time seemed to slow as the samurai looked at Noboru's hair dancing across his battle enraged face. Noboru then pressed the blade diagonally into the chest of the samurai's leather armor.

"Yōkai…" the samurai muttered in fear.

192

Only when the blade had made contact with the samurai's armor did Noboru apply force to his downward swing while giving a wild scream. The samurai's chest spilled blood as the blade came downward across the chest. Noboru finished the death by thrusting the sword into the heart. Noboru had made good on his promise; the man was first to die.

The other three shinobi had started their chosen fights; even in the midst of battle the samurai noticed that their leader had fallen, fear began to penetrate the remaining three.

Itsuki had taken on a short but broad built samurai. The man had obviously been trained well, but Itsuki had a newly found lust for revenge. This was the first battle since Hekison's downfall for the Iga shinobi, each death would be a payment for their fallen comrades.

Itsuki's style was much more patient than Noboru's, he parried with the samurai, thoughtfully reading his moves while looking for a mistake. When the samurai saw that his comrade had fallen, Itsuki took advantage of the distraction and applied pressure. The samurai was backing up across rocks and grass, hilly terrain advantageous to shinobi. Itsuki played the fool as if the samurai had knocked him off balance; the samurai took the bait by making an excessive frontal jab at Itsuki's chest. Only when Itsuki saw that the samurai was committed did he twirl his body while raising his sword two-handed above his head. With the samurai's arms outstretched, Itsuki's black blade came hammering down on the victim's wrists, releasing flesh from man. The samurai screamed as his hands fell to the ground, Itsuki gave the man mercy by freeing the samurai from his head with a lateral slice. Even in battle Itsuki was surprised as the black blade gave no resistance as it flew effortlessly through the air, the lifeless samurai's body fell to the floor along with its former head.

Kaito had taken the samurai that had been writing a letter. Even with his new superior light blade and training over the winter months, Kaito's inexperience showed, and the samurai took advantage of it. Kaito was on the defense, keeping up with the samurai's swings that bore down like an avalanche. Kaito kept his wits, Itsuki and Noboru's aggressive training had taught him what to do with a superior skilled foe. He had practiced everyday with three companions more skilled than himself.

"If the enemy is better with a dagger, then use a sword. If he's better with a sword, then use a bow. If he's better with a bow, then cheat. Use something he does not have." The voice of Itsuki's training rang in Kaito's mind.

Kaito began retreating from the samurai as if fleeing, but with his other hand the young man grabbed a sealed tube containing a blinding powder, a remnant of Hekison. Confident for the first time, Kaito gave an aggressive downward stroke that caused the samurai to go on the defense for once. Simultaneously, Kaito held his hand out with the blinding powder and blew the contents into the samurai's face. The man cursed Kaito's trick, but the move that his father had taught him in swordplay was already in motion. The first time he had experienced it was when he was only twelve. Kaito called the move a trick and called his father a cheat, but if the enemy was better *"then cheat"* still rang in Kaito's mind.

The samurai instinctively jumped back to rub his eyes, but he made the mistake of using his sword hand. Kaito's training from his father kicked in and he stepped forward to grab the samurai's wrist while twisting the hand. In one fluid motion Kaito stabbed the samurai in the shoulder and then thrusted the samurai's sword into the owner's throat. The samurai died by his own blade. Kaito pulled the black blade from the victim's body, surprised to find that such a light jab had penetrated the samurai's shoulder clean through.

Tsubasa was taking the longest out of all the shinobi with his attacker, but it wasn't for lack of skill, it was from enjoyment. Tsubasa was smiling as he fought the samurai. *This sword is the best I've ever felt,* Tsubasa thought as he continued to bring an onslaught of sword swings upon the samurai.

Noboru could see Tsubasa taking his time and yelled, "Stop getting cocky, kid. Finish him off, or I'll do it for you."

The comment seemed to fuel the samurai's anger and his determination to live strengthened. The samurai took a hard swing at Tsubasa, but the young shinobi deflected and took a backward roll, creating space between him and the samurai. With blinding speed Tsubasa quickly released two kunai throwing daggers from his hip. Tsubasa threw one kunai directly to the left of the samurai, causing the man to flinch right. Another kunai came trailing the original, causing the samurai to commit to a roll. Tsubasa then released a third while simultaneously running toward the samurai. Once the samurai evaded the final throwing kunai with his roll, Tsubasa sliced the man nearly in half at the waist with a running stroke. A final rasping breath accompanied the man's life as his body fell to the ground like a felled tree.

Tsubasa smiled but he soon felt a hard hit on his head.

Noboru was standing over him. "I told you not to get cocky. Never prolong a fight, regardless of the man's skill." Noboru sheathed his sword and couldn't help but smile and gave Tsubasa a pat on his shoulder. "But still, a good kill. I saw your father do something like that once."

Tsubasa nodded in approval; he could not help but feel smug.

Suddenly, a single applause could be heard, and the four shinobi looked back at the cave entrance. The mountain priest sat on the hill above the cave where they had gotten the swords.

"Nice of you to warn us, priest," Itsuki scoffed.

The priest smiled and rocked back and forth cross-legged excited as ever. "I had to be sure, sure as pain."

"Sure of what?" Itsuki responded.

"That you were the four," the priest stated. "If not, I would have killed you, it was my charge to reap the unworthy."

"Killed us?" Tsubasa stated doubtfully.

"Yes, you." The priest's smile disappeared. "You and you and you."

The shinobi did not believe the priest had the skill, but they had no reason to see him as a threat, so they let the comment pass.

"I don't understand." Kaito stated, cleaning his new blade.

"Your father knew, in time you will too?" the priest rhymed excitedly. "Come, shinobi. There is a stream, a stream to make yourselves clean."

The four shinobi looked at each other and shrugged their shoulders. They grabbed their belongings and followed the priest up to a remote spring. The spring did not connect to any of the other waters in the shrine to avoid contamination. The shinobi took off the top of their traveling garments to wash in the spring and cleanse themselves from battle. Noboru and Itsuki were bloodstained from their close quarter kills and began scrubbing their skin.

Tsubasa washed his face with clean water. "What's your name, priest."

"Names, names, I have many names, but your father called me Hiraku."

"Speak plainly, priest. What is it you mean by the four?" Noboru spoke as he washed.

"The four, four swords for four sons, four blades, four shinobi I see," the priest riddled as he rang his ringed staff.

"We do not share a mutual father, priest. What do you mean?" Itsuki stated.

"Father, father, no mortal father. Sons of the tengu, Sōjōbō, are the inheritors of his feathers."

"You babble in riddles," Noboru scoffed.

"It is the world that speaks in riddles, I speak as plain as day," the priest retorted.

"You said you knew my father," Kaito spoke. "In what way?"

"Yukimura, Kazuki, yes, the Hundred Shadow Man, man of snow, man of wind. He came to me with the tengu feathers, blades of woe. He charged my tribe to guard them, hold them, protect them, until the four arrived. The four to protect the old ways, the ways of the gods. Only the true four could find the blades, Kazuki told me so."

Itsuki looked at Noboru. "What do you think? We were with Kazuki when the blades were found, but he had forbidden us to use them. If the swords were meant for us, why not give us some clue?"

"Itsuki Hayashi, man who stands as strong as trees." The priest's eyes looked back to Noboru. "And you, Noboru Tsukino, man who dances with flames. Kazuki always suspected you two to be part of the four, but he did not know it at the time. The Hundred Shadow Man spoke much of you two, he spoke of your trials of the pit."

"You know nothing," Noboru retorted.

"The brand on your back says I know much more," the priest quipped back.

Noboru only growled and mumbled obscenities under his breath at the priest's comments.

"And us?" Tsubasa butted in. "Did our father speak of us?"

"Guesses only guesses, your father only knew you as his sons. He did not know that you two would be part of the four," the priest responded.

"I don't know who you take us for, Hiraku, or whatever your name is," Itsuki spoke gruffly. "We came for the blades because we knew of their masterful origin. We needed the blades for justice, nothing more. We are no protectors."

"Not yet, shinobi. Time can change, time will flow, work is to be done, paths paved. My task of protecting the blades is done. Now my job is to prepare the way of the four. The time of this shrine is done, I am the last, the last of many."

"We need no help, priest. Our goal is Nobunaga's death," Itsuki stated determined.

The priest laughed. "Yes, yes, all men owe a death, one death. This will be a good test of your will. But when you are done bringing death, what will you do after?" the priest questioned, jingling his staff.

The shinobi looked at each other as if seeing the future for the first time. Since the fall of Hekison none had considered a life beyond vengeance. Their village had fallen, scattering all family and comrades. The past was obliterated, the present was revenge, and the future contained nothing.

"You four live in the present, no matter, the present needs attending. I will attend to the future. I will gather the shinobi while you gather Nobunaga."

"Hekison is no more, priest. There are none to gather." Itsuki rubbed his eyes from the water of the stream but when he looked up to see where the priest was, the man had disappeared.

The four shinobi searched for the priest but to their dismay they could find no sign of him.

"What the hell is going on?" Tsubasa stated in frustration by all the riddles of the journey.

"Was he a spirit, left to guard this shrine?" Kaito questioned.

"He looked real enough to me," Noboru smiled, admiring his new sword. "Who cares? We have what we came for. Now let us see what we can gather from our freshly dead samurai, shall we."

The shinobi made their way down to their previous battlefield. Kaito stood over the dead samurai and scanned his fallen foe. The man's eyes were still blood red from Kaito's blinding powder, the fallen samurai appeared as a possessed puppet that a demon had cast aside. Kaito searched the pack of the samurai finding some food provisions and a letter. The correspondence was an unfinished letter that was to be sent to the late samurai's wife. Tsubasa took notice at his brother's sudden concern of the letter.

"What is it?" Tsubasa called out as he walked over.

Kaito paused and then looked at the letter. "This man had a son that he has never seen. The letter was for his wife... I feel sorry that we had to kill — Oi!"

Tsubasa snatched the letter from Kaito and ripped up the parchment, leaving the pieces to the wind before Kaito could protest.

Tsubasa locked his eyes with Kaito. "This man would have killed you without remorse. These men are responsible for the death of our father. I would gladly make orphans of all their sons if I had the chance."

Kaito hesitated, "Yes, but—"

"But nothing!" Tsubasa's anger flared. "Hesitation will get you killed; your resolution must be absolute."

Kaito gave a nod of submission. Tsubasa took a deep breath and gave a pat on the shoulder of his brother, remembering that he should not be the direction of his anger.

"Find anything?" Kaito asked eagerly to change the subject.

"Some food and a map. Actually, of Yamashiro Province, where Kyoto is," Tsubasa stated, unfolding the map.

The map contained an outline of the province with roads, towns, cities, and landmarks of the area. The parchment had deep folds from excessive use.

"Here, you're better with maps than I am," Tsubasa stated, handing over the parchment.

"May come in handy," Kaito stated, stuffing the map into a pocket.

Noboru gave a yell. "Oi, you girls done fondling those corpses over there?"

Tsubasa gave an obscene gesture back to Noboru.

"Already protective of your dead girlfriend?" Noboru taunted. "Come. We found something."

Itsuki and Noboru had pillaged the samurai of goods as well, but Noboru had found something more valuable.

"What is it?" Kaito questioned.

"Dispatch orders." Itsuki raised a piece of parchment. "From the looks of it, these samurai were headed to Kyoto. To meet with…" Itsuki scanned the correspondence. "Their commanding officer, Nobutada Oda, the brat of Nobunaga himself."

Kaito looked at the insignia that was over one of the samurai's shoulders. "This crest, I've seen it before." The crest contained three circles with curved tails swirling to make a larger circle. "The crest of Susanoo, the god of storms," Noboru pointed. "It is the crest that Nobunaga uses for his special auxiliary squad; a troublesome group that specializes in reconnaissance. I remember the first time encountering such a squad. Remember, Itsuki? They would have killed us if it weren't for Yamada and his men."

"You know I do... Yamada died." Itsuki peered at the dispatch. "That was at the beginning of the siege of our homeland."

"So, what of the dispatch?" Kaito asked eagerly.

Itsuki looked up at the young shinobi. "What do you think?"

"Well... it means that if they are regrouping in Kyoto, there will be more of Nobunaga's men, probably a gathering for new orders."

"Exactly," Itsuki stated as he folded the dispatch and put it in his pack. "That is where we must go to find out Nobunaga's next move."

"That reminds me," Kaito said, pulling a piece of parchment from his pocket. "There was a map of the Yamashiro Province on one of the samurai. It should come in handy if we're heading to Kyoto."

Itsuki waved a hand. "Keep it, you can show us the best way to get there."

"Yes... of course," Kaito stated slightly surprised at the responsibility. "So, Kyoto then."

"A two-day travel from here on foot, but for once we are not in a terrible rush, we can camp here tonight," Noboru stated, looking up at the setting sun in the sky.

Itsuki nodded. "We can get a good night's rest here and have a lazy start tomorrow."

"What of the bodies?" asked Kaito.

"Who cares?" Tsubasa blurted out.

"I don't care about the corpses, but I would take care of this place, and I would not anger the spirits who care for it by leaving corpses to rot," Itsuki said, looking around.

Noboru nodded in agreement. "The shrine of Mount Kurama is no place for dead samurai. You two don't have to bury them but we want them outside the grounds."

Tsubasa looked at the bloody bodies. "Ugh. Why?"

"Because your father left you a gift here in this shrine, and we will not have it defiled," Itsuki said curtly, standing up as if waiting for the young shinobi to challenge him.

Kaito could see the tension and broke it with a pat on Tsubasa's shoulder. Kaito grabbed the first body and started dragging it down to the torii at the entrance of the shrine. Tsubasa reluctantly walked to the other body and followed his younger brother down the stone steps. In silence the Yukimura brothers walked down past the wood torii and dropped the two bodies into the forest outside the shrine. As they made their way up to gather the remaining two bodies, they could see that the two older shinobi had started making camp. Noboru was gathering wood to start a fire and Itsuki was gathering foliage to make bedding. The last two bodies were much more bothersome to dispose, as one lacked a head, and the other was barely in one piece. The brothers groaned at their job but were happy to be almost done. As the Yukimura brothers made their way down to make their last corpse drop, Tsubasa broke the silence.

"Kaito," Tsubasa said, glancing in the direction of Noboru and Itsuki to check that they were out of earshot for once.

"What?" Kaito looked at his brother confused.

Tsubasa let the samurai fall to the ground and gestured Kaito to crouch by the fallen samurai. "Do you remember what the priest said about our friends over there?"

Kaito scanned his memory for a moment. "Something about Noboru eating from a hearth?"

"Shhh, not so loud. But anyway, I have only heard the term used once by our father when he spoke with Yamato years ago, they were yelling at each other."

"You always did like to spy," Kaito smiled and shrugged his shoulders. "So, what does it mean?"

"I do not know," Tsubasa stated, looking concerned. "The hearth of Yomi-No-Kuni is of the underworld, a symbolic meaning of sorts. All I know is the saying is from the old laws of Hekison, the original laws, and that it was never openly spoken except among the elders of the village. I know it is some sort of punishment, for what I cannot say, but the ceremony for the hearth of Yomi-No-Kuni is something few have ever heard of or seen. From what I gathered the event can skip generations. Whatever Noboru did, we should not take it lightly."

Kaito contemplated the weight of his brother's words. "Well, I trust them. They have brought us to our father's legacy."

"Trusting as always, brother." Tsubasa shook his head. "I do not deny their contribution to us, the training, the swords, the chance to avenge our father. All I'm saying is that they withhold much… and that many of their intentions are masked. They are shinobi after all."

"Our father obviously trusted them. Why not just ask?"

"They are as tight lipped as a mute when it comes to things of their past. It was only out of concern for our safety that Noboru told us of Itsuki's familial loss."

"So, what are you saying?"

"I'm saying... I'm saying that one who deserves a punishment as severe as the hearth of Yomi-No-Kuni cannot be taken lightly. In fact, I have never heard of any surviving it. I don't know what I'm saying, brother... just keep your guard around them and your tongue with such matters."

Kaito gave a nod of understanding, it was rare that he had ever seen his brother so disturbed. After all, family came first with the Yukimura clan.

"For a moment I thought you were going to challenge Itsuki again," Kaito stated, changing the subject.

"I thought better of it," Tsubasa stated bluntly.

Kaito laughed. "Because he would have you on your back in seconds and made it look easy."

Tsubasa came out of his gloom and smiled. "Maybe, but I'll become stronger, as strong as father."

Kaito gave his brother a hard punch in the shoulder and ran off. "But not as strong as me."

The brothers taunted each other in laughter, and after their task was complete, they returned in high spirits. Noboru had a roaring fire going and gestured the brothers to come warm themselves. The tree grove that sheltered them filtered the quickly appearing stars from the heavens above as night enveloped the shrine.

A cool calm breeze gave a song to the grass and trees as they swayed in the wind. The smell of mountains was in the air and the running of water sang through cascading streams. If the samurai had never come to start battle, one would say that the place was a shrine meant to calm the soul.

In the village of Hekison it was rumored that Mount Kurama

had been the birthplace of ninjutsu; the art of shadows and honing the mind to be one with nature, reaching a totality of being. In times of old it was a common tale that the Lord of the Tengus, Sōjōbō, had made the mountain his throne to counsel and teach.

Noboru and Itsuki sat while discussing about the mysterious priest that had disappeared. The shinobi had all agreed that the man was no specter, but a wood spirit or kitsune was still up for debate. In any case, Hiraku the priest seemed to have been a friend of Kazuki and the subject was left at that. Noboru unsheathed his black blade and looked at it while smiling as if he was in a dream. Each shinobi held their blade close as if it were one of their limbs and would only remove them reluctantly when it was time to sleep.

Kaito looked at his sheathed sword and spoke aloud, "Do you think Muramasa knew what he was making when he started to forge these blades?"

Noboru's smile faded to a melancholy tone as if hearing that an old friend had died. "I would like to think so; I was about your age when I had met Muramasa with your father. As I said, we vowed not to speak of our journey. But I will tell you, even at my young age I felt that Muramasa had the wisdom of many generations. At times he seemed very clear and accepting of his role in life, but he would have fits of riddled words."

"What do you mean riddles?" Tsubasa interjected.

"He was ancient or…" Noboru trailed off.

"A genius, but sick of mind," Itsuki stated. "His sword craft obviously never left him, but he had trouble recalling memories and simple tasks at times." Itsuki pulled the book of Muramasa out of the pack and handed it to Tsubasa.

"Remember the last entry that we read in the cave?" Noboru stated.

"Yes, what of it?" Tsubasa questioned.

"Well here is the next," Noboru said as he directed Tsubasa to the right page.

The writings of the book had drastically changed. The words were jumbled together with no spacing, no consistency of character height, and appeared to be the handwriting of a different owner.

Watching. Watching. Watching.

Masamune is laughing at my method, but the Tengu Lord is watching. Masamune was master of the soshu kitae, three steels, seven layers. The starry night blades.

But the Tengu Lord teaches much and demands more. His feathers will not be made in the ways of men.

Watching. Watching.
The first blade it speaks, it speaks to me. I argue with it often. It calls for a mountain, one I do not know, one it calls home. Watching.

I must finish four.
Watching. Watching.

"It goes like this for a while, writings in riddles, but..." Noboru flipped the book around so the two brothers could see the next entry, but the next page wasn't an entry at all. The page was the drawing of a yōkai demon, the tengu from Muramasa's dream.

The creature did not look anything like the statue in the cave or of any other tengu depicted in the country. The drawing looked as if the man who drew it had seen the creature in real life. The drawing was dark and ominous. The depiction showed a hint of crazed genius at the reality of the creature. Large wings worn like a coat, the face of a bird, talons of a demon, and the eyes as black as the blades which the shinobi held. Both Yukimura brothers were disconcerted by the dark drawing.

"Do you think... do you think that Muramasa spoke with a tengu, I mean was it a dream he had?"

Itsuki looked up at the stars through the filtered treetops. "There are nights I wonder. There is one thing I do know. Whether the yōkai appeared to him or not, I think that Muramasa believed that it came to him, dream or not."

Kaito's countenance changed from a look of interest to trouble. He peered at the blade in his lap with new feelings of reverence, fear, and wonder.

"He asked your father to continue the tale of the book that he had started," Itsuki continued.

Kaito's head perked up. "You mentioned this before, why have we not read it?"

"It would have made little difference," Itsuki stated. "It is encoded, look."

Kaito and Tsubasa both looked at a very large number of entries in the book of Muramasa for the first time, the entries themselves contained more writings than Muramasa had. Although the words were jumbled, they used the same kanji symbols of their native tongue, but everything was out of order.

Kaito laughed when he realized what it was. "It needs a cipher."

Noboru and Itsuki, both perked their heads up. "What?" the older shinobi stated together, eagerly awaiting an answer.

Kaito laughed, enjoying the reversal of roles, knowing a bit of knowledge that his superiors did not know.

"Why should I tell you?" Kaito joked.

Noboru's anger flared not liking Kaito's newfound superiority. "Listen here. You tell us what it says or—"

"Relax," Tsubasa stated, enjoying the moment just as much as his brother. "He does not know."

Noboru's posture relaxed. "Speak plainly."

"It is an encoding our father taught only to family members." Tsubasa saw that Itsuki and Noboru looked betrayed, as if Kazuki had shared all with them.

"Sorry," Kaito laughed, still enjoying the torture they were giving their superiors. "Our father taught us how to encode secret messages if anything were to ever happen. To translate, a cipher is needed, a single word, which allows you to rearrange the jumble of words to form a coherent text. Without the cipher we cannot show you how to read it. See, look. He left some blank pages after the entry; this is for the reader to write down the translation."

Noboru and Itsuki's optimism faded at the end of Kaito's words.

"A single word that we must find," Itsuki stated disheartened. "Unless we just stumble upon the cipher, his words will remain sealed."

"Do not fret," Noboru stated. "We cannot have everything at once, we have the blades at least."

Tsubasa let out a deep exhale and watched his breath fade into the cold night air. "In any case, I am grateful however this blade came to be. I have never held a sword so light before. When I had first wielded it against the samurai, I feared it would break, but when the blade met my opponent... it felt..."

"Powerful," Itsuki said, looking at the fire and then smiling at Noboru. "As Noboru adeptly showed you. A bit reckless, but you were true to your word. He was the first to die," Itsuki spoke in a mocking Noboru voice.

"What can I say? I'm a man of my word," Noboru joked in his growling voice and pulled out a gourd of sake that he had taken off the samurai. Noboru unstopped the sake gourd. "To Sengo Muramasa, the bladesmith." Noboru gave a long swig and wiped the remains off with his sleeve. He then handed the gourd to Tsubasa to pass around the circle.

"Why are they black?" Tsubasa asked. He drank from the gourd and passed it to Itsuki. "Even rumors of swords being made this way don't exist."

Noboru pondered for a moment. "All we know is that Muramasa found some new technique, new material to combine with the steel. Something that drove him mad at the same time. I have no doubt its superiority is linked with the color. Its knowledge is lost with Muramasa or hidden in the book, probably by your father."

Itsuki drank from the sake gourd and let out a long exhale. "Ahh, that's smooth. It has been too long since I've had sake like this. Nobunaga's ghost squad gets the best. Anyway, Kazuki believed the blades to be sacred to the shinobi clan."

"Sacred how?" Tsubasa probed.

"I am not sure," Itsuki admitted. "But do you not find it curious that a bladesmith making his masterpiece chose to do so in the form of a long wakizashi and not a full-fledged katana."

"Lack of material," Kaito suggested.

"Perhaps," Itsuki contemplated. "Then why not three katanas? We shinobi prefer a wakizashi over a katana. A katana cannot be worn across the back, too long for stealth, and cumbersome indoors. A katana excels in open field battle, but a wakizashi is suited for all shinobi needs. I believe this method of thought is linked to your father's reverence for the blades."

Noboru chuckled in memory. "In any case, Itsuki and I coveted them the moment we saw them. Your father eventually had to threaten to take our sword hands after our tenth attempt to try one. Kazuki forbade that they should be used until he found their proper owners. It was not until Yamato had died that I believed the blades truly belonged to Itsuki and myself. Until that moment all four belonged to Kazuki."

Itsuki rubbed his bald head and gave a smile. "I will not lie to you two. Noboru and I had spoken of not giving you the blades, but I do not count our journey as complete coincidence."

Tsubasa had a look of betrayal on his face at hearing the comment of Itsuki and instinctively grabbed his sword. Noboru saw him flinch and gave a shove to his shoulder.

"Relax, Tsubasa. We aren't going to take it." Noboru threw the gourd of sake to him. "Itsuki and I discussed the matter; the two blades belong to the sons of the Hundred Shadow Man."

Tsubasa's tension seemed to go out of him. "What do you mean? When you said they belonged to our father."

"Kazuki seemed to understand something we didn't, he told us the blades would be protected by him. I suppose he never believed them to be his, but more that he was the keeper of them. I was angry beyond belief when your father said the blades were not to be used, but I was just a boy then."

210

"Our Father," Kaito whispered under his breath. The sting of his father's death was abruptly felt. Since leaving Hekison he had few times to stand still from the chaos of the blade quest. His father, Kazuki, had always gone on missions for the Iga shinobi, but he had always returned. The thought made Kaito wish that he had spent more time with him. Tsubasa on the other hand had become angrier since the fall of Hekison. Kaito had seen the look of his brother for a split second as he had battled the samurai outside the cave; the enjoyment of revenge was clearly on his brother's face. Kaito looked over at his older brother, remembering the rage in his eyes after the fight. Kaito took a long swig of sake to dull his senses.

"I miss him," Kaito stated.

"I miss him too but avenging him is what concerns me at the moment," Tsubasa responded with his usual restlessness.

"Patience is what your father would have told me. Anger can be a powerful tool, Tsubasa, but like fire it can consume you unchecked," Itsuki counseled.

"Easy for you to say, you didn't lose your father," Tsubasa mocked.

Itsuki looked at the young shinobi with a stare that could have killed a corpse all over again. Tsubasa diverted his, eyes knowing he had misspoken.

Noboru tried breaking the tension. "When I was younger, on starry nights like these my father used to tell me the story of the gods. He would say there is power behind tales of old, that repeating the deeds of the gods would bring blessings upon our house. It reminds me of… of better times."

"You have never mentioned family before, Noboru," Kaito said. "Did they survive the siege?"

Itsuki eyed Noboru, wondering what his response would be. Noboru shifted nervously thinking of old memories. "I lost them years before the siege," Noboru lied.

Tsubasa stared at the stars. "Then tell us the story your father taught you," Tsubasa stated in a melancholy tone. "To remind us of better times."

The night grew dark, and Noboru began his tale of the first gods, Izanagi, and his wife Izanami. The two gods through their marriage formed the great islands of Japan. Izanagi with his jeweled spear named Amenonuhoko, drove forth the weapon from the heavens into the sea, pulling out the great islands of Japan. Noboru continued the tale of how Izanagi lost his wife Izanami to the underworld. Izanagi formed other gods: Tsukuyomi the moon, Susanoo the storms, and their sister, Amaterasu, the sun goddess. Noboru acted out each scene with great enthusiasm as if he had an audience of 10,000. Into the night Noboru told the tale and acted out the scenes while the other shinobi laughed at his excitement. For a brief night they all forgot the ghosts of their pasts and were reminded of better times.

18

The Descent

-Yamashiro Province, Base of Mount Kurama-

The shinobi had begun their descent south from the top of Mount Kurama, leaving the holy place of Sōjōbō, Lord of the Tengus, to his throne in peace. Infused with power from their new blades and the imparting wisdom of the shrine, they made their way toward Kyoto with a renewed feeling of vigor. The shinobi all felt a sense of nostalgia as they left the mountains. Although they had left on various missions in the past, this was the first time that they would leave such landscapes with no assurance that they would be returning. Even though they had left the mystical shrine, the shinobi were glad to be about their goal once again. Noboru had an aura of enthusiasm surrounding him that did not go unnoticed. His pace was swift and after a break he would be first to leave. He hummed a song as he traveled and talked as if he were going to a party.

"You're in light spirits," Itsuki spoke as they walked.

"And why shouldn't I be. We found the blades, Itsuki. It seems a lifetime ago that we made it out to the island, out beyond the world."

Itsuki could not help but smile, glimpsing the inner child of his friend once again while remembering the days of their youth. Noboru being an impetuous longhaired ruffian with no patience at all; Itsuki being a shy wary boy. "I agree, the wonders we saw I will never forget."

Noboru nodded in agreement. "Ha, indeed. We are masters of our own fate. We are… free. Much has happened in these past months, but we are in a way free to rule ourselves. Hekison is no more, but we owe no allegiance to anyone with all the shinobi scattered. I never wished Yamato Akiyama's death, but you must admit the man wished our deaths along with Kazuki more than once. Kazuki taught us in the old ways, Yamato wanted to unify with the feudal system, we are free of Yamato and his judgement. In a way I am glad for all that has happened."

Noboru looked at Itsuki and saw his face turn to a melancholy stare at the mountains. "Sorry, I did not mean to imply that I'm glad you lost…"

"It's all right, you mean well." Itsuki gave a half smile. "I can't blame you for the joy of freeing yourself from the judgements of Hekison."

"Do you still dream of them, the burned village?" Noboru questioned carefully. "I did not wish to stay there… over the winter…"

Itsuki could feel the sincerity in Noboru's voice and could not help but forgive him. There had always been an air of tension left between the two friends since the storm-ridden night that Noboru and Itsuki had quarreled. The argument about staying in Itsuki's former home had almost ended in a deadly altercation.

"The dreams change, but my anxiety is still present while I sleep. I was too late."

"Blaming yourself for the tragedy is a natural thought," Noboru responded. "But you were hunting a mile out, providing for your family. Your village was closest to the border, it was the first to fall and the beginning of Nobunaga's treachery. No man can see the future. I mourn for them, I do, but your wife and child walk outside mortality. They say one who dreams of the dead will soon walk with them."

"I dream of them because they have need to be avenged. Only then will my sleep have peace."

Noboru gave Itsuki a nod. "For your sake I truly hope you are right, I will see it through with you."

"I have no delusions of grandeur," Itsuki admitted. "This will be a difficult assassination to pull off. I doubt we will have a chance of performing the task unnoticed."

"Nobunaga is no fool," Noboru grunted in his low raspy voice. "He will have an honor guard by him at all times. We will need all four of us at our best to be successful."

"Yes... If only we had more time to train the brothers. You can see flaws in their skills due to a condensed training. They have much to learn."

"Were we any different? We were forced to adapt or die, thanks to Yamato and his misplaced justice. Ha, I remember every time we would come back from a mission alive; Yamato would have a sour look on his face."

"Well, in any case, we haven't told them the truth about the hand seals. You know they can never master them without the final step."

Noboru for once seemed troubled. "Yes... Tsubasa is too eager to brush with death, he should be well prepared before given this knowledge. The best we can do is continue to train till the test."

215

Itsuki nodded. "It was not so long ago that you had problems with diving headfirst into battle… you still do."

Noboru laughed. "True, true, but you know I do not rush in without a plan anymore. Kazuki beat that out of me years past."

"That he did," Itsuki agreed. "Tsubasa will need that lesson as well, unlike Kaito. He is too hesitant to deal death… he is no killer. I feel there is a special place in hell for us, leading such a boy to the evils we commit."

"What choice did we ever have, born into an age of war and into a society that trades information and lives for money. We were not so lucky to be born into an era where such choices of peace were an option."

"I suppose," Itsuki shrugged. "But who are we to teach such lessons? Matters of such debate were to be left to the elders of the village."

"The elders of the village were pawns of Yamato. We do the best we can. As we always have."

Itsuki always appreciated the optimism of Noboru, a trait that had lifted the hearts of his comrades many a time. "That we can do," Itsuki sighed. "Well I suppose we had more time with them than anticipated. They show promise, but I do not wish to add the Yukimura's deaths on my conscience. Not to mention, the legacy of these blades could fall into unworthy hands if we fail."

"With a little luck, all will come together," Noboru stated optimistically. "We have trained the brothers well; we will continue to do so. We must accustom ourselves to these new weapons as best we can."

The shinobi made their descent to the lower valley toward Kyoto. Kaito made good use of the map that was found on one of the samurai they had killed. He used the map to orienteer the group through several shortcuts and used the landmarks to gauge their position in reference to Kyoto. Although Itsuki and Noboru were much more experienced, the older shinobi used every opportunity to hone the skills of the Yukimura brothers. Throughout their travels they would continue teaching stealth, orienteering, meteorology, espionage, military strategy, and disguises.

When the shinobi made camp, they practiced with their new blades, even Noboru and Itsuki were not fully aware of the potential of their new weapons. When sparring, they used wood practice swords to avoid any real injury. Every night they would train against each other, Noboru against Tsubasa, and Kaito against Itsuki.

Noboru would try to beat the lessons into Tsubasa's thick skull to show the flaws in his speedy fighting style. Several times Noboru would give a lump on the side of Tsubasa's head, each time saying, "Dead." Tsubasa would try again and get another bruise from Noboru's practice stick. "Dead again," Noboru would repeat.

"You are fast, Tsubasa, but you give away your movements with your frustration," Noboru would state. "Emotions can be powerful, but they can also be used as a map of your intention."

Itsuki would be pushing Kaito into a corner with every blow, being aggressive as possible. Kaito would parry each blow but when an opportunity would present itself, he would keep on the defense, being conservative with every stroke. Eventually Itsuki would kick him in the chest and Kaito would be on his back.

"Dead," Itsuki would state. "Your defense is adequate, Kaito, but sometimes you need to be on the offense to win."

On the second day of the descent, finding a regularly used

clearing, they made camp early, just on the outskirts of Kyoto. Noboru and Itsuki had decided to train with each other, an event that had not been seen since before the times of the siege of Hekison. The Yukimura brothers took special interest and watched to see who would win. Noboru, as expected of his fighting style, came whirling at Itsuki with his wood training sword, his hair flowing like wildfire. Despite Noboru's intimidation, Itsuki stood his ground still as stone, letting Noboru's fiery blows bounce off his own sword. The Yukimura brothers watched with fixed eyes at each parry and blow, waiting for one to get the upper hand. At one point of the sparring practice, Itsuki kicked Noboru's legs out from under him, but Noboru countered by putting a hand down on the ground, twirling his body and kicking out Itsuki's legs in turn. Itsuki countered with a back handspring, both shinobi ended in a defensive stance looking at each other, swords in hand.

Itsuki's hard stare turned into a smile. "That's a new one Noboru, I thought I had you."

"Someone has to keep you on your toes."

"Do you always end in a standoff?" Kaito questioned.

Noboru glanced over at Kaito coming out of the fog of his bout with Itsuki. "Sometimes. We have fought with each other too much. We can read each other's moves like a book. Sometimes I best him, sometimes him me."

Itsuki sat down by the fire. "It is good to know your comrade's strengths and weaknesses so you can accommodate them in a fight. I'm sure the two of you know we have a distinct advantage with these blades, but you two must be ready to help each other when a superior foe is presented."

"That also goes for your hand seal training, your natural

abilities can be used to step in where your comrade may lack that strength." Noboru looked at Tsubasa. "Your training of Retsu, the mastery of time, will be complemented by Kaito's training of Kai, the sensing of danger."

"An offensive and defensive hand seal combination," Kaito stated, comprehending the lesson before it was taught.

"Your intuitive mind is a testimony to why Kai is the first hand seal we set you on," Itsuki nodded.

"Why not train us in both?" Tsubasa questioned. "The winter months we had nothing but time."

Itsuki shook his head. "Mastering one hand seal is hard enough. Learning two at one time would create a battle in your mind. You would be trying to command your mind to enhance separate emotional states of your life. You must fully master one before you even consider taking on another. There is no quick way to learning hand seals."

"You two can barely remember the names of them all," Noboru scoffed in disapproval. "List them if you can."

Kaito spoke, eager to impress. "Rin for strength, Pyō for energy, Tō for harmony, Sha for healing, Kai for intuition, Jin for awareness, Retsu for time, Zai for elemental control, and…" Kaito trailed off.

"Zen for enlightenment," Itsuki finished. "Which we all lack."

Tsubasa looked off down the valley impatient as usual. The adolescent had been a prodigy of the physical aspects of ninjutsu. Since he was a child, all training had come easily to him. Where other boys his age would struggle with ninjutsu training, Tsubasa would quickly excel. Because the physical aspects of Tsubasa's training came so quickly, he would often neglect the more conceptual lessons that took more time. A bad habit that still lingered.

"It is only recently that Itsuki and I took on training in another hand seal," Noboru stated. "And the task is still proving difficult."

"Do you plan on learning all of them?" Kaito questioned.

Tsubasa gave his brother a nudge. "Remember, they said no man has ever mastered them all, even our father only learned three in his lifetime."

"In any case, I hope the two of you have tried to practice your hand seals when the opportunity presented itself," Itsuki spoke.

The Yukimura brothers nodded. Since the monastery, and frequently during the stay in Itsuki's old village, they had tried to mimic intense emotional states and merge them to their perspective hand seals by focused repetition. Every time Tsubasa would spar or battle, he would take mental note of the battle rage he would feel and the slowing of time. Although Tsubasa was not one for literary learning, training by doing was a task in which he excelled.

Kaito would try to calm his mind to be aware of all surroundings. He would study people, animals, and nature. He would attempt to enter a heightened state of sense, focusing on sights, sounds, and smells to be aware of all before others.

"Good," Itsuki nodded. "We will only be four against many when we go after Nobunaga. Even though we will do so in secrecy, we must not have any of us making novice mistakes. Keep at your sword play and especially your agility for stealth."

"One man can be easy to kill," Noboru stated. "But even more so when he does not know you're coming. The blades we received are superior weapons, but we must not forget that we are shinobi, our strength comes from ninjutsu."

Noboru grabbed his pack and pulled out a curious looking blue flower, examining it to see that the plant was still intact.

"Flowers for your hair?" Tsubasa jested.

Noboru ignored the joke. "A flower that grows only in the mountain ranges of Iga. It has many purposes in herb lore. I know of an herb shop owner who pays much for such flowers, I will need supplies for my powders."

"Powders for what?" Kaito questioned.

Noboru opened his mouth as if to answer the boy, but his eyes glared at the trail and became alert. It did not take long for the others to take notice, but they could see in the distance a six-man squad bearing the Nobunaga crest and coming up the mountain. Instinctively they all hid off the trail in the forest.

"I do not believe they saw us," Noboru stated.

Itsuki nodded in consideration. "We could always…"

"Ambush them," Tsubasa grinned eagerly, "let us set a trap."

19

Kyoto

-Yamashiro Province, Kyoto City-

Rin Kurosawa entered the city of Kyoto with Hideyoshi's Hashiba's caravan. Kyoto had been the Capital city of Japan and the central power of the Shogunate prior to the Ōnin war; Kyoto was still considered the Capital even though the country was in a state of civil war. The city was situated some miles southwest of Lake Biwa, not far from the ever-watchful eye of Nobunaga's Azuchi Castle. A large wall surrounded the city and inside the perimeter the streets were planned in a rough grid system with the river Kamo running north to south. The exterior wall showed the past scars of sieges and conquests. Two giant wood doors creaked open as the gatekeepers pulled them open with large, twined ropes.

Upon entering, the noise of everyday city life surrounded Hideyoshi's caravan. Local peasants bowed as they saw the banners of Hashiba, the general of Nobunaga trotting into the city proudly. Kyoto gave great praise to Hideyoshi not only for his status but also for his personal investment in the city. In the past, Nobunaga Oda had charged Hideyoshi with the care of the city. Hideyoshi had rebuilt roads and walls to better protect the city from siege while improving daily commerce. Not to mention his wife, Nene, was held in great favor by nobles and common citizens alike. Their welcome was as if they had just returned from winning a war.

Always a spectacle, thought Rin. *This man prances around more than a geisha.*

Rin trotted her black horse just behind Nene and Hideyoshi but left a great enough distance that it did not seem a mere servant was interrupting Hideyoshi's triumphant entrance.

"Pardon your leave, masters, but I have business within the city. If I am to serve you effectively, I must gather a few items."

"Make sure you check in, my dear," Nene chimed in. "I will want to know the state of Kyoto and how it is doing. Any gossip that will help me in the courts will be expected as usual."

"Yes, Lady Hashiba," Rin nodded.

Hideyoshi was smiling to the people bowing as he passed as if not listening. "You're not trying to avoid the meeting with Chuugo are you? Ha, you will surely be missed by him."

Rin couldn't help but cringe. "I'd be lying if I said I would miss the fat slob, but if my lord requires—"

"That will not be necessary, my dear," Hideyoshi said. "I shouldn't be needing your skills, and you'd only distract Chuugo. I need him focused on the conversation. You may go but take this token with you. When you return the guards will not let you into the noble quarters without it."

Hideyoshi flipped her a small coin containing the Hashiba crest. Rin caught the coin in the air and nodded at Hideyoshi. She then dismounted the horse and gave the reins to one of the foot soldiers. As usual, Rin did not want to be noticed and walked away, blending into the crowd while leaving the caravan.

Kyoto was a typical castle town of Japan but on a much larger scale. An overhead view would show hundreds of streets outlined by thousands of tiled roofs. Near the center of the city was the royal palace and a castle that was manned by the local governor loyal to Nobunaga. In peaceful times Kyoto had been the center rule of the Shogunate supported by the royalty of Japan, but that had been in the days before the Ōnin war that started the long civil unrest.

Outside the governor's castle the housing consisted of royalty and government buildings; further out was the crime infested sections and slums. The city was dotted with many Buddhist shrines, a growing religion that was starting to trump the pure Shinto shrines that remained in the city. At the outskirts was the residence of peasants and the merchant trading streets; this is where Rin Kurosawa intended to dwell for her stay.

Rin walked the streets until she found a familiar inn. The place was nothing of prominence; just a plain wooden building that accommodated a traveling middle class citizen. Upon entering, the innkeeper looked up in surprise to see a beautiful woman occupying his doorway. The innkeeper had large round eyes with a short stature and a bald head that could reflect light better than a mirror.

The man looked up from his chair. "Oh, what is a young lady like you doing in my humble inn? How may I help you?"

Rin played the maid with a naive girl's voice. "Yes, my husband told me to get an inn for us, he was granted a small respite from war. I would like to prepare the bedroom for him. He would appreciate not letting anyone know that I am here. I am a lone woman in Kyoto until his return."

Rin slipped the man a few copper coins and one silver coin for the man's discretion while giving a flirtatious smile. The fat man blushed as Rin's hand lingered on his as she gave him the coins. "Do not worry, young lady. I, Hiroshi, will keep you safe in my inn. If there is anything that you should need, I will serve." "Just your discretion, kind sir," Rin responded. "And a room with a window away from the main street. I sleep better in silence."

The man nodded. "Right this way, young lady."

The man took her up the stairs and Rin held onto his arm as they walked up as if needing him for support. The first door on the right slid open to show her a humble room with a floor mat, closet, small desk, and a bowl of clean water.

Rin nodded in approval. "This will do nicely, sir. My husband will be glad to hear that a strong man took it upon himself to watch over me in his absence. I will make sure he rewards you."

The innkeeper beamed with pride. "Not a soul will bother you under my watch. I could even keep you company until your husband comes back."

"Ah... thank you, but I am tired from travel, sir, and I must rest." Rin smiled and slid the door shut.

Rin's smile faded from her face instantly at the absence of the innkeeper. She reverted to her old self and slung her travel pack upon the floor. She took out a pair of worn peasant clothes and dressed into them quickly. She washed what makeup she had on her face and then opened the window to the city. As requested, the window faced an alleyway. With usual expert agility, she climbed down to the city streets below.

The time was midafternoon, and the streets were alive with merchants and shoppers. She walked by a hundred booths with each merchant yelling about their products. "Fish for sale, clothes to make you shine, beads for chants," all the merchants yelled. As she walked by one booth, she stole a conical straw hat as the merchant argued with a customer over his goods. When she was out of eyesight, she put on the hat to help conceal her face and hair.

Rin ignored all the pestering vendors and made her way to the outskirts of the city slums. There were few people on the street and the few present were most likely thieves, smugglers, or prostitutes. Rin passed an open walled bar where people were drinking, gambling, playing the game go, or a combination of all. One man sitting by the outskirts of the bar showed signs of a sickness which locals called the Fading, he was leaning back and forth rubbing his bald head. The man mumbled words to himself drifting between whispers and yells as Rin walked by with her head held low. The street she had turned on was shadowed by the tall buildings and narrow alleyways. A single sign hung above a door which read, "Herb Shop." She pushed open the door to find a store that one could barely walk through.

The herb shop appeared more like a cluttered home than a store. From the ceiling hung rare oddities of items both domestic and far off foreign lands. Plants, herbs, and spices were lazily shelved on surrounding wooden cabinets. In the back of the shop was a service desk that seemed to be abandoned.

"Hello? Osamu?" Rin questioned, peering her head around to see if anyone was there.

Like a rabbit popping from a hole, an old man's head bolted up from behind the counter. The man was bald except for the a few white hairs that clung to the old man's dome, stubbornly refusing to die. He was also very short and had but a few teeth due to his age. Rin became perplexed as she saw the man had two brass rings strapped around his face that contained glass circles magnifying the size of his eyes.

Rin laughed. "What are those?"

"They are called spectacles," the old man responded. "I bought them from a foreigner of the far west. A man of Portugal or something or other, one of the white barbarian traders, smelled horrible. Anyway, they help you to see better. Who are you?"

"If you could see, you would know who I am."

Osamu took off the odd brass rings and squinted his eyes. "Ahh, Rin, good to see you again. What will it be this time, dragon tears to make your face stay young forever?" Osamu grabbed a bottle off his shelf. "Or, ahh, I know. This liquid I acquired from a man that traveled to the top of Mount Fuji..."

"Osamu."

"He said he took the liquid from a spring at the top of the mountain in a full moon," the old man continued.

"Osamu," Rin stated again impatiently.

"The curative properties have to be unbelievable."

"Osamu!"

"Well you don't have to yell, just say my name normally and..." the old man drifted off as he started to stare at Rin's chest.

"Hey, old man, up here, I need you to focus," Rin said, snapping her fingers.

"Yes, yes." The old man shook his head back into reality. "But are you sure you don't want a potion?"

"I don't need any of your wild potions. I need this." Rin slid a slip of paper with a list of items.

Osamu took the list and peered at the entries as he walked the rows of his shop looking at items. "Hmm, yes, yes, many of these

I have here, but this item… this blue flower of Iga, this will be a hard one to acquire. One might say these items could be used for mischief."

"Maybe yes, maybe no, maybe none of your business," Rin stated curtly.

"Yes well, in any case, I used to get this flower from a man who lived in those parts. But since Nobunaga's siege on Iga started, I have not seen him."

"So I've heard," Rin stated. "Can you get it?"

"Hmmm, the blue flower. I may have to go through one of my competitors to get this… this means it will cost more… or you can pay in other ways." Osamu grinned and squeezed Rin's backside as he made his way back to the counter.

"Watch it, you perverted little goblin." Rin whirled around looking down and pointed at the grinning short old man.

"Fine, fine," Osamu stated as he put his hands up in defense. "The usual method will do."

Rin slammed a couple of gold coins on the counter.

"This is why I like you, Rin," Osamu said as he gummed on the coin to see if it was real. "You pay up front. Hmm, no promises but I believe a week or two's time I can get the blue flower. How long is your stay in Kyoto?"

"I should be here longer than that. I will come back in a week to make sure you're not using my money on cheap women and even cheaper liquor at the bar," Rin spoke as she gathered her pack and started to walk for the door.

The old man became serious, and his gaze was hard as stone. "I would never buy cheap liquor."

"And cheap women?" Rin jested while making a dramatic pause before exiting.

"We can't all be perfect. Why leave? I have more potions that you would be interested in, eternal beauty. We could discuss your travels over sake, comfort an old weary man, maybe something more?"

Rin shut the door as the herb shop owner was still speaking. Rin donned her newly stolen conical hat once again and started to make the trek out of the slums. She walked until she came upon a popular bar, a place she had visited many times before. The bar was of dark wood and polished floors made smooth from years of use. The air was filled with liquor and fresh cooking. Nobody noticed as she entered, the place was crowded and boisterous. Soldiers told stories of battles as women pretended to sound interested, others talked of trade and how the wars were affecting the economy. Rin sat in a small corner and ordered a meal with sake. A food-stained waiter promptly came with a bowl of rice, vegetables, and chicken. The waiter finalized the meal with an unstopped, small clay bottle of sake. Rin said no words but nodded in satisfaction. Rin began to eat her meal while listening for any gossip within the bar that would come of use to her. Just as Rin thought she would hear nothing of value, other than the usual gossip of war, she caught the conversation of two men.

A man with a large mustache and bald head spoke as he drank his sake. "Strange dealings I have heard around Mount Kurama."

"In times of war there are always strange dealings," the fat merchant replied that stunk of sweat and sake.

"Not like this," started the bald one, leaning closer. "Rumors... yōkai of old have returned."

The fat merchant only gave out an unbelieving laugh. "You have always been gullible; stories of yōkai are to make sure children behave."

"It's true. I heard it from an associate of mine, he saw it with his own eyes."

The fat merchant seemed skeptical but somewhat interested in an eyewitness account. "I didn't know you associated with half blind merchants but go on. Tell the tale."

The bald merchant started despite the received skepticism and recounted the tale in a low tone. "My friend was taking the mountain pass through the base of Mount Kurama, heading north. A trading errand, spices and such, so there was not much to carry. A shrewd man, always has been. He said he knew better than to go near the higher peaks of Mount Kurama, there have always been strange rumors of creatures of other realms living in such places."

The fat merchant nodded in agreement. "I have heard of Shinto shrines being started by priests, some even rumored to be high in the mountains, but they have repeatedly become abandoned."

"Anyway, it was near dusk, and my friend came to a clearing to set camp before nightfall. A spot he had used many times, but then…" The bald merchant looked around for eavesdroppers but failed to notice Rin behind him with her back turned acting as if eating. "He heard screams just before the camp. He told me that he mustered the courage to poke his head around the bend. He found six soldiers bearing the Nobunaga seal, dead. One was being dragged into the forest while clawing at the dirt, pleading for his life."

"What? Dead?" the fat merchant said out loud.

"Shh! Quiet now. We had nothing to do with it, but no reason to give soldiers here reason to question us. Nobunaga's troops would skin a child if they suspected them to be a traitor. Anyway, my friend was obviously struck with fear. The only reason he lingered was his legs were frozen with terror. The deaths had been brutal, nothing a man would have done. He found one body strung upside-down, hanging from a tree branch without a head. The other bodies had all been killed in peculiar fashion, ways in which men do not kill. That is when he saw..."

"Saw what?" the fat merchant questioned eagerly for the first time.

"Shadowed figures where the last soldier had been dragged into the forest, too hidden to distinguish," the bald man nervously spoke. "The figures had long black claws, yōkai of old. Perhaps sent to punish these lands for the blood we have been spilling for generations."

The fat merchant shifted nervously. "So, what of your friend?"

"He froze in terror, thinking he was next, only to see the shadowy figures disappear into the forest. Only then did his legs give haste. He ran back to Kyoto. When I saw him, his face was white with fear. I questioned him as to why he had not departed. It is then he recounted this dark tale."

"These are troubled times," the fat merchant stated seriously. "War, death, tales of yōkai, this all brings bad trade for us."

"Indeed," the bald man said. "Let us speak of business and not demons."

Rin thought about the tale she had just heard, it was certainly out of the norm, even for her. In a strange way it reminded Rin of stories she had heard in her childhood, but that felt like a lifetime ago. In any case, mysterious creatures killing troops bearing the Nobunaga seal was something to take note of, especially so close to Kyoto.

Rin traveled back to the inn and entered the side alleyway.

Instead of climbing back into her room she climbed to the top of the roof. She sat down and unstopped her unfinished clay bottle of sake and surveyed the city. From the top of the inn the city of Kyoto looked like a thousand little islands of tiled roofs. Toward the center of the city the larger castles and imperial palace could be seen towering over the whole city. In the distance the sun was setting on the mountains, giving the sky a large burst of orange and red colors mixing with the streaming clouds. Rin sat, contemplating the strange tales she had heard, and her thoughts wandered to her childhood; Rin wondered if she would see anyone from her home ever again.

20

The Snow Monkey
-Yamashiro Province, Kyoto City-

Hideyoshi Hashiba's caravan had passed through the normal residence section of Kyoto; he now came to the front of the inner gate separating the peasants from the nobility. A member of the imperial court of Kyoto had come in person to greet him and his wife. All formalities were given to the couple; the court official had greeted them with the heads of his household, giving every courtesy. After the long welcome, the official bowed low and gave the Hashibas leave to their quarters.

A servant in lavish robes bowed low. "Lord and Lady Hashiba, I'm to take you to your quarters, by your will."

Hideyoshi and Nene gave curt nods of approval and followed. At times it even surprised Hideyoshi the respect that he would receive from the courts. Hideyoshi had been born into a humble birth and started his military career as a simple foot soldier. Hideyoshi had climbed his way through the ranks eventually becoming a samurai through willpower, cunning, and savagery. Unlike many samurai who had been born into the privilege, Hideyoshi had proven himself worthy of the title and was given the honor by Nobunaga himself. Hideyoshi's humble beginnings gave the opportunity to be tempered through battle and the result was the creation of a brutal enemy. Other men would flaunt their family name for respect, Hideyoshi had earned respect through victory and skill. Nene on the other hand was born into the life Hideyoshi had earned. At times the difference showed, court etiquette and procedure were second nature to her. Hideyoshi wore the robes of nobility; Nene had the skin of nobility that could never be removed.

The architecture inside of the palace was masterfully crafted. The wood pillars beamed with a dark black sheen, but the floor mats and walls of the buildings were a sandy gold. Tapestries and rugs of religious history lined the hallways of the palace. The Hashibas followed the servant until they came to the last door down the hallway.

The servant slid the door open and bowed low. "If there is anything that you require, food, entertainment. In any case, a servant will be posted outside the door, you only need but ask."

Hideyoshi nodded. "Send for my servant, Kyou, I have need of him."

"And send for my other handmaiden, Haruna. Rin is currently out on errands," Nene prompted.

The servant bowed and scurried off.

The quarters given to the Hashibas had been the best that could be offered. The floor bedding consisted of white silk sheets and feather pillows. The ceiling had a cross beamed structure of black lacquered wood creating square tiles. Each square had a gold-colored inlay design of an intricate tree.

In the center of the room was a sunken hearth for warming tea and providing warmth to the room. A single clay sake bottle had already been placed with cups for pouring. Hideyoshi grabbed the clay sake bottle, took out the wood stopper, and poured a cup for his wife and then himself. No sooner had they toasted a knock came at the door.

"Enter," Hideyoshi barked.

Kyou had slid open the door, quickly followed by Haruna; they both gave a small bow. Kyou was a man of small stature and a rat face with two teeth sticking out. The gods had not given him the physique of a warrior, so Kyou had learned from an early age to focus his efforts on reading scrolls of business and history. A man of his talents had not gone unnoticed, and he soon became Hideyoshi's unofficial secretary.

Haruna was your typical handmaiden: quiet, obedient, and attentive to her lady's needs. She dressed in a kimono of her status, but never near the quality of whom she served. She quickly went to Nene's side to see what her lady's needs were for preparing to attend the courts.

"Lord, you summoned me?" squeaked Kyou.

"Yes. What news of Chuugo?"

"Chuugo has agreed to meet and has invited you to his own bathhouse. The Snow Monkey."

Hideyoshi scowled. "Snow Monkey?"

"Yes, sir," Kyou stated, fearing his master took the response as an ill joke.

"That man presumes too much," Hideyoshi stated. "One does not summon me like some dog, especially to a place as that."

Kyou diverted his eyes as if Hideyoshi's wrath could burn him. "Chuugo said that the noble residence has eyes and ears. Business with a man of your stature should be done in discretion, not to draw the notice of unwanted eyes."

Hideyoshi stared at Kyou. "Very well, summon Kenji. I will not be going into Chuugo's den alone."

"May I remind you, dear," Nene chimed in, "that your presence will be required at dinner tonight. Do not have too much fun at Chuugo's."

"The Emperor is only a ceremonial figurehead, even more so when Nobunaga disbanded the Shogunate without consulting. Sometimes I wonder why we bother; the daimyōs are who truly rule Japan."

"When this civil war finally comes to an end, the power will return to the Capital. You will ensure our power with the daimyōs; I will ensure our power with the royal family." Nene spoke as if she could see into the future.

"Right as always. I will see you tonight." *Formalities with nobles to keep your spoils of war, but men's lives are what pay for them,* thought Hideyoshi.

Playing the game of flattery with the imperial court was necessary. In times before the civil war, the shōgun would rule in Kyoto alongside the imperial family as the military ruler. Hideyoshi put on a jacket still befitting of his status but to the common citizen he would only be recognized as a noble. His goal was not to draw attention to himself; Kyoto was filled with spies and Hideyoshi was a known general.

Kenji came in hastily with his katanas at his waist. "Sir, I take it you'll be needing a guard if you are meeting with Chuugo."

Hideyoshi nodded. "Yes, but not a battalion, I need protection with no attention."

Kenji smiled. "I thought you might say that. I have taken the liberty of using two of my best men to trail us, but with distance. Chuugo has never betrayed you, but Chuugo—"

"Does what's best for Chuugo," Hideyoshi interrupted. "That's why I shouldn't have to fear him as long as I'm giving him the best deal. But your men are welcome as long as they do not go noticed." *Kenji has a one-track mind, but he is good at what he does,* Hideyoshi thought.

Kenji nodded and then followed his master closely as they walked through the palace. Guards stood at attention as Hideyoshi exited. Hideyoshi made a point to go through one of the auxiliary exits of the castle grounds where his absence would go less expected. As they left the huge doorway of the castle grounds, Hideyoshi and Kenji made their way through the noble's quarters until they came to the bathhouse called The Snow Monkey.

Hideyoshi looked up at the sign and shook his head. "Only Chuugo would name a business after a monkey."

The bathhouse of The Snow Monkey may have had an odd name, but it did not lack in comfort. Although called a bathhouse, the business was a place where men of means could drink, do business, gamble, regale geishas, or soak in the hot springs. As Kenji and Hideyoshi entered, a man in a blue kimono with beady eyes bowed before them.

"Master Chuugo has been expecting you, this way if you please."

"More like he knew we were on our way," Kenji muttered under his breath.

The three men passed by the gambling tables where men played their money at games of chance. Nobody noticed Hideyoshi as he made his way through the den of Chuugo. In the back he was utterly invisible passing the private rooms of geishas entertaining groups of nobles. As Hideyoshi walked through the hallway, he saw one geisha playing a stringed instrument called a shamisen while the other danced to the slow plucked melody. At the very end of the bathhouse, a stairway led up to Chuugo's private quarters.

The man with the beady eyes stopped and bowed. "Master Chuugo awaits inside."

Hideyoshi gestured Kenji to wait outside the door and entered the room. The room was very large and was attached to an outdoor balcony that overlooked the springs of the bathhouse. In the center was a large table and small sunken hearth for tea. At the large table sat a very large, very plump man eating a meal that could feed four people. Chuugo Matsushita had a very large head even for a man of his stature; his head was bald all except for a small topknot at the crown. Hiding his dark brown eyes were two square eyebrows that moved up and down. His eyes moved rapidly, constantly scanning his food and whereabouts. Chuugo had developed a nervous tick from his excessive paranoia that affected his speech.

Chuugo's belly hugged the table as he hunched over to pick at the fish he was currently attacking with his chopsticks. He then slurped down the meat as he looked up at Hideyoshi. "Ahh, Daimyō Hashiba, good of you to come, huh. It has been a while since I have seen you last, once a common soldier now a great general for Nobunaga, huh."

Hideyoshi looked at Chuugo and hid his disgust as he came to sit at the opposite side of the square table. "We have business, yes. This could have been done at a barracks."

Chuugo smiled mischievously. "Huh, you'd like that wouldn't you. Huh, all those eyes and ears to watch me. Bad for business, huh. I keep all my clients in the dark, nobody knows who I do business with."

238

"So you can give arms to their enemies," Hideyoshi stated coldly.

"Maybe, maybe not, huh. My reasons are my own. War is good for business."

"So, you will have no problems supplying me some extra mercenaries," Hideyoshi retorted.

"Huh, why should I help a general of Nobunaga. If Nobunaga succeeds in conquering Japan, I will be out of business," Chuugo spoke as he wolfed down some rice.

"You mean unite Japan under one rule. You must know at this point that Nobunaga has already established his dominance on the majority of this land. With or without your help, Japan will be under one rule. I am giving you a chance to help the winning side." Hideyoshi put down a gold coin. "Such generosity of your services would not go unnoticed."

Chuugo's eyes widened at the gold piece, and he licked the grease off his fingers. Chuugo was a man whose lust for gold was as big as his appetite for food. "Huh, well, in any case, I suppose I cannot pass up a business opportunity."

Hideyoshi smiled. "Well, I need seasoned men, those who can take orders well."

Chuugo nervously shifted his weight, scooting his fat body awkwardly as he sat cross-legged. "Huh, yes you need men, men for killing. I have men and weapons to give but they cost money, huh. Eat, Hideyoshi. You make me nervous. A man who does not eat is not relaxed, huh."

"You eat and are always nervous, Chuugo. I have money, but I want to know what I'm buying."

"Huh, big man now, you have money to buy lots of men I see. I am not like one of your fool daimyōs. The first time you came to me you were but a simple soldier needing more men for a mission. I know your true origins, Hideyoshi. You act like a noble, but they will never accept you as one of them, not truly, huh."

He wants to be the bigger man. "You may be right, Chuugo. A humble man like myself has need of your connections," Hideyoshi stated.

Chuugo smiled as if he had won an argument. "Huh, yes, I am right, Lord Hashiba. Men I can give, it just so happens that I have dealings with the mercenaries of the black fox. A group of 200 men, murderous cut throats that are notorious for their archery. And then I have the men of the six rising suns also, and don't forget—"

"I'll take all of them," Hideyoshi interrupted.

"Huh, all you say?" Chuugo's eyes widened under his thick brows. "What is your game, Hideyoshi? You don't need all my men to take on the Mōri clan. I know Nobunaga has supplied you with sufficient forces, huh."

"Yes, what of it?" Hideyoshi stated, annoyed that Chuugo was so well informed.

"Don't look surprised, Hideyoshi, huh. You deal in battles, information and war are my trades. I knew you'd be here just as I know you have two more guards in my bathhouse besides the one outside this door."

"Precautions, my dear friend."

Chuugo spoke with a muffle as he crammed down a huge piece of beef. "Precautions indeed, huh. So why do you need my men?"

Hideyoshi smiled. "What was the phrase you used. My reasons are my own, it's good for business."

Chuugo furrowed his brow. "Huh, war brings me business, but your business is war, Hideyoshi. Huh, the only reason you would need that many forces... You are planning something bigger afterward. Huh, no matter Hideyoshi. You bring me good business; I will make the arrangements if you have the coin." "Coin I have," Hideyoshi stated. "If you have the men, let us talk price."

"Then sake is needed!" Chuugo clapped his hands together and an old lady with gray hair came in holding a tray with cups and a clay sake bottle. The old lady's hands shook so much that you could hear the rattle of the cups. The wrinkles on her face seemed so thick that it was impossible to see her eyes. As she slowly shuffled her feet into the room, taking what seemed to be an eternity, Hideyoshi couldn't help but turn and look.

Geisha's downstairs and he has an old woman serving him? thought Hideyoshi.

Chuugo gave a nod of approval and for once wasn't shifting nervously. The old woman gave a large smile as she set down the tray and then exited the room, slowly shuffling her feet.

"Something to celebrate our business ventures, to the downfall of the Mōri clan, huh." Chuugo raised a cup to toast with Hideyoshi. They both drank down the sake and then Chuugo clapped again. "Some entertainment while we talk price." Shortly after, the same old woman from before came into the room shuffling her feet holding a tray with more food.

Chuugo rolled his fat body to get himself off the ground and yelled. "What are you doing coming back? Not you, go back to the kitchen!"

The old woman threw a rag at Chuugo, her hands waved in the air in defiance as if hearing the tantrum of a little child as she exited the room. Shortly after, two geishas came in with elaborate kimonos and shamisens.

Hideyoshi looked at Chuugo. "Who was that?"

"Who was who?"

"The old woman?"

Chuugo shifted nervously. "Huh, my mother of course. She's the only person I trust, huh."

21

The Blue Flower
-Yamashiro Province, Kyoto City-

The long stay in Kyoto had taken its toll on Rin, she had become utterly bored. Hideyoshi Hashiba had been preparing for his upcoming battle campaign and would be leaving on the morrow. He and Nene presented a few tasks for Rin, but nothing worthy of her skill as of yet. One day she had dealings with the fat arms dealer Chuugo; all the man did was try to get her out of her clothes and into a private dance room. Although the days had been at best dull, the city of Kyoto had new people pouring in every day to make the streets come alive.

Troops had been coming to rendezvous with Hideyoshi's main force. Every day Hideyoshi was organizing men, meeting with the captains, and preparing for his march upon the heart of the Mōri clan. With Hideyoshi's recruitments, there had been a flow of mercenaries and unsavory characters alike. There had already been several murders in the city and fights in the bars had become more frequent. Even Rin had kept her guard up in the slums of the city. She was a capable woman, but even a large group of men looking for some entertainment could pose trouble.

Rin had stayed at the inn she had chosen the first day she entered Kyoto. Nene had insisted Rin come to the castle from time to time to report on rumors and to perform tasks that required a certain discretion, but Rin would leave as soon as possible. Rin would always have something worthwhile to give Nene to ensure her freedom outside the castle. Rin enjoyed the perks of spying for the Hashibas, but she relished her time outside the courts.

Rin looked out from her second story window upon the city of Kyoto. The sun hung midway down the sky and the streets were bustling as usual. The innkeeper had been infatuated with her since the day she arrived. Rin's boredom got the best of her and she decided to check if Osamu, the herb shopkeeper, had the supplies she ordered a few weeks past. Rin went to her travel pack and clothed herself with a simple kimono and conical straw hat. She stepped out from her window and climbed down into the alleyway below with the agility of a spider. When she landed, she put her sandals on her feet and assumed the role of a peasant out on morning errands.

She made her way to Osamu's shop on the outskirts of the merchant slums. Rin kept a dagger close, hidden in her robe. The influx of soldiers had made some streets dangerous even in midday; not to mention the stink that had accompanied the slums with the overpopulation. Rin eventually came to the simple store with the sign saying, "Herb Shop" above the door. She moved her hand to slide the door open but stopped short with curiosity when she heard the arguing of two men inside. She quickly walked to the side of the building and found a small window eight feet from the ground. Rin nimbly climbed up to the window to peer in, tensing her wrist muscles to support herself so she could see what the commotion was about. Inside the herb shop, Osamu argued with a rugged longhaired man over some supplies at the counter.

"Your goods are rare, but you act as if they are the jewels of Izanagi's spear." Osamu glared in defiance.

"How long have we done business? I haven't changed a thing, old man. You've lost your wits just as you have almost all your teeth," the rugged man grunted back.

That had only made Osamu stiffen up more. "Times change, supply and demand. Your supplies are rare but the powders you want have gone up in price, its simple business."

Rin smiled at the window. *The old man loses all business sense around a busty young woman, but the second he deals with a gruff looking man he's as shrewd as ever.*

"If you believe that you can get my goods from someone else, then maybe I'll take my business elsewhere." The man started packing the goods into his sack.

Osamu tried to hold his bluff till the last moment but finally gave in. "Fine, I will make a deal for the flowers and the roots, but the others I have no use for. Give me the rest and I can get you the powders."

"Get the powders and I'll give you my goods," the man haggled.

"The flowers for down payment, the powders I can have ready in four days, then you give me the rest." Osamu stared at the man grim faced, the few white hairs on the back of his head seemed to stand up in defiance.

"If you try to swindle me, old man, I will knock out what few remaining teeth dangle from your gums. And do not try to sell me those male endowment potions that you gave me last time," the man rebuked.

Osamu took the flowers. "I'll have you know that my potions are a work of perfection. Just because you don't know how to use your manhood properly is no fault of mine."

The rugged longhaired man seemed to be tired of arguing. "Fine, old man, the powders on the fourth day, no later." The man pointed at Osamu as he would a child. He then gathered his things and headed for the door.

As the man exited the shop, Rin silently dropped to the floor of the alleyway. She poked her head around the corner to see the man prodding off in the opposite direction cursing under his breath about an old man and how his tooth was probably the size of his manhood. After the man had turned down the alley, Rin walked into the herb shop.

Osamu sat behind the counter with a glum look on his face as if he had just been robbed, but his expression changed as he looked up at Rin. "Ahh, Rin. You do these old eyes of mine good. You could do me better by giving me a kiss."

"I'd sooner kiss a toad," Rin quipped back.

"Ah, toads I have here, one's oils that are known to grow the chest of a woman two full sizes. It would help you find a noble husband; you are so gamey... but still so beautiful my dear."

"Enough with the flattery. Do you have it?" Rin questioned.

"Yes... actually your timing could not be more perfect, the blue flower of the Iga mountains just came in, the trader just left a moment ago," Osamu stated, wondering a little on the timing of Rin.

"The man just now?" Rin stated, sounding disinterested.

"Yes, you are lucky. With the siege on the Iga Province, I almost did not expect he would be coming by anytime soon."

"Then how did he come by the flower?"

Osamu thought a moment. "Well I always supposed he was from the Iga Province, but he never would tell me. He comes in every year with local Iga herbs, roots, and plant life. Useful items, trades them for store credit, usually for some powders."

"Powders for what?" Rin spoke as she pretended to adjust her robe but conveniently bore more skin.

Osamu stared with the blank stare of a fish and the brain of an insect but somehow squeezed out words. "Powders? I could find out. I suppose he will be here in four days, same time as today."

Rin perused items in the store looking disinterested. "No matter, old man, I'll take the flowers. Here is the remaining payment." Rin pulled out a small bag of coins and threw it on the counter. The jingling of the coins seemed to wake Osamu from his hypnosis.

Osamu quickly opened the bag to peer at the coins. "Seems a little light my dear."

"Spare me your haggling, old man. I always pay in full," Rin scoffed.

"Very well." Osamu slid a couple of blue flowers bound together by twine. The flowers were exquisite, the blue was vibrant enough to give a faint glow in the shine of the light. The petals did not flower out but stayed tightly together with a dark violet center. The stem was dry but had a dark green that almost looked black.

Osamu looked at the flower. "A beautiful flower. What do you need it for if I may ask?"

Rin put the flower bundle into her pack and then looked around suspiciously to see if anyone was in the shop. She then leaned over the counter, gesturing Osamu close and whispered, "You really want to know?"

Osamu leaned forward quite curious and looked into her travel pack. "Well... Yes."

Straight-faced Rin looked at Osamu. "It's for a potion to increase one's manhood, I'll sell you a vial when I'm finished."

Osamu frowned and waved his hands in the air with disapproval. "Yes, yes, all secrets with you Miss... What is your family name?"

"Rin, old man, just Rin." She blew a kiss toward Osamu as she exited the herb shop. She then put on her conical straw hat to cover her features, leaving only her smile for Osamu to see.

Upon entering the street, she could see clouds overhead and the smell of rain in the distance. A light sprinkle came down as she traveled through the streets of Kyoto, she made sure to keep the contents of her pack covered. For once the busy streets of Kyoto seemed clean; the rain had begun to wash away the grime of soldiers, beggars, and merchants. Rin did not rush out of the rain as the other villagers did; she walked through it enjoying every step. The rain was clean; the cool drops gave her renewed vigor as she made it back to the inn. By the time she made it back, her kimono had become damp, but she still opted to climb through the window.

Upon first glance, Rin always seemed a humble female villager, but as she climbed the inn to the second story, a different being appeared. She had slender limbs as she climbed, but her skin showed the protrusion of hard lean muscles. Her agility also showed, as if she were born in the treetops and fostered by a forest spirit.

Rin entered her humble quarters, removed her wet kimono, and replaced it with a light silk one, the color of the blue sky. She then took out the blue flower bundle and put it on the low-rise table on the floor along with the other items she had previously bought from Osamu. She began crumbling ingredients together for the beginnings of a recipe. As she worked the materials her thoughts went to the woman who had taught her such skills, but that was another lifetime ago. That was when she had still been a child. Rin was only nineteen years old, but she had experienced more than others would in a whole life. Her face was innocent, but her eyes betrayed her. Rin had the same eyes as an old woman full of experience, wisdom, and loss.

The man that brought the flowers may know what happened, Rin thought. But now was not time for such thoughts, spying would have to come later. The potion Rin was making was the same that she had used at Azuchi Castle on the guard that barred the jail of Masanari Hattori, master of arms of Hekison. A sleeping potion that left the victim disoriented and with a short-term memory loss, much like a drunken stupor. Such potions were extra effective when blended with her well-practiced charm that she wielded as gracefully as calligraphy in her service to Hideyoshi Hashiba.

As her thoughts drifted toward Hideyoshi, she realized that today would be the last time that she would meet with him on the eve of his departure. When she finished making the ingredients, she poured everything into a pot with water and watched the ingredients blend as they heated over the sunken hearth. Rin then ate a simple lunch of water, rice cakes, and vegetables that she had saved.

Rin went to the closet and clothed herself in handmaiden clothes to meet with Hideyoshi. The kimono was a lavish white and pink with flowers on top. She braided her hair to hang from her head and then put in the small blade that appeared to be a comb at the top of her hair. Before leaving, she took the pot that had been steaming with the ingredients off the heat so that the liquid could settle. She wore the face of a naïve woman once again. As she made her way down the stairs, she could see the innkeeper eagerly awaiting her presence, it took everything Rin had to not frown.

"Ah, Rin," beamed the innkeeper. "Out for a walk, a woman such as yourself should not be out alone amongst such unsavory folk. Might I accompany you?"

"Oh, Hiroshi," she smiled. "I am to meet my husband so there is no need."

Hiroshi the innkeeper furrowed his brow. "But still with all the mercenaries that have come in, a lady should not walk alone... and I have yet to meet your husband. Will you two be coming back for your things?"

"Yes of course, although he is a busy man. Who knows what important matters he has to attend. I thank you for the offer." She scuttled out of the inn before the fat bald man could give a word of protest. After a while she made her way to the noble quarters. At the gate stood two guards that looked at each other, surprised and wondering why a noble's attendant was walking alone through Kyoto.

"What are you doing alone?" the guard spoke.

"Oh, I got lost shopping and was stuck in the rain. I had to wait until it had cleared. I was a little scared until I saw the gate."

"Lost?" the guard said suspiciously. "Pardon, but I must ask for a token pass. With all the unsavory lot about, security has gone up."

"Oh, of course." Rin fumbled through her small purse as if she could not find the pass. "Is this what you mean." She handed the guard the small gold coin. The guard's face showed a look of surprise to see the crest of Hashiba but gave an approving nod.

"My apologies," the guard said as he made way for Rin. "One cannot be too careful."

Rin smiled, putting a hand on the guard's soldier. "I will be sure to inform Lady Hashiba of your vigilance. She should know that the grounds are so well guarded."

Rin passed the gate and the stink of the common city faded. Unlike the common area of the city, the noble quarters had wide streets and gardens. She made her way to the familiar area of where the Hashibas had taken up residence. Only a few people took notice of her until she made her way through the palace of sandy gold and black lined pillars. A man stood sentry outside the door of Hideyoshi's quarters.

The guard stood firmly. "Master Hashiba is not to be disturbed."

"I suppose I should delay my lady's errands then?" Rin questioned innocently.

"No... no of course not." The guard reluctantly let Rin pass.

"Yes," an authoritative voice came from inside.

"It's me."

"Come."

Although Rin had seen Hideyoshi's quarters before, she was still impressed by the lavish gold and black décor. The ornate ceiling beams and crossing pattern with artistic tree design gave off a large presence. Hideyoshi was mulling over a table containing several maps and letters. The room had obviously become the central place of Hideyoshi's planning for the siege on Bitchū Province.

"Nene?" Rin questioned.

"With the governor's wife," Hideyoshi answered. "Do not worry. Haruna is taking care of my wife's needs."

"How goes the plan?"

Hideyoshi did not look up as he read a letter. "On schedule, I will be departing with the brunt of Nobunaga's army tomorrow at sunrise. Nene will be staying in Kyoto and so will you."

"Is that a good idea?"

"The Capital noble quarters are the safest place in Japan. Even if Kyoto is attacked, no one would dare defame themselves by attacking noble blood. Everything should go as planned."

"And how is the other plan?" Rin lowered her voice a bit.

Hideyoshi gestured her close to the table and lowered his voice. "I have spoken with Daimyō Mitsuhide Akechi, and when casually discussing war plans, I subtly presented him with an opportunity that he could not pass."

"Him?" Rin questioned. "The man hates you because you have continually beaten him over Nobunaga's favor. You trust him?"

"Absolutely not. Even if I'm wrong about his future actions, I merely steered his decisions and said nothing that could incriminate me. He truly hates Nobunaga, which is why his loyalty is now questionable. Do you forget? Nobunaga has continually insulted him and recently had his right-hand man committed to seppuku. Nobunaga was trying to appease too many parties and it cost him the loyalty of Mitsuhide. He was commanded to stay with our lord to protect Omi Province while I make the attack on the Mōri clan. In any case, my spies tell me that Mitsuhide is in agreement. When I arrive in Bitchū Province, I will ask for more reinforcements from Lord Nobunaga. I will say that in order to quell the Mōri clan, I will need more men. A reasonable request as before the winter Mitsuhide was taking on the Mōri clan from the south. I will explain that a two-siege force is necessary for success. Terumoto Mōri will have centralized his forces and I will say that his condensed forces were larger than anticipated."

"That will leave Nobunaga only with his honor guard. Would Nobunaga leave himself so exposed?" Rin pointed to the map.

Hideyoshi rubbed his balding head. "Nobunaga is no fool, but sending forces will show that he is still leader of this campaign. It will show Japan that without him I could not take Bitchū Province. If he wishes to unify Japan, he will not let this opportunity go. When Nobunaga dispatches Mitsuhide, he will not join me but stay behind outside Kyoto in waiting."

"And if your prediction is wrong and Mitsuhide has other plans?"

Hideyoshi smiled. "That is why I have you, my dear, and I have need of your skills once again. I have a man in Mitsuhide's army, if Mitsuhide deviates, word will be sent to you. You will stay in Kyoto, monitor communications here to ensure that he plays his part. If he fails or waivers from his task, he becomes a liability. Well... you know what to do. And you will send word, understand?"

Rin did not smile for once. "A man surrounded by an army, that will not be any easy task. And you've never divulged this much to me. Why are you telling me all this?"

Hideyoshi gave Rin a sideways glance from the maps and sighed. "I have accepted the fact that you would somehow find out anyway, like you always do, and if you ever did cross me, you would just be another forgotten corpse. But we both don't want that and if I tell you my details up front you will spend less time sneaking around looking for what I have not told you. Besides, you have not failed me yet, I have faith in you, my dear. Remember, if I rise, so do you."

Rin rolled her eyes. "Yes of course, but if I'm caught, that could affect my future employment with your wife."

"If all goes to plan, you'll need to do nothing. Consider this your last assignment until my return."

"Very well, Lord Hashiba, till you return from Bitchū Province."

"Till then, you must go now. I have captains coming. I would rather not explain why you were here without my wife." Hideyoshi gestured to the door.

"I'm already gone," Rin said as she walked toward the door.

Rin made her way out of the palace and through the noble quarters and back to the inn. She was grateful to find that Hiroshi, the fat innkeeper, was not at the front desk. She made her way upstairs and checked the liquid that had been settling in the pot. She approved of the color and then transferred the contents to a bottle and placed a stopper on the top. She looked at the window and could see that the sun was hanging low in the sky, orange rays filtered into her room. Night fell and Rin retired to her bed. As she fell asleep, her thoughts returned to the man at Osamu's herb shop. *How did he get the blue flowers?*

The next few days were hard for Rin to keep busy. Rin found that her curiosity about the rugged man at Osamu's shop had not been satisfied. When the day came, Rin decided to don her peasant clothes once again and venture out to Osamu's herb shop. She took her usual route out the window and to the merchant section of town. This time she went to a nearby restaurant and bought some food to eat. She dined on pieces of grilled fish with rice, vegetables, and a cup of sake. She ate them eagerly, for the day had given her hunger. When she had finished, she exited the restaurant and went to the alleyway across from Osamu's herb shop. She climbed the building and sat on the roof out of eyesight from the public. From her vantage point she waited, watching Osamu's herb shop for the mountainous longhaired man. Rin waited till sundown; her vigilance never wavered.

When her backside started to ache from sitting on tiles, she stood up and considered leaving. When she was about to gather her things, she saw the man walking down the alleyway toward Osamu's herb shop. Only this time two other young men were with him. She watched the three of them enter the herb shop, then she climbed down to the pitch-black alleyway below. Her knees bent deeply when her feet hit the floor, recovering from the landing. The alleyway was dark without vision. Rin was deciding whether to wait for the man to exit, or spy from the window. Suddenly, a powerful force emerged from the shadows, grabbing her hair, and pulling her back with the weight of a mountain. Rin was about to fight the unknown being when she felt the familiar shape of a kunai at her throat.

22

A Past Life

With one hand, Itsuki Hayashi had a death grip on Rin's hair and with the other hand, a kunai at her throat. The only thing he told her was, "You scream, you move, you die. We are going to wait for my friend to conclude his business. And then we will have a chat about why you have been spying on him."

It had been a week since the shinobi had arrived in Kyoto. Their group went completely unnoticed when they entered the city gates due to the influx of daily travelers being so large in numbers. The Yukimura brothers had been astonished by the size of the city; the largest community they had known was the town of Iga, the Capital was on another level. For a short time, the brothers had forgotten why they had come to the city; every street vendor, geisha, bar, and entertainer would catch their attention.

The shinobi had made humble accommodations at an inn with the pillaged money from the samurai they had killed. Four days past, Noboru had gone alone to Osamu's herb shop to trade for some powders meant for his kayakujutsu weaponry. He had returned to complete his trade but brought along the Yukimura brothers. On the day of his negotiations with Osamu, Noboru had noticed Rin in the window spying, which is why Itsuki had taken the precaution of trailing behind the group. While Itsuki had Rin by the hair, Noboru was conducting business with the three-toothed old man.

"You have my powders, old man?" Noboru grunted.

Osamu, the herb shop owner, scowled at Noboru. "Yes, yes, I'm a man of my word, do not doubt me. Powders for the rest of your herbs, that was the agreement. Who are these young men? Do you now need guards to conduct your business with me?"

Noboru produced a bag of herbs for trade and began inspecting the various goods he received. "Pay them no mind. Where is a scale? I need to know if the ratios will be sufficient."

Osamu pointed to a scale in the corner of the room surrounded by other oddities of the store. Noboru nodded and began to use the device to measure the weight of the powders. Osamu looked over to see Noboru distracted and then smiled through his few remaining teeth at the two adolescents. He saw Tsubasa and Kaito looking at various shelves and items, curious as ever. Tsubasa stopped on a small withered black plant and touched it with his finger.

"Careful with that," Osamu called out. "That's black fox bane."

Tsubasa looked back at the shopkeeper. "So?"

Osamu came down from his stool and walked around the counter, carrying a small stepping stool. The short man was no taller than five feet, partially due to his advanced age. Osamu stood up on the stool to grab the plant. "So, it is very rare, meant for making a powerful drink to increase one's strength."

Kaito looked at Tsubasa while shrugging his shoulders, squinting his eyes, and pursing his lips in skepticism. If it was disbelief of how the old man was still living or what he was saying, Tsubasa did not know.

"Ahh... I see your friend is unbelieving," Osamu scoffed.

"As he should be," Tsubasa quipped back. "Abilities come from training, not potions."

Osamu raised his brows and taunted. "Oh really?" Osamu put the plant on top of his counter and then stood on his stool to open a cabinet. After opening the cupboard, the old man moved around various bottles while mumbling to himself and then finally retrieved a painted black clay bottle.

Tsubasa stepped forward to the counter. "And this is your supposed miracle potion."

"Yes of course, but it would not work for a boy like you."

Kaito had come forth as well to watch his brother. "And why not?"

Osamu folded his arms. "I can tell that he is not strong enough, the potion only works for a man... not a mere boy."

Tsubasa gave a look of disapproval. "You think me a boy?"

Osamu acted uninterested. "You are a boy."

Kaito gave a loud mocking, "Ha."

"Give me that," Tsubasa declared. Annoyed at his younger brother's taunting, he grabbed the strange drink from the countertop.

Osamu smiled while giving no resistance. Just as Tsubasa unstopped the bottle, Noboru had turned around from weighing the powders just in time to yell, "No!"

But it was too late, Tsubasa had fallen for Osamu's guise and had taken a swig of the bottle. For a long moment everyone awkwardly locked eyes in silence and anticipation to see if something would happen. Noboru slapped his hand over his face in frustration as if expecting Tsubasa to turn into a toad or explode.

"I don't feel anything. It's as I thought, a charade old ma—"

Tsubasa's stomach grumbled, his face turned white, and then he keeled over in pain. Noboru put his fingers between his eyes as if he were about to receive a migraine.

"What did you give him, old man?" Noboru grabbed Osamu by the kimono leaving the old man's feet struggling to find the floor.

"N-n-nothing. I gave him nothing; he grabbed the bottle and drank."

Noboru glared a look of death at Kaito.

"He did," Kaito responded, diverting his eyes from Noboru's wrath.

Noboru looked at Osamu in disgust. "I know you, old man. You goaded him into it."

Osamu played innocent. "I did nothing, I warned him that only a man could drink it for the potion to work, and he's clearly just a boy. It's not my fault he got sick."

Noboru let go of Osamu's kimono and growled between his teeth. "All your potions make people sick. If he is injured, old man—"

"H-h-he will be fine," Osamu assured. "Give the boy thirty minutes, or maybe four hours... I can't remember."

"How can you not remember?"

"You said it yourself, I'm old, my mind has a lifetime of knowledge in it."

"More likely your mind is as disorganized as your store!" Noboru shook his head in disbelief and picked up the bag of powders he came for. "You better hope I do not come back here with a dead body, or I'll come back and start testing potions on you until your last three teeth fall out."

Osamu licked his precious three teeth in fear. "You wouldn't."

Noboru glared at Kaito. "Pick up your brother. Let's get out of here before this little imp curses us all."

Kaito could not help but chuckle under his breath as he put his shoulder under Tsubasa's arm. The three shinobi exited the building. Twilight had just passed and upon exiting the herb shop Noboru heard the squawk of a crow. Noboru did not speak but only gestured for the boys to follow the sound of the bird. The three of them made their way toward a dark alley. There in the back of the alley was Itsuki with his kunai at the throat of Rin. Upon further inspection, Noboru saw that it was a feisty young woman with long hair tangled over her face and breathing hard with adrenaline. Itsuki was mumbling something at his captive about not moving when he saw them approach.

"Is this the one?" Noboru came closer to get a better look. "Yeah, I thought it was a boy at first, she's the one that was spying on me last I was here."

"She was spying again, on the roof this time," Itsuki said as he kept the dagger close to her throat. "The question is why... what, what is that noise?"

Three paces back from Noboru in the dark alleyway, Tsubasa's stomach was groaning loudly, followed by a waterfall of vomit on the alleyway floor. Itsuki looked at Tsubasa in disgust and then at Noboru in confusion.

"What the hell happened to him?"

Noboru looked back and sighed. "He drank from one of Osamu's bottles."

"Why did you let him do that?" Itsuki contested.

"Like I would let him. I didn't want to bring them in the first place for that exact reason. You're the one who insisted on it."

Tsubasa was breathing heavily. "Ooh... I feel so much better."

Kaito started to chuckle, followed by Noboru and Itsuki joining in with thunderous laughter. Rin looked wild-eyed at her captors with a look of disbelief that she may meet her end to such a group. She would have protested for her life, but Itsuki had stated quickly that if she made a sound that he would gladly slit her throat. Only when the shinobi stopped laughing did they seem to notice their captive again.

Noboru gestured toward Tsubasa. "Sorry about my friend over there but he seems he can't hold down his poison very well, but now I need answers."

Itsuki brought the dagger to the skin of her throat. "Why were you following him?"

Rin coughed, struggling to speak. "He brought the flowers. I was the buyer that had been waiting for them."

"Not good enough," Noboru threatened. "Do better or my friend here will put a smile across your neck. Or... I could test out one of Osamu's mystery potions on you."

Rin's eyes widened; the fear of Osamu's mystery potion was worse than the threat of death. "I knew the flowers came from the Iga mountains..." Rin hesitated and eyed her captives in attempts to read them.

Itsuki looked at Noboru to see if the other had an answer. "How do you know where they come from?" Itsuki threatened, pulling her hair taught and bringing her throat closer to the dagger.

"Because she's from there," Kaito interrupted. "Her name is Rin Kurosawa, I almost did not recognize her, it has been a while."

Noboru and Itsuki looked back at Kaito in disbelief. Rin peered through her hair to get a better look at Kaito as he came out of the shadow of the alleyway. Her eyes grew wide as she saw a ghost from another life.

"How can you be sure?" Itsuki questioned, still not convinced.

"She has a tiny chip in her front tooth."

"Smile," Noboru commanded, leaning only inches from Rin's face.

Rin reluctantly gave a mocking smile and sure enough to Noboru's inspection, Rin showed a tiny chip in the corner of her front tooth. Noboru nodded in reluctant approval.

"Kaito?" Rin said in disbelief.

"How do you know this girl?" Itsuki looked at Kaito.

"We both do," Kaito said, gesturing to Tsubasa. "She is from Hekison. It has been years, but I know it's her. She was a close friend to us as children. Itsuki, maybe you could let go of the kunai."

Itsuki still held the dagger close. "That still doesn't explain why she was spying, and why she has a comb in her hair that's really a dagger. Speak and get to the point, quickly."

"I was sent by Yamato Akiyama," Rin blurted out. "As a spy, to keep tabs on the Oda clan. When the first siege on the Iga shinobi was plotted, I am the one that sent the message warning Hekison, at great risk I might add."

Itsuki loosened his grip on Rin, still holding the kunai dagger, still wary.

"You're a kunoichi," Noboru bluntly stated. "An infiltrator."

Rin straightened her clothes and gathered her messy hair

262

back. "Yes," she stated defiantly. "Yamato had his suspicions of Nobunaga long before the siege. I was sent to infiltrate, pose as a castle servant."

"That would be over three years ago, that would have made you far too young for this mission," Noboru stated doubtfully.

"I was sent because I was young," Rin stated bitterly. "Nobunaga is known for rooting out spies. I had to establish a known history among the servants."

Noboru and Itsuki looked at Kaito for verification.

"I do not know anything about a mission she was sent on," Kaito stated. "She was our friend. All I know is that Tsubasa and I trained with her in the basics of the shinobi arts. Yamato had trained her personally at times. Then one day she was gone, my father told us not to ask about it."

Tsubasa's face was still pale, but he nodded in uncaring approval and returned to the important duty of spitting out his leftover dregs of vomit. Itsuki and Noboru's stance seemed to relax a little at the approval of the Yukimura brothers. Even if Rin were playing them for fools, she could have never counted on the Yukimura brothers being present.

"So why did you spy on us?" Noboru questioned.

"Osamu told me that you were the man that brought in the flowers I ordered."

"That dumb troll."

Rin smiled in agreement. "I know they are only from the Iga region, and only a person who knew the area well would be bringing them. I have been out of contact with Hekison over a year now. If you want more details, I suggest we not speak in the open, there are other spies in Kyoto."

The rest could all agree on that much, they were not in the most favorable part of Kyoto, and they had already started a commotion. Itsuki nodded and gestured everyone to follow.

"I will need to gather my things," Rin requested.

Itsuki grumbled. "Very well, but I am coming with you. I will meet the rest of you at the inn."

"But—" Kaito interjected.

"You can catch up with lost friends later," Itsuki stated bluntly.

Noboru left with the Yukimura brothers but gave a look of warning to Itsuki as they took off. Itsuki did not respond but only nodded in understanding that neither one of them trusted Rin; Itsuki would keep her at arm's length. The groups split, Itsuki following Rin while keeping his hands at the ready to grab his dagger if necessary.

Rin could feel Itsuki's apprehension. "You can relax. I'm only a girl."

"You're a kunoichi," Itsuki said coldly. "You were trained in Hekison, and you've been in deep cover for years. You would not be alive if you weren't apt and dangerous. I'm sure 'I'm only a girl' is a line that you used on many men before slitting their throats."

Rin frowned; she was not comfortable having someone know her true identity. For years she had been a mystery to all men, and she came to enjoy the control. She thought better of pushing the subject of her innocence and decided to submit to Itsuki's will, for now. Once they got to the front of the inn she looked up at the window. "I would rather avoid the innkeeper, we could—"

"We'll go through the front door." Itsuki gave a mocking smile. "Together."

Rin nodded reluctantly and started to walk through the entrance. "Yes, but—"

"Ahh, Rin. I was beginning to worry. It is after sundown." Hiroshi the inn keeper quickly scanned Itsuki's scarred face and sword at his belt. "And… this must be your husband?"

Rin wrapped her arm around Itsuki's and leaned on his shoulder. "Yes! This is my husband. He has finally come to me."

Itsuki tried to muster a smile but only gave an uncomfortable smirk and nodded.

Hiroshi did not take his eyes off Itsuki and his weathered garb. "What happened to your kimono, Rin? It seems slightly torn and is not your usual attire."

"Mud," she answered quickly. "My kimono was ruined, such a sad thing, but my husband bought me this so I would not go home filthy. Better homely than filthy is what he said. Isn't that right, dear." Rin gave Itsuki a nudge with her elbow; Itsuki uncomfortably gave a nod of approval.

Rin spoke before Itsuki could stumble any further. "I am here to gather my belongings. We will be heading out tonight."

Hiroshi seemed convinced and let the couple assume their quarters upstairs. Before entering, Itsuki knocked on the door and then let Rin pass first.

"You're good, that inn keeper would do anything you want."

"A necessary skill, and one you obviously lack with that scar on your eye and ghastly performance you just gave. You might as well have been holding up a sign." Rin stood defiantly with hands on her waist and in a mocking male voice said, "Me Itsuki, me assassin, me kill for you."

"Enough, start packing," Itsuki grumbled.

She was not wrong; ever since Itsuki got the scar he honed his covert skills more than that of an infiltrator. Posing as a farmer or priest he would get too many questions about his scar. A scar he never wished to receive but would receive it again gladly, considering the price.

"It was no interest of mine to play husband for the innkeeper." Itsuki couldn't help but defend himself.

"It is, if you don't want trouble," Rin quipped back. "The man thinks me a lady of means. If he thought ill of you, he would have notified city guards. Then where would we be? I've been doing this daily for years; it's amazing that you get by at all."

"I get by," Itsuki stated annoyed.

"Barely," Rin said, marking a spot on her face to mimic Itsuki's scar placement. "Where did you get it?"

"Just keep packing," Itsuki spoke coldly.

Itsuki found the girl to be clever and witty, obvious reasons why Yamato had chosen her for such a task. He kept scanning all his memory for something that would give a hint to her identity. While Itsuki watched her pack, he noticed mixing bowls and a clay bottle. He inspected the materials closer, suspicious of its contents.

"Is this what I think it is?" Itsuki pointed to the bottle.

Rin looked at it as if deciding her answer. "Yes, what of it?"

Itsuki removed the wood stopper and sniffed the bottle's contents to verify the sleeping potion, satisfied, he then put it in his travel pack. "I'll be taking this for safe keeping."

Rin defiantly swung her bag over her shoulder and stormed off. "Let's go... my husband."

This time Itsuki lead the way but with the girl always at his side, never behind. Itsuki walked with the countenance of somebody alert, he scanned everything and everyone, as if expecting a threat at any moment. Rin seemed to accept her fate for the time being, knowing her usual tricks would not work on someone so vigilant. Eventually they came to an inn brimming with mercenaries. A few men gave looks at Rin wondering what a girl was doing there, but only a glance.

"It's like these men have never seen a woman before," Rin scoffed.

"Oh yes they have," Itsuki chuckled.

"What?"

"The only women that come into this inn tend to be whores; they're wondering how much."

At the comment Rin held onto Itsuki's arm a little tighter. "It would cost them an appendage they would loath to lose."

Itsuki permitted a small smirk at the comment and continued upstairs through the busy inn. When they reached the door, the Yukimura brothers could be heard arguing on the other side with vigor.

"She always beat you on the climbing tree. She was nimbler than either of us."

"I doubt she could now."

Itsuki slid the door open, and Rin entered smiling.

"For your information, I could still beat you at the climbing tree," Rin stated, looking at Kaito. "Tsubasa, you're looking healthier, which of Osamu's miracle potions did you try? Was it the one to increase your manhood? I would have hoped that these past years you would have grown into a man by now."

Tsubasa's face reddened. "You're as annoying as I remember."

"And you're much gloomier than I remember."

Noboru sat in the corner of the room, methodically mixing powders in the premeasured quantities into small bowls. He stopped to look at Itsuki and Rin. "Any trouble?"

"No." Itsuki nudged Rin in the back. "Have a seat. And let's hear this tale of yours."

"It's been years. Where do I start?" Rin responded.

"From when you left Hekison. Just give the short version for now," Itsuki stated.

"As I said earlier, I was sent by Yamato Akiyama to infiltrate the Oda clan as a serving maid. I was ordered to find out any of Nobunaga Oda's military plans. I would meet with a contact monthly."

"What was the contact's name?" Noboru asked.

Rin saw through the trick question. "You know as well as I that we never use names. In any case, I played my part for the better of two years. I found out what information I could, and I would send it to Yamato through my contact. I eventually gained employment in the house of Hideyoshi Hashiba."

"Wait, wait, wait," Itsuki interjected. "Daimyō Hashiba, the general of Nobunaga?"

Rin nodded. "I took the opportunity because he was becoming one of Nobunaga's closest confidants. My last correspondence was a year ago, right before the second siege of the Iga Province, after that my contact never came back. Since then, I have stayed under the employ of Lady Nene as a handmaiden. By her order I'm to keep tabs on the comings and goings of Kyoto."

"You spy for those you spy on?" Kaito stated in disbelief.

"Of course, a serving maid can only find out so much, what greater way to receive vital information than to become a spy for your enemy."

"Why did you not come back to the village, especially if you knew of the siege?" Itsuki probed.

"That is the exact reason I did not go back," she spoke as if Itsuki was daft. "How do I get to such a village as a lone woman, surrounded by thousands of Nobunaga's troops."

"What happens if you don't check in with Lady Nene?" Itsuki looked at Rin with concern. "Will there be a search for you?"

"They know I'm a spy and use me as such," Rin stated. "They just don't know I'm of Iga. It's not uncommon for me to not check in for a week... provided I bring them good information."

Itsuki stared at the girl, weighing her words carefully. The little room held an awkward silence for a few moments. Kunoichi were the female term for a shinobi. The difference is they emphasized more in skills of espionage and trickery in place of combat; societal norms allowed woman to spy in other places than men. A woman, years in deep cover, and under the nose of a general surpassed any accomplishment of any other kunoichi that Itsuki had known.

"I take it Yamato died?" Rin spoke, staring at the floor while thinking of her past conversation with Masanari in Azuchi Castle.

"Yes," Itsuki looked at Noboru and remembered how they left Yamato to die while choking on his own blood. The chaos of Hekison had happened so fast that the memories almost felt surreal. "We were there at his death, by arrow fire."

"Did he die well?" Rin probed.

"Yes," Itsuki lied.

"We have heard survivors have gathered in Osaka, some in the town of Iga, but in submission to Nobunaga's rule. When we are done here, we could take you there to your relatives," Noboru stated, trying to change the subject.

"I have no family," Rin responded. "Part of the reason Yamato chose me. I have told my tale, the least you can do is tell me yours."

Kaito was about to open his mouth in eagerness when Noboru

cut him off. Itsuki and Noboru told a modified tale of how they came to Kyoto from Hekison. They specifically left out parts about the swords and retrieving them. Although all the shinobi wore the swords on their belts, the worn-out sheaths made it look like they only concealed low-grade weapons. Rin listened intently, only asking questions where she dared. She could feel that they were leaving something out of their story, but she had as well.

"There is a flaw in your story," Rin stated at the conclusion.

"Oh?" Itsuki raised his eyebrows.

"I heard you deserted the village before it fell."

"The village was lost; the wall had fallen." Itsuki folded his arms. "And who told you this?"

"Masanari Hattori." Rin stared at the four comrades, waiting for a response but only received a long awkward silence.

"He was our commanding chūnin at the wall of Hekison," Tsubasa stated in disbelief. "He's alive?"

"What's left of him," Rin nodded. "He was in the dungeons of Azuchi, missing an eye and looking like hell. Although for your sake, you may want him to stay there."

"Why?" Kaito questioned.

"He swore revenge on you two for deserting. He said he saw you two with... I'm assuming these men," Rin spoke, gesturing to Noboru and Itsuki, "climbing over the wall retreating, while he stayed to defend the village."

Tsubasa and Kaito looked at each other in wariness. They had not been long under the command of Masanari Hattori, but the man had proved to be a powerful shinobi. Any man would be a fool not to fear the wrath of Masanari. He proved to be a stern man, killing subordinates for trying to escort survivors from Hekison when ordered to stay and defend the wall. Masanari had stated that a man who could not do his duty was a danger to all and was better dead, at least dead bodies could be trusted.

"Masanari Hattori..." Noboru growled.

"I take it you are old friends?" Rin questioned.

"Best friends," Noboru stated with contempt.

"Fair enough," Rin responded. "In any case, I can't imagine Masanari escaping the Azuchi prisons without assistance."

"We'll deal with Masanari if that time ever comes," Noboru nodded. "We have bigger things to take care of."

"Like killing Nobunaga," Rin stated bluntly.

The four shinobi looked at each other waiting for someone to respond.

Rin broke the silence. "It's pretty obvious. Why else would you be here and not with the remnant survivors? A four-man squad is usual protocol for an assassination of someone as high up as Nobunaga. Not to mention he is the reason we no longer have a home. Plus, I know where to find him."

"Where?" Itsuki questioned.

"First, I want something."

"What do you want?" Noboru responded, wondering what this price of information was going to cost.

"I want in." Rin smiled, showing the look of death she had given so many men.

23

The Oda Legacy
-Omi Province, Azuchi Castle-

Nobunaga was looking over Lake Biwa from the same balcony that his younger son, Nobukatsu, had stood pondering the day after returning from the Iga campaign. The recent nightfall brought a full moon, and the reflection could be seen in the inlet; the lunar image distorted as the water ripples danced. Nobunaga contemplated the soon to come battles as a genius contemplates a game of go, the man's mind never stopped planning the oncoming scenarios. *If I sleep, another man will usurp my position,* Nobunaga often thought. His gift was his military genius, but his curse was his ever-pondering mind.

His eldest son, Nobutada, came out from the hallway to find his father pondering as he had often seen. He wore a casual kimono and a jacket to keep warm in the cool spring air. Nobutada, unlike his younger brothers, took after his mother with exception for his father's long nose. His hairline was still young and vibrant in contrast to his father's gray-streaked hair.

"Father, you sent for me," Nobutada stated.

"Yes," Nobunaga said, still gazing out over the inlet. "I have need of you, and we will be mobilizing forces soon. I need every man at arms."

"As you say... will we be meeting up with Hideyoshi Hashiba?"

"Perhaps, but if all goes according to plan, Hideyoshi is already in Bitchū Province to meet Terumoto Mōri in battle and begin the siege upon his main castle. I will monitor his progress and decide accordingly."

Nobutada shifted uneasily, clenching his fists as if annoyed. "Father, I do not understand why you gave the honor to Hideyoshi to be the vanguard against Terumoto. I am more than capable to quell the Mōri clan. Why do you give the man such prestige?"

Nobunaga sighed. "I suppose it is because I see myself in Hideyoshi. The first time I met Hideyoshi he had no armor and a weapon you could barely call a sword. I joked he looked like a monkey. But that monkey was successful at every mission received, he eventually became one of my sandal bearers and is now one of my head generals. Throughout my conquest of Japan his use in battle command has been proven multiple times. The Oda clan was never a prestigious one until I came along and raised it. Hideyoshi does not even come from a noble family and look where he is now. Hideyoshi has ambition and I must make good use of him. If I do not, he would be drawn by one of my rivals. Do you understand?"

Nobunaga shook his head when he saw the confusion in his son's eyes. "My son, balancing the men underneath you is like playing a game of go. You must weigh each piece's value and worth. Hideyoshi is loyal but ambitious. I show him honor in battle so he views me as a lord that will raise him up. I must sync his ambition with my goals, otherwise he will view me as an obstacle to his progress."

"But he was born a peasant, he would not dare rise against his lord," Nobutada blurted out.

Nobunaga put a hand on his son's shoulder, imploring him to understand. "Unfortunately, it happens all too often. In these long years of civil war, I have seen powerful daimyōs fall under a peasant's sword. This land is in a state of chaos, each clan putting their lot into this war, each hoping to come out on top. I must convince all that throwing their support behind me is the best way to help everyone. A harsh reality to become shōgun is to convince emperor, common man, and everyone in between of your worth as a leader. Only then, will there be unity."

Nobutada's fire seemed to dwindle from his eyes as he listened to his father's words. "I believe I understand, but what of Mitsuhide Akechi? You speak of convincing all the daimyōs, yet you have shown Mitsuhide much disgrace. You must admit, the seppuku of his captain was ill timed. And now you have Mitsuhide on hold as if he is some old man or young boy not ready for battle. I cannot imagine the man will be enthusiastic to any future task that you give him."

Nobunaga gave a long sigh. "Mitsuhide had failed me too many times in battle. I pray to the gods for wisdom in such situations. Sentencing his subordinate to seppuku was the only path I could set to balance the competition of daimyōs. There is a time for killing and there is a time for reward. I will admit it was a hard choice, my son, hard choices you will have to make some day."

In glimpses like these, Nobutada would see the age of his father come out, the weight of his mighty burden. The ambitious goal of his father had taken its toll; Nobutada felt nothing but admiration for his father making it this far.

"Father, you carry a large burden. I would still like to prove myself, to help you achieve your goal."

Nobunaga smiled. "You already have. When I unify Japan, I will need my eldest son to rule after I die."

Nobutada's pride filled within him. "Certainly, I will do as you command. What is the task that you would have me do?"

Nobunaga gestured his son to follow. The father and son followed their way through Azuchi Castle, servants bowing as the two men passed. Tradition dictated that all lower caste must bow to samurai as they walked by; not adhering to this custom could even mean one's head, depending on the samurai of status. At the end of a long hallway, they came upon Nobunaga's quarters. A single sentry sat outside guarding the study, Nobunaga barked an order to find someone to bring tea.

Nobunaga slid the door open to his room. The walls were lined with various weapons of war and the lantern light danced across each object giving a life to the room. At the end of the room sat Nobunaga's samurai armor on a post, appearing as the skin of a demon waiting to be worn. A large table sat in the center of the room with a map of Japan. Stone pieces of various colors sat on the map, signifying forces of differing loyalty.

Nobunaga pointed to the city of Kyoto. "Hideyoshi has currently left Kyoto, using the city as a rendezvous point for my forces before heading to the Bitchū Province."

Nobunaga pointed further west on the map of Japan to a stone piece signifying Terumoto Mōri's land rule. "For the better part of a year, Hideyoshi has chipped down the defenses of the Mōri clan, while Mitsuhide Akechi barely kept the land south in hold. As

275

you can see, I control the land east, but in order to take the Bitchū Province with a final strike, Hideyoshi will need the majority of my forces. I have Ieyasu Tokugawa touring the lands of the southeast from the victory over the Takeda clan to oversee integration of the locals into my rule. He can keep the east and shoreline protected while surveying the newly acquired land. I have rid myself of the troublesome groups in the interior of my rule such as the Iga shinobi. Although I have my two major generals protecting my land on either side, loyal daimyōs are all guarding other borders from minor clans. This has left little forces with me."

Nobutada nodded. "I see, the Iga shinobi were an unknown loyalty that could be used against you. They were too close to Azuchi Castle to be left alone."

Nobunaga stroked his mustache. "Yes, the blasted shinobi had betrayed me once already. I believe they would have done it again. An enemy could have hired them to bolster their forces or attempt an assassination on my life."

Nobunaga then pointed back to the city of Kyoto. "I have my special auxiliary forces that will be coming back from their specific missions, I rarely have them meet together. I will not have a large quantity of men to protect me, but I will be damned sure to have quality men. You will travel to Kyoto and assume command of these troops. I am not so proud to believe that I am invincible, even in the center of my rule."

Nobutada scratched his chin. "You are spread very thin, father. I do not like this. Azuchi Castle is also a well-known target, leaving you here with little forces would give any of your enemies an excuse to come after you."

Nobunaga held Nobutada in high esteem. Over the years he

had not only proven himself as a loyal son, but he had become a grown man and a friend to council with.

"Your old man can still take care of himself, and I have a few tricks left to teach you. I will be leaving Azuchi to meet you in Kyoto. If Hideyoshi has not finished his task, we will set out to meet him and finish the siege. If any of the scattered clans in the northeast decide to unite instead of squabble and come after me, they will go for Azuchi without me inside. Azuchi Castle will be an empty prize, and minor clans don't have the manpower to hold it once captured. Although it is highly unlikely they would attempt it, I will not leave anything to chance. There is no reason for them not to believe it isn't fully armed."

Nobutada nodded in approval. "A sound plan. What of mother?"

"I will have Nōhime come to Azuchi with her guard; it will help protect the castle and keep her safe. As I said, Azuchi will not be much of a target without me inside. Now you see why I need you close and not off in battle. I would only trust my kin to guard me."

A knock came at the door.

"Enter," Nobunaga barked.

A servant held a tray with teacups and a large kettle of steaming tea. Nobunaga gruffly nodded as the servant set down the tray and abruptly left. Father and son sat as they discussed the progressing war plans in detail. Nobunaga was enjoying his time with his eldest son with great enthusiasm. Very few moments allowed him to discuss the legacy he planned to leave behind to his son. They were interrupted yet again by another knock at the door.

Nobunaga rolled his eyes and barked, "Enter."

"Sir, urgent news, a courier has been sent from Hideyoshi."

"Let him enter."

The courier came in sweating profusely from his run to the upper levels of the castle and had obviously ridden a hard journey. The man bowed low, his eyes suggested nervousness as if the message would mean his life.

"Have you no tongue. Speak your message!"

The courier stammered, obviously not eager to bring the news. "Lord Nobunaga, General Hideyoshi has requested more troops. Scouts report that Terumoto has fortified his castle and if Hideyoshi is to meet the deadlines that you gave him, additional forces will be needed."

The courier handed Nobunaga a sealed scroll with a detailed written correspondence from Hideyoshi himself to verify the authenticity of the message. Nobunaga opened it and read the details concerning the siege with deadly efficiency.

Nobutada scowled. "What troops can be spared?"

Nobunaga nodded as if not surprised. "I will send Mitsuhide. Maybe he will be able to redeem his honor and turn the tide to help himself and that monkey, Hideyoshi."

24

A Trap

-Yamashiro Province, Kyoto City-

After Rin's proposal to join the group, Noboru and Itsuki had abruptly gone outside the room to have a private chat about the upcoming situation. This left the Yukimura brothers looking at a young woman who had once been a playful childhood trainee in Hekison.

"So how did you get stuck being with the brute and a stiff?"

Kaito smiled wide. "They were friends of our father, and under his command... it's a long story, about seven months."

"Hmm," Rin responded, looking out the window in boredom. "You could tell me the rest some time."

The brothers looked at each other. "Not likely soon, Noboru and Itsuki have only just started to trust us. It will take time before you can have the same trust," Tsubasa stated bluntly.

"Very well, tell me what you can, it's been years since I was able to speak of home."

Kaito spoke mostly of times before the siege of Hekison, of training, friends, family, and daily tasks. Tsubasa mostly remained silent. The walls that Rin had always put up naturally as a barricade for emotional protection slowly decayed as the conversation progressed. The Yukimura brothers were people she had known, trained with, she had even eaten at their home on occasion. For a while the three childhood friends had felt as if time had gone backward, and the memories of fonder times had returned. Rare moments as these were to be cherished; they were a short glimmer of light between the overcast skies of a warring country.

Behind doors, Itsuki and Noboru stood outside of the room discussing their options.

"I do not trust her," Itsuki stated bluntly. "And on top of that she is very apt at what she does. She knows how to make a phantom drink, few in Hekison had the skill or knowledge to do so. She seduced the innkeeper to the point he would fight to the death for her. The girl is beyond skilled; her loyalties could have changed with so much time passing and no check from Hekison."

Noboru nodded. "Not to mention she was sent by Yamato himself. I've never heard of someone under cover for so long, two years at most. Why would Yamato send such a young girl for such a dangerous infiltration?"

"Maybe he didn't expect her to last? Yamato was cold-hearted, but in any case, she has survived, and no doubt become extremely deadly because of it."

"There's no doubt, she is not just a normal child of Hekison." Noboru tapped the hilt of his sword in thought.

"Kurosawa." Itsuki looked at the closed door. "The name is often used with orphans. The brothers say she was raised with the other orphans among Hekison, but orphans are rarely trained in fieldwork, there is something more to her."

"Yes, she looks familiar."

"Knowing you, probably a barmaid," Itsuki joked.

Noboru chuckled. "Well, in any case, we do not trust her, but isn't that even more reason to let her join? If we let her go, she will be free to do as she pleases. With her close at least we know she cannot cause us trouble, and if she does —"

"We kill her," Itsuki finished Noboru's sentence.

Noboru rubbed his sideburns thoughtfully. "Well then, let's get back in there before Kaito opens that fat mouth of his and tells her something she shouldn't know."

Itsuki couldn't help but smile. "Yes. But let us act as if we are not convinced. She will be more willing to give us information if we feign interest."

The older shinobi entered the room to find Rin and Kaito laughing about an old story. Even Tsubasa was chuckling at the story of Kaito falling out of a tree during training which ended with Rin throwing a bird's egg at his head, smothering his face in yolk. Rin laughed at the memory, a true laugh she had not experienced in ages. But as the elder shinobi looked on her, the carefree memories of a past life disappeared and her face assumed the serious expression she wore like a mask.

Rin rubbed the tears of laughter from her eyes while looking at Itsuki and Noboru. "So, what have you decided?"

"We can get to Nobunaga without your help. We don't need you," Noboru stated bluntly.

"Eventually," admitted Rin. "I have no doubt, but you know as well as I that this will not be the first assassination attempt on his life. He is well prepared, but I know when he will be most vulnerable, and I know how to get close to him. More importantly, I have this information now; it will take months for you to gather the information to pick an appropriate time to strike."

Rin was not wrong; shinobi took their enemies out through opportunity, not force. No point in killing an enemy in his fortress when one could wait for them to come out. Itsuki and Noboru contained their enthusiasm, careful not to take the bait, hiding their emotions from Rin to not seem over eager.

"Speak then of this plan," Itsuki said, studying the girl.

"First I want your word." Rin met Itsuki's gaze. "I want in."

"Fine," Itsuki nodded, "but only if this information is as good as you say."

Rin smiled. "How about some tea. This may take some time."

"And food," Noboru stated. "I'm starving."

The group ordered some humble meals from the inn in which they took residence. Rin began her explanation of the plan by first describing the updates of all the generals' positions and power throughout Japan. As she explained, she would give the shinobi insights of her various tales of how she came about the information. Halfway through her tale the food arrived. The group began to eat and discuss their plan further.

Rin shoved a rice cake in her mouth, enjoying the lack of requirement for manners. "So here's the deal," she said with a mouthful of food. "As you can tell from the state of Kyoto, Hideyoshi has recently left for Bitchū Province to fight the Mōri clan. Ieyasu Tokugawa and his army are in the south provinces, integrating Nobunaga's rule into the local populace. Most of Nobunaga's sons are on minimal military assignments elsewhere. This comprises the majority of his forces, leaving only outposts with minimal forces to defend his borders. Nobunaga's military is fully occupied."

"The majority, not all," Noboru stated as he swigged a bit of sake.

"Exactly," Rin agreed. "But I know for a fact that Hideyoshi has asked for more reinforcements in the Bitchū Province, Mitsuhide Akechi will be dispatched to augment the invasion."

The four shinobi looked at each other in skepticism.

"And you know this... how?" Kaito questioned.

"Because I heard him say it," she casually stated while wolfing down rice. "I'm a spy. Remember?"

Itsuki and Noboru gave a look of skepticism but probed no further.

"Assuming this is true," Itsuki responded. "How do you know where Nobunaga will be?"

"Nobunaga has a pattern when he spreads his forces thin, a pattern I have picked up on while working in Azuchi. If Nobunaga has to send more forces to Hideyoshi, he will rendezvous with his special auxiliary forces for protection. Nobutada Oda is now gathering the auxiliary forces here in Kyoto. Follow the son and you'll find the father at a time when he is weakest."

Noboru nodded in agreement and looked at Itsuki. "Show her."

Itsuki pulled out the dispatch orders of the samurai that they had killed at Mount Kurama. He put down the note for Rin to read.

"It seems you've already met the auxiliary force," she stated slightly impressed. "We could use this."

"What do you mean?" Tsubasa questioned.

"Infiltrate," Itsuki stated bluntly. "She means that we could join Nobutada's forces as samurai and follow him to Nobunaga... a risky plan."

"With high reward," Rin quipped back. "I am quite familiar with the protocol of this force."

"We would be unknown troops; how will that work?" Tsubasa spoke up.

"That's the beauty of the special forces squad." Rin picked up the dispatch orders again. "They are often separated and meet rarely; it is uncommon that the squads know each other. The list of their names on the signed dispatch orders here will be proof enough for Nobutada. The only thing we'll need is some armor."

"We?" Itsuki raised an eyebrow. "You're a woman."

Rin nodded. "You are right, I may be a kunoichi, but I am no shape shifting fox, although I have been called one. I cannot impersonate a samurai, but I have taken note of their mannerisms and such. I will need to teach you certain military protocol that they use, you do not want to insult a general due to your lack of discipline."

The shinobi could not help but be convinced. Rin Kurosawa had years of information on their enemy. Typically, an infiltration unit would have to do a month of reconnaissance before going under cover this close to an enemy. Impersonating a street vendor was one thing; a personal guard of Nobutada Oda was a completely different realm. The opportunity was too tempting for the shinobi to simply let it slip by. Revenge was in their grasp.

"We will need to make preparations now." Noboru stood up and looked out the window. "If we are to impersonate Nobutada's men we will have to ambush them before they group up with the main force. They will most likely be entering through the eastern gate of the city."

"Then we lay a trap," Rin stated. "But I'll need to borrow Kaito."

Kaito looked nervous at the other shinobi and Rin. "Me? For what?"

"Don't worry," Rin smiled mischievously.

They all continued their meals as they discussed their plans through the night, careful to leave no details out. The plan would need to involve them stealing someone else's identity without any civilian finding out. Late into the night the group slept, unknown to the others, Itsuki and Noboru took turns pretending to sleep, always keeping an eye on the kunoichi.

After a day's preparation Kaito was on the street wearing a conical straw hat and a plain blue kimono with sandals. He yelled to all. "Food and geisha for entertainment, take time for rest in these troubled times of war."

The group had rented out an old dingy vendor shop with a back-entertainment room near the eastern city gate. The place was hardly a palace but suitable to their needs. The shinobi had promised rent to the landlord within a week, a promise they did not intend to keep.

Behind Kaito, Rin Kurosawa was in an elaborate geisha kimono of red, white, and gold. Ornate markings of flowers and cranes lined the Kimono. Her hair was back and tied tight; she had a powdered white face, and deep red lips. She held a traditional fan to show the crowd a peak but never her whole face. Men who were interested came up asking when she was available for appointments and her entertainment specialties. Kaito would pretend to write down names and addresses for future appointments.

Each day the group proceeded with their plan, fishing for their target. Each night they would retire and refine their plans further. When Tsubasa and Kaito would get the chance, they would often talk with Rin about where she had been these past years. Despite their small age gap, Kaito had often had feelings for Rin in his younger adolescence. He had had a boy's heartbreak when the girl had disappeared. Itsuki would only speak with Rin when necessary and always curtly. On one night when Kaito and Noboru were out on reconnaissance to find out where Nobutada's forces gathered, Kaito could not help but be curious.

"Why does Itsuki seem to hate Rin so much?" Kaito probed as they walked the streets.

"Who knows?"

"I think you do," Kaito quipped back.

Noboru kept his eyes on the street and sighed. "It is better you hear from me than get a punch in the face from Itsuki. But you are not to mention this. Understood?"

Kaito nodded in agreement.

"Rin…" Noboru hesitated. "As you know Itsuki lost a wife, child, parents, everything at the beginning of the siege. He was a man much more lighthearted before this mess. I fear he is only a shell of what he once was."

Kaito did not dare speak but only listened while Noboru took his pause.

"Rin, although slightly younger, she has the appearance of Yuna, his wife. One would think they were sisters."

"You don't think that…"

Noboru looked at Kaito in confusion and then a wave of understanding came over him. "Oh no, he would never. Why do you think he's so hostile toward her? I know why you ask. I have seen the way you look at her."

Kaito gave a look of denial.

"Do not lie," Noboru stated. "And do not trust the woman. She may be close to your age, but she has been in cover for years. The life of a kunoichi will add years on a woman."

"But—"

"Not to be trusted." Noboru held up a finger. "I will admit she is of use. But her past is shaded, and before the siege the shinobi villages were never truly united. Nobody knows what intentions she had when she left Hekison."

Kaito took note of Noboru's serious demeanor; the man usually opted for a joke and drink over a sobering chat. Shortly after the conversation, Noboru returned to his usual self and got distracted by a street vendor. He started looking for a bar and pointed at a young woman that passed by. Four days passed in preparation and execution of the group's plan. Kaito pretended to solicit people for the use of geishas. Eventually their plan paid off, and on the fifth day a squad of five samurai came down the street, all bearing the symbol Susanoo, God of storms, representing Nobunaga's special forces. Tsubasa was the first to spot the squad; he sat on a roof to gain a bird's eye view of the gate. Tsubasa turned and then made the birdcall passed onto him by his father. When Kaito heard the signal, he began to animate himself even more, waiting for the men to approach. People bowed as the samurai passed, Kaito saw his opportunity and closed in on the group, bowing low.

"Master samurai, it would do me great honor to provide entertainment to your squad."

The samurai eyed Kaito and the geisha. "We have no time. My men and I are weary from travel."

The squad leader gestured to keep moving but Kaito stepped forward more eager. The streets were alive with similar offers, but Kaito knew he had to stand out. "As you should be, inside I can offer private quarters with food." Kaito gestured Rin closer. "And entertainment, compliments of the house for those under the command of Lord Nobunaga Oda."

The squad leader showed no emotion at Kaito's offer, but his men contained eager faces to take the bait. Kaito kept his head bowed low in respect, a single bead of sweat rolled down the back of his neck. Kaito knew that this opportunity may not reveal itself again. A long tense moment followed.

"If it's free... very well," the squad leader submitted.

The men of the squad all seemed a bit relieved that their weary travels would soon be over. Rin took the squad leader by the arm and smiled while guiding him into the fake teahouse. Kaito rambled on of food that could be offered and the honor that awaited Lord Nobunaga Oda once Japan was unified.

The squad leader eyed the emptiness of the tea house, "Where are all the other patrons?"

Kaito was quick to react. "Ah, we pride our establishment on its privacy. This way." Kaito slid open a door.

The room was moderate and poorly lit. The plainness was also apparent, a single hearth in the center of the room contained a kettle boiling with cups.

"Merchant," the squad leader barked at Kaito. "More light, and the food that you promised."

Kaito bowed low. "Yes, as you command."

Kaito slid the door shut and left Rin to her work. She daintily put her fan on the floor and began to pour the tea into each cup slowly and methodically as a geisha would. Two of the samurai were so thirsty they drank the tea down instantly. The squad leader watched the geisha tentatively while the other three soldiers put down their belongings. When one of the soldiers that drank the tea started to yawn, Rin stood up and started to wave her fan and dance. The situation was awkward with no music, but the distraction was necessary. Rin pulled out her comb, letting her hair fall around her shoulders.

When one of the other samurai went to take a drink of the tea, the squad leader suddenly slapped it out of his hand. Two of the soldiers that had previously drank the tea were starting to bat their eyes until they passed out on the floor.

Rin did not wait for the remaining samurai to act. She held the dagger that looked like a hair comb in her hand and lodged it with force into the nearest samurai's throat. Blood streamed as the man instinctively grabbed his throat to defend himself, but the damage was done. Not a second later did Noboru, Itsuki, and Tsubasa fall from the ceiling rafters, blades pointed downward. Two more soldiers fell with coughs of blood. The blades of Tsubasa and Noboru were pulled from the backs of the soldiers. Only the squad leader escaped the trap due to his vigilance. The squad leader backed toward the entrance with both swords drawn.

"Assassins! Soon the city will know of you."

The three shinobi and kunoichi stood relaxed with swords down and stared at the man. Only when Rin smiled that look of death she had given so many men did the samurai realize his fate.

The black blade of Kaito Yukimura protruded through the chest of the samurai. Kaito had stabbed the man through the sliding door, causing him to slowly fall to the ground with blood at his lips. Kaito quickly slid the door open, only then did Rin notice the shinobi with their blades black as oblivion, as if sucking the light from the very room.

Rin stared at the shinobi. "Where did you get—"

"We'll explain later," Noboru grumbled. "Quickly now, strip the bodies, keep the blood off the clothes. Dead bodies will arouse suspicion; dead samurai will provoke an investigation."

The group made quick work of the bodies, bagging the necessary clothes and armor into large sacks. Rin cleansed herself of the geisha makeup and disrobed the bright kimono, revealing a plain blue one underneath. They left the bodies to rot; the unlucky landlord would discover corpses instead of the rent.

Taking one last look before exiting, the group all nodded in approval and disappeared into the busy streets of Kyoto.

25

Ghosts of Nobunaga
-Omi Province, Azuchi Castle-

It had been a week since Nobunaga had dispatched his son, Nobutada, from Azuchi Castle to Kyoto. Trust did not come easily to Nobunaga Oda, but it came easily with his sons. Nobunaga's plan of unifying Japan had been a slow process, the corpses left in his path could fill a lake, but the fruits of his labor were on the brink of being harvested. Nobunaga was no longer a young man, and his goal was becoming a race against time. Any setback in his campaign led to the possibility that Nobunaga would not live long enough to see a time of peace.

The sun had retired, and the moon was rising in the sky. The hour was late, and the hearths of Azuchi Castle were burning, giving off a clash of warm air fighting the cool night breeze. Nobunaga was in his study alone writing a letter to his wife, Nōhime, and younger children, an act he enjoyed, but rarely had the opportunity to perform. He smiled as he wrote, recalling the memory of his youngest daughter riding a horse for the first time. His smile soon became a frown as his joyful memory was replaced by the image of a small girl the same age as his daughter, choking on blood in the streets of Hekison with an arrow in her back.

Nobunaga distracted himself by drinking sake and fumbling over maps. Most of the inhabitants left in the castle had retired, but once again sleep did not come easily to him. His genius mind showed no fatigue, constantly thinking of every situation to come in the upcoming military battles and political courts. The ebony and inlayed gold map, still cracked from Nobunaga's past spurt of rage, lay on the table containing all the locations of his current allies and enemies. The map contained a red stone in the Iga Province, a memento Nobunaga was reluctant to move, and his eyes lingered on the stone while he remembered the fires.

"They should not have betrayed me," Nobunaga muttered to himself.

Nobunaga hobbled to a seat with a clay sake bottle in his hand, he slumped down in the chair and the memories of past enemies began to envelop his mind. The sake had begun to take its effect and Nobunaga's mind became clouded. Whether Nobunaga was asleep from exhaustion or just in a slight drunken stupor, he could not tell.

"They should not have betrayed me," he muttered once again. "My father and I called you friend, Yamato; and you betrayed us."

"I did no such thing," a voice responded. "You asked for something that could not be given."

The figure of Yamato Akiyama, alive and whole, appeared before Nobunaga as if he had had been invited into the room. Yamato stood before the table of maps; the specter thumbed a small white rock between his fingers as he inspected Nobunaga's plans.

"I asked for a sword," Nobunaga responded, as if speaking with the dead was a usual thing.

"A sword that I said did not exist. And you asked for more...

so much more, Lord Nobunaga. Submission." The specter walked to the map on the table and tapped the red pin on the map. "We were shinobi. We did not wish to take part in your war, yet you brought it to our homes."

Nobunaga shook his head. "I wanted loyalty, not submission. I offered you terms to join my cause, to help unify Japan."

"A unified Japan?" the specter mocked. "A dream, a state this country has not seen in almost one hundred years. If you know your history well it was the daimyō's decision to reject the Shogunate rule, your kind caused this era of war. Your arrogance is beyond what I thought if you believe you could bring the daimyōs under your wing. The great Fool of Owari Province, Nobunaga's great Shogunate. A noble goal, Lord Nobunaga, but you will not be the one to achieve it. You are a mere steppingstone."

"A steppingstone? You act as if you are the great orchestrator of Japan," Nobunaga scowled. "You wrote back that you would unify Japan, but by your own means. Then to further your insult, you tell me that the sword of Muramasa was not to be delivered like we agreed. I could not let your people stand in defiance so close to my stronghold. I did not wish your death."

"Yet you came for vengeance and steel."

"Yes, I came, vengeance and steel be damned," Nobunaga spoke as if he had just swallowed something bitter. "To unify Japan I must make sacrifices, some I wish I did not have to make, but I would make them again. Daimyōs squabbling over scraps, families slaughtered in the streets, and the Iga shinobi in the middle of the chaos. This nation lost its civility a century ago and I must beat it into submission. Without destruction there is no creation, there is no change. My will is unyielding, and I will move forward bathed in blood to finish the task."

"Blood to end blood," Yamato nodded, showing no emotion.

This time when the specter turned, his face was pale, and three arrow wounds were slowly starting to pool with blood upon his chest. The specter threateningly stepped closer while holding a dagger, filling Nobunaga with fear. "Maybe you are not the steppingstone I though you to be!"

Nobunaga woke up with a gasp of air. His study looked the same as his dream but with no specter in the room. The empty sake bottle he finished had fallen on the floor; he looked at the bottle with disgust and rubbed his pounding head. He drunkenly stumbled to the entrance of his study and barked at the guard outside to send tea for sobering.

Nobunaga began to look at the large map on the table, once again calculating any battle risk to the upcoming plans. Soon Hideyoshi would lay siege on Terumoto's main castle, the heart of Bitchū Province. Nobunaga's reserve army of Mitsuhide Akechi would help bring the final blow swiftly. Ieyasu Tokugawa would be integrating the southeastern provinces to prepare the upcoming unification. Nobutada would soon be taking command of the special forces in Kyoto where Nobunaga would rendezvous. Loyal daimyōs could hold their respective areas with their own forces. Nobunaga nodded his head in approval after days of looking for errors in his plan. *It is within my grasp, Japan may be unified yet*, he thought.

Nobunaga's mind wandered back to his sons, especially Nobutada and Nobukatsu, at times the worries of the country wore heavy on his shoulders and gave little time to think of his children. Nobutada had shown large promise over the past years, becoming a fine military tactician and warrior. Nobukatsu had shown the same promise but being the younger sibling had always constantly pushed himself to be the better. In comparison, Nobunaga truly thought Nobukatsu to be the better successor, but he could never tell his eldest son. Even if he did unify Japan, the country would be but a fragile sapling, creating a dissent in his family would undo all that he had dreamed. *Nobutada will be a great leader and rise to the challenge*, Nobunaga thought.

A knock came at the door. "Enter," Nobunaga stated gruffly.

The door slid open, and a serving maid entered carrying a teakettle with steam coming out of the spout. The girl had the appearance of his daughter, but it had been a long while since he had seen her. The life of war and travel had left little time to see his wife and daughters.

The girl noticed her lord staring. "Is there something more I can do for you, my lord?"

Nobunaga came out of his deep thought. "No, no that will be all. Actually, I would ask, do you have a father still living?"

The girl nervously shifted. She was obviously not used to having the daimyō acknowledge her presence. "Yes, I do. I mean yes, my lord."

Nobunaga smiled at the nervousness of the girl. "And what does he do? Your father."

"He's a fisherman of Lake Biwa at the local village. He sells prime fish," the girl spoke, diverting her eyes to the floor.

"A man spared from the wars around him, a rare thing in these times. Would you say he is a peaceful man?" Nobunaga took up a cup of tea waiting for it to cool.

"Yes," The girl smiled, showing a bit of pride.

"Does he provide well?"

"Yes, as best he can," the serving maid spoke, feeling less nervous.

"And if the war came to his house, would he defend his family?"

"He is no warrior... but I believe he would."

"Even if it meant killing friends that sided against him?" Nobunaga asked, looking at the girl intently.

The girl became extremely nervous at the question.

Nobunaga drank the tea. "This is good tea, by the way."

"I'm glad you think so," the girl said, trying to avoid the question, but Nobunaga's gaze showed that he had not forgotten.

"Do not worry, girl. I want honesty. If I want compliments, I would speak with one of my generals."

"I... I believe he would sacrifice for his family, but I do not brand my father as a killer. I know such a task would weigh heavy on him," she stuttered.

"Such a task would weigh heavy on any man with a soul," Nobunaga confirmed, nodding his head. "When I killed for the first time I did not hesitate, I had been trained to do so. I felt no... I'm sorry, girl. I can see that such subjects trouble you."

"My lord... forgive me," the girl spoke more nervous than ever.

"I wish your father may die a fisherman, and I mean that as a compliment. In a way I envy such a thing. Go now. And thank you for the tea."

The girl bowed and scurried out, glad to be out of the presence of Nobunaga. Nobunaga shook his head as she left. *I have focused so much on my reputation; to lead this nation I have become a frightful demon in the sight of serving maids. For my country I have sacrificed my soul.* Nobunaga could not help but laugh in irony. His occupation was war, and the world would remember him for it. Not as a father, son, or husband, but as a mighty warlord bathed in blood.

26

The Plan
-Yamashiro Province, Kyoto City-

The group had taken refuge in an abandoned granary to discuss their last-minute plans for infiltrating the samurai forces. The storage had a musty smell from the damp wood and years of disuse. The group decided that disguising as samurai at the inn would not be prudent. They carefully laid out the samurai armor that they had stolen.

"We have three usable uniforms; the others are too bloody and tattered to use," Kaito stated, inspecting the clothes.

"We'll make it work," Itsuki stated. "Tsubasa can stay with Rin."

"What? Why not Kaito?" Tsubasa stated defensively.

"We have our reasons; the deception will work better. You know Kaito is the better performer."

"Fine," Tsubasa admitted.

"Well let's gear up then, shall we," Noboru stated excitedly. "Rin, a word please, I need to go over a few last things on samurai protocol. As I will be playing the unit leader, I will be doing most of the talking."

"Very well."

Noboru brought Rin over to the other side of the granary and started to ask his questions. Itsuki asked Kaito to fetch a pail of water to wash off a bloodstain on one of the uniforms.

"Tsubasa," Itsuki waved. "Give me a hand with this armor. There is another reason we are having you stay behind," Itsuki whispered.

"To keep an eye on Rin," Tsubasa responded with no surprise. "Noboru doesn't need any last-minute tips, does he? He's been going over his disguise for days."

Itsuki couldn't help but smile. "No, he does not, but it gives a chance to chat with you in private."

"You're never going to trust her, are you?"

"I have my reasons, Tsubasa, but I trust you. Which is why I'm having you stay behind. If she is as trustworthy as you say, then you have nothing to worry about. All I'm saying is that she is not the girl you once knew; kunoichis often must develop a kill or be killed mentality. Their life is more about deception than truth, these attributes can harbor a new personality within oneself. Being from Hekison I'm sure you've heard the stories."

"Yes," Tsubasa nodded reluctantly. "Kunoichis in extensive deep cover, coming back with different personality traits, often forgetting the life they once had. So what? They all adjust."

"Not all," Itsuki stated darkly. "Some were killed, Yamato's orders. He believed that they had turned into the very people they were trying to impersonate. He believed that if you act like an enemy supporter long enough you may start to think like them, even have feelings for them as you spend enough time with them. I do not envy the life of a kunoichi. Anyway, I am getting off subject; I just want you to be vigilant until I am sure about the identity of Rin. For now, I will keep her at arm's length. Which is why—"

"I'm to keep an eye on her," Tsubasa finished Itsuki's sentence. "Fine, fine. I got it. You have my word. I will mark her."

Itsuki smiled and nodded as he finished cinching the last piece of armor around the waist.

"Absolutely not!" Noboru retorted across the room.

"What?" Itsuki waved.

Noboru looked over and Rin wore a stern look on her face. "She says we need to leave our swords and only bring the samurai katanas."

"It is customary to kneel and present one's sword to a general as a token of service," Rin spoke stubbornly with her hands on her hips. "I don't suppose you'll have a good answer for Nobutada Oda if he decides to inspect your wakizashi."

Noboru rolled his eyes, Itsuki stood in silence as if contemplating his options. In that moment Kaito had returned only to find his comrades in an awkward tense moment.

"Has something gone wrong again?" Kaito asked disheartened.

Tsubasa stepped forward. "She's right. You can't take the swords, but you can hide them."

The two older shinobi shared a silent look of communication, a look the Yukimura brothers had seen all too often.

"Very well," Itsuki reluctantly agreed. "We will follow your advice, Rin, but I'll hide my sword on my own."

"As will I," Noboru agreed.

Kaito just shrugged his shoulders.

When the group had been fully dressed, they quickly made way to the barracks where the special auxiliary squad had been ordered to rendezvous via the dispatch orders they had stolen. Noboru, Kaito, and Itsuki made accommodations to hide their swords, double backing with paranoia to their hiding spot.

As planned, the infiltration had begun. Noboru, Itsuki, and Kaito entered through the barracks door to see a gathering of Nobunaga's auxiliary corps. Most of the men inside were without armor and leisurely sat discussing trivial things such as weather and swordplay. Luckily, the auxiliary force's armor was light compared to the average samurai, the shinobi did not have to put on much to complete their guise.

Noboru took the place of squad leader; his age was appropriate, and his natural gruffness could be taken for the pride of a samurai. Itsuki strode close behind with his chin held high. Kaito followed, young but fit for duty, his age would protect the group, as most samurai would not expect younger troops to know much or have a reputation. In the barracks, tables were everywhere. Even though the samurai were technically one unit, there was not much mingling of squads. Some soldiers ate, gambled, talked, or simply slept. For them, there was no need to be alert, they were in Kyoto, the Capital, and surrounded by allies. The shinobi were in the den of the enemy, they would have to stay vigilant to keep up their disguise.

Nobutada's second in command had been assigned the duty of welcoming all reporting squads and leading them to Nobutada Oda for orders. The shinobi came to the end of the barracks; they were bidden enter through a sliding door by Nobutada's second in command. In a small room, Nobutada Oda sat in front of a table, reading a letter with great intent. Noboru, leader of the squad, came forward and bowed low while holding a katana out as a token of service, the rest of the group followed in example.

"Squad eighteen reporting for duty. I humbly ask that you accept the service of my men and our lives if necessary." Noboru showed strength in his voice, but at the same time a loyalty that all samurai showed toward their lords.

Nobutada Oda looked up and nodded in approval. "Accepted. I had started to think that no more squads would show because they were dead. What delayed you?"

Noboru came up from his bow and produced the dispatch orders that they had taken from the samurai. "We were ordered to patrol the outskirts of Lake Biwa after the Iga incursion. The purpose of which was to kill any remaining shinobi from infiltrating Azuchi Castle."

"And did you?" Nobutada questioned while verifying the dispatch orders.

"It took more than a month to track the group that had skimmed by Lake Biwa, but we hunted the rats and exterminated them. Unfortunately, we did lose a man in the process, this is the reason for our delay. If I had given up on our hunt, I would have dishonored myself and your father," Noboru replied with confidence.

Nobutada seemed to be pleased with the response but still questioned Noboru further. "I would have your names before I give you leave."

Each of the shinobi gave a name from the stolen dispatch orders. Nobutada looked at his second in command and the man gave a nod of approval as he checked his paperwork.

"We will wait for no other squads to return," Nobutada spoke, looking at his second in command. "The rest are dead or scattered, we have the bulk of the force here and I have received orders from my father. We will gather the men in the barracks. I mean to tell them of my father's plan."

The shinobi were escorted out into the common area with the other samurai. The plan seemed to be going well, but there was no need to let their guard down.

"What do you think?" Itsuki whispered to Noboru.

"Well let's just wait and see about this plan."

For about a half hour nothing changed: men sat, chatted, ate, and drank. The shinobi spoke with each other nonchalantly to keep up appearances and only spoke when spoken to, remaining friendly but forgetful. After a long wait, Nobutada Oda with his second in command came out of the office. All the samurai in the room stood up at attention to see their new commander.

Nobutada lifted a hand for silence. "I am not my father, but I am humbled that he gave me command over such tested men. I can only hope that I can give you the loyalty you all deserve from a commander."

Nobutada paced back and forth, pulling out the letter from his father. "This letter contains orders from my father. As you know, Hideyoshi Hashiba began his siege of the Bitchū Province, but it seems he has hit trouble, biting off more than he could chew."

A low rumble of chuckling came from the troops.

"Hideyoshi has requested more troops from my father. I say he should have sent us in the first place."

A thunderous "Ho!" came from all the men in the room.

Nobutada smiled. "Nevertheless, my father will oblige Hideyoshi by sending him the rest of Mitsuhide's reserve army. That will only leave his personal guard with him. My father is coming here, to the Capital, to bolster his force with ours so that he may protect himself and Kyoto. His enemies are great, you have all personally battled them. You showed your strength during the quelling of Iga Province against the farmers who play assassin. My father will need that strength here in Kyoto."

In this moment, the shinobi's eyes widened in excitement. It was more than they could have hoped. Nobunaga would be coming to them, and they were already disguised as his troops.

"I know you have just arrived, but my father would ask on you again." Nobutada raised his fist. "Will you protect your future shōgun?"

Another thunderous, "Ho!" came from all the men.

Nobutada raised his hand for silence. "In three days, my father will be here in Kyoto. And for three days I would have you enjoy peace in the city before you continue your days of war. Enjoy this time to be reminded of why my father is trying to unify Japan. To bring about peace so that you may all return to your families once again. The squad leaders are to stay and receive their assignments. The rest may go, enjoy the city and report back on the morning of the third day for dispatch. Dismissed."

At a wave of his hand, Nobutada Oda was done. He had taken after his father for being a leader. In one speech he praised the men, asked for their loyalty, and rewarded their past deeds. Whatever misgivings the soldiers had of him would likely be alleviated. As for the shinobi, they all looked at each other but dare not speak the words in the den of the samurai.

"We'll I guess that's my cue," Noboru nodded. "I suppose I will see you two back at the granary."

Itsuki and Kaito nodded in agreement, knowing that Noboru needed to complete the infiltration and find out what orders they would receive.

"We will be outside," Itsuki stated. "At the bar, I need a drink."

Meanwhile, back at the abandoned granary, Rin and Tsubasa were having a heated discussion while sitting cross-legged from each other.

"You should have more reservations about following those two," Rin stated.

"Why? They knew my father and have only helped me get closer to avenging him," Tsubasa replied.

"They are helping themselves. You really think Itsuki would let you give the killing strike? He's blind with revenge, you know better than that. Not to mention Noboru being on trial."

"Noboru on trial?" Tsubasa exclaimed. "And why have you not mentioned this before?"

"Openly discuss this in front of them, I think not. Besides, I wasn't exactly sure it was him at first."

"How would you know of such judgments? They are not done openly; you would have never been allowed to view such a ceremony. It is only done before the elders of the village, the accused, possible witnesses, and an advocate."

"I always stuck my nose where I wasn't supposed to be, you know that, Tsubasa. It was just this time that I stumbled upon something more... interesting."

"So out with it then," Tsubasa urged.

"Well, I still remember; it was an autumn night. I heard voices outside my window, and I decided to get a better chance to hear what all the commotion was. I found your father and Yamato arguing. I still remember Yamato saying that a shinobi had come back all bloody, the rest of his squad dead, and that the mission had failed. They did not state the details, only your father was arguing to postpone the trial. He wanted to speak to the accused."

Tsubasa understood the weight of the words that Rin spoke. Under the laws of Hekison, to fail at a mission was an embarrassment. To be the only survivor of a failed mission was worse, the implications could only mean one of two things: cowardice, or betrayal.

"Anyway," Rin continued, "I followed your father and Yamato to the pit in front of the Hall of Four Rings. There were a couple of elders waiting, but the one kneeling in the pit was Noboru."

"Noboru?" Tsubasa questioned.

"Yes, although I did not know him at the time. His hands were bound behind his back. Furthermore, he was bruised and bloody with a swollen left eye."

"So, what happened?" Tsubasa stated impatiently.

"Something odd. First off, the trial was moved outside the village grounds into a forest clearing with a single campfire. I followed as close as I dared, but your father could always hear a leaf fall when wary. His mind was obviously distracted, so I did risk tailing at a distance." Rin paused, trying to recall old memories.

"And?"

"Well that's just it, I couldn't get close enough without being seen. What I do know is that the elders had said the word murder a couple times between arguing. And that it looked like Noboru was to be sentenced to death until your father suggested something about a hearth."

"The hearth of Yomi-No-Kuni," Tsubasa stated gravely.

"How... did you know the name?"

"Spying, same as you. It is a very old ceremony of Hekison, involving what, I know not. So? What happened next?"

"I saw a brand was heated, but I was forced to leave for fear of being caught. Next, I heard..." Rin hesitated at Tsubasa's knowledge. "Screaming in the distance, some of the worst I've ever heard."

"Why would my father wish the trial of Yomi-No-Kuni on Noboru?"

"I can't say for sure, knowledge of it was burned with Hekison. But from the screams, a death sentence may have been kinder. As I said, I saw the brand before it was used, and when I caught a glimpse of Noboru's back... How old is he?"

"Twenty-five maybe, I'm actually not sure."

"The age fits."

"Yes," Tsubasa deducted. "So that's how you recognized that Noboru was the same man you saw that night." Tsubasa sat for a long time in silence, taking in the information. A flood of scenarios was running through his mind. The Noboru, Tsubasa knew was a man quick to laughter and one to lift the hearts of his comrades. The man Rin had described had been accused of cowardice and possible betrayal by murder.

Why does Itsuki show such loyalty to a man accused of possible murder? Tsubasa thought.

"Tsubasa," Rin stated, breaking the silence. "It is not my place to say, but Noboru and Itsuki may just be using you and your brother for a means to an end. They may quickly leave you for dead if it suits their purposes."

"I wouldn't take it that far," Tsubasa stated thoughtfully, still contemplating the information. "But our goal is the same for now. After Nobunaga's death we can always part ways with them. I will consider what you have said, but not jump to any conclusions."

"Fine, think on it," Rin stated, folding her arms and appearing somewhat defeated. "At least let me see your sword. You four are all secrets about these dark blades. I know I will not be told the whole tale out of mistrust, but will you at least let me inspect it?"

Tsubasa hesitated for a moment, then pulled out his sword. "I'm just as protective about my sword, so I hold the handle."

"Fair enough."

Rin slowly inspected the battered sheath; it was weather worn from being in the damp cave of Sōjōbō, years it had pretended to be a feather. Only when she unsheathed Tsubasa's blade could she inspect the masterful legacy of Sengo Muramasa.

Rin methodically ran her hand from guard to the tip of the blade. She investigated the blade while peering down the tip at a sideways glance and became slightly hypnotized by the beauty.

"The blade is black, almost like obsidian but... rotate please."

"No sheen or reflection, just a dark gray line at the edge," Tsubasa stated while turning the blade over.

"Yes, that's it, almost a shadow made metal. How do you know they were made by Muramasa? Have you checked the tang for his engraving?" Rin questioned with her eyes fixed on the blade.

"No, but so say Noboru and Itsuki," Tsubasa stated. "They were with my father when they were originally found, a mission to find and commission Muramasa."

"Yes, but why black? And how? This method of forging is unheard of," Rin pondered. "I don't suppose —"

Rin's trance was interrupted by the loud voices of Noboru, Itsuki, and Kaito. Tsubasa quickly sheathed the blade; he preferred not to explain why Rin was inspecting the weapon so closely. Noboru entered abruptly with an extremely large grin on his face.

"Well?" Tsubasa stated.

"Honnō-ji Temple," Noboru stated enthusiastically. "We are assigned to be guards for Nobunaga Oda." Noboru's smile faded as he saw the serious looks on the young faces before him. "What were you two talking about?"

"Nothing," Rin said with a serene smile. "Just old memories around the hearth."

27

Honnō-ji Temple
-Yamashiro Province, Kyoto City-

The setting sun in the sky was making a brilliant set of amber colors on the horizon that faded into a deep dark blue. Low clouds filtered the sunlight to give Kyoto a brilliant show before letting the night sky envelope the city. Nobunaga Oda had arrived that morning and taken up residence at Honnō-ji Temple. It was Nobunaga's tradition to take a tea ceremony and reside in the temple every time he stayed in Kyoto. The city was to be his final foothold before continuing his conquest of the west after Hideyoshi's siege of Bitchū Province.

The shinobi had arrived at sunset to relieve another squad from guard duty. Noboru handed over the dispatch orders to the group, proving the legitimacy of their squad. Noboru had adeptly volunteered to guard at night, saying that his squad works better at night, a truth, but a lie at the same time. In full samurai garb, the shinobi acted as guards outside the perimeter of Honnō-ji Temple. The group studied the other patrols as best they could in preparation to know their whereabouts. Kaito and Tsubasa had previously climbed a nearby building to gather as much information on where guards would be and how many men were in the temple grounds. Currently, Noboru, Itsuki, and Kaito were playing the ruse of patrol, waiting for the others to arrive.

The stars could be seen amply, and the heavens blessed the night sky as the shinobi waited for the dead of night. One would call such a night beautiful; a thin crescent moon let the stars show evermore brightly and gave a dark concealment to the shinobi's mission. The task the shinobi had would be completed not by force, but by speed, agility, and cunning. The plan would begin by penetrating the temple from the section they had been dispatched to guard. They had counted a few sentries from higher vantage points that they would have to eliminate. Farther in, the groups would split, one for diversion and the other for assassination. If all went well, the groups would meet at the proposed rendezvous outside the city walls with their possessions stowed away and ready for travel.

As planned, Tsubasa and Rin rendezvoused with the others late at night, carrying a large pack of supplies and clothing. There would be no point in assuming the ruse of samurai, the armor made noise, and they would be stopped for questioning if they tried to make their way to the interior temple grounds. In a nearby wooded garden the group put on their shinobifukus. The shinobi were glad to be in their preferred clothing. Even Rin had an earth toned shinobifuku fitted for a female that she had long saved; her current life rarely necessitated the garb until now. She had always kept it in hopes she could be the hunter of the night instead of the friendly face knocking on a door. They all wrapped their three-foot long cloths around their faces to conceal their identities.

Itsuki took out a small collapsible paper lantern no bigger than a hand and gave it to Kaito. The four men had their black blades slung across their backs; Rin had a normal wakizashi short sword. Noboru had his two kunai bombs, Kaito his bow, Itsuki his weighted chain, Tsubasa his throwing kunai, and Rin had tucked away a simple dagger.

Noboru handed two previously prepared arrows with cylindrical powder bombs attached at the shafts to Kaito. "Use them well, they make more of a show than damage," Noboru whispered. "Use only if necessary. Ideally, we will be gone before an alarm is raised. Give the signal when the targeted sentries are dead."

The group could not help but flash smiles under their face cloths, the nervousness before going behind enemy lines, and the invigoration of pulling a mission off without getting caught. The whole scenario made their blood come alive, true shinobi lived for moments like these. Once everyone was ready, Tsubasa being the tallest made his way to the high wall and faced the group. Itsuki went first and ran straight at Tsubasa, jumping up only a foot before colliding with the young man. Tsubasa used the palms of his hands to vault Itsuki's foot, elevating Itsuki to the stone wall. Noboru followed and took a crouched position on the wall.

"I know how you like to be first," Kaito gestured to Rin.

Rin playfully bowed and followed the group, Kaito shortly after, and Tsubasa was helped up the wall last by his brother. Once on the wall, the group headed toward a tall building overlooking the perimeter of Honnō-ji Temple. They ran in the shadow of a three-story building as best they could to avoid detection from any far-off sentries. They stayed in single file as much as possible, Itsuki and Noboru leading the way. They used hand signals for commands to stop, go, and wait. The whole group moved like water, a fluidity that showed the discipline of their craft. The group had split between alleyways when a lone guard was walking toward them.

Itsuki gave the signal to wait; he silently took out his chain, gripping it firmly. Only when the guard had come right to the corner of the building did Itsuki make his move. The chain went over the guard's neck and twisted into the man's throat; the guard instinctively clawed at his neck. Itsuki did not dare loosen his grip for fear the guard would scream. Once the guard had gone limp, Noboru helped Itsuki put the body in the shadows behind some barrels. The group continued to the base of a tall building and began to climb; to the men's amazement, Rin had easily taken the lead.

Just as nimble as ever, Tsubasa thought, trying to keep up with her.

The three-story building contained a square, 360-degree view balcony that encompassed a top chamber and contained two guards. The group waited below for the right moment when both guards were out of each other's view. Noboru flipped over the balcony railing, silently he slid a kunai through the guard's neck. The kill only made the slightest of noises, but when the other guard questioned the noise, it was too late. Rin had made a similar scene of the adjacent guard's throat.

The group convened at the balcony, crouching at the railing.

"Here is where we split," Noboru stated, pointing to a building. "Over there, you see."

The group peered for a while to see a single guard sitting on a roof.

"He must die before Noboru and I can move farther toward the temple grounds, he has a clear view of our entry," Itsuki whispered. "If not eliminated he will surely see us and raise the alarm. When he's dead, give the signal so we know how to proceed. Then distract as needed and kill if necessary, use your best judgment. Understood?"

The three youths nodded in approval.

Noboru pulled down his face covering for a moment to speak to the Yukimura brothers. "Your father would be proud of you two, make sure you keep it that way. Tsubasa, you have great skill, but don't get overzealous. Kaito, have faith in yourself, you're stronger than you know."

Tsubasa gave a reluctant nod. Still prone to rash anger, he could not help but feel the approval from his dead father. Kaito eagerly agreed with the sentiment.

"Rin, you too. We could not have made it here so quickly without your help."

Rin hesitated only for a moment. "I should tell you something," she whispered to the group.

Itsuki waved his hands. "Hey, we'll have time for sentiments after the job is finished." Itsuki had no patience; only revenge was on his mind for his wife, Yuna, and his young daughter, Natsumi. All other motivation came secondary.

The group split, the brothers and Rin headed down the railing in silence. Noboru and Itsuki stood together looking out over Kyoto. The city was silent and slumbering.

"Noboru," Itsuki stated, staring at the temple.

"Yes." Noboru looked over while struggling to see his friend's face in the pale moonlight.

"I want to kill him without help, even if it means my death."

"But..." Noboru contended but quickly sighed. "Very well. But promise me that it will bring you peace, my friend."

"Promises are for children, an empty gesture that one hopes to control one's fate," Itsuki said, thinking of promises he gave to his daughter.

"If promises are for children, then I say fulfillments are for men. And let us fulfill our purpose this night, live or die."

Itsuki almost smiled, Noboru always had a knack to say just the right thing. The mountain range where Mount Kurama stood was watching over the city. The two shinobi looked out with a panoramic view surveying the night. The lanterns outside the homes dotted the city with dim yellow light. There was a slight wind blowing where they stood as if the kami were watching in anticipation for the coming events.

"It reminds me of the islands," stated Itsuki, "and the light of yōkai we found."

"Yes," Noboru stated pensively. "The demon's blood we found out in the isles beyond the world where Muramasa forged the swords. I'd be lying if I didn't say I wish Kazuki was with us, it was him that started us on this path. I have the same feeling I had when the three of us set sail off the island of Honshu in search of Muramasa. My blood flows like fire."

As the words left Noboru's lips, the pair could not help but feel that Kazuki was with them in spirit. The night had a familiar magic; broken only by the movement of their comrades awoke Itsuki and Noboru from their nostalgic memories. In the distance they could see the targeted guard and what looked like Kaito sneaking slowly behind him. Kaito was squatting and sliding his feet to reduce noise.

"Here it comes," Noboru stated.

In the distance you could see a sword protruding from the man's chest and Kaito putting a hand over the man's mouth.

Shortly after, Tsubasa and Rin climbed on the rooftop. The group studied the temple perimeter for a long while. Noboru and Itsuki watched them intently.

Kaito pulled out the small collapsible paper lantern and lit it. He then repeatedly put his hand over the lantern light eight times.

"Eight guards," Itsuki stated, reading the signal.

Then after a long pause Kaito blocked the light over the lantern repeatedly at greater speed.

"Scattered," Noboru nodded in confirmation.

Itsuki and Noboru swiftly jumped down the railing, climbing down to the lower rooftops. For the first time since before Hekison, the two could unleash their full potential. In their recent journey they had always reserved themselves, parting some of their focus on keeping the Yukimura brothers safe. Like a dam breaking, Noboru and Itsuki flooded their path where the guards stood sentry. The two comrades' rage and skill could finally be unleashed. The guards would have to be killed in series and hidden swiftly to not rouse their next target. Itsuki and Noboru positioned themselves for their first attack.

Noboru rolled off a rooftop with his blade pointed downward and swiftly made contact with the first guard. Noboru muffled the man's grunts and dispatched the body into the shadows. Itsuki waited at a corner, blade ready in hand. The guard came and Itsuki sent the blade upward through the guard's ribcage. Itsuki simultaneously put his hand over the man's mouth to muffle the gasp.

The two shinobi quickly continued their assault. Itsuki and Noboru did not have to use hand signals or wait till the other was ready, they had worked so much together that they were of one shadow and mind. The shinobi eagerly used the legacy of

Muramasa, each cut was clean, precise, and swift. Repeatedly they made their way closer to the temple, silently killing each of their targets until only two remained.

The last two guards were talking with each other, leaving no blind spot for the shinobi. They waited only a moment in the shadows of an alleyway, their dark shinobifukus and black blades made them nearly invisible. Itsuki and Noboru silently climbed to the roof of an adjacent home. Itsuki dislodged one of the roof tiles and then dropped it into the shadows, making an abrupt shattering ceramic sound. The guards hastily broke their conversation and headed toward the sound with their lanterns held high.

"What the?" the guard stated, looking at the tile.

Naturally, the two guards looked up, two black shadows with blades coming down were the last things they ever saw. The black tengu blades continually impressed the shinobi; even now the cuts they had made had gone deeper and faster than any other blade previously handled. Despite Noboru and Itsuki's best efforts, blood splatters had stained their shinobifukus, the two gave each other a nod and headed to the temple wall. One boosted the other up the wall, and the following pulled the other with conjoined hand in a continuous flow like water running between rocks. Together Noboru and Itsuki felt unstoppable, the Hundred Shadow Man had taught his disciples well.

In the temple grounds Noboru and Itsuki knelt on one of the roofs, upon inspection they found too many attendants and guards within the grounds. For success they would have to find and kill Nobunaga Oda in one strike and escape before the alarm was sounded. In the center of the grounds stood the main temple building draped with a cloth that bore the Nobunaga family crest.

The building had a single entryway with sliding doors and an encompassing square patio. Long pillars and elaborate lit windows lined the perimeter of the building. The typical curved and pointed tile roof was their goal of entry. Itsuki and Noboru silently made their way toward the building, a mere hundred feet, they stayed in shadows and moved slowly and silently. Only once did a guard look in their direction thinking that he had seen something move in the night, but when the guard moved to investigate, he found nothing.

At the very end, the two shinobi scaled the building from the back, planting their feet on the roof. They searched the roof, hoping for a weakness in the building. As per common architecture, the building had a vent for the hearth inside. The shinobi simultaneously pried open the grate from each end, the wood creaked ever so slightly. The two entered, balancing on the thick wooden beams supporting the ceiling.

They creeped over to the darkest corner to catch a glimpse of their target. The temple was a very large room used for religious assemblies. The center was open, but the elaborate dark wood columns came down around the perimeter, holding up the roof structure above. Below, Nobunaga Oda was awake and alert with his sandal bearer, Ranmaru Mōri. As described, Nobunaga was in his late forties, with a large nose hanging over a large mustache. Just as Rin had warned, Nobunaga had a tendency not to sleep; the man was on guard and vigilant. Nobunaga's identity was confirmed by the way his subordinate addressed and spoke to him. Nobunaga was currently turning the coals of the fire, peering into the changing colors of the embers. Despite not being in his armor, Nobunaga had his two swords at his waist, armed and dangerous as usual. The place where Nobunaga was standing made it impossible to drop on him or land a blow silently. The shinobi would have to confront the two men to kill them, but once alerted they would soon be outmatched by the guards. So Itsuki and Noboru waited silently in the shadows of the rafters, waiting for an opportunity.

Nearby the temple walls, the Yukimura brothers and Rin made their way closer, keeping an eye out for stray guards and potential threats.

"Do you think they're inside?" Rin whispered.

"I imagine so, they took off in a hurry after the signal," Tsubasa answered.

The group observed the temple perimeter, very few guards could be seen. In all reality, Nobunaga Oda had the least amount of protection since before his rise to power. His generals were all out on war and Nobunaga had a sense of security, Kyoto being the center city of his military hold. If Itsuki and Noboru raised an alarm it would be up to the Yukimura brothers to distract guards from closing in on them.

"Rin," Kaito whispered.

"Yes?"

"Will you come with us when this is over?" Kaito whispered.

Rin kept her eyes on the city. "I... I hardly think this is the time to ask that."

Then it came, the war horn of an ocean conch and the distinct glimmer of a torch line. In the distance hundreds of torches were lit near the perimeter of the city walls. A rumble of an army could be heard coming through the city gates.

"What the hell?" Tsubasa said.

"Mitsuhide Akechi, Nobunaga's general," Rin muttered.

"Who?" Kaito spoke. "Is he here to lend Nobunaga support?"

"No," Rin spoke nervously. "He's here to kill Nobunaga, I'm sorry but there's no time to explain."

At this point the whole city was waking up, and soon the streets would be full of panicked citizens. The Yukimura brothers and Rin flattened themselves on the roof; alert eyes would soon be upon them. A file of torches could be seen in the distance, making their way toward Honnō-ji Temple.

"What are we going to do?" Kaito questioned, looking at Tsubasa.

"This." Tsubasa grabbed one of the black powder arrows out of Kaito's quiver.

"That's only for emergencies," Rin blurted out.

"What do you think this is? If we don't act now, a thousand soldiers will be at Nobunaga's door with Itsuki and Noboru inside."

"But..." Rin's anger flared. She did not know what to say.

Tsubasa ignored her while tossing the arrow to Kaito and then quickly rummaged through one of his shinobifuku pockets. Kaito, instinctively knowing his brother's thoughts, grabbed his bow and loaded the arrow.

"Ready?" Tsubasa said, getting out the flint lighter next to the bomb's fuse.

Kaito nodded and in three tries Tsubasa lit the fuse. Kaito aimed high to compensate for the weight and let the arrow fly into the night sky. It disappeared toward the men with torches. They waited and for a moment feared that the wind caused the fuse to go out. Then finally, in the distance there was a large flash and boom near the men with torches.

"Is that supposed to stop them?" Rin mocked.

"Of course not, it's to make them cautious," Tsubasa declared. "To buy time for Itsuki and Noboru. Kaito, one more."

Tsubasa and Kaito repeated their rigging of the arrow and let another fly; their position had been compromised. An investigating guard had seen the second arrow fly and blinked in surprise at the shinobi, as if questioning his eyesight.

"Assassins!" the guard yelled.

Kaito did not let him yell again as he released an arrow into the man's chest. Tsubasa unleashed his sword and Rin reluctantly followed.

"Stay on the rooftops," Tsubasa stated. "If we fight in the streets, we'll be dead. We need to draw Nobunaga's troops to engage with the intruders, only fight if necessary."

A wave of fear rushed over Tsubasa and then he steeled himself with a kunai in one hand and his sword in the other. The group was about to be caught between Nobunaga's guards and Mitsuhide's troops. Time seemed to stop as responding warrior yells from each side were given, followed by a sprinting of feet. The first part of Mitsuhide's troops and Nobunaga's guards met with a giant clash of sword, spear, and blood.

Kaito had unleashed what few arrows he had and soon drew his sword. In a flurry Tsubasa had thrown all the kunai daggers hanging from his torso at guards daring to climb up to the rooftops. The Yukimura brothers and Rin eventually made battle with the slow trickle of soldiers coming up to their terrain. Tsubasa and Kaito stood back-to-back while wielding their tengu blades with deadly efficiency.

Tsubasa slashed his enemies away with his usual astonishing speed. The quality of the first wave of soldiers was low; Mitsuhide did not believe he would receive this much resistance. Kaito was finally coming into his own with the battle as he kicked a guard off the roof to fall to his death. Even Rin's sword skills were proving more than efficient, another secret she hadn't divulged from her long-shaded past.

Now that the Yukimura brothers and Rin had successfully baited the forces of Nobunaga and Mitsuhide into battle, the diversion strategy had shifted into surviving. It was soon obvious that to stay and fight was futile, so they began to leap from roof-to-roof to distance themselves from the armies. Buildings surrounding the temple grounds were starting to go ablaze, including the one that the Yukimura brothers were fighting on. By now most of the city was awake and chaotic, but Mitsuhide Akechi had ordered that the citizens of Kyoto were not to be touched. If Mitsuhide's coup d'état was to work, he would need the support of the common folk. Only those who gave resistance were to be dispatched.

Tsubasa jumped to the next adjacent rooftop. "C'mon we have to get out of here."

Kaito went to follow but was caught by a soldier wielding a spear, metal shimmering with each jab. The two parried and jabbed at each other until the soldier was able to trip Kaito. As Kaito landed flat on his back, the samurai put a foot on Kaito's hand, pinning his wrist and causing him to let go of his sword. The soldier positioned the spear for Kaito's chest. A wide-eyed Kaito gasped, bracing himself for the killing blow. At the last moment, blood sprayed on Kaito's face, but to his surprise he found that Rin had skewered the soldier with her wakizashi. Kaito breathed heavily, blinded by the soldier's blood and head dizzy with adrenaline, he frantically looked for his dropped sword.

Then, as if a sixth sense had run across Kaito's spine, he noticed a slender hand twirling a dark black blade as if testing the balance. Rin had taken the tengu blade. Kaito turned, still on his bruised knees while Rin looked at the blade, coveting its beauty. Rin's hair had become unbound and blew wild in the wind with the fiery embers of the roof dancing around her.

"What are you doing?" Kaito said astonished. "We have to get out of here."

"Come with me," Rin stated. "Leave the others to die with Nobunaga. Tsubasa will follow if you come with me."

"W-w-what? They're my friends?"

"Grow up. Your friends? A man with a death wish, and the other a murderer. Both left Yamato to die in his blood and both ready to kill me if I so much as even questioned their actions. They're just a renegade squad who abandoned Hekison when they were needed most."

Kaito stared at Rin, at a loss for words.

"If you're not coming, I'll be borrowing your sword."

Rin ran to make an escape and Kaito bolted after her, grabbing the spear of the dead soldier. She jumped to another rooftop and Kaito caught up with her. Kaito swung at Rin, and she parried with lightning speed. Nevertheless, Kaito twirled with efficiency and swung at Rin with deadly intent, the spear heading for her neck. Wide-eyed Rin rolled back. Kaito came again, blind with rage and swinging downward. His spear came down perfectly, but Rin parried and slid her other hand to Kaito's spear handle. She finished her attack with a gut-wrenching kick to Kaito's stomach. Kaito gasped for air while Rin held both blade and spear, he had been no match for her. Rin slowly brought the tip of the tengu blade to Kaito's chest.

"I saved your life, letting you die would have been easier."

Kaito grabbed the black blade with his right hand. "Then go, but the sword stays with me," Kaito stated bitterly, his voice enveloped in rage.

Rin's gaze pierced Kaito's eyes. As if a veil had been lifted for the first time, Kaito saw the woman Rin had become over the past years and not the girl he once knew. "I have a mission to complete, for Hekison," Rin stated coldly.

Rin pulled the sword away from Kaito with his death grip still on the blade. Kaito screamed with pain as the palm of his hand poured blood from the wound. Rin jumped down to the streets and ran into the screaming crowds. Kaito attempted to follow, but when he put his wounded hand on a wall to gather his balance, he slipped from the blood, bashing his head on roof tiles. Soon after, Tsubasa was behind to help his brother up.

"We have to get it back!" Kaito screamed, trying to break Tsubasa's grip.

"I know," Tsubasa stated sympathetically. "I saw the whole thing, but you know her. By now she is just an ordinary frightened woman in the city, we'll never find her here. And we'll be dead if we stay, we have to get to the rendezvous and pray Itsuki and Noboru are successful."

Noboru and Itsuki stared at each other in surprise when they heard the large boom outside the temple. The noise could only have been one of the powder bombs Noboru had given the brothers. Nobunaga's honor guard was alert as ever. Noises could be heard outside, and a guard came running into Nobunaga's quarters.

"What is it?" Nobunaga demanded.

"Men bearing the Akechi clan banners," the guard said while frantically catching his breath. "Mitsuhide Akechi has betrayed you. He has brought his troops to Kyoto and seeks your life. We must get you out of here."

"Go where?" Nobunaga fumed with anger but showed no surprise by the news of the betrayal. "We are only but a couple hundred, Mitsuhide has thousands. I am the one who sent them. No... we will stand fighting. The alternative is to die running and I will not have that be my last act. You know my orders, now go."

The guard nodded and Nobunaga could hear the barking of commands and the running of soldiers toward the perimeter temple walls.

Ranmaru Mōri came forward. "My lord, it will be an honor to die by your side."

Nobunaga could not help but smile. He had chosen Ranmaru to be his sandal bearer because of the man's great skill of sword, bravery on the battlefield, and undisputed loyalty.

"We will both have a death to be remembered," Nobunaga said, putting a hand on Ranmaru's shoulder.

Itsuki, believing this to be his only opportunity, slid down one of the columns from the rafters to confront Nobunaga. Noboru followed down another, knowing that if they succeeded this would be a sloppy assassination. A shinobi never confronted an enemy head on unless absolutely necessary, but the present circumstances left them no choice.

For one of the few times in Nobunaga's life, the man was genuinely surprised by the two ominous shadowy figures. For a short moment Nobunaga thought that the two figures were deadly yōkai coming for his life before the end. He and Ranmaru both looked at the shinobi while drawing their katanas.

"Shinobi-no-mono." Nobunaga clenched his jaw. "It seems I had not finished what I started in Iga."

Noboru and Itsuki unsheathed their black wakizashis from their backs; the looks on the samurai's faces were of surprise and disgust.

"Tainted blades," Ranmaru spoke. "What corrupted swordsmith made such abominations?"

"Muramasa," Noboru stated.

Nobunaga's eyes widened at the comment. But before a response could be given, Itsuki came at Nobunaga with full force and Noboru at Ranmaru like wildfire. Itsuki had a drive in him that he had never felt, he was having difficulty keeping his emotions in check. Despite Itsuki's tengu blade, Nobunaga still wielded the legendary blade of Masamune, an arguably better crafted sword. Nobunaga's strokes were heavy and strong, a strange methodic motion that weakened Itsuki at every attack. Itsuki was cautious while fighting Nobunaga, the man was battle hardened and had years of experience on him. Itsuki dared not use one of his usual tricks, he could never take both hands off the sword hilt in fear of Nobunaga taking advantage of a one-handed grip. Held up by the vengeance of his family, Itsuki focused himself with every parry against Nobunaga.

Noboru was wildly yelling at Ranmaru as he twirled, trying to land aggressive blows on the samurai. The samurai stood his ground not wincing once; he was not intimidated by Noboru's strength and aggressiveness. Noboru saw that the ploy was not working and slowed his pace so he would not wear himself out. Ranmaru read the change, and decided that the shinobi was starting to fatigue, Ranmaru instinctively changed to an offensive style. Ranmaru came with a downward swing and Noboru blocked the blow with his sword. Ranmaru then unsheathed his small dagger and made a swipe, nearly taking Noboru's throat. On and on Ranmaru's blows came, wearing Noboru down with each strike. Noboru's speed was starting to fade. Noboru took advantage of an opening to recollect himself. He flipped backwards, leaving a ten-pace gap, and stared down Ranmaru while breathing heavily. Noboru fought to keep his anger at bay and contemplated how he would overcome his enemy. Ranmaru paused and looked at Noboru waiting for his next move.

"Come, shinobi," Ranmaru taunted, "I have other men to kill."

Noboru pulled down his face covering letting it hang around his neck. Noboru's face perspired with sweat and a look of defiant determination pierced Ranmaru. Noboru stabbed his wakizashi into the floorboards as if giving up. To the surprise of Ranmaru, Noboru closed his eyes as if praying in the temple. Noboru slowly interlaced his fingers together to make the Kuji-in hand seal of Retsu. Noboru fearful for his life, but not yet overcome with terror, concentrated to conjure the mental state of time, to give himself the boost needed to defeat his foe.

For the first successful time in Noboru's life, he conjured his second hand seal. The flood of a battle sense came over Noboru, the feeling of time slowing; a more intense state of battle awareness draped his entire being. With a renewed vigor, Noboru came at Ranmaru with a fierceness that caught the samurai off guard. Ranmaru felt as if he was fighting a new foe and being pushed to his limit, the fear of death pushed Ranmaru to fight harder. Noboru came with a one-handed sword position for piercing and Ranmaru countered with the same. With lightning speed Noboru was able to grab Ranmaru's sword-hand and pull the arm to expose the man's armpit. With all the swiftness Noboru could conjure, he led his tengu blade to sever the arm of Ranmaru while still holding onto the wrist. Ranmaru almost ended Noboru if it weren't for the pain; in his final defense, he stabbed Noboru's chest with a tantō, but only enough to break skin. Noboru still held the samurai's arm while delivering a final stroke against Ranmaru's chest. Noboru yelled in victory.

Itsuki continued his battle with the fierce Daimyō Nobunaga Oda. At this point Itsuki was breathing heavily but Nobunaga stood as if he was teaching a student for the first time of how to use a sword. Itsuki backed away from Nobunaga and made the Kuji-in hand seal of Jin, for awareness. Nobunaga squinted his eyes at the seal with a new caution but came at Itsuki with force. Itsuki focused on Nobunaga's movements to predict his next attack. For the first time in the battle Itsuki was keeping up with Nobunaga and even making him step back on a few of his blows. Nobunaga had a look of frustration on his face, but only briefly, something had changed.

Nobunaga Oda shifted his fighting stance to a wider footing to balance his center of gravity. Nobunaga Oda's blade came at Itsuki with a swift swing, nearly landing on the collarbone. Then after one of Itsuki's blows, Nobunaga counterattacked with a lateral slice, almost taking out Itsuki's bowels. The brief wave of confidence that Itsuki gained from his hands seal had become replaced with frustration. Itsuki was outmatched.

Itsuki's hand seal mind state could no longer predict Nobunaga's moves because the samurai was using a fighting style completely foreign to Itsuki. The frustration of not completing his goal became unbearable and Itsuki screamed with anger. Itsuki gave a final desperate sword swing fueled by emotion. Nobunaga parried and then expertly sliced Itsuki's ribs.

Itsuki yelled with pain and clutched his bloody side, the wound had lost him the battle. Itsuki braced himself for Nobunaga's final blow. *I will go back to my family without a head and as a failed fool*, Itsuki thought with panic.

Nobunaga raised the sword of Masamune high as if to take Itsuki's head. Noboru only looked on in panic as he saw his friend clutching his ribs while hobbling away from the mighty warlord. Then with steady composure, Nobunaga stepped back and sheathed his sword while looking at Noboru and Itsuki. For a moment it seemed as if time had stopped; there was no battle outside, only a simple sparring match between colleagues.

"Unsheathe your sword." Itsuki tore off his face covering. "This is not over."

"A blind man could see that it's over," Nobunaga stated calmly, mulling over the situation. "The two of you may have been able to take me out, but that is no longer an option. We both know you lack the skill to kill me, especially with the wound you now have."

"You mock us," Noboru said threateningly.

"Hardly," Nobunaga stated bluntly. "The last man I saw do that obscure hand gesture the way you two did took out several squads by himself and gave me this scar on my jaw." Nobunaga stared at the pair as if weighing his options and sighed. "Those blades... they were what you found when I requested Yamato find me the final blade of Muramasa?"

Itsuki and Noboru only stood dumbfounded, not knowing what to say. The plan they had set out to do was obviously now in the hands of Nobunaga.

"It matters not. In the end I suppose there's no point."

The sounds of fires could be heard in the distance along with the fighting of men. The heat of the flames was already starting to make its way toward the inner temple grounds.

"What I propose is for my country. If you disagree, we may continue our fight."

Itsuki winced at his pain, frustrated that he could not complete his sworn task. With great reluctance, he gave a curt nod. Noboru looked on worriedly as if guards would come in any moment.

"I will die here today, I have no delusions," Nobunaga stated. "But I would rather die at your hands than by the traitorous Mitsuhide Akechi. That swine will parade my head around Kyoto as a trophy, weakening this country's unification that I have sought all my life. People do not take lightly the display of conquered enemies; it will surely allow Mitsuhide to rally people to his cause. I have sons to think of which leaves me in a dilemma. My sons could continue my cause to unite Japan, but I must prevent Mitsuhide from gaining power. I must commit seppuku."

"Your samurai suicide?" Noboru spoke puzzled.

"An honorable death, and I would have you help me," Nobunaga stated, looking at Itsuki.

"What?" Itsuki stated confused.

"I would have you be my number two, to take my head as I commit seppuku and then burn my remains in this temple."

"You would give me your life," Itsuki responded unbelievingly. "You could call for guards to do it. What trick is this?"

Nobunaga could not help but scoff. "From the smell of the fire… I have no time to call guards." Nobunaga looked at Noboru sternly. "And you have killed Ranmaru, not an easy feat. You are an enemy worthy of the task and I have no options. I will have the

329

death of a samurai, you will get your revenge, and Mitsuhide will have no recognizable remains to display. I do not fear death, I fear for the future, I will not see a unified country, but I will die for one."

Itsuki and Noboru were dumbfounded. Nobunaga Oda was nothing like anything they had pictured, a man of prudence, wisdom, and skill, very similar to their mentor, Kazuki Yukimura. Despite Nobunaga's logic, Itsuki cursed that he could not kill the samurai in a proper fight. The man was directly responsible for the siege that ended the lives of his family. Itsuki had no reason to indulge the daimyō in his proposition, but at the same time he thought of the consequences if he refused. He would surely die, and Noboru would surely follow.

"I do not care for your conquest," Itsuki stated bluntly. "But I'll gladly take your head."

"You never use names I have heard." Nobunaga could not help but smile. "But a dead man cannot tell them, I would have them before I go."

"Itsuki Hayashi."

"Noboru Tsukino."

"So, it is settled then, we have little time." Nobunaga knelt. "You must wait until I disembowel myself. Strike true, Itsuki Hayashi, make sure my death is clean. Noboru Tsukino, I would have you start the fire afterwards."

All Noboru could do is nod, a conversation with their sworn enemy was the last thing he expected. Itsuki wrapped his ribs with the three-foot cloth that had been his face scarf to tend his wound and stood behind Nobunaga with his sword held high.

"It will take one swing. I promise you that." Itsuki gripped the handle of his tengu blade.

Nobunaga untied his kimono, baring his chest and stomach. He then took a deep breath and unsheathed his wakizashi short sword. Nobunaga looked out from his temple quarters; the curtains that bore his family seal blocked the view of the battle outside. The sounds of men dying, fires burning, and cries of city folk could be heard. Nobunaga thought back to his childhood and what brought him here. He could not help but smile at the fact that he should die by a shinobi acting as his number two in seppuku. He had no death poem, a tradition a samurai kept before committing seppuku, so he simply spoke.

"I have no regrets," Nobunaga stated proudly.

Without hesitation Lord Nobunaga Oda took his wakizashi and carefully placed the point at his stomach. Then with the strength of his battle worn arms he thrust the blade into his abdomen, dragging the blade laterally across his bowels. Nobunaga Oda did not cry out in pain but gave a struggled grunt as he kept his eyes focused on the Oda crest that fluttered in the curtains.

Itsuki yelled and swung his black blade through the air. In a spurt of blood, Nobunaga's head fell to the floor, his body falling to the side like a timbering tree.

Lord Nobunaga Oda died on an early summer morning. Itsuki breathed hard, if it were the adrenaline or the pain at his side, he could not tell. He only stared at Nobunaga's head looking with ghostly eyes up at his own. Only when Noboru grabbed Itsuki did his hypnotic gaze end.

"Itsuki?" Noboru stated, shaking his shoulder. "Itsuki."

"Yes," Itsuki said, gathering his thoughts. "We must leave, you'll have to help me escape... the wound."

"Of course, but first let me do what I do best," Noboru stated.

He then pulled down the tapestry cloths from the walls and set them ablaze with the hearth fire in the center of the room. "Can you climb?"

"Yes," Itsuki winced. "But not those pillars, we can't go out the way we came, and guards will be near the front door."

Noboru nodded. He pulled out one of his kunai bombs, lit the fuse with his flint box, and threw the kunai at the back wall. A loud thump sounded as the dagger stuck into the wood siding. The two shinobi took cover at the other end of the room. A small explosion erupted from the bomb and wallboards became splintered and weak. Noboru kicked a hole in the wall to finish the job. The two shinobi exited out the burning quarters. Outside, Mitsuhide Akechi had the perimeter nearly surrounded; a few of Nobunaga's guards remained.

Noboru helped Itsuki hobble away from the inferno, making their way to the rear temple grounds wall, but soldiers were in pursuit. Noboru boosted Itsuki up and over the wall; Noboru was nearly hit by a spear throw as it stuck to the wall inches from his head. With lightning speed, Noboru lit his last kunai bomb and threw the missile at the pursuing soldiers. The kunai hit one man's shoulder, the fuse still sparkling as the soldier looked at the lodged kunai in panic. Noboru climbed over the wall and jumped, landing with his knees deeply bent. The explosion of the kunai erupted on the other side of the temple walls. Noboru's skill of kayakujutsu had ended his pursuers.

The two shinobi ran into the streets, the citizens screamed at the sight of the two men in bloody attire. It did not matter to Itsuki and Noboru, the fear of the people was the least of their concerns. Chaos consumed the city of Kyoto. In the shadows Noboru and Itsuki made their way out of the city into the dark forest, hoping that they would find the Yukimura brothers at the designated rendezvous. They had left a city burning while escaping into the wild, a similar scene they had witnessed on the day Hekison fell.

28

The Opportunist
-Yamashiro Province, Omi Province Border-

Ieyasu Tokugawa was in the midst of traveling back from his mission of integrating the locals of the Takeda lands under Nobunaga Oda's rule. Ieyasu had been ordered by Nobunaga to return to Kyoto after the completion of his tour. Ieyasu's troops had taken camp on a small stream in the south of Yamashiro Province, taking a break before returning to Kyoto.

The grass was green and high with the life of early summer; Ieyasu Tokugawa savored the glimpses of peace between the bloody obligations of a daimyō. Ieyasu had introduced Masanari Hattori and the shinobi to his troops, although the shinobi's story of escaping Azuchi Castle was kept a secret. All Ieyasu's troops knew was that these shinobi were here for a negotiation of service. Masanari had returned to his former self after a few months of recuperation from the cells of Azuchi Castle. Ieyasu sat with his new ally while discussing their alliance when a messenger from Kyoto had brought news of Nobunaga's death.

"Word travels fast," Masanari stated while looking at the scroll with his one good eye.

"It's an opportunity," Ieyasu Tokugawa said, walking by the stream. "The first to kill Mitsuhide Akechi will be crowned the successor to Nobunaga's rule. I fear returning to Kyoto will put me in the hands of my enemies."

"And why should my men and I continue to follow you when Nobunaga's dead? It seems my revenge has been taken from me."

"Nobunaga has died, but all that he has built can be for the man that can take it. What better revenge than to see that his legacy is not passed to his sons."

Masanari was mute for a moment as he mulled over the words. "You easily betray your lord?"

"It is true I had no love for Nobunaga; under his command I was forced to order my own son to commit seppuku. It was a just death, but a harsh one, and one I would not recount." Ieyasu furrowed his brow at the memory. "As I have said before, I foresaw Nobunaga's death, even warned him about it. When Nobunaga would not heed my advice, I made plans for the future. The reports say that his successor and eldest son, Nobutada, died in the fighting outside the temple. Nobunaga's other sons will not be able to carry the influence their father had. I mean to unify Japan and bring back the Shogunate. I offer you a position in helping, to continue the deal I had with the Jōnin, Yamato Akiyama."

Masanari looked up surprised. "What do you mean, the deal you had with Yamato Akiyama?"

"I apologize for the secrecy, but I had to wait to see who you really were."

"And who am I?" Masanari questioned skeptically.

"A leader," Ieyasu stated bluntly. "I have heard your men have given you the new title of jōnin, the highest title among the

Iga shinobi. I have also heard you've received a new nickname for your fierceness, Hattori the Demon Hanzō. A new name for a new life."

"Between us, Hanzō Hattori will do," the newly dubbed Hanzō chuckled. "But for my enemies... well, they can address me by my new name."

Ieyasu was well informed. The now named Hanzō Hattori was the one that kept the shinobi together in the fall of Hekison and was the man that had planned the escape for the prisoners of Azuchi Castle. The remnants of Iga had acknowledged his pivotal role and loyalty to Yamato in the siege of Iga. Granted, most of the remnants were all men, but once word got out, surely the families would rally to them.

"I did not save you and your men solely for your skills," Ieyasu explained. "When I was convinced that Nobunaga would fail in his campaign, I began gathering support secretly where I could. Yamato Akiyama and I had an agreement, to help me rise to the title of shōgun. In return I would respect the Iga lands and give the shinobi a position within my reign, with all rights serving under the house of Tokugawa."

"Our home has been destroyed, and as for being servants..." Hanzō scoffed.

"Not mere servants. Yamato knew that the shinobi could no longer survive alone in the misty mountains," Ieyasu reassured. "Nobunaga and his siege are proof of that fact. Living in a partnership with the Shogunate would allow your clan to continue your ways, while still surviving."

"At what cost?" Hanzō questioned sternly.

"Loyalty to the Shogunate," Ieyasu responded with composure. "You are free to lead your men as your conscience dictates. I am not Nobunaga, if the Iga shinobi do not wish to join my cause I will not compel them to do so. As long as your clan does not take up arms against me, I bear them no ill will. But I do not offer any of the benefits of serving me either."

Hanzō looked at Ieyasu with his one eye, studying the man. Despite losing vision with one eye, his judgement of character was not diminished. So far, Ieyasu had given Hanzō no reason to doubt him. The daimyō at great personal risk helped orchestrate the escape of Hanzō's men. Their current situation gave the Iga shinobi no homes and no real power in the world.

Hanzō was convinced of his path.

"Very well, I am your man," Hanzō said with all conviction. "I would like to seek proof of Yamato's agreement."

"I have someone for that," Ieyasu stated. "But all in good time. In a way this deal is recompense for you and your men, a new beginning. For me it's the long fight…"

"For what?" Hanzō questioned.

"The Shogunate. My rival, Hideyoshi Hashiba, will surely rally the support of the daimyōs to his name. He may even further Nobunaga's campaign, but he will never become shōgun."

"Why? If he has the power, why can't he just take the title?"

"Blood," Ieyasu stated, looking over the land.

"Blood?" Hanzō raised an eyebrow.

"Hideyoshi is baseborn; the imperial court will never acknowledge him as shōgun."

"The Emperor has no power," Hanzō mocked.

"Only a formality," Ieyasu responded. "But a formality that must be completed. Without the Emperor's approval he will never gain the support of the nobles or the common people."

"So, what's your move?" Hanzō questioned.

Ieyasu nodded his head repeatedly. "That, my friend, is what I have been losing sleep over. I am thinking to rally support now and make a declaration of rule, but as I stated before, the person to kill Mitsuhide Akechi will have the advantage. And currently I am only with my honor guard, not an army."

Hanzō stroked his beard. "Years ago, on a mission, my squad and I were traveling through a mountain pass. In the distance we could see rival predators, a lone moon bear and a pack of wolves fighting over a freshly killed carcass. A curious thing if ever I saw. Anyway, the wolves must have been starving because they attacked the bear to defend their kill. The bear instinctively fought back, killing all but one wolf before dying."

"What of the lone wolf that survived?"

"Ah," Hanzō said while stroking his beard. "The wolf simply lay down by the carcass unable to feed due to injury. I thought the scene was finished but I saw a small fox come from the bushes. The fox hesitated only but a moment, then freely ate. The wolf was too injured and could only watch. I often think of this peculiar event because the fox is much like a shinobi. An essence we live by, to wait till the absolute right moment to strike."

"You would advise me to wait?" Ieyasu questioned, appearing mad at the suggestion.

"Wait too long and the meal could spoil or be taken. The lesson I take from the beasts fighting over a prize is to know which predator you represent. I would advise you not to be the bear or the wolf, running in for the kill without caution, but be as the fox. To know all the players in the game before making your strike. Your rival, Hideyoshi, will undoubtedly make his move. Just make sure that when you strike it will ensure that you win the prize."

Ieyasu could not help but chuckle.

"Why do you laugh?" Hanzō looked at the man with his one eye.

"My intention was to let things unfold," Ieyasu smiled. "But I wanted to know if you would advise reckless glory or sound advice. Returning to Kyoto with so few forces could mean submission or even death. Who knows what the chaos has created. I must get back to my own lands in the Mikawa Province, gather my forces. I fear going back the way we came will put us into my enemy's hands."

"My men and I will guide you through the Iga mountains. None but us know the paths, and you will be as the fox, Ieyasu Tokugawa, hidden from your enemies," Hanzō stated with a smile.

Ieyasu pondered a moment and nodded with a visual relief. "The roles have reversed. This time my life is in your hands."

29

Fox in the Darkness
-Yamashiro Province, Yamazaki-

At the Katsura River by the village of Yamazaki, a battle had just ended. Hideyoshi Hashiba had put an end to the betrayer Mitsuhide Akechi's uprising. When word of Nobunaga's death had come, Hideyoshi had forced a quick surrender from the already battered Mōri clan and combined his power with loyal Oda forces along the way.

Hideyoshi had confronted Mitsuhide's army on the banks of the Katsura River, an easy battle as Hideyoshi was bolstered by the brunt of Nobunaga's troops. When the fighting was over, Hideyoshi received reports that Mitsuhide had died at the hands of farmers; an ironic ending to the man that had defeated Nobunaga Oda and declared himself shōgun of Japan.

The night had come, and Hideyoshi Hashiba sat in his command tent contemplating the recent events and his next move. The deep running water of the Katsura River, the chirp of crickets, and the occasional rustling of guards in their tents sounded about the camp. In the silence, a familiar shadow slipped its way into Hideyoshi's tent.

340

Hideyoshi did not look up from the map in the center of his tent, only a small smirk crawled on his lips. "None thought you dead, but I knew you would come back."

"My apologies, but as you know the recent events have changed many things."

"You served well, but I would not stay long. If my men see my wife's handmaiden with a sword on her back... well, that's a story I will not be able to explain."

Rin was not in her usual kimono in which Hideyoshi was accustomed. She wore her earth toned shinobifuku robes; unlike a dress, they did nothing to hide the deadly intent of Rin's body. Her face was uncovered, plain and clean but for a few fresh scratches on her cheek from fighting. Rin's hair was held back tight in a ponytail, her sandalwood eyes peered through the shadows toward Hideyoshi.

Rin spoke softly, staying hidden from sight. "The sword and clothes have been necessary as news of Nobunaga's death has spread; thieves, bandits, and small lords' ambitions have grown. Kyoto became very dangerous while you were away."

"You are a spy, not a soldier. You have no need for a sword," Hideyoshi spoke with offense. "In any case, you are correct that Nobunaga has left a void in the land, a void I intend to fill."

"It seems Mitsuhide Akechi played his part well," Rin responded.

Hideyoshi gave a scoff. "No thanks to you. If you remember, you were to keep a close eye on his whereabouts. As predicted, my subtle influence over Mitsuhide and his weakness for rash decisions caused him to kill Nobunaga Oda. But he did so blatantly under his own familial banners. On top of that I intercepted a letter sent to Terumoto Mōri, asking that he and

Mitsuhide join forces to destroy me. Luckily, Terumoto never got the letter. Mitsuhide declaring himself the shōgun of Japan and betraying me was a mistake he shortly lived; a life that could have been shorter if you stuck to your assignment. But... I suppose it turned out better than I expected."

"Better?"

Hideyoshi almost smiled. "I have killed the betrayer of Nobunaga Oda and by doing so it will allow me to gain the support of the daimyōs with ease."

"Not all of them," Rin doubted.

"No... the sons of Nobunaga will need convincing, especially Nobukatsu. Not to mention Ieyasu Tokugawa will surely try to seize this opportunity to rally followers. Allies will soon become enemies; in any case, the game of go has begun. I have a plan for the Oda clan, but I must move swiftly. Did you run into any trouble while keeping an eye on Mitsuhide? What have you learned? What happened at Honnō-ji temple?"

"I was forced to hire assassins as back up if things went wrong," Rin responded. "And things did go wrong."

Hideyoshi gave a smug look. "Don't be coy, Rin, I have more than one spy, they were shinobi, and more likely they used you. I know they're not the squabble that Ieyasu rescued. So, who were they?"

"Angry men looking for revenge." Rin chose her words carefully, not underestimating Hideyoshi's knowledge. "The Iga tribe is no more, but there are splinter groups looking for vengeance."

"How many of them did you connive into this mission? Do they still live?"

"Four and unknown," Rin stated.

"Four?" Hideyoshi scoffed. "Four v. ible to gain access to Nobunaga?"

"They attempted assassination the night Mitsuhide attacked, I am unaware of how far they were involved in the events of Nobunaga's death," Rin stated, still as stone in the shadows.

Hideyoshi peered at the dark corner of the tent at the silhouette of Rin while trying to read her thoughts. "And now that Nobunaga is dead what is to stop such a group from coming after me if their revenge was not to satisfaction."

The sound of soldiers approaching could be heard in the distance.

"Pay them no mind, they are only four, a remnant soon forgotten to history. A tale I will finish in better circumstances. I will return to Kyoto, by your wife's side." Rin cautiously listened to the rustling of guards outside.

"Is that all you have to report?"

"Yes. Now I must make my leave before your guards—"

"They know you're here," Hideyoshi stated smugly, "this chat of ours was just to buy time."

"Why?" Rin stated, looking defensively at her surroundings.

"Because you're a spy, and not my spy," Hideyoshi chided. "You tell me to not worry about a group of shinobi. My spies and interrogations of Mitsuhide's troops tell me otherwise. Reports of demons, monsters, and shinobi killing men on rooftops. Those four are undoubtedly after more than Nobunaga and may soon be after me, all thanks to you," Hideyoshi stated with finality. He then waved to the entrance and two guards came through the tent flaps unannounced.

"If you knew, why kill me now?" Rin tensed in a crouch as an animal waiting to spring.

"I did need you, but you served your purpose. As I said earlier, Nobunaga is now dead, friends will soon become enemies, and your true master is my rival, Ieyasu Tokugawa."

Hideyoshi nodded to the guards, and they approached Rin with swords in hand. Rin quickly pounced, not toward the exit, but toward Hideyoshi, unsheathing the black blade and bringing it under his neck. The guards stopped, looking to Hideyoshi for orders.

Rin pressed the black blade's edge under Hideyoshi's chin, blood began to trickle to the floor.

"Men always think a woman will choose to flee rather than fight. You didn't even have your sword in hand." Rin glared at Hideyoshi's eyes. "How many guards are surrounding the tent?"

"Five," Hideyoshi stated through clenched teeth.

At the response Rin twisted the blade.

"Fourteen," Hideyoshi corrected, "not counting the two inside."

"I'm flattered." Rin gave a mock smile and then turned her gaze toward the guards. "Oi, ugly, cut a hole in the back of the tent large enough to walk through. And you, ogre face, tell the guards outside to gather at the entrance."

The guards hesitated not knowing which one was ugly and which one was the ogre face.

Hideyoshi rolled his eyes and gave the little nod he could, approving the command with the blade at his throat. "You can't have me at sword point forever, and my archers will have you marked."

"Don't worry, my lord," Rin stated calmly. "We just need to take a walk to the tree line."

Rin gestured for the newly made tent flap, Hideyoshi slowly walked toward the exit and stepped through. As expected, Rin saw a cluster of guards, many with bows aimed at the original entrance. Their torchlit faces were stern and full of the intent to kill. Rin studied the darkness like a wild beast looking for the tree line, but not letting her fear get the best of her she turned her gaze toward the Katsura River.

"Change of plans, my lord." Rin nodded to the river in the distance. "Tell your men to keep their arrows in their quivers and keep a comfortable distance, in return you won't have to take a boat ride."

Hideyoshi did as he was told and his soldiers reluctantly followed the orders, bows lowered but still in hand. Hideyoshi instinctively started walking toward three small skiffs at the shoreline. Rin guided Hideyoshi's footstep with the sword point, each partner sidestepping as if a dance, Rin defensively eyeing her entire audience. Human speech was absent as the two made their way to the river. Their intimate dance was accompanied by the wind blowing through the grass, the shifting soil of their feet, the running water, and the chirping crickets. The short walk took an eternity, the locked eyes of Rin and Hideyoshi held a long conversation, absent of words but no less communicative.

"Release two of the boats," Rin commanded, gripping the blade firm.

Hideyoshi untied the boats and they lazily floated down the river into the darkness. Rin looked in the distance to see that the guards were not too close. Satisfied, Rin gestured Hideyoshi to turn as she released the rope holding the last skiff in place and fluidly entered the boat. Only as the boat lazily floated away did the black tengu blade release Hideyoshi's chin. Hideyoshi instinctively grabbed the cut to catch the small droplets of blood as he watched Rin's figure quickly become a shadow on the deep wide river, shrouded by the dead of night. Hideyoshi caught one last look at Rin's moonlit face before it receded into the shadows. It was the only time he could remember she was not showing her fake smile as she took her leave. The guards came running, bows in hand, and shot a few arrows with futility into the darkness.

"My lord." It was Kenji, Hideyoshi's main captain.

"I'm all right," Hideyoshi stated, trying to keep the anger at bay. "What, what are the men muttering about?"

"My lord..." Kenji stated, "the sword she had, was it black?"

Hideyoshi turned back in disbelief and glared at the Katsura River as the water quietly flowed into the darkness.

30

Lost

-Yamashiro Province, Kyoto Outskirts-

Kaito awoke from nightmares filled with anxiety and pain. Bewildered, he took a moment to recall his surroundings. The all too familiar sore pain of his hand, his black eye from falling on the roof tiles, both a sharp reminder of what had happened the night Nobunaga Oda died.

Kaito's memory came back like a crashing wave. The army that had come invading Honnō-ji, yelling for the death of Nobunaga Oda, Noboru and Itsuki returning bloody and injured. The group had taken refuge in a remote inn, since injuries were common after the events of Kyoto, the innkeeper did not think twice, especially when they paid a week's advance to ensure silence.

Kaito looked over to see Itsuki in the adjacent bed, bare-chested except for the bandages wrapped around his ribs, his clothes which hung on a chair were stained maroon from old, dried blood. Itsuki seemed to sleep, but his face was drenched in a cold sweat, showing signs of a bad fever. The room was dark and Kaito could hear voices from outside. With the loud creak of the door, a man entered and made his way to Itsuki.

The man lit a lantern, knelt by Itsuki's bed, and began to remove the bandages around his ribs. The man inspected the newly stitched wound and gave it two long sniffs of his nose; he seemed to be satisfied and began wrapping Itsuki with fresh clean bandages.

"Will he live?" Kaito asked with a hoarse unused voice.

The man looked up somewhat startled, previously under the impression that Kaito was asleep.

"Yes… and no, his body heals but his spirit grows cold, cold as stone, alone to atone."

Kaito blinked twice as if making sure the rhymes coming from the healer were not from his head injury. The room was dark, and the only distinguishable feature was that the man was bald except for a long braid at the back of his head.

"Where are Noboru and my brother?"

"Fire and wind, they both are gone, to find some herbs to bring Itsuki along."

"Who are you?"

The man's face came into a ray of light from the nearby window, only to reveal a wide smile and a leathery face. Only then Kaito noticed a staff with four intersecting rings propped in the corner of the room. The same staff he had seen being wielded by the strange priest of Mount Kurama.

"Hiraku," Kaito stated, putting his head to the pillow.

Hiraku stayed silent, only smiling, still working on Itsuki's wounds. When he was done, he came to Kaito's bedside.

"Hold up your hand," the priest commanded.

Kaito did not hold up his hand, fearful of what he may find out next. An evil countenance came upon the priest, a stark contrast to the carefree attitude the priest seemed to always have.

The priest grimly stated once more, "Hold up your hand, I'm not asking."

Kaito slowly raised his bandaged right hand, and the priest began to unravel the dressing to show the fresh wound.

Kaito's hand was bruised and scabbed with a perfectly straight cut that traveled horizontally across the palm. The cut had been stitched skillfully and seemed to have saved his hand, although there would be a large scar. Kaito dared to clench his hand into a fist, but the slightest movement sent an unbearable jolt of pain. Hiraku grabbed the wrist, rotating the palm and inspecting the wound while looking for signs of infection.

"Try to make a fist," the priest stated.

Against the raging pain, Kaito tried to make a fist, finding that he could barely curl two fingers.

"It will likely be a lame hand," the priest stated bluntly. "At least one tendon was severed… there will be a lot of scar tissue. If you are lucky your hand may heal, but your dexterity will be forever lost."

The reality of what Hiraku had said sat deep with Kaito; he had lost his sword hand. What skill he ever had with a blade would have to be relearned by his left hand, a process that would take years. Hiraku redressed the wound, cinching the bandages tight.

When Hiraku finished, he looked at Kaito grimly and stated, "This will hurt."

Hiraku thumbed the lame hand of Kaito with immense pressure. Kaito's world started to twirl around him, and he thought he would pass out from the pain.

"Son of Kazuki, your sins, your sins have come. You have lost the blade and the soul, now you will pay the toll. You must get it back to mend your hand, if you fail so will your clan. I was charged, charged to protect the blades, but now gone are the sacred days. Retrieve the blade to plead your case or another will come to take your place."

What seemed a lifetime of pain had finally passed only at the finale of the priest's sermons. Kaito had a cold sweat and was breathing heavily; he stared at the priest, preparing for another threat. Hiraku stood, bowed, and smiled as if nothing had ever happened. The awkward tense moment was interrupted by the sounds of Noboru and Tsubasa coming up the stairs toward the room.

"Ah, Fire and Wind. Enter, enter," Hiraku stated happily.

Noboru walked through the door, looking healthy as ever, but the countenance on his face only showed that he was exhausted and had not slept well. Tsubasa looked somewhat the same but cracked a smile on his face when he saw that Kaito was awake.

Noboru handed the herbs to Hiraku, nodding for the man to get started on Itsuki's medicine.

"We have much to speak of," Hiraku stated, looking at Noboru. "Much to be done."

Noboru only nodded. The weight of the world seemed to be on his shoulders. Noboru went to the desk in the corner of the room, gave a very long sigh, and began to write a letter on a piece of parchment, a letter to long forsaken kin.

Tsubasa sat by Kaito's bed, taking off his dusty traveling items. "How's the hand?"

"Lost," Kaito stated.

"What can I do?"

"Train my left hand," Kaito stated with conviction.

"Don't worry, brother. We will get the sword back," Tsubasa stated, attempting to lift the spirits of his brother.

"If she doesn't return it first," Kaito stated, looking at his wounded hand.

"Return it?" Tsubasa questioned, wondering if Kaito's head injury had done more damage than just a black eye.

"I know it sounds absurd," Kaito defended, "but she said 'borrow,' and I think she meant it. It doesn't matter, the hunt will begin regardless."

"For the sword?"

"Not the sword," Kaito stated with finality. "The hunt for Rin."

Historical Note

In 1467 Japan, a conflict named the Ōnin War started from a dispute over the succession of the shōgun. The emperor was the ruling leader by title and tradition; but in practicality the shōgun was the nation's leader by authority and control. Events escalated as rival clans started fighting over land, power, titles, and vengeance. As no peace could be agreed upon, Japan plummeted into an age of civil war known as the Sengoku period, meaning "the age of warring states," lasting from 1467-1603.

During this Sengoku period there were three unique warlords given the title of the Great Unifiers. This group included Nobunaga Oda, Hideyoshi Hashiba (later surname to be Toyotomi), and Ieyasu Tokugawa. All three contributed to gradually unifying Japan and ending the great civil war.

In the Sengoku period the power of the Iga shinobi, or ninja as they are more commonly referred to in the modern era, was at its peak. It should be noted that the term shinobi is the accurate name translated from historical records. The term ninja was adopted later and gained popularity after the 1950's. Their specialization in covert-ops and unconventional tactics were utilized by rival warring states. The Iga Province contained an enveloping mountainous terrain, resulting in a geographical isolation that created a unique governance and culture different from the surrounding feudal system. A campaign named the Tenshō Iga War was put upon the shinobi. The first invasion was met with failure in 1579, as Nobukatsu Oda met high resistance in mountainous terrain and guerrilla tactics. In 1581, Nobunaga Oda came to rectify his son's failure with 42,000 troops and surrounded the Iga Province, massacring the populace and demolishing the infrastructure. The completion of the campaign left scattered survivors and destroyed a unique culture. Masanari Hattori, also known as Hattori the Demon Hanzō, was one of the few leaders that remained from the dwindling Iga shinobi. Hanzō Hattori was known for many exploits and his allegiance with Ieyasu Tokugawa.

Nobunaga Oda's death did occur in Kyoto at Honnō-ji temple in 1582, whether he died by seppuku or by fire is debated amongst historians. Nobunaga's general, Mitsuhide Akechi was responsible for Nobunaga's death, reasons for Mitsuhide's betrayal are contested. However, there are several documented instances where Nobunaga was known to publicly insult and demean Mitsuhide Akechi.

During the age of the Sengoku period the blades of two unique swordsmiths were used in battle. Goro Masamune lived from approximately 1267-1343, while Sengo Muramasa was born before 1501, whose exact life span is unknown. Both are considered the best swordsmiths of Japan, each known for their superior craftsmanship and induction of new unique designs. Goro Masamune's blades were considered to be beautiful, effective, and brought the wielder stillness. In contrast, Sengo Muramasa's blades were considered to be evil to the point that if unsheathed the wielder would be required to spill blood, even if it was their own. The origins of such reputations are disputed, but most likely legends and tales were spread to add to the mysticism of owning such blades.

The original and primary religion of Japan is Shinto, literally translated as "the way of the gods." Although a complex religion, a brief description is that it incorporates the polytheistic worship of ancestors and nature spirits. These spirits or gods, referred to as kami, are supernatural entities believed to inhabit all things. Shinto has a very in-depth mythology of kami and their exploits with human beings. From within the traditions of Shinto sprung the folkloric yōkai, a term that has no direct translation in English, but can be defined as sprits, demons, or monsters ranging in appearance and motivation. Tales of such creatures were spread and believed openly, especially amongst the commoner populace. It can be surmised that the beliefs and actions of people living in the Sengoku period were influenced by the creatures known as yōkai.

About the Author

Kyle Mortensen is the author of the Sons of Yōkai series. To read **Chapter One of the sequel to Mists of Iga** and other upcoming projects, visit **www.Kyle-Mortensen.com**

Made in the USA
Monee, IL
05 December 2022

19635910R00215